With a burst of energy fueled by rage, I sprinkled powder into the muzzle and rammed a bullet down with the long rod. Tear down our store, would they? Well, I'd show them a thing or two.

Flinging open the door, I stepped outside.

Frozen open-mouthed, too startled to move, the four Indians in front of the store stared at me as I strode across the yard through the dim evening mist.

"Get out of here," I ordered. My hands steady, I pointed the rifle at the stocky, older Indian who seemed to be the leader.

He laughed, a guttural sound. "Brave squaw."

My body stiffened. My pulse drummed frantically inside my head.

Another stepped toward me. Grinning smugly, he raised his hand to reach for my gun. I cocked it and glared at him, fury blazing from my eyes. He hesitated, watchful.

"This is my house. This is my store," I said. Good Lord! Would I really have to shoot them? Did I have the nerve . . . ?

Also by Susan Hatton McCoy
Published by Ballantine Books:

A FRONTIER WIFE

EDEN VALLEY

Susan Hatton McCoy

To Grace,
with best wishes —

Susan Hatton McCoy

BALLANTINE BOOKS • NEW YORK

Library of Congress Catalog Card Number: 91-91891

ISBN 0-345-36845-2

Manufactured in the United States of America

First Edition: August 1991

To my parents,
who from my early childhood
enriched my life with
story, song, and poetry.

Author's Note

The characters in this book and the town of Eden Valley
are fictitious. Their story, however, represents the
authentic history of the time and place.

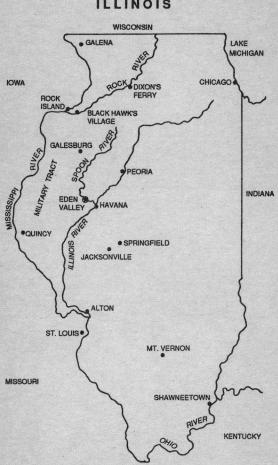

ILLINOIS

WISCONSIN

• GALENA

IOWA

ROCK RIVER

ROCK ISLAND •

BLACK HAWK'S VILLAGE

GALESBURG •

SPOON RIVER

MILITARY TRACT

MISSISSIPPI RIVER

• QUINCY

EDEN VALLEY

• HAVANA

ILLINOIS RIVER

• PEORIA

• SPRINGFIELD

JACKSONVILLE •

• ALTON

ST. LOUIS •

MISSOURI

• MT. VERNON

SHAWNEETOWN •

OHIO RIVER

KENTUCKY

LAKE MICHIGAN

CHICAGO •

DIXON'S FERRY

INDIANA

CHAPTER 1

SOUTHERN ILLINOIS—1821

"So help me, someday I'm going to kill that whole damn Nichols tribe!" Uncle Amos roared as he stormed through the back door. "It's like living next to a den of rattlesnakes."

I stared with eery fascination at his flushed face, twisted with anger, uglier than ever. This short, squat man, dressed in plain farmer's clothes, was the owner of the crowded log inn where we lived, which was beside the post road, heading north from Shawneetown. Now he planted himself in the middle of the inn kitchen, his barrel chest rising and falling with the quick rhythm of his noisy panting.

Aunt Flora, thin and haggard-looking, glanced up from the fireplace where she was frying ham for the inn guests' supper. "Nellie, you go ahead and carry the plates and tableware to the dining room," she told me, wiping her hands on her spattered apron. "Now, Amos, what did the Nicholses do this time?"

He glared at her as if it were her fault. "They let my calf run out through a break in the rail fence, that's what. Those Nichols boys probably broke that fence on purpose, damned spiteful whelps. So naturally I went over on their land to bring my calf back."

"And they didn't like that, I suppose," Aunt Flora said wearily.

"Soon as I got there, there came Old Man Nichols, galloping his horse over to call me down for trespassing. Talk about gall. If I'd had a club along with me . . ."

A pleading look clouded Aunt Flora's eyes. "How long will this go on?"

1

My uncle spat into the fire. "Someday I'm going to show that ugly devil. You just watch me."

I gathered up the pile of plates, trying to look busy, staying out of his way. At least if he was raving about the neighbors, he was not attacking me for some mistake or oversight.

"This is no way to live." Aunt Flora wrung her hands. "Why, you two have been going at it for over ten years."

He seized her shoulders and shook her violently. "Whose side are you on, woman? I tell you, someday I'm going to kill those people. I'm going to kill the whole damn family."

A shiver of fear snaked down my spine as I regarded his reddened face and pale, bugged eyes. It made no sense to me, this nasty feud that Uncle Amos kept picking like a sore. Only the wide pasture separating the inn and the Nichols farm prevented open warfare between the two stubborn men.

It was not my fight. I had only lived here five years, since my mother had died. After Mama's funeral, Aunt Flora, her older sister, told my papa they wanted me to come to Illinois and live with them.

There was another reason it was not my fight. I was in love with Johnny Nichols.

After supper I stood alone in the kitchen, engulfed by the mingled smells of fried ham and boiled cabbage hanging in the sultry air about me. I had finally finished washing and drying the mountain of dirty pans and supper dishes. I wiped the last piece, a long iron ladle, with a damp dishtowel and hung it on its hook under the mantel.

Johnny's note rustled in my apron pocket as I moved. Almost unconsciously I drew it out and held it to my heart. I reached into my pocket again and fingered the brooch of fresh-water pearls he had secretly given me for Christmas.

Johnny loved me. In all my eighteen years, I had never known such joy. Me, a skinny redhead with a freckled nose. But he thought I was pretty. Best of all, he understood my desperation here and promised to help me get away.

The sound of hearty male laughter drifting in from the dining room disturbed my reverie, and I quickly slipped the note back into my pocket. That bunch of men in the next room, those peddlers, speculators, hunters, travelers of all sorts, were laughing at another hunting story. Stretching the truth a bit, I didn't

2

doubt. Every night brought another session of drinking whiskey and telling tall tales around the fireplace or out on the front porch. The faces changed, but the stories sounded pretty much the same.

I could hear Uncle Amos's loud, twangy voice adding his share to the senseless boasting. Aunt Flora, feeling poorly again, had retired early to their cramped quarters off the kitchen.

My heart tripped wildly in my chest as I stood stock-still, listening to the rumble of voices from the next room. Again I cautiously slid Johnny's note from my apron pocket and smiled as I read his scribbled words once more: "Meet me by the oak grove tonight. I love you."

Johnny. Handsome, laughing Johnny Nichols. He was my only friend here, the only joy in my grim life.

A gust of cool evening breeze wafted through the open doorway and struck the beads of sweat moistening my brow. I stepped to the back door, tense and alert, fully aware of the danger if, as Johnny asked, I slipped out after dark to the inviting grove of oaks behind the barn. I lived in constant fear of my uncle's violent temper.

From the grove, the lonesome coo of a mourning dove called to me, enticing me to a rendezvous among the trees. I must see Johnny, for I loved him more than life itself. Just to gaze at him was exquisite pleasure. In the precious stolen moments I had spent with him, I had memorized his face—those high cheek-bones and that fine straight nose, those deep blue eyes, that crop of unruly black curls. How I loved his wide, lopsided smile. Oh, yes, my love for Johnny was much stronger than my fear of Uncle Amos.

Over a year had passed since Johnny and I first began chatting over the fence behind the oak grove whenever I went out to lead the cow into the barn for milking. Though I quickly sensed the sparks that flashed between us at each glance, like steel against flint, I could see Johnny only rarely—and always secretly. From the start, we both understood that if my uncle found out, he would forbid Johnny even to talk to me, much less to court me.

Overhead a veil of filmy clouds, pinkened by the lingering glow of sunset, drifted toward the western horizon. The mourning dove beckoned me again. The heavy shadows of the grove looked peaceful and inviting.

3

Dare I go out there now, without the cloak of night to hide me? I yearned for just a moment of repose. Since dawn I had been working without pause—cooking, hauling in wood for the fire that magnified the summer's stifling heat, churning butter, rubbing dirty towels and bed linens with lye soap in the huge iron kettle of hot water until my knuckles cracked and bled. Just a moment of rest was all I asked. A moment to collect my thoughts before night fell and Johnny came.

Footsteps. I heard the dull thuds on the rough kitchen floorboards and stuffed the note back in my pocket. I turned and saw my uncle's eyes devouring me. He always stared at me like that, a loose-lipped stare that turned my blood to ice. I was no beauty, just a scrawny redhead with work-worn hands, but the lust simmering behind his eyes terrified me.

"You done with this kitchen work, girl?" he muttered, his eyes fixed on me like a swamp snake on its prey.

"Yes, sir," I said, and hung my head to avoid his burning stare. "I'd better run upstairs and see if the Cranford kids are tucked in." Warily, I walked a wide path around him . . . toward the dining room door.

"Let Cranford mind his own damned kids," he snarled, but I was through the dining room and halfway up the stairs before he finished.

The night lantern on the upstairs landing spread a golden glow over the worn floorboards, lighting my way as I opened the door to the women's quarters. The stifling hot room housed no women tonight, only two small boys sharing one bed, and a pretty blue-eyed girl lying on a cot in the corner.

Perspiration glistened on the children's brows. Their eyes gleamed wide and anxious in the dim light. "Ain't you kids asleep yet?" I asked gently.

My heart twisted with sympathy as I gazed at these solemn children. New settlers from back East, the family had traveled this far when the mother came down sick with some mysterious fever. They stopped at the inn, and I helped nurse the woman the best I could, but she died within a week. For two months now, her grief-crippled husband had stayed on with his children, unwilling to turn back, unable to go on to settle his claim of land somewhere up in central Illinois.

"Tell us a story, Nellie," the youngest child, little Eddie,

4

said. I smoothed his rumpled dark brown hair. He was only three, but the most talkative by far.

The others, Hugh, seven, and Sarah, five, were silent, as usual, for their load of grief sapped all their strength. How well I remembered that bitter, crushing pain.

"Why, sure. I'd be glad to tell you a story," I said, hoping to coax a smile to those small grave faces. "Let me tell you about my little sisters and the games we used to play, back when I lived down in Kentucky."

I kept the story brief, for my thoughts were all with Johnny. A short time later, I tiptoed from the room and back down the open stairway to the empty dining room. Uncle Amos and the inn guests had moved to the benches out on the front porch. The noise of their chattering covered my footsteps as I crossed through to the kitchen and over to my tiny closet of a room on the other side.

After brushing out my heavy thatch of long hair, wishing it would curl in pretty tendrils about my face, I gathered it neatly at the back with a piece of yellow ribbon. My green gingham dress was faded, but it was the best I had. As I slipped off my apron to smooth the wrinkles in my skirt, I drew my pearl brooch from the apron pocket. Just this once I would dare wear it to meet my beau.

When I tiptoed outside to the back stoop, cheerful choruses of katydids greeted me in the refreshing night air. The dove cooed once again, calling me to the grove.

I hurried across the yard, toward the barn looming huge and black against the darkened sky. From inside came the nicker of a restless horse. The pungent barn scent drifted to my nostrils as I passed. Clinging to the shadows, I crept toward the dark mass of towering oak trees beyond the barn, drawn as iron to a magnet.

Anger flared inside me when I recalled the reason for all this stealth. Why should Johnny and I suffer for some ancient feud between his father and my uncle? Why would anybody bear such bitter grudges, drag on the hostilities year after year? It made no sense at all.

Of course, logic never seemed to play any part in my uncle's thinking. He was always mad at the whole world. I supposed he was simply born that way.

As I entered the grove of oaks, stillness closed about me like

5

a cave. The air felt cool against my skin, fragrant and clean after the inn's stuffiness. Sinking down on a log, I gazed up at the dark canopy of leaves and heaved a weary sigh.

The night flowed over me. A gentle breeze caressed my face and murmured softly in my ears. Peace. Tranquility.

I was young and alone in the world, for my aunt and uncle were more like slave drivers than relatives. What did the future hold for me? All I wanted—all I cared about—was Johnny Nichols.

And any moment now, he would come to me.

CHAPTER 2

I had been living at my uncle's inn for three months when I first met Johnny. By then, all the events of my life leading up to that time had become blurred in my mind. I could only dimly recall the exuberant, bubbling child I had been, running freely about our cabin yard in Kentucky, before Mama died giving birth to a stillborn baby.

Pa's gloom and silence afterward frightened me. I recalled his grim visage when the relatives came, and his unquestioning agreement when they divided up his children, me and my three little sisters, as if we were so many plates or cooking pots.

Since I was the oldest, thirteen, I already had plenty of experience with all the hard work of settler life. Sometimes I helped Pa with the farm chores, too—even driving the hay wagon.

When they saw how able and energetic I was, Flora and Amos spoke up quick. "We'd like Nellie to come and stay with us," Uncle Amos told the other relatives.

Aunt Flora's eyes glistened. "Yes, the child will take the place of our poor lost babies. Every one of them died of croup or whooping cough, all those many years ago.''

"Pack up your things now, girl," Uncle Amos said. "We'll have to be heading North real soon."

I climbed up to the loft and stood beside the bed I shared with my sister Meg, folding my flannel nightgown and my few dresses into a small cloth bag. Tears rolled unheeded down my cheeks.

When I climbed down, Pa met me at the bottom of the ladder. "Here, you take this." Averting his eyes, he handed me Mama's prized tortoiseshell hairbrush.

My lips quivered. I grabbed up my apron to wipe away the fresh torrent of tears. "When can I come back? The littles ones will miss me." I glanced at the sad faces of my sisters, crowded close around me.

"Things are tough just now," Pa said, grimly shaking his head. "You know I can't look after all you kids myself. You're darn lucky you have such nice relatives to take you in."

It was hard to feel lucky when I had to kiss my little sisters for the last time and bid them farewell. How long would it be before we could all be together again? I bit my lips to keep from crying as I climbed up in the buggy beside Aunt Flora and started down the narrow, dusty road.

We hadn't even reached my aunt and uncle's place up in southern Illinois before I realized the truth. They only saw me as a source of cheap help for the constant round of heavy chores around their busy crossroad inn.

"At least this one won't be marrying and taking off right away, like all those other hired girls," Uncle Amos told Aunt Flora as we rode up a dusty cart path, the only road leading north from the ferry across the Ohio River. He glanced back at me with a scowl. "Skinny little runt, ain't she? And that hank of red hair and all those freckles don't help."

"Why, Amos! She's as cute as a ladybug. True, she is a mite small for her age, but she's big enough to help with the garden and the kitchen work and washing," my aunt said.

"I should hope so!" he growled.

"Yeah, poor child. Keeping busy will probably be the best thing for her, too. Help take her mind off having to leave home so young."

Yes, they were real thoughtful about keeping me busy. Steamy summer days spent bending over the kitchen fireplace, frying

7

bacon or stirring pots of stew. Up to my elbows in greasy dishwater as I scrubbed the stacks of dishes and serving bowls. Backbreaking baskets of sheets and towels to lug outside and hang over the fence to dry. The cow to milk, and cream to churn into butter for all the supper guests I could hear chattering in the next room.

Uncle Amos, I soon learned, hated to part with a penny. He raised most everything he used at the inn, so his operation was almost pure profit. He kept hogs and a few cattle in a prairie pasture out back of the copse of oak trees behind the barn to provide meat for the inn's table. A cow gave him milk and butter, and a flock of clucking chickens supplied eggs and fried or stewed meat. Corn bread, along with vegetables from the big garden out back, filled in for the rest of the travelers' meals.

While I worked out in the garden, weeding or picking beans or pulling carrots during the hours after breakfast, I saw many travelers passing on the busy road in front of the inn. "Who are all those people?" I asked my aunt.

"Don't know. New settlers, I reckon."

"Settlers? Where are they going?"

"Land sakes, this whole territory's opening up," she said. "Though I suspicion half those folks will end up squatting on government land."

"What's squatting?"

"Oh, folks just move onto some land and act like it belongs to them. Some of them file for deed in a few years, after they've made a crop or two."

"Don't they get in trouble for it?"

She waved her hand in dismissal. "Lord, child, you ask too many questions. I got more important things to think about than sneaky squatters."

Still I watched them, the people riding by on horses or driving wagons, pulling carts completely loaded with household goods. Those who stopped by the inn overnight were up for an early breakfast, then were quickly on their way again. I longed to talk with them, to ask each one a hundred questions. My aunt and uncle, always faithful to their goal, kept me too busy for any such frivolity.

I missed Mama and my sisters. At first the pain was sharp and cutting, but gradually it faded into a constant ache. At night I lay awake, clinging to Mama's hairbrush as I tried to recall her sweet, gentle voice. My little sisters' faces began to blur and run together in my mind and I panicked, struggling desperately to remember each one's separate features and personality. If I forgot them, would that mean they had forgotten me?

A deep resentment burned inside me each time I thought of my pa, sending us all away with just a casual word of farewell. Couldn't he at least write, to let me know how he and my sisters were doing? But the months went by without a single word.

One day, as my uncle stopped to wash his hands in the pan set on the small table beside the door, Aunt Flora approached him nervously. "Amos, can I please have a few cents . . . so Nellie can run down to the store and buy us a dozen candles?" she asked, her head hung in apology. "Just enough to tide us over till I get time to make some more."

His shoulders stiffened; his face turned red as flame. "Buy candles? Damn it, what are we keeping this kid here for? I figured when she came, she could keep all that stuff done up."

She shrank away from him. "I'm sorry, Amos. You know I don't like to ask for money, but we've been so busy picking and drying all the beans and garden truck before it gets too cold. There just ain't been an extra minute."

"If she's got time to run to the store, I'd say she's got time to dip candles," he said, glaring at me.

Aunt Flora wrung her hands. "We'll get on it right away, I promise. Just as soon as we get all the apples sliced and dried. But we need some candles right now—just enough to tide us over the next few days. Please, Amos. With all these people here at night, we have to have some light. I don't know what else to do."

He exhaled a long sigh. "Half a dozen. No more," he growled. "I can't be spending all my money on things you can make here at home."

"I'll put her to making them soon as we get a spare minute."

"I have to save my money to buy more land," he said, folding his arms across his belly. "Someday I'm going to own twice as much as that damned Nichols. Let him stick that in his craw." He turned to leave, then stopped and reached into his pocket. Grudgingly he drew out a few copper pennies and handed them to me.

I nodded my thanks and drew back from his touch, for the

9

man—with his loud, belligerent voice and his constant reek of whiskey and tobacco—repulsed me.

After receiving strict instructions from Aunt Flora, I wrapped a shawl around my shoulders and strolled down the road to the small general store that sat beside the blacksmith shop in the little crossroad settlement. I welcomed this brief moment to myself, this respite from the endless round of work and tension at the inn. The fall air smelled crisp and spicy; the gold- and orange-colored leaves brightened the thick stand of woods across the road.

When I entered the store, a rangy, rawboned man greeted me from behind the counter with a snaggletoothed grin. "Morning. New around here, ain't you, missy?"

I nodded. "Yes. I'm living at the inn."

"Well, I swan! I heard tell old Barton had some kinfolk working there now, but you're nothing but a mite."

Flustered, I held out my pennies. "Can I have six candles, please?"

"Why, sure." He reached back to the shelves behind his wooden counter. At that moment, I heard footsteps on the porch and turned to see a boy with curly dark hair pull open the plank door and step inside. He was a fine-looking boy, two or three years older than me, clean-cut and slender. His eyes, deep blue and gleaming, spoke of intelligence and good humor. "Hi, there, Red," he said, grinning inquisitively. "Do you live around here now?"

"Yes, I do . . . And my name is Nellie, thank you," I said, with a defiant flip to my curls. "I just moved up a couple of months ago. I'm living with my aunt and uncle—at least for a while."

"You'll be the only redhead in school." He pointed down the road. "They hold it in a little cabin just down the way. It'll be starting in a couple of weeks. I'll be seeing you there, won't I?"

I suddenly recalled that Uncle Amos never said a word about me going to school. Back home I had looked forward to our winter school sessions, for I thoroughly enjoyed reading and writing and ciphering, learning new things. In fact, the teacher sometimes held up my work as an example to a few of the older boys who didn't like to sit still and mind their lessons all day long.

"When does school start? I'll have to tell my aunt about it," I said.

"Middle of November. Looks like we're going to be classmates."

I nodded, blushing at the unaccustomed attention.

"Maybe I should welcome you with a licorice stick. Can I have two of those, Mr. Snider?" he asked the storeowner, pointing to a glass jar filled with assorted-colored candies. He presented me the treat with an exaggerated bow. "I expect you'll be seeing me around here quite a bit. I live just down the road. My name's Johnny Nichols."

Nichols? The very sound of the name sent shivers down my spine, for I had heard it cursed by Uncle Amos almost every day. "I live down that way, too," I said hesitantly. "Down at the inn."

He turned and stared at me. "The inn? You mean your uncle is Amos Barton? Crazy Amos Barton?"

I hung my head, confused. "My—my mother died. They brought me up here to live with them."

"Oh. I'm sorry. Real sorry," Johnny said softly.

Leaning forward to catch our conversation, Mr. Snider winked at Johnny. "Amos Barton ain't likely to cotton to you talking to his niece. We wouldn't want to start a war around here, now would we?"

"A little licorice stick's not likely to start a war. But, look, she doesn't even know what we're talking about."

The storeowner wagged his head and grinned. "Oh, I'll wager that's not the first time she's heard the name of Nichols mentioned. Right, missy?"

"Yes, I've heard my uncle talk about the Nicholses." I hesitated, at a loss for words. "You all live across that big field from the inn, don't you?"

"We do," Johnny said. "Why don't we step out on the porch and I'll tell you how all the problems started."

Mr. Snider looked amused, as if it were some fine joke. I quickly paid him for my candles and followed Johnny outside.

His young face was cast in solemnity. "That rail fence between your uncle's land and ours marks the old battle line. It must have happened over ten years ago, 'cause I remember I was just a little kid. Old Amos Barton built that inn there, and then he started putting up a zigzag fence. The only problem

11

was, he started about twenty feet over on my dad's property."

"So that's what caused the fight," I said.

"That's it. Dad knew where the surveyor's stake had been, but somehow the thing had disappeared," Johnny continued. "Dad hired a surveyor to lay it out and mark the boundary again. Amos Barton argued with him, said he wouldn't move the fence, so Dad took him to court. They had to go way down to Shawneetown to settle it. Barton was mad as a hornet, I can tell you."

"Yes, I can guess that," I said. "But it wasn't your fault, was it? He just built his dumb fence in the wrong place."

"My thoughts exactly. But I suppose you've seen some samples of his temper. And, of course, when Dad won the lawsuit, that just made him all the madder. Now Dad makes sure all us kids never set foot near your place." Johnny grinned, shaking his head. Abruptly he clapped his hand over his mouth. "I'm sorry. I shouldn't be talking to you about your uncle this way."

"He's not my blood uncle, anyway. He's just married to my mother's sister. I didn't want to come here in the first place."

"No, I don't suppose you did." His eyes softened with sympathy. "Look, kid. Don't give this silly feud stuff another thought. I'll tell my sister and my younger brothers to watch after you at school. No reason why we all should let this worry us, is there?"

I shook my head, grateful for his kindness. The thought of school gave me the first ray of hope I'd had since coming to live in Illinois. And now I wouldn't be a total stranger. I'd see Johnny's familiar, friendly face there on the first day. I would meet other kids there, too—girls my own age that I could talk with, younger girls like my little sisters. Johnny Nichols said he had a sister, too. Maybe when I started school, this painful ache inside my soul would ease.

After I returned to the inn, I asked Aunt Flora about signing up for school. She merely shrugged, an anxious frown clouding her face. Later that evening, she broached the subject with my uncle. "Amos, I was just wondering," she said, then stopped to clear her throat. "Was you planning on sending Nellie down to school? It's starting soon, you know."

"Now just why would I be paying good money to send her to school? She can already read and write, I've noticed. More'n

12

she'll ever need to know. I suppose you just figured I'd hire somebody else to do all her work while she was gone."

"She's only thirteen, Amos. She could go on another year, anyway," Aunt Flora said. "She's real bright—just like my poor sister was, God rest her soul."

Grimacing, he spat into the fire. "An educated female's about as useful as a crowing hen. The answer's no, and that's my last word." He stomped out the back door, slamming it behind him.

She glanced at me with an apologetic shrug. "Well, I guess that's that."

"But I really want to go to school," I protested, my eyes smarting with tears. "There'll be other kids there, and I love book learning. I could catch up with my housework here at night. And anyway, there won't be any garden work in the winter. Please, Aunt Flora. Oh, please. I promise I won't ever ask for anything else."

Her face froze in a stern, adamant expression. "One thing you'd better learn quick, child. When Amos says no, that's just what he means. It don't pay to cross him."

Already I had learned that. My uncle never hesitated to emphasize his orders with a quick slap—or to punish my childish mistakes with a few whacks with his belt.

I didn't go to school. I couldn't even go to the little village church, for I always had to help fix Sunday dinner for the inn guests. I wasn't allowed to go anywhere, except out to the garden, or to the back pasture to bring in the cow for milking. If an inn guest or one of the local people stopped to visit with me for a moment, Uncle Amos always seemed to appear from nowhere with a scowl. He knew just how to discourage anyone from stopping my work, even for a little chat.

Though Illinois was technically a free state, I soon realized that I was nothing but a slave. I began to dream of escape.

Would Pa marry again someday and send for me? When could I go back to Kentucky and see my little sisters again? If I didn't hear from him, maybe someday, when I was just a bit older, I would go back and make a home for them myself.

Four years passed, and my father never wrote me, not a single letter, not even at Christmastime. For all I knew, he had moved far, far away from our old home in Kentucky. And what had happened to my sisters? I had not the slightest clue.

13

With all the hard work at the inn, I grew up strong and healthy, though I was still a mite too thin. My hair was fiery red, my eyes a fiery green, and in my heart, my anger and resentment forged another kind of fire. I vowed I would never let Uncle Amos break me down the way he had Aunt Flora. Though I was forced to obey him, to avoid his ever-ready blows, my spirit remained my own. I was only biding my time, daily promising myself that things would change.

Through the years, I caught only an occasional glimpse of Johnny Nichols as he tore down the road on his spirited black gelding or galloped across the pasture near the fence that divided the Nicholses's property from ours. Sometimes he saw me, too, and flung a friendly wave in my direction.

From the distance, I watched Johnny grow from a gangly adolescent to a handsome young man. His curly hair and his frank blue eyes remained the same, but his cheekbones gradually took on a craggy, grown-up look and his nose grew longer, with a proud, high arch.

One evening, after I had just turned seventeen, Johnny rode over to the dividing fence as I was bringing the cow in from the pasture for milking. "Hi, Red!" he called, waving to me.

"You shouldn't be over here," I said, with a quick glance toward the inn. What if Uncle Amos saw him? But the thick grove of oak trees between the barn and pasture blocked the view.

Johnny's smile was as warm as the summer sun. "Hey, I'm a grown man. Stay and talk to me a minute. I'm not afraid of Crazy Amos anymore." He jumped down from his horse and strode over to the fence.

"I reckon I'm the one has to be afraid of him. You can just jump on your horse and gallop away."

Still, I hurried over to the fence to meet him. After watching him so often from a distance, I wanted to see how he had changed close up. His sun-bronzed skin accented the deep blue of his eyes. I caught my breath at the sight of a jagged scar, still bright pink, curving across the right side of his forehead. "What—what happened to your face?"

His fingers rose to the scar. "This? Oh, just a little throw from King here. I landed on a wagon tongue and split my head. It's nothing, really. Does it look that bad?"

"No, you look fine, Johnny. I haven't seen you for so long."

14

"It has been awhile, hasn't it? Why won't Crazy Amos let you go to any of the cornhuskings and frolics like the other folks? What are you, a prisoner over there? You're growing up, Nellie. He can't go on holding you captive like this."

"I know. I'm seventeen now."

"And you're growing up so pretty."

My cheeks grew warm. I hung my head and brushed back a stray lock of hair. "No, I'm not. You're teasing me."

"You are! You're like a ray of sunshine, with all that shiny red hair. Why, it cheers me up just looking at you." His eyes played over my flushed face with frank interest. "Stay and talk to me a minute, Nellie. It's been years since we've talked."

"I can't stay. My uncle's out by the barn somewhere. He'll notice if I'm gone too long. But I come out here every day about this time . . ."

"I'll watch for you. I'm usually helping my dad with the horses, but I can get away." He pointed to the small herd grazing at the far end of the pasture. "Some of those are racing stock. We have a big herd of cattle, too. Yes, I have plenty to do, helping Dad raise grain and take care of all that stock."

"Your dad does well, I reckon."

"Real well." He smiled into my eyes. "It's good to talk to you again. I suppose you get tired of talking, though, with all those people stopping at the inn."

I snorted. "You must be kidding. I'm just the kitchen help. Uncle Amos plays the host and entertains the guests. My aunt and me just do the dirty work."

"Sounds like him. But it's not fair. Not fair at all. Can't some-body say something to him?"

"Who? Aunt Flora? Me? He knows how to keep us both in line. I used to hope my pa would send for me, but . . . I have to go now, Johnny."

"Come back tomorrow. I'll be watching for you."

I nodded, gazing at him one last time before I turned to leave. How beautiful it was to have a friend to talk with.

We started meeting then, just a few stolen moments talking across the fence. At first we only exchanged mundane obser-vations about the weather or our work, but soon Johnny began telling me all his dreams for the future.

"Someday I'm going to buy a piece of land of my own down the road a piece," he told me one afternoon. "I'll build a fine house there—and raise prize cattle and racehorses. There's no end to the opportunity here, if a fellow's not afraid of hard work."

My dream was simpler. "All I want is to leave that inn and make some kind of life of my own. Someday I'd like to quit being just a kitchen slave. You won't believe it, but I was always a cheerful, happy person before my mother died."

"Do you remember her?" he asked, his eyes warm with sympathy.

Gazing off into the distance, I swallowed back the lump in my throat. "Most of all, I remember her voice. She used to sing us the sweetest song, all about Barbara Allen."

He reached across the fence and took my hand. At his touch, a surge of heat flowed up my arm and through my body. "Sing it for me, Nellie," he said softly.

"Next time. I'll try to remember all the verses." My face felt hot. Strange, confusing new emotions stirred inside me. "Right now I'd better hurry back and milk this cow."

"You always have to hurry." He bent down to pick some wild daisies and handed me a bouquet. A slight smile lingered on his lips as he gazed into my eyes. "When are we going to have time to really talk, Nellie? Can't you ever get away?"

"You don't know my uncle like I do. But we could write notes. See that flat rock under the big oak near the fence? I could leave a note there for you sometimes. And you could leave one for me."

"A note's better than nothing, I suppose. But someday, Nellie"—he stood tall, his spine rigid—"someday we're going to have to face that man and let him know you're not his slave."

I stared over at the big oak by the fence, thinking of my uncle's size and strength, his insane temper. Where would I ever find the nerve to cross him?

Suddenly I saw a movement in the grove of trees. My uncle's bulky form appeared, moving with clumsy speed toward us.

"Go now, Johnny. Quick." I said, tugging on the cow's rope.

Uncle Amos waited like an angry giant, both hands on his hips. When I came near, he slapped me full across the face. His eyes bloodred, he glared at me, for a moment too angry to

16

speak. "A Nichols?" he sputtered. "When my back's turned, you're sneaking out here talking to a Nichols?"

My face stung from his blow. I bit my tongue to hold back the tears. "I was not sneaking! I just came out to bring the cow in for milking," I protested. "I . . . We just were saying hello."

"I have to watch you every minute! I try to keep you out of the dining room, away from all those traveling peddlers and their kind. And here you are, out making eyes at some damned Nichols kid. I've got a good mind . . ." He drew back to strike me again, but I dodged him and dashed back to the kitchen, leaving him to bring in the cow.

"What is it, child?" Aunt Flora asked as I rushed in the door. "Did you milk the cow already?"

"No, it's Uncle Amos. He . . ."

She breathed out a weary sigh. "Men. You stay here and stir these beans. I'll go and see to the cow. You know Amos gets riled real easy after he's had a few drinks. Just try to stay out of his way."

After that, my uncle watched me much more closely. I could only talk to Johnny those rare times when I was certain Uncle Amos was nowhere around. As I had promised, I left notes for Johnny under the oak tree, painfully written with lead pencil on little scraps of paper. I found I had nearly forgotten how to write or spell.

Johnny answered me with short but precious messages, telling me to keep my spirits up. Nothing lasts forever, he wrote. I was growing up—and would not have to stay in my prison much longer. Johnny's notes, his thoughts, the knowledge that he really cared about what happened to me, gave me a thread of hope to cling to. My life was going to change. I knew it for a certainty.

Just before Christmas, I found a little package by our hiding place. Fingers trembling with excitement, I unwrapped it to reveal the lovely pearl brooch, the most precious gift I had ever received. Best of all was the note folded in beside it: "With love from Johnny."

Love. Yes, now he had put a name to the wild new emotions churning within my heart. I loved him, yearned to spend each moment with him, cursed anything that kept us apart.

One day, when I had finished working in the garden, I hurried over to our hiding place. I found a note there, written in Johnny's

17

neat, square hand: "Can you come out tonight after everybody is asleep? I'll be waiting here for you."

A hundred sleepless nights I had sat beside my tiny bedroom window, gazing at the moonglow over the wide, rolling meadow separating me from Johnny's house. I pictured his beloved face, his shining eyes, his warm smile, his strong, lean form. Tonight I would put aside my fear and go to him.

I waited in my room, fully clothed, until all the noises at the inn had stilled. The moon was dark, the whole yard swathed in blackness when I eased my body, feetfirst, through the narrow window opening and dropped onto the earth outside. Stealthily I crept through the darkness toward the woods behind the barn. A horse neighed as I passed. Mysterious noises and flutterings sounded in the trees and grass around me. Still I pressed on, all my senses alert, my pulse hammering in my head as loudly as the blacksmith's hammer striking on his anvil.

My eyes searched the woods around me, so familiar in daylight, but now a confusing mass of black and dark gray forms. The air smelled of wildflowers and fertile soil and rich green vegetation. I heard the grass rustle ahead of me. A whisper. "Nellie?"

"Yes, it's me."

The darkness enshrouded him, but his hands reached out to take my arms. "Are you all right? Nobody saw you, did they?"

"No, I don't think so. If my uncle catches me, I'm dead."

"This is no way to live," he said, gently brushing back my hair from the sides of my face. "I don't want to sneak around like this. I want to come and talk to you, take you to my house for supper, take you to the dances like normal people do."

I shook my head in disgust. "Nothing about my uncle is normal. I learned that long ago. But let's not waste time talking about him. Tell me what you've been doing since I saw you last."

"Working with the horses, same as always. My sister Blanche was real sick with the fever last week. We had to have the doctor come and bleed her."

"I've never even seen your sister, except from a distance. How old is she?"

"Twenty-two. Just two years older than me. She always tried to boss me around when we were younger. I suppose most big sisters do."

18

I chuckled softly. "Does she still boss you?"

"Sometimes she tries. I stay out of her path. The only good part of my life is when I get to see you, Nellie." He squeezed my hands and drew me closer to him. His voice was low, rich as velvet. "Tell me you feel the same way, too."

"Oh, Johnny! You know how I feel." My throat choked with emotion. "You're my only friend. You're the only thing that makes my life worth living."

He slipped his arms around my waist. "How long are we going to have to go on this way?"

"Someday I'm going to stand up to him and demand my rights. I turned eighteen last month. I'm of age now. It's just . . . I'm afraid of him, Johnny. He's crazy. He hits me for the smallest things, and he beats my aunt if she takes my part."

"I'm going to help you, Nellie. Somehow." His lips pressed against my brow. "I'm not going to let that man hurt you anymore. We'll think about it. We'll start making plans."

"I'd have to run far away from here. If I stayed anywhere close by, he'd come after me sure. I think he'd kill me without thinking twice. You don't know him, Johnny."

"He's been making threats against my dad for years. He's never done a thing about them. Just talk. Seems like he'd rather pick on women." Johnny drew me close against him, his embrace tightening. "We didn't come out here to talk about your crazy uncle, did we?"

I lifted my face to him. His breath felt warm against my cheek; his scent was sweet as clover. His lips sought mine and lingered there, gentle and yet urgent. Our bodies locked together, swaying with emotion. I felt dizzy and exhilarated, like a falling star flying through the night sky. Strange new sensations, warm and liquid and aching, surged through my whole being.

"I love you, Nellie," he murmured, his warm gaze soft as an embrace. His finger traced a path across my nose. "I love your freckles where the sunshine kissed you. I love your shiny hair and pretty green eyes. I'm going to help you. I'm going to get you out of that hellhole they've trapped you in."

"Oh, Johnny. Can it be true?"

"It is true. Trust me. I'll figure out a way."

His kisses brought me joy—and a confidence I'd never known before. Yes, with Johnny I could find escape . . . and so much more—a love and fulfillment I had never dreamed existed.

19

A cat squalled out by the barn. Reality suddenly intruded. "It's getting late, Johnny. I have to get back," I said, reaching out to trace the craggy line of his cheek and jaw. His whiskers prickled sharp against my fingers.

He took my hand and pressed a kiss in my palm. "I love you, Nellie. Just hang on a little longer. I'll figure out a way to get you out of there."

We clung together for a final fiery kiss. Reluctantly I tore myself away from him and crept back to the inn. As I squeezed back through my tiny window opening, his words rang over and over in my ears.

Johnny loved me. Everything would be all right.

CHAPTER 3

And now, tonight, we would meet again. As I waited beneath the trees for him, my whole body tensed with anticipation—and with dread.

The grass behind me rustled. A dry twig snapped. Love blazed up inside me like a torch flame. I jumped up from the log, sensing Johnny's presence before I could distinguish his form in the darkness.

"You came." His voice hushed and urgent, he seized my hands and pressed them to his lips. "Oh, Nellie, Nellie. You're my girl, aren't you?"

"I am. I have been, ever since we first met," I whispered, stroking the warmth of his smooth-shaven cheek. Could this really be happening? A ragged veil of clouds drifted across the pale moon. In the darkness, the whole world seemed soft and misty as a dream. I felt transported to a new, enchanted world.

Johnny wrapped his arms about my waist and drew me close

to him. "I love you, Nellie," he murmured, his breath warm against my ear. "I have to see you more. I can't stand to be away from you—not even for a day."

Suddenly I froze. "Listen! Did you hear that sound back by the barn? Do you think Uncle—"

"Hush. It's just a horse moving around in his stall. Forget your crazy uncle. There's nobody here but you and me."

I gazed up at his night-enshrouded face; he was smiling at my fears. Light as gossamer, my fingertips brushed over his lips. The intoxicating, masculine scent of him, so close to me, set my heart aflame. "You're right. My uncle doesn't matter anymore."

Johnny held me close, gazing at me in the dim moonlight that filtered through the leaves. A tense urgency came over him. "I love you, Nellie. I want to marry you. I'll build you a fine home, just up the road a piece."

He bent and kissed me, his lips like searing velvet. His warmth surged through me, turning my blood to flames. Trembling, I clung to him, savoring his touch, longing to make this enchanting moment last forever. Yes, my dream had come true. We would be married, be together always, always close like this.

But the danger of our meeting intruded like a chill wind; I drew away from Johnny with a sigh. "My uncle is a cruel man," I said bitterly. "He would never let us—"

A voice shot out of the night. "You're damn right I'd never!" I spun around and saw Uncle Amos looming there, dark and threatening, his huge body silhouetted in the faint light.

We froze, startled as he lunged toward us, leveling a long-barreled pistol at Johnny's stomach. Even in the dark I could see the crazed sneer on his twisted, haggard face. He spat a smelly wad of tobacco at our feet. "Just like a damned Nichols, dallying with my girl behind my back. You bastards will do anything to get at me, won't you?"

Johnny's voice was taut. "Look here! I wasn't—"

Rage blazed inside me, making the whole world seem aflame. "You leave Johnny alone!" I stepped in front of my uncle's pistol and glared at him, jutting out my chin. "I'm going to marry him. I'm of age. I don't need your say-so."

His arm sprang out and knocked me to the ground. "When I get done with him, he won't be marrying material for anybody," he snarled.

Quick as an arrow, Johnny hit Uncle Amos in the jaw. The pistol shot instantly cut through the still night air. I screamed. The bullet had missed; Johnny was unharmed. But Uncle Amos flipped the gun and used its heavy butt to strike at Johnny's head and face. The dull, rapid thuds of metal against flesh made me ill.

Now they were on the ground, battling like grizzly bears, snarling, kicking, gouging, biting. I tried to interfere, but all I saw was churning movement in the darkness. Then my uncle's voice came, harsh with hatred. "I'll kill you, you rattlesnake! I won't rest until the world is rid of all you Nichols bastards!"

He grabbed Johnny's head and pounded it against a tree stump. All movement stopped. Johnny lay still as death. I shrieked and rushed to him, but my uncle seized my arms and held me fast.

"Let me go! Johnny! Johnny!" I yelled.

"You little slut!" He jerked me toward him. "I turn my back and you sneak out to meet some damned Nichols. You're not going to get away with this."

"I wasn't doing anything wrong! Let me go!" I shouted, hoping someone from the inn would hear. I tried to twist my arm from his clasp. "What have you done to Johnny?"

His piercing eyes bore into me like lanterns in the darkness. He slid his arm around my waist and pulled me closer toward him. "I'll kill him. I'll kill you both before I let some Nichols have you."

"No! You let me go!" I shrieked, beating my fists frantically against his chest.

He pulled me, sobbing, back toward the inn. The door opened, and Aunt Flora peeked out. "What's all this noise? Is something wrong out there?" she asked in her meek voice, holding out her flickering candle.

"Not a thing," my uncle growled, glaring at her. "I just caught this little slut out here with that damned Nichols kid. I'm going to have to lock her up like some bitch in heat."

"Now, Amos. You know Nellie's a good girl," Aunt Flora protested mildly. "She just wants a chance to talk to somebody her own age."

Sucking in a quick, raspy breath, he released my arm and stepped toward her. "Don't you contradict me, woman!" he snarled, shoving her violently against the doorframe.

Fury exploded from me like a cannonball. I lunged at him,

shrieking, "You leave her alone! Leave us all alone! I won't let you hurt her one more time!"

He seized me in a viselike grip. "Ingrate! Wildcat!" He dragged me, kicking and biting, to the small smokehouse behind the inn, threw open the door, and shoved me inside. I heard a key turn in the lock. "I'll teach you to cross me. That Nichols kid is going to wish he'd never been born," he shouted through the door. His heavy footsteps disappeared into the distance.

Frozen in shock, I stared into the surrounding blackness. Odors enveloped me—ham and lard and smoked sausage—so strong and greasy my stomach lurched. Tears flowed, scalding, down my cheeks. I sobbed and cried and called my uncle vile names. I was alone, totally alone.

Outside, the dull thud of horse hoofs. They paused, then faded into the distance.

My stomach drew into a rock-hard knot of panic. Where was Johnny? Was he badly hurt? Oh, it was all my fault. I never should have gone out there to meet him. I knew full well how crazy Uncle Amos was.

I gasped for breath. The dense hot air of the windowless room was suffocating. Feeling my way, I crawled across the rough floorboards to the wall and scratched at a spot in the mud caulking between the logs. I dug and scratched until my nails were broken to the quick and my fingers bleeding. Finally I cleared a tiny hole and sucked in the fresh air that came rushing in.

What if Uncle Amos came back later? The thought of being at his mercy, cornered in this dark, smelly smokehouse, filled me with icy terror, for he had been acting stranger than ever lately.

After hours of anxious dread, flinching at the slightest noise, I curled up on the hard floor in the cavelike darkness and tried to rest. I prayed my aunt could somehow keep Uncle Amos away from me. My mind rolled with images of all the misery of my life, this endless nightmare that had begun the day my mother died.

If it weren't for Johnny, my whole life would be a living hell. But Johnny, handsome Johnny Nichols, loved me. Oh, the wonder and magic of it all. Soon we would be together. Nobody, not even Uncle Amos, could ever destroy this wondrous love.

Chills racked my aching body. Was Johnny all right? How badly was he hurt? We had left him lying on the ground unconscious, his eyes closed and still. Oh, God! He had to be all right! He had to be!

My rage and tears flared anew. The minute anybody let me out of this smelly smokehouse, I would run away. I had to be with Johnny. And Johnny wanted me with him.

Hours later, I finally curled up in a corner and fell into a fitful sleep.

Toward dawn, a rooster crowed out in the chicken yard, and I awoke with a start. Where was I? A cloying, greasy smell surrounded me. My whole body ached. As I recalled last night's trauma, my mind churned with turbulent emotions. I would run away. Yes, I would make a whole new life with Johnny.

A faint, ragged shaft of sunlight beamed through the hole I had dug in the mud caulking between the logs, bringing a dim relief to the oppressive darkness. Where was Johnny now? Oh, darling Johnny—we will be together soon, I thought.

A short time later, Aunt Flora, wary and apathetic, crept out and unlocked the smokehouse door. "Amos said you can come in now," she murmured. "You and me have to get the fire going for breakfast."

"Oh, God! Thank you, Aunt Flora."

"He's gone out to the back pasture to see about the cattle." She averted her eyes from me. "For Lord's sake child! Don't do anything else to rile him up today!"

I stumbled outside onto the dew-sprinkled grass and sucked in great breaths of cool, clean air. Though the sunlight blinded me, the slanting golden rays had never seemed so beautiful.

As Aunt Flora started back to the inn, I glanced about the yard. Uncle Amos was nowhere in sight. My heart in my throat, I ran to the oak grove and searched for some sign of Johnny. Only a bit of crushed grass and a patch of dried blood on the tree stump gave any evidence that he was ever there.

I threw myself down on the grass beside the stump and buried my head in my arms. My mind spun in a whirlwind of confusion. What would I do if Johnny was badly hurt? I could not bear to think of life without him, without the joy his presence brought me. Oh, he had to be all right. I would go to him. If he was badly hurt, I would care for him.

I glanced back at the inn. The weathered log building looked tranquil, white smoke curling upward in a lazy spiral from the wide stone chimney. I knew my aunt, grim and silent, was already busy in the kitchen, gathering the pans and eggs and corn-meal for cooking breakfast. She would expect my help, as usual. Uncle Amos would soon be back, his sly, evil eyes watching my every move.

A vision of my grim life at the inn passed through my mind. Suddenly my feet assumed a life of their own. They carried me over the rail fence and through the wide clover meadow—toward Johnny's large brick house in the distance.

The meadow grass was cool and moist beneath my feet, the sky a wide blue arch overhead. As I dashed forward, panting for breath, I saw a dozen horses galloping far down the field, their long manes flying out behind proud, stately heads. They looked so free. So gloriously free.

CHAPTER 4

I ran stumbling across the field. As I neared the large brick house, I slowed my pace, hesitating. Would his family let me see him? Did they hate me as bitterly as my uncle hated them?

When I approached the front steps of the house, the door opened and a tight-faced young woman stepped out on the porch. It had to be his sister Blanche. Why, she was only two years older than Johnny, but already she looked like an old maid as she stood tall, pole-thin and motionless, glaring at me with pale eyes as frigid as a February midnight.

For a moment, her chilly expression held me back. "Are you Blanche?" I asked tensely.

"Yes. What are you doing here?"

"I have to see Johnny. Is he all right?" I dashed up the porch steps and to the door, trying to brush Blanche aside. "Please let me see him. Where is he?"

Her arm barred my way. The nostrils of her long nose flared. "He's asleep," she snapped, her thin lips barely moving. "You can't see him. Get off our land."

"Is he all right?" I grabbed her stiff, bony arm. "Please tell me how he is. Is he hurt bad?"

"He's still alive, no thanks to you." She brushed me off as if I were an insect. "We weren't sure of that when Amos Barton dumped him on the doorstep last night. But the doctor said he'd be all right in a few days."

"Thank God."

Her eyes and voice were cold and hard as ice. "Now you get out of here. This whole thing is your fault. You're always chasing after Johnny. You're going to ruin his whole life." She wheeled and started walking into the house.

"No! Please!" Frantically I seized her arm again. "I love Johnny. Please tell me when I can see him. I have to talk to him."

"Your crazy uncle tried to kill him last night. I don't believe Johnny will ever make the mistake of seeing you again."

"Please, Blanche. I have to talk to him. Oh, please." Tears burned my eyes, blurred my vision of her livid face.

She smirked. "He hates you."

"No! I know that's not true."

"This is all your fault. I've been watching you for months from my upstairs window. I've seen you calling him over to the fence—and you knowing full well all the bad blood there is between our families." Her glare burned into me. "You're going to pay for this."

My mind whirled. Speechless, I leaned against the house, fighting the dizziness and confusion that engulfed me.

"Get out of here. Johnny said he never wants to hear your name again." She turned from me, stomping back into the house and slamming the door to punctuate her words.

She was lying. I was certain of it. Yet the very thought of losing Johnny dropped a curtain of despair so smothering I could not breathe. I sank down on the steps and buried my head in my arms, trying to shut out the wretched thought.

Blindly I rose and staggered back across the pasture, toward the inn, her words echoing inside my head. Johnny hated me. Everything was my fault. Tears flooded my eyes and coursed down my cheeks. I cried in painful, desperate sobs. I could not go on without him. What was left for me?

Somehow I must escape my crazy uncle. But when could I see Johnny? How?

I hesitated on the back stoop, brooding over Blanche's cruel words. Johnny hated me. No! He loved me. He had told me so. But Uncle Amos had beaten him so horribly. Did he really blame me? Now I loathed my uncle even more, with a hatred that seared my very soul.

As I entered the kitchen, Aunt Flora rushed to me and seized me by the shoulders. "Good Lord, child! Where have you been? Amos was in here looking for you. I told him you'd gone to change your clothes. If he finds out you were gone, he'll whip us both to a pulp. Run in and change your dress quick, lest you make a liar out of me."

Wordlessly I rushed to my room and changed into my old blue homespun.

When I returned, Aunt Flora glanced at me with a nervous frown. "Come on. We have to hurry and get breakfast out."

With a nod of my head, I stepped over to the fire and stirred the mush. The familiar morning smells of fried bacon and boiled coffee filled the room. I must try to act normal while I decided what to do next. "Is this about ready to serve?"

"Yes . . ."

I took a stack of small wooden bowls from the shelves that lined the plastered log wall and dipped them full of mush. As I carried them and a platter of bacon on a tray through the doorway to the crowded, noisy dining room, I glanced down at my clean dress and blessed Aunt Flora for covering up for me. That took courage, I knew, for she was terrified of Uncle Amos. Curse that man. I would show him. But first I must get through this insane day.

Smiling stiffly to mask my turbulent emotions, I nodded to the usual group of tavern guests crowded along both sides of the long plank table in the center of the dining room. Though the faces of the guests were always changing, to me the results were all the same: stacks and stacks of sticky, greasy dishes to be washed and dried and set away.

But among the handful of traveling preachers and land spec-ulators and surveyors were some familiar faces—those of the three sad-faced Cranford children and their father Daniel, a tall

Yankee, solemn and intelligent-looking with his dark brown beard and high forehead. As I passed, little Eddie tugged my skirt and gave me a shy smile.

"Morning, Eddie," I said briskly, hoping to mask the quiver in my voice.

"Will you tell us more stories today?" he asked.

"Not today." The sight of his innocent face looking up at me wrenched my heart. I hurried out of the room after I had served the mush so no one would see the scalding tears welling in my eyes.

Back in the kitchen, my tears spilled over, trailing down my cheeks. I brushed them away with the back of my hands and blew my nose on my pocket hanky. This was no time for tears. I must think clearly now.

As I stared down at the pan of gray greasy dishwater, Uncle Amos suddenly loomed beside me like a grizzly bear. I would not look at him, would not let him see my tears. "You, girl! Get to work!" he snarled. "I had enough trouble from you last night. I hope to God you learned your lesson."

I raised my eyes and glared at him, focusing all my anger and hatred on his ugly face. Our eyes met and held in a war of wills. He scowled. "I'll kill that bastard if he ever comes sniffing around you again."

How could he say such vile things to me? Why, I was just a girl, innocent as a child. "We weren't doing anything . . ."

With three steps he was upon me. His hand lashed out and slapped me full across the face. "Don't you back talk me! If you ever set foot near that Nichols kid again, I'll shoot him square through the heart. I swear I will."

His breath came in agitated pants, his enormous body stiffened with rage. I stared at his glazed, reddened eyes and chills slithered down my spine. He meant it. He had beaten me, many times. There was no doubt in my mind that he would kill Johnny.

Eyes downcast, my sight blurred by fresh tears, I fished the dishrag from the gray water and began to scrub a dirty, sticky pan. Though my face stung from his blow, I felt hollow, empty, lifeless. I tried to remember Johnny's sweet words, but instead, my uncle's curses rang in my head. I tried to visualize Johnny's beloved face, but all I saw was his beaten form, sprawled under the tree. Had my uncle won? Was his hatred stronger than our fragile love?

By the time I had finished all the breakfast pans and dishes, my eyes were dry. My heart felt frigid and hard as granite as I filled a pail with hot water from the kettle on the fire and began to scrub the grease spots under the dining table with a corn-husk brush. If I stayed cold and detached, surely I could figure out how to escape from Uncle Amos and make a life of my own.

Would it be a life without Johnny? Without a single glance from his blue eyes? No. Surely he would come back. At least he'd put a note in our hiding place. After all, he said he loved me.

Turmoil colored my whole day. How could I bear to live without the hope of someday being with Johnny? The prospect turned my blood to ice.

But even if I could not be with him, I knew I had to get away from here. I would run away. Anywhere. It would not be easy, I knew. A girl alone was easy prey to the unscrupulous. Still, I would have to strike out on my own. I could not stand the sight of Uncle Amos. The very thought of him repulsed me.

That night, sleep would not come to me. I lay wide-eyed, tossing until I had twisted the coarse sheets on my rough corn-shuck mattress into ropes. I cried for Johnny, prayed that he would somehow get in touch with me. He was not a coward. He had assured me he was not afraid of Uncle Amos. If he really loved me, he would not change his mind so quickly.

Three weeks passed, day after endless day without a single word from Johnny. The day after the fight, I had slipped away and hidden a note for him under our special rock. Time after time I checked that hiding place and found my note still there, undisturbed.

He could have sent me a note. Even if he was afraid to come himself, he could have had someone bring a message to our hiding place, telling me that he was all right. Surely he could have done that much, knowing how I cared for him. Only a coward would let my uncle scare him from even sending me a note. It was becoming painfully clear to me that Johnny never really loved me.

Each day my heart sank lower. Maybe Blanche was telling the truth when she said he hated me and blamed me for the whole mess. Had he decided I wasn't worth the trouble I brought along with me? There were other, prettier girls—girls whose parents could provide a generous dowry at their marriage rather than a passel of ugly family squabbles.

Still, at night I dreamed of him, vivid images of him charging down the road astride a white horse, coming to rescue me. My body yearned for his touch, my lips for his sweet kisses.

Then one day I looked under our secret rock and found my note for Johnny was gone. I stood and stared at the spot, my mind reeling with pain. There was no note for me. No message swearing eternal love. Just the damp, dark earth and an ugly worm.

I returned to the spot again and again. No note. Not a word. Agonizing as it was, I must accept the bitter fact. Johnny didn't love me. Or he was so afraid of Uncle Amos, he didn't want to see me anymore.

Johnny had become an expert at avoiding me. Though I tried to keep an eye on all the people coming and going at his house across the field, I never caught a glimpse of him. My pain was a raw, bleeding wound. The very sight of Johnny's house became a torture to me. I began to mourn the Johnny I had loved as if he were already dead.

Somehow I had to find the strength to leave by myself. I would bide my time, for I dared not rile my uncle. But someday soon, I vowed I would escape this wretched prison.

I trudged about the kitchen, working like some dumb beast of burden through the long days. The anger churning inside me was the only thing that kept me going.

"My lands, you sure do look peaked," Aunt Flora said one day, watching me from across the room as I dully wiped a wet dishrag across the worktable. "That Nichols boy didn't ruin you, did he? Oh, Lordy! What will Amos do if that boy got you in trouble?"

The sudden fury in my glare silenced her. Ruined? My life was ruined, all right, but not by Johnny's tender kisses. Uncle Amos had ruined it by forcing me to be part of his senseless feud.

After breakfast, Daniel Cranford left his children in my aunt's care and rode out to his rented fields to inspect his livestock. Aunt Flora glanced at my haggard face and patted my shoulder. "Here, Nellie. You take these young'uns out for a little walk. Do you all good to get out of this place for a spell."

With a silent nod, I numbly gathered the three children around me. They looked as forlorn as I felt. Hugh, the oldest, all of seven, could pass for an old man with his solemn bearing, as dignified and pensive as his Yankee father. His dark brown hair lay neatly brushed; his blousy shirts were always properly tucked into his short dark trousers.

Sarah, blond and blue-eyed, was at five already a miniature of her delicate mother. Proud of her pretty lace-trimmed frocks and dainty slippers, she obviously disdained our rugged frontier ways.

Only little Eddie, the renegade, ever displayed any childish enthusiasm. Often he looked bewildered, his deep-set hazel eyes darting from face to face, seeking answers to all his unspoken questions.

"Come on, kids. Let's go over and wade in the creek," I said with forced cheerfulness, leading them across the road and through a sun-dappled stand of timber.

The sound of water rippling over rocks drew us toward the delightful little creek that wandered through the cool, green woods. Sunlight danced on the bubbling water, flashing in gold and silver sparks of radiance. At the sight and sound of it, my agitated soul began to ease.

"May we take off our shoes and socks?" Hugh asked in his proper, low-pitched voice.

"Sure. Go right ahead," I said, kicking off my own old clogs. "Kids in these parts go barefoot all summer long."

As I watched the children splash timidly, quietly, among the rocks in the shallow creek, I recalled their loss, and my own troubles faded temporarily from my mind. The Cranford family had stopped by the inn one warm day in early summer, on their way to settle a piece of land upstate. When they reined their covered wagon to a halt, we learned that some strange fever was raging within the mother.

Her face was flushed, her speech faint and delirious. We were used to seeing people with ague and other kinds of recurring fevers, but this was worse. Much worse. We called the doctor.

"You just stay your distance. I don't want you catching nothing," my uncle told Aunt Flora. "Let Nellie do the nursin' if there's any to be done."

With the help of Mr. Cranford, I installed the bone-thin blond woman in the end bed in the ladies' room, and I nursed her the best I could. This lady from New York State was so delicate and

31

fair-skinned, she appeared in imminent danger of breaking, like some precious porcelain cup. Even with her raging illness, she was clearly a beauty. Graceful tapered fingers fluttered like butterfly wings at the ends of long, white hands. Her soft, melodic voice rambled in an unfamiliar Yankee accent, calling for faraway people and places.

Doc Spencer came and bled her, thrusting his thumb lance into a pale, thin arm already scarred from frequent bleedings. He dosed her with calomel and thick, smelly castor oil.

Her husband Daniel, tall and grave and silent, paced the floor beside her bed. He gently smoothed sweat-dampened strands of blond hair back from her face and spoke to her in tender, loving tones.

The children wept far into the night, there in the same room, for we had no other place to put them. I stayed and tried to comfort them.

The lovely Mrs. Cranford died. Her family, devastated by the loss, stayed on at the inn, and her husband rented pasture for his livestock from a local farmer while he pondered his next move. Now he spent his evenings talking with the changing group of tavern guests after his three children had been tucked into bed upstairs.

One evening as I cleared the supper table, I heard the voices of the men, as always, on the porch benches out front. How often I had longed to sit down after supper, too, to talk with the occasional women guests or just to stare up at the stars.

The sound of Daniel Cranford's deep voice drifted through the open door. "Yes, I'm a veteran of the War of 1812," he said in his strange-sounding Yankee accent. "I fought with General Scott in the Battle of Lundy's Lane, up by Niagara Falls."

"Back in '14, wasn't it?" one fellow asked.

Cranford grunted agreement. "Talk about hard fighting. I don't know who was stubbornest—us or the British. It's a wonder we're not all still up there shooting at one another. One thing about it, though. The government did give me a nice piece of land for my service."

I moved closer to the door, intrigued by the conversation. I caught a glimpse of the half-dozen men lounging on the benches, contentedly smoking their pipes.

"They gave you land?" somebody asked him. "Is that up in the Military Tract?"

"Yes, that bounty land up between the Illinois and Mississippi rivers. Have you been there?"

"Nope. Not many have."

"My land's first-rate, they tell me. We veterans had to draw lots to see which plot of land we each could claim. I was made a field officer, so I got three hundred and twenty acres, twice as much as most. A couple of weeks ago, I rode over to the government office in St. Louis and copied the surveyor's notes. I'm hoping I can find the boundaries of my claim when I get there."

"You're going up soon, are you?"

Mr. Cranford paused, then continued in a tight voice. "I just don't know. My wife and I had been waiting for years for them to survey the land and divide it into plots—so we could come out here and claim our share. It just doesn't seem possible we'd get this far and then . . ." His head bent; his gray eyes stared unseeing at the floorboards.

The other men puffed their pipes and shook their heads in the sympathetic silence that followed. I reflected on the uncertainties of life. With all the mystifying diseases and fevers that threatened us, which one of us could depend on being here next week? We could all understand Cranford's dolefulness.

"You planning on going back East?" one fellow asked.

"No. I don't want to go back." Daniel Cranford sounded perplexed. He hesitated, rubbing his neat dark beard. "This land grant is an opportunity I could never duplicate back East. But . . ." With a shrug, he hung his head again.

The men around him nodded and scratched their heads and beards. "Could be mighty dangerous up there. I hear there's still a right smart heap of Potawatomis hanging round. Sauk and Fox. Some Winnebagos, too," grunted a rough-looking hunter. His shaggy hair and unkempt beard, the long sheathed knife stuck in his snakeskin belt, made him look as fearful as any Indian.

"You couldn't pay me to live anywheres near them heathen Indians," the traveling peddler said. "I still remember all the troubles we had with the Kickapoo around these parts. Not so long ago, neither. I tell you, it was like living in a battle zone."

"Yeah. Remember how the Indians burned down Fort Dearborn at Chicago during the war? They stirred up plenty of mischief in Peoria, too. Oh, they made dandy allies for the British,

33

didn't they? Hell, around this state the Indians gave us ten times more trouble than the British did.''

A heavy silence followed, softened only by the mesmerizing drone of the cicadas outside. Daniel's voice was low and thoughtful as he gazed into the darkening woods across the road. ''There've been no real Indian problems here since they signed the treaties after the war, have there?''

''Hell, I wouldn't trust those red devils as far as I could throw them.'' The hunter wiped his hand across his shaggy beard. ''Reckon you'll have to send those young'uns back East, anyways.''

Stiffening his spine, Daniel Cranford sat up straighter. ''No. My children stay with me,'' he said in a firm tone. ''That much I know for certain.''

I drew in a sharp breath. Never once had my father inquired into my welfare after he sent me away. I suspected my little sisters had been treated with the same indifference. This cool, grave Yankee, Daniel Cranford, was evidently of a different breed.

His concern for his motherless children won my deep admiration. I recalled how fondly he hugged them every day before he left them in my aunt's care and went out to work with his livestock in his rented field. He sought the children out as soon as he returned. Though he bore his own grief like a wearisome burden, I knew how hard he tried to bolster the spirits of his little ones.

In the two and a half months since their mother's death, I had become attached to the children, and I begged Aunt Flora to let me spend more time with them. I sympathized with them, of course, remembering my own loss. I tried to cheer them up by inventing games and singing songs with them.

Though my success was meager, the time I spent with them was a tiny ray of sunshine in my gloomy life. For those few moments, I could forget all the hostility and vile threats from Uncle Amos, the endless, grueling drudgery of kitchen work and heavy cleaning and laundry. In truth, these children, and the few moments I could steal away to talk with Johnny, were the only things that made my life endurable.

Now Johnny came no more. And each passing day seemed further proof he never would.

* * *

The next morning, Daniel Cranford brought his children to the kitchen as I washed the tall stacks of breakfast bowls. "Hugh has begged and begged to work with me, so I finally gave in. I'm taking him out to help cut some hay this morning."

"I can do it, Papa. You'll see I can help," the boy said, with more eagerness than I had ever seen him display.

The sight of their identical gray eyes, both pairs looking somberly out upon the world, brought a grudging smile to my lips. "You're quite a frontiersman, Hugh. All set to go out and tame the wilderness."

The boy grinned up at me.

"The two of us could tame quite a piece of it, I'll wager," his father said, smiling as he clasped Hugh's thin shoulder.

An idea struck me like a bolt of lightning from the night sky. I shook my head to dispel this strange and disturbing thought. Still it persisted. Before I could change my mind, I followed the man out the back door and laid my hand on his arm. "Mr. Cranford . . ."

He stopped and glanced at me, frowning. "Yes? Something wrong?"

I sucked in my breath to calm my racing pulse, and the words came bursting forth. "I could work for you. When you go up north, I mean. I could look after your kids and work out in the garden and take care of your house and everything."

He stood stock-still, staring at me, his brow furrowed above puzzled eyes. "I don't understand what you're saying."

"It's simple." My words were hushed and quick. "You need someone to take care of your house and family. I need to get away. I'll work for you. I'm strong. You know I'm a good worker. You've seen all I do around here. Why, back in Kentucky I even drove a wagon to help my pa bring in the hay."

With a tentative smile on his thin lips, he shook his head. "You don't know what you're suggesting, Nellie. It's not possible."

"Sure it is. I have to get away from here."

A look of sympathy and understanding crossed his face as he met my anxious gaze. "Your uncle works you awfully hard, doesn't he?" But then he shook his head again. "No, it's just not practical." He turned to leave.

"Well, think about it, anyway," I said as he strode out to the barn to get his horse, little Hugh close by his side.

All day I walked a knife's edge, wondering, hoping he would change his mind and hire me to work for him. As Aunt Flora, mumbling to herself, flustered about her work at the inn, I saw what a broken, lusterless woman she was. I knew beyond a doubt that if I stayed I would soon become just like her.

When Uncle Amos came and went with his chores around the inn and barnyard, I returned his sullen, lustful glances with angry glares. My rage was like a prairie fire, blazing high into the heavens, consuming everything that lay in its path. My uncle had driven Johnny from me, but I'd show him. I would work for Mr. Cranford. He needed me. No man alone could settle new land and still watch over a house and three little kids.

I imagined going north with them—and my heart began to race. A whole new life, an adventure, settling the wilderness. A real home, with me to run it, with no shouts or curses if I moved a bit too slow. There would be freedom there, a wild and glorious freedom, like the horses as they galloped across the meadow. I could taste it. I could feel it in my bones.

By midafternoon I was already watching for Mr. Cranford to return. I kept walking to the door, peering far into the distance, straining to catch the first hint of the sound of his horse's hoofs. When I went outside to fetch the towels I had washed and hung over the wide fence to dry, I lingered, squinting to see farther down the dirt road out front, hoping I could catch sight of him coming back. This was it, my one chance to escape.

Uncle Amos crept up behind me and grabbed my arm, his rough hand deliberately brushing my breast. "Dawdling again, girl? Damn it! Can't I never let you out of my sight?"

I jerked away from him. "Don't you dare touch me."

His mouth dropped open, but I was already running back to the kitchen, hugging the clean towels to my chest. It would not be long now till I'd be far away from here.

The sun sat low in the western sky, throwing long shadows ahead of Daniel Cranford and Hugh when they returned at late afternoon. After making certain Uncle Amos was nowhere in sight, I ran out and met them by the stable. Hugh climbed off his horse and dashed to join his brother and sister on the front porch.

Pulling myself up to my fullest height, I inhaled a deep breath and faced the man boldly. "Well? Have you thought over my offer?"

His brow furrowed. He chewed the side of his lower lip as he gazed at some spot over my shoulder, pondering. "Well . . . Naturally I'd like to settle my land as soon as possible," he said in a low voice. "But you know I just lost my wife less than three months ago."

"I know all that. I want to help you. And help myself to get away from here."

He sighed, shaking his head. "Surely you realize it is impossible. Oh, it would suit me just fine to be able to get up to my land. And I know you're a hard worker . . . and you're good with the children, but . . ."

"Please," I said, fidgeting with impatience. "Just give me a job. I have to get away from here. I can't stand it any longer."

His frown deepened. For the first time, his clear gray eyes met mine directly. "I can't just take off with a young woman like you," he protested. "The fact is, we'd have to marry. You know that I'm still grieving for my wife. It's too early to even consider marrying again."

"Marry?" I stared at him, agape. "Who said anything about marrying? I don't want to marry you. I just want a job, that's all."

"Yes, but . . ."

"Why, that's plumb silly. We scarcely know each other."

"I know that. But you see . . ." He sighed deeply, shaking his head. "Otherwise we couldn't possibly travel together. It would be a major scandal. I know how these things go. Your reputation would be ruined forever. Mine, too, for that matter. As I said, it's impossible."

My heart sank to my feet. The fear of scandal had never crossed my mind. I only knew I had to get away, and I needed some way to support myself. But marry? Marry someone I hardly knew? A Yankee who seemed almost like a foreigner to me?

Never in my life had I thought of marrying anyone but Johnny. There hadn't been a single word from him for three weeks now. Clearly he had given up, for fear of Uncle Amos.

Johnny was a lost dream, gone forever.

I swallowed hard, painfully, and stared at Daniel Cranford, this tall, neatly dressed man with his high brow and dark beard.

What did it matter now? He was nicer than most men I'd seen. He was kind to his children, tender to his wife when she was ill. Anything was better than staying here.

"Oh, well, all right," I said, with a shrug. "Let's marry then, if that will make you feel better. All I want is to be shut of this place."

His gaze bore into me. "You just don't seem to realize . . . Look, I'm thirty-four years old. That must be nearly twice your age."

"I'm eighteen." For the first time, I noticed the fine lines around his eyes and across his brow.

"I've already been married once. Lenore was everything to me—" He broke off and stared down at the ground, his cheeks flushed, his eyes glistening.

I shifted from one foot to the other, not knowing what to say.

"I knew her from the time she was a girl," he continued in a distant-sounding voice. "So beautiful. So refined. I courted her for three years. Never thought I'd win her. She finally consented to marry me when I went off to war. We lived together eight years. Eight happy years." He paused, his jaw clenched tightly. "It's been hard . . ."

"Please, I have to get away from here," I said, trembling with intensity. "I can't stand another day around my uncle."

He glanced at me, his gaze dark and far away. "I know you have a hard life here. I'd like to help you, really I would. But you're young and pretty, Nellie. Just stick it out a little longer. You'll find yourself a beau and set up your own household. You don't have to settle for some old widower with three little ones."

Tears burned my eyes. My heart thudded with the agony of remembering. "Johnny Nichols was my beau. Uncle Amos beat him, threatened to kill him. Now he's afraid to see me anymore. And I'm in for another beating myself if my uncle catches me talking to you like this."

"No. I won't let him hurt you, Nellie."

I gritted my teeth to hold back the anger and frustration. "I hate him. I'm scared to death of him. I have to get away."

"Don't you realize I'm going up to wild country?" he said. "It just wouldn't be fair to you. There're still Indians up there, lots of them. I'll have to build a house and clear land and try to make a living. It's going to be a tough scramble for a long while."

38

"You're not scared, are you?"

"I've been through a war. It takes quite a bit to frighten me now," he said. "As far as I'm concerned, it's a great opportunity. A free grant of land. The best farmland anywhere, they tell me. I can start a business up there later. Start a whole town, if I like. It's a dream Lenore and I shared for years."

I thought of Johnny, of my own dreams, and the pain was staggering. My uncle had robbed me of my dreams. But this man had dreams, ambitious and adventurous visions for the future. What a thrilling, wondrous thing that seemed to me. "Take me with you. I'm strong. I can work hard."

He wrinkled his brow, studying my face for some clue to my jumbled thoughts. After a taut silence, he murmured, "You do like my children, don't you?"

"Oh, yes," I said, nodding briskly, a lump rising in my throat. "I feel for them. I lost my mother, too. That's when I had to come up here to live with my uncle."

His expression softened. He gazed at me with sympathy. "You lost your mother, too?"

"Yes. And let me tell you, it's a sorry way to grow up. Well?"

Chewing his lip thoughtfully, he jammed his hands into his deep coat pockets and kicked at a loose clod of dirt. "Oh, I don't know. I suppose there's been many a marriage for convenience sake. Lenore—Lenore would probably want me to think first of the children."

He studied my face, thoughtful, measuring. "Who knows? Might be the best thing for both of us. But still . . ."

I heard my uncle's voice from inside the inn, then heard the back door slam. "That's Uncle Amos coming. I have to go."

"I— Give me some time to think about this, Nellie."

CHAPTER 5

Three days of strained silence followed. On the fourth day, as I was carrying a handful of sun-dried towels in from the fence, Daniel Cranford came to meet me in the side yard. My heart quickened when I saw his tall form striding toward me.

"Are you still of the same mind you were the other day?" he asked.

I flushed at his blunt approach. "You bet I am. The sooner the better."

By now I knew for certain Blanche had told the truth. It was clear Johnny blamed me for everything. I would never hear from him again. The knowledge sliced my heart to shreds, for I loved him and longed desperately to be with him. But somehow I would learn to live without him.

Mr. Cranford gazed into the distance, slowly nodding his head. "It seems the most practical solution as far as I'm concerned. Obviously my children still need a lot of care, and I can't possibly do it all myself—not and settle new land."

Could this be happening? "I'll take good care of them for you. And I can cook and clean and garden, too. You won't be sorry, Mr. Cranford."

"No, I don't suppose I will." His gaze rested on my face. "My main concern is you. Are you sure you know what you're getting yourself into?"

"I know that any place would be better than here."

His gray eyes studied me with careful scrutiny. "Well, if you're certain this is what you want, I'll go and tell your uncle."

"No. Let me have the pleasure of telling him myself." I hurried over to the low log barn, where Uncle Amos was cleaning out the stalls. Daniel Cranford followed close behind me.

A pungent barn smell assailed me as I stepped out of the sunshine, through the wide door, and searched around for my uncle in the shadowy light. Hearing a scraping sound from the farthest stall, I rushed down the straw-littered center aisle.

Uncle Amos halted when he saw me, his pitchfork half full of wet and smelly straw. "What the devil . . . ?"

In my eagerness, words tumbled from my mouth. "You'd better call the preacher here, soon as he can come. I'm marrying Mr. Cranford—and going north with him."

My uncle's mouth dropped open. He stared at me for one long moment. Then he jabbed the pitchfork into the dirt floor and seized me by the shoulders. "You're doing nothing of the kind!" he shouted, shaking me violently. "You can't leave here! I'll—"

Cranford stepped around the corner of the stall, his tall form looming over Uncle Amos. His voice was deep and threatening. "Take your hands off that girl."

This was something new. Someone standing up to defend me.

Wide-eyed and slack-jawed, Uncle Amos slowly released his grip. He stared at Cranford uncertainly. "She's my ward. She's under my authority."

"I believe Nellie is of legal age now. That would entitle her to make her own decisions." Cranford's crisp Yankee accent gave his words authority. He pulled himself to his full height and met my uncle's stunned stare. "She has agreed to marry me."

"Marry!" Uncle Amos said, sneering. "What kind of man are you? Your wife just died, and here you are, already talking of marrying this ripe young thing."

I backed away from him and hung my head. Trust him to color everything obscene.

"I would have preferred a proper mourning period, sir. My wife certainly deserved that." Daniel Cranford hesitated just a second. "But she would be the first to want our children well cared for. And they already know and like Nellie."

"I need her here," my uncle snarled. "Who you think is going to do all this work?"

"I won't stay! You can't keep me here!" I wheeled and started out the stall.

41

My uncle grabbed my arm. Cranford seized his wrist and squeezed until he released me. "She's of age, Mr. Barton. Do I have to call the law on you to make you set her free?"

A tense silence hung over the pair. My uncle turned and sneered at me. "Last month it was that Nichols kid. This month a boarder at the inn. Who's it going to be next time? Maybe a traveling salesman?"

Cheeks flaming, I hurried from the stall, away from his vile mouth.

"Take her!" His words echoed off the barn walls. "The sooner the better! Take her out of my sight and be quick about it!"

I ran back to the inn and burst in through the kitchen door. Aunt Flora, startled, looked up from her work.

"Call the preacher, quick," I told her breathlessly. "I'm going to marry Mr. Cranford."

She raised a hand to her heart, staring at me, her eyes as big as dinner plates.

Two days later, just after breakfast, we were married at the preacher's house down the road. I wore my plain green gingham dress, the best I owned.

After we walked back to the inn, Aunt Flora, still looking stunned, pulled me aside. "Try not to be too scared at what happens to you tonight," she whispered ominously. "All men are beasts. That's just the way they are."

I gulped, wondering what I had let myself in for. Though my uncle was certainly a beast, it was impossible for me to imagine Mr. Cranford in that role.

Aunt Flora served the wedding cake she had baked for us, fussing around the dining room and blinking back tears. I brought out mugs of coffee and milk for all of us. The three children gathered close, quiet and puzzled-looking, staring at Mr. Cranford and me.

Uncle Amos was absent, seeing to the cattle in the far pasture. With Daniel Cranford standing tall by my side, with that authoritative military bearing, my fear of Uncle Amos drifted away.

Yes, it was only a marriage of convenience. Mr. Cranford needed help with the children and the housework. I needed to get away. Yes, we were practically strangers. And he was a stiff and formal-acting Yankee, speaking in that funny-sounding way.

But of all the men I had seen at the roadside inn, I admired this one most. Though he appeared strong and determined, I knew he was a caring man as well, from the tender kindness he always showed his children. He was intelligent and well educated. I was woefully lacking in that department, and stood in awe of anyone with learning.

I understood how deeply he still grieved for his wife—and knew that I could never compete with her. After all, I was just an ignorant backwoods girl. But I knew how to work hard. I had good health and drive and energy. Before long Daniel Cranford would surely recognize how valuable I was to have around.

For now, just the thought of being free from my uncle was enough. I felt lighthearted, almost eager for the future. And for the first time since my mother died, I felt a budding sense of family.

If thoughts of Johnny Nichols sometimes floated through my head, I quickly banished them to that dark and silent region where old memories of my parents and my little sisters dwelled.

Daniel was strangely quiet. "Would you excuse me for a few minutes?" he asked in a low voice. "I should pay one last visit to the cemetery."

Lenore. Somehow I knew she would always be with us. "Do you want the kids to go, too?"

"Yes, I think they should."

While they were gone, I tried to make idle conversation with Aunt Flora. An uneasy sense of foreboding crept over me. Still, I wanted to leave quickly, to avoid any further contact with Uncle Amos.

"Ready to go?" Daniel asked when he returned.

I nodded, and he hurried out to the barn, returning a short time later seated on a wagon pulled by two stout horses. This covered wagon, packed months ago in Shawneetown with all his family's household belongings, had been stored in my uncle's barn.

As the three children, silent and anxious-looking, watched from the front porch, Daniel hopped down from the seat and quickly tucked their clothes trunks back into the corners of the wagon bed. I handed him my small box of clothes and little keepsakes. Yes, I had slipped the pearl brooch that Johnny gave me in there, too, right beside my mother's tortoiseshell hairbrush. These were the only treasures I owned.

43

"You're sure you can drive this wagon?" he asked, turning to me with a dubious frown.

"Shoot, there's nothing to driving a team. They just keep going down the road." I grinned as I climbed up on the seat and took the reins.

"I sure hope you're not taking on more than you can handle."

He disappeared again—and returned driving another wagon, this one hitched to a yoke of oxen and loaded with farm tools, bags of shelled corn, food supplies and seed, a crate of squawking chickens, and half a dozen shoats. He led out a milk cow and a dozen steers and tied them with leather lines so they could trail along behind his ox wagon.

Their young sheepdog, Shad, had traveled with them all the way from New York and had been staying with a nearby farmer. Now he stood, wagging his tail, eager to lead the whole outfit on this new adventure.

Aunt Flora observed us closely as we prepared to leave, her hand fluttering against her chest. "Oh, Lordy! I just can't believe all this is happening."

Neither could I.

"Come on! Hop up in the wagon," I called to the children, hoping my bright smile would ease their doubts. "We're on our way to your new home."

The three hesitated on the tavern porch, wide-eyed and speechless. I could tell by their grave faces they still didn't quite understand why I was going with them.

Hugh, somber as an old man, glanced up at me, then looked away. "I'd better ride with Papa," he said.

"Fine, fine," I replied. Daniel boosted Sarah up on the high seat of my wagon, and I slipped my arm around her thin shoulders. "Come on, honey. You can help me drive this here team."

She jerked away from me as if I had the plague. "You talk funny," she said, flicking a dainty finger on the flowered print of her dress.

"Why, honey, I talk the same as everybody else in these parts. You're just used to square-cornered Yankee talk."

Daniel lifted little Eddie up, and the child slipped in beside me. This lovable child, too young to understand the situation, snuggled close to my side. Sarah, ignoring me, took her brother's small hand and held it tightly.

"You're sure you know how to drive a wagon?" Daniel asked

44

me. His brow furrowed, he surveyed the team and wagon. "I had originally planned to take only one, but with all this live-stock and the farm tools I've picked up since I've been here . . ."

"Nothing to it. Why, I used to help my pa bring in the hay when I was not much bigger than these kids," I said, glancing at the wary faces of the children beside me. I grinned at them, hoping to entice a tiny smile, but all to no avail.

"Well, I hope it all works out. I'll lead the way, and these fellows should just follow along behind my wagon."

I looked at the dusty road before us, heading northward, away from here. It beckoned me to follow it to a whole new life.

Daniel held up a sheaf of papers. "I have some rough maps here to follow. We go straight up this road for quite a-ways. If you have the slightest problem, just call and I'll stop and take care of you." His frown deepened. "I'm really sorry we're burdened down like this."

"You'll need every bit of this plunder when you get up to your place."

He nodded somberly. "Yes, I suspect we're going to be out on our own for a good while." Still he hesitated, glancing from my face to the children's and back to me again. "Well, I suppose we might as well be on our way."

He climbed up on his wagon, gave a sharp yell to his oxen, and the great beasts started down the trail. I glanced once more at teary Aunt Flora on the porch and felt a rush of sympathy. I was escaping, but her life would go on, as miserable as ever. Thank God Uncle Amos was still nowhere in sight.

Holding tightly to the reins, I clucked to the team of horses. They stood stolid and unmoving. Oh, no! It had been years since I had driven horses. I had assured Daniel I could do it. What would he think of me?

"Giddap," I said, and clucked again, jerking on the reins. The horses twitched their ears, looking at each other dubiously.

"Giddap, you stubborn varmits!" I yelled, fearful now that I could not control them. I grabbed the whip from the post by my side and cracked it in the air. The horses reluctantly pulled away from the inn, following after Daniel's wagon. I breathed a long, relieved sigh.

We rattled slowly down the dusty rutted trail through the trees, and with every turn of the wagon wheels, the oppressive weight on my heart lightened. At long last, I was free.

When we passed Johnny's house, I stared straight ahead, trying to ignore the painful lump that rose and swelled in my throat. Johnny didn't want me, not enough to cross my uncle. Well, all that was far behind me now.

As I watched Daniel's wagon bouncing ahead of me, kicking up dust in the rutted road, I mused once again on my new husband. We'd both agreed ours was a marriage of convenience only. I knew he was a good man, devoted to his children, a gentleman in every way. Since I knew I could never have Johnny, I would have settled for far worse than Daniel Cranford just to escape from Uncle Amos.

Eddie, a small, cuddly child, snuggled close to me on the wagon seat and began to suck his thumb. I slipped my arm around him, smiling over at his sister. "Exciting, ain't it? We're going to your new home."

Sarah sat up straight and prim, her eyes fastened on the wagon ahead. "Papa says *ain't* is bad English. We are not allowed to talk like that."

"Oh. Sorry."

She turned to me with eyes like blue ice; her voice was just as chilling. "You are not my mother. I will never call you Mother."

I drew in a long breath, steeling myself against this small foe. "No, I'm just Nellie. You can call me Nellie."

"My mother was beautiful. She was a lady. She always spoke good English. Her voice was soft, her hands were white . . ." Tears glistened in Sarah's eyes, but her small chin was firm as she glared at me defiantly. "She wasn't anything like you."

"No, I reckon not." My cheeks flushed. I could see myself through this child's critical eyes: a thin and wiry young woman with a thatch of red hair and a patch of freckles across my nose. My hands were rough and weathered from hard work and harsh lye soap.

My throat tightened. No doubt my new husband was making the same comparison. I must try to remember not to say ain't. Still, out here on the frontier, delicate females didn't last for the long haul. They'd soon learn how well I earned my keep.

I knew Daniel still grieved deeply for his wife. And I grieved just as much for Johnny, ached at the very thought of him. How could I endure the agony of knowing I would never see Johnny again?

I clenched my fingers tighter on the reins and stared at the feathery heads of the tall prairie grasses beside the trail, bobbing in the wind. Life must go on. Youthful dreams of true love and romance might do for other girls. As for me, I could not afford such frivolous luxuries.

Our two wagons and the retinue of livestock jogged along in a discordant parade as we plodded northward, mile after mile up the narrow road, an ancient Indian trail winding through woodland and prairie. Driving the horses was not proving too hard, for I found they followed stoically along behind the ox wagon.

Wooden wheels creaked and groaned under their cumbersome loads: harnesses clicked; pots and kettles, dangling from broom handles extending out the back, clanged against one another; chickens squawked and piglets squealed—all to the steady, sluggish rhythm of the horse and oxen hoofs, of milk cow and beef cattle.

We forded a shallow stream and passed through heavy timberland, the leaves above us alive with the flutterings and melodic song of birds. Then, suddenly, the sun was beating down on us as we left the woods and moved out to a wide, flat stretch of prairie. Man-high grasses, sprinkled with brilliant late summer flowers, billowed in the breeze like waves upon the sea. Ahead of us, a hawk soared in lazy circles over the grass. My heart leapt with delight at the sight of such freedom and grace.

Shad, the shaggy brown sheepdog, seemed to feel he was in charge of the whole party. He trotted nervously from one wagon to the other, worrying over all the people and the livestock entrusted to his care.

An hour later, Daniel pulled his wagon to a halt beside the road in a stand of tall timber. "Are you all right?" he called, looking concerned as he walked back to us.

I smiled. "Fine! Just following you." Despite Sarah's continued enmity, every mile I traveled brought a steady lifting to my spirits. This journey was an exciting adventure, taking me into a new and unfamiliar world, one where bitterness and old feuds had no part.

"Why don't we all get down and stretch a bit?" Daniel said. "This is going to be a long trip. We need to break into it gradually."

Eddie and Sarah scrambled down from the wagon seat and

joined Hugh to play tag among the trees, while their father watched them fondly. Then he turned to me with a shy smile. "I do appreciate what you're doing, Nellie. Coming along to help me with the family, and all."

I nodded, at a loss for words. It felt strange, being alone here in the woods with him, far from the inn, the other guests, my aunt and uncle.

His gray eyes turned serious as he gazed at me. "I just wanted you to know . . . I—I won't force myself on you," he murmured nervously. "We both understand this is only a marriage of convenience."

My cheeks burned crimson. "Yes." To hide my embarrassment, I hung my head and focused on the low grass at my feet, but his black boots loomed there before me, dusty from the trail. Well, thank heavens Aunt Flora had been mistaken. After all, Daniel and I hardly knew each other. Wedding ring or not, I was just the hired girl.

"Pretty spot here, isn't it?" I flicked my hand toward the canopy of leaves overhead. A yellow finch flitted from limb to limb, a lovely touch of color in the trees.

"Very nice." He breathed out a long sigh. "But we'd better be on our way. I'll go collect the little ones."

We all climbed back to our seats, and the horses and oxen began trudging faithfully, towing the creaking wagons along the narrow trail. Soon the road opened again onto a vast expanse of level prairie, where wildflowers dotted the tall grasses like pieces of a crazy quilt. Sunflowers, black-eyed Susans, goldenrod, violet ironweed, and scores of other blossoms bloomed in reckless profusion. Overhead, fleecy clouds glided slowly across the immense blue arch of sky.

The prairie teemed with life. Red-winged blackbirds circled overhead, scolding us for trespassing into their domain. Large flocks of prairie chickens scuttled through the grass, and in the distance herds of tawny deer grazed serenely until, startled by the clamor from our weapons, they fled in graceful, arching lopes.

We passed only a few scattered settlers' cabins along our way, a few fields of flourishing corn and pumpkins, small herds of cattle and sheep grazing on rich prairie grass, peaceful as a painting in the wash of yellow sunlight.

As the sun glided toward the western horizon the first evening, we set up camp in a walnut grove beside a shallow creek. Oh, it felt so good to be down off that jolting wagon. I headed straight for the creek to wash the gritty road dust off my hands and face.

The children helped me gather fallen limbs and twigs from beneath the tangle of trees and underbrush, while Daniel dipped up a kettle of water from the creek. He braced up planks from his wagon to form a fence around his piglets, then strolled off with his gun to bag some game for supper.

We carried a kettle of live coals hanging underneath the wagon frame, as most travelers do. I used a few of these to start a fire, and soon had a crackling blaze for the coffeepot and the kettle of beans I set on for tomorrow's journey.

After digging through the boxes in the wagon to find supplies, I mixed some cornmeal in a wooden bowl with water from the creek, then baked a batch of little round corn dodgers on a griddle over the fire. The children scampered beneath trees gilded by the late sun, filling small pots and sacks with fallen walnuts.

Daniel returned in twenty minutes with his trophies, three plump prairie chickens. "Congratulations, sir!" I said, with a wide grin. "You sure must be a darned good shot."

He nodded, looking real pleased with himself. "Yes, I did my share of hunting back East."

After he had deftly cleaned and plucked the trio, I roasted them on green sticks skewered over the fire.

I felt cozy and relaxed when we all gathered around the fire to eat our supper. Here at last was a glimmer of the warm companionship I had anticipated when I joined this family.

Daniel turned to me. "You must be exhausted from driving that team all day, Nellie."

"Not me. I was enjoying all the sights. It's the first time I've been anywhere since I came up from Kentucky."

"Looks like you may make the best traveler of this lot."

I breathed a deep, contented sigh as my glance skimmed from Daniel's sober bearded face to the children's smooth and youthful miens. "Why don't you tell me all about your trip out from New York? I've never been to any of those places."

Instantly I realized my unforgivable mistake. Lenore's death had interrupted that trip. I'd really stuck my foot in it this time.

Horrified, I clapped my hand over my mouth, but it was too

late to undo my thoughtlessness. "Sorry I brought it up," I murmured, lifting my eyes to Daniel.

He smiled gently, sympathetic at my embarrassment. "I'm sure you would be interested in knowing how we got all the way out here."

"We came down the Ohio River," Hugh said softly, a faraway look clouding his eyes. "Such a big, wide river."

Sarah hung her head. "My mother was so sick."

Staring thoughtfully into the flickering orange flames of the campfire, Daniel cleared his throat. "We sold our home and land in New York State and started this journey last spring. We drove a wagon down to Pittsburgh, then bought a keelboat there and stocked up for the rest of the trip. We bought all kinds of things there for the new house—tinware, brooms, glassware, salt, flour, candles, needles, thread, soap. Heavy clothes and shoes for the whole family, too. Bought a spinning wheel and churn. Farming tools."

"Was the trip hard?" I asked, plunging ahead, not knowing how to turn back.

He blew out a long exhalation. "We had our share of troubles. The Ohio River's not easy to navigate. It's full of islands and sandbars, and there're dead trees under the water that can puncture your boat. Planters, they call them. And sawyers, too—bobbing up and down."

"Lordy me! That sounds real dangerous," I said.

"They can be. That keelboat cost a good bit, but the people out in Pittsburgh told me it was much safer than a flatboat. Anyway, I sold it for a respectable profit after we landed in Shawneetown. We bought the team of horses and covered wagon and transferred all our belongings to it."

"Mother felt better when we got to Shawneetown," Sarah murmured, tears welling in the corners of her eyes.

Laying his dark curly head on my lap, Eddie began to suck his thumb as he fingered the faded homespun of my skirt.

The burning logs hissed and flared. A spark shot upward into the deepening dusk. Daniel looked pale, a frown flickering on his face. "I thought Mother would feel better here in Illinois," he said numbly. "I kept hearing about the clean air and healthy living out here. Lots of people come West purely for that reason."

Sarah leaned against Daniel's arm. A dam of tears broke loose from her eyes; she began to cry with deep, heaving sobs. He lifted the child to his lap and cradled her in his arms. As I glanced around the circle of mournful faces, I felt a complete outsider. Quietly, unobtrusively, I gathered all the dirty tin plates and flatware and washed them with hot water from the kettle on the fire.

That night, my wedding night, I slept in the wagon with the two younger children, while Daniel and Hugh stretched out on blankets in a tent pitched by the fire. I had expected nothing different.

I was thankful Daniel hadn't been the beast of my aunt's warning. And with all the children here, too, to make it all that much worse. Still, I lay awake a while, pondering the mysterious relationship I knew existed between a man and wife. It frightened me a bit, for I recalled the brutish matings I had seen among the barnyard animals.

If Daniel meant to be a real husband to me, I hoped he would at least give me time to get to know him better.

My thoughts drifted to Johnny. My body tensed and my heart beat faster as I recalled the warm passion and urgency of his kisses. How very different a wedding night with Johnny would have been. Just the thought of it set my being aflame.

But after the arduous day of riding over bumpy, dusty roads, I let the darkness settle over me and drifted to sleep, lulled by soft, soothing sounds of whippoorwill and cricket chirps, of night breeze rustling through the leaves.

A few hours later I suddenly awoke to Shad's sharp bark. Peering out the back of the wagon into the thick blanket of darkness, I saw an eery ring of glowing green eyes circling the fenced-in piglets. Wolves.

The piglets squealed in terror. Daniel, hastily belting his trousers, stood outside his little tent. All the glowing eyes now stared at him with hungry intensity. A pack of wolves. They snarled at Shad's frenzied barking, restlessly pacing back and forth. They stared, the reflected firelight making their eyes glow like beacons in the black night.

"Quick! Get in the wagon!" Daniel yelled to Hugh. The boy scrambled from the tent, up the wagon frame beside me, where he watched out the rear opening, trembling.

Daniel raised his arm, brandishing a piece of firewood at the wolves. One of them lunged at him with a vicious snarl. From

51

the fire, Daniel grabbed the far end of a burning limb and swung it at the beast, singeing its fur. The wolf jumped back with a sharp yelp.

Another instantly sprang forward in its place. Daniel yelled, seizing another burning brand. He struck the beast sharply on the head, then turned to strike a third.

I leapt from the wagon and dashed for the rifle lying beside his pallet in the tent. "Get back!" he shouted.

Snatching up the rifle, I yelled at him over the din of snarling, growling wolves and squealing piglets. "Is this thing loaded?"

"No! Get back, for God's sake!"

I held the rifle by the barrel like a club and swung it as a wolf leapt for me with bared fangs. Daniel struck another with his flaming stick. The wolf's fur caught fire and it ran yelping through the trees. I hit one with the gun stock as Daniel rushed at the pack with his burning branch. Finally the wolves retreated, growling and confused. After a hurried, grumbling conference, they skulked away into the darkness.

The children watched the ferocious battle in stunned silence, peering from the wagon with terror-stricken eyes.

As I tried to calm the shrieking but unharmed piglets, Daniel bundled up an armful of dry limbs and tossed them on the dying fire. It blazed high, brightening the jet-dark night. He walked over to me and took my quaking hands. The flickering firelight danced over the planes of his cheeks and brows. "Why didn't you stay in the wagon? I can take care of you."

"I know you can. And in a pinch, I can help you, too."

A puzzled frown creased his face. He shook his head and chewed his lower lip, staring at me as if I were some bizarre creature from a circus show.

Naturally, I'd always known that Yankees and frontier folks look at things a mite different. My family had settled down in the Kentucky hills long years ago, and I grew up knowing I had to look out for myself. I wasn't about to sit around and let a pack of wolves eat all those shoats. Not while I still had two good arms.

I suppose that meant I'd never be a proper lady, like those Daniel had known back East. Like his lovely lost Lenore. Oh, well. So be it.

At Daniel's urging, Hugh stayed up in the wagon, to sleep in greater safety with the other children. With the blazing fire as protection, we all crept back beneath our blankets. I breathed deeply, trying to still the racing of my heart, but now every rustle in the trees, every owl's hoot, every subtle night sound assumed ominous proportions.

My sleep came only in fitful spurts. I dreamed of immense packs of green-eyed wolves—and woke each time Daniel rose to stir and feed the fire.

CHAPTER 6

Dawn finally appeared. How wonderful those ribbons of rosy light in the eastern sky seemed. Exhausted as I was, the daylight looked so fine I somehow felt refreshed.

We arose and, after a hasty breakfast, continued on the trail northward, toward the Military Tract. Daniel told me this was an enormous wedge of land—three and a half million acres and shaped like a piece of pie—located between the Illinois and Mississippi rivers. He said that when he turned in his warranty for his war service, the government officials had allowed him to draw a lot for a half-section of land, three hundred twenty acres, because he had been promoted to officer. Most veterans received only a quarter section.

His land grant, situated along the Spoon River, appeared to be a choice plot—with the river as assurance of the two essentials: timber and water. He felt himself singularly lucky in his draw. Some of the veterans had drawn plots that were nothing but prairie, and everybody knew the prairie, very difficult to break for farming, was more suitable for pasture. Of course, his land probably contained some prairie, too, so he had brought along the cattle. "Might as well put this tall prairie grass to good use," he said.

"I may start a business when the Military Tract builds up," he told me later on in the trip, his face gleaming with intensity and zeal. "Might even start a whole new city. There's just no limit to the opportunity. The fellow in St. Louis told me I'll be one of the first ones on the scene."

"It all sounds so exciting! I can hardly wait to get there," I said. "But why hasn't it been settled sooner? The war's been over for years."

He shook his head with disgust. "These government affairs always take twice as long as you think they should. We had to wait until they signed treaties to buy the land from the Indians there; then they had to survey the territory and lay it out into plots."

As we traveled north, we saw fewer and fewer signs of settlement, yet Daniel's enthusiasm continued to grow. "Just look at all this!" he shouted, gazing about him, awed by the vastness of the unbroken, flower-strewn prairie stretching to the wide horizon.

"It's beautiful!" I called back to him. His wagon brushed aside the stems of man-high grass and wildflowers. A gentle south wind flowed across the prairie, tugging at my dress and hair, billowing the canvas wagon cover. In the distance, dark groves of trees appeared like small islands in this endless sea of grass.

"Look there, Sarah! See, Eddie?" From my high roost on the wagon seat, I pointed to the boundless sweep of prairie, to the winding streams and rushing creeks and tangled forest groves teeming with birds and game. Snakes and foxes and wild turkeys scuttled through the grass as we approached.

We saw great flocks of wild pigeons that blackened the sky, and trees with limbs broken from the weight of pigeons roosting for the night. Green plumage of parakeets glittered in the sunlight. Cardinals' wings flickered like flames among green leaves and branches in the wooded glens.

At midday we stopped beside a shady brook for a picnic. "Bears have been here," Daniel said.

"Where? Where?" the children asked.

He pointed out the signs where the bears had wallowed in the tall grass and had tossed aside a decayed log in their search for worms and beetles. Luckily none had so far crossed our path.

It was late September, the best time for traveling. The road was dry; the streams and rivers low enough to ford. Every day we met one or two travelers coming toward us on horseback or in wagons, and we had to pull over in the tall grass to give them room to pass.

"Why don't we ever see any other settlers heading in our direction?" I asked when we had camped for the night.

"Don't worry. They'll be pouring in before long," Daniel replied. "Just look around you. This is God's country."

In some places, though, green-headed flies attacked the horses and oxen without mercy, leaving the animals dotted with tiny spots of blood. I stopped and shooed them away, but after buzzing around a few moments, they returned to their feasting spots.

"We're going to have to travel by night to give these poor beasts some relief," Daniel said after pulling to a stop beside a creek. He groaned and kneaded the small of his back. "I expect you'd appreciate a little rest yourself."

I chuckled. "Oh, I'm pretty tough, you know. I'm just enjoying all the scenery."

"You're still young enough not to notice aches and pains. I'm starting to feel them, myself. Well, I'd better find some fresh meat for our dinner."

He picked up his long rifle and strode out onto the prairie. The children ran down to the creek to splash and wade, and I joined them there to wash out some dirty clothes.

From a blue silk sky, dotted with fleecy puffs of clouds, the sun smiled down on the prairie. The fragrant air was alive with the song of meadowlark and thrush, soaring on wing or perched on swaying milkweed plants.

"Hey, try this, kids!" I called, laughing as I chased the milkweed seeds that came bursting from their pods like delicate white fairy wings.

We tried to catch a bit of rest during the heat of the afternoon, lying on quilts spread in the shaded grass beside the creek. That night we traveled on by moonlight. From the distant prairies came the long, eery howl of a coyote, and later, from the timber, a startling panther scream. Yet despite the frightening sounds and the jarring wagon ride, after an hour or two my head nodded and my hands loosened on the reins.

I awoke with a start and gazed about me, yawning. The children were fast asleep, sprawled out on quilts back in the wagon. A dull fatigue bored into me, casting the moonlit prairie in a dreamlike mistiness. An image drifted into my mind—Johnny, standing there before me on another moonlit night, his face pressing closer for a kiss.

No. I must forget him. That was all behind me. Daniel was my husband now, and I would make the best of this new life. But would we always be so awkward around each other? Would his Yankee accent always grate on my ears? And would these children ever come to care for me? Maybe little Eddie might, but what about Sarah and Hugh? I had hoped that someday we could be like a real family.

We had been traveling slowly northward for almost a week, our trail like a tunnel through the high grass, when we came to a fork in the main road. Daniel stopped to study his maps and compass. "Yes, this is it," he said, nodding decisively, and our noisy retinue continued up a narrow pathway, an Indian trail, heading toward the northwest.

Each time we crossed the steep-banked creeks that appeared at intervals, we stopped while Daniel wandered up and down the banks, searching for the best fording spot. At one fair-sized river, he located a wide, shallow strip and waved for me to start driving the wagon through the water. Halfway across, the horses halted, struggling as the wagon wheels sunk and became locked in the spongy, sucking mud of the riverbed.

"Don't worry! I'm coming to help you!" Daniel shouted. He leapt from his wagon seat and sprinted down to the water's edge, while the rushing water swirled and eddied, bubbling around my mired wheels. After yanking off his boots, he hastily waded out to my wagon. "Just sit still, everybody. I'll have you out as soon as I can."

The horses heaved and pulled, snorting as their clusters of gnarly back muscles rippled with the fevered effort. The sunken wheels refused to budge.

"You and Eddie go back in the middle of the wagon and sit still," I told Sarah. I pulled off my old leather shoes, crawled to the back opening, hiked up my skirt and tucked it into my apron band, and then started to climb out the rear end of the wagon.

"Nellie! Stay inside! You'll be all right," Daniel said as he wrestled with the iron frame of the wagon.

To his surprise, I ignored him and jumped into the mud beside him, the cool water swirling up past my bared knees. "I guess I'm not about to sit there and let you do it all." Jutting out my chin, I reached down and grabbed hold of the heavy frame. "I told you I'd work for you, Mr. Cranford."

Spots of crimson appeared in his tanned cheeks. "Yes, I guess you did, didn't you?" he said, with an embarrassed grin. He heaved on one side, while I heaved and strained with all my might on the other.

Sarah peered out the back of the wagon, her blue eyes wide, her small face tight with disapproval. Eddie, in childish bewilderment, began to cry. From the bank, Hugh watched, helpless and distressed.

Finally, by our combined brute strength, Daniel and I dislodged the mired wagon. The horses ceased their thrashing and wearily dragged it through the remaining stretch of water and up the other bank.

"I thank you for your help, but a woman shouldn't strain herself that way," Daniel murmured. He gazed at me, a curious expression in his eyes. "I hope you're all right. I didn't mean for you to have to—"

"Don't give it another thought." I supposed that he, like Sarah, wished I acted more like a lady. Well, it was too late now for me to change. I was not cut out to sit and wring my hands in times of trouble.

"Ooh," Sarah said, squirming and wrinkling her nose. "You're all wet."

Glancing down at my soaked skirt, I wiggled my toes in the sticky clay mud. "I don't reckon I'll shrink." With a grin, I scooped up a handful of water and splashed it on her and Eddie. "And now you kids are just as bad as me."

A giggle trilled from Eddie. Sarah stared at me, her blue eyes wide with surprise. Then just the slightest hint of a smile trembled on her lips. Well, that was something, anyway.

I glanced over and saw Daniel's steady gaze on me, the warm look in his eyes.

"Come on, Hugh," he called, wading back out of the river. "Let's unload some of these heavy tools and supplies from this other wagon. We'll have to bring them across in two trips so we don't get stuck again."

When they had crossed, and we were all set to start up the trail once more, Daniel strode over to my wagon. "The Illinois is the only deep river we have to cross," he said, with a reassuring smile. "I'll get some logs and float the wagons over that one. You won't have to push it there."

With a burst of laughter, I flicked back a straggling lock of my unruly hair. "Well, Mr. Cranford, if anything needs pushing, I reckon I'll get out and push."

As we rode on, I glanced down at my roughened hands. An image of Lenore's delicate-looking fingers flashed through my mind. She never could have made this grueling trip, I realized with sudden clarity. No, Lenore's refined beauty would have served for little in these parts.

Later that afternoon, Daniel pulled to an abrupt halt. He strode back to my wagon and pointed to an Indian village perched beneath the willow trees along a winding creek. The mat-covered lodges looked like a cluster of haystacks in the distance.

A wave of panic rose in me. My stomach cramped with fear. "What—what do we do now? We'd better turn and go a different way."

"I'll take care of this," Daniel said. "If we show them we mean no harm, I'm certain they won't bother us. After all, there are treaties—"

Suddenly three barebacked braves leapt on spotted ponies and galloped our way.

Sarah shrieked. Trembling, she hid her face in her hands. But Eddie's eyes glowed with interest as he watched the approaching Indians, their bare copper arms and chests glimmering in the sunlight. "Can we go and talk to them, Papa?" he begged. "Maybe they'll let us see their little houses."

"You all stay here. I'll handle this."

I had heard too many tales of Indian massacres in old Kentucky to remain as calm as Daniel. My heart hammered a rapid drumbeat and my breath lodged in my throat as the three riders tore across the prairie, coming ever closer.

Unperturbed, Daniel walked out to meet them, his hand held up in a sign of peace. How stalwart and fearless he appeared, his body tall and straight among the swaying prairie grasses.

The Indians, dressed only in fringed buckskin leggings and breechcloths, with necklaces of small pierced mussel shells, remained mounted on their ponies. Daniel gestured and spoke with them for a few moments, then strolled back to his wagon

58

and pulled several twists of tobacco from a wooden box. He handed them to the copper-skinned men with a confident smile. They nodded and waved us on, allowing us to pass without another word.

"Whew! You got us out of a tight spot," I said when Daniel came back to the wagon. "I thought for sure we'd all be scalped."

"Oh, that wasn't anything. They just wanted a little tribute for crossing their land. I was expecting that."

Soon we were under way again. Eddie crawled to the rear of the wagon and peered out through the opening until the village of domed lodges and the herd of grazing ponies were out of sight. "Did you see those fast horses they were riding?" he called to me, excited. "Did you see those shiny things around their necks? I saw some little boys, too. Just my size."

"Indians scalp people," Sarah said, her voice quavering. "I didn't know there would be Indians up here."

"Now don't you worry, honey. Your pa will look out for you." I patted her clenched hand. "Didn't you see how fast he made friends with them?"

But she pulled away from me and stared straight ahead, her eyes like round blue saucers. I followed her gaze to our narrow pathway through the prairie. This time we had avoided trouble, but I was gripped by a disturbing apprehension. Unknown lands and unknown people encircled me. Sometimes even this man and his children seemed as foreign to me as the Indians. Would I ever feel at home up in this vast unsettled wilderness?

I had already seen plenty of evidence that Daniel was brave. But was his courage a match for all the dangers ahead, when we were living in an unpopulated territory where few whites had ever ventured?

Well, he has no choice, I told myself, clenching my jaw. And neither do I. This place will probably call for every last ounce of courage from us all.

What about the children? Sarah, so delicate and fragile, so desperately unhappy. My heart went out to her, understanding how her mother's sudden death had crushed her. I could not blame her for resenting me. But would she ever soften enough to accept my help and affection? I only hoped this little hot-house rose would prove hearty enough for this harsh, demanding life.

Eddie was a different story. Though he was hardly more than a baby, he faced this new life as a great adventure. Hugh still grieved for his mother, too, but I knew he would prove strong and steady, like his father.

And what about me? I harbored no doubts about my own strength. The hardships and grueling work I had endured for all my eighteen years would toughen anyone. I looked on this move, this new life, as an exciting challenge.

Once I had nurtured exciting, romantic dreams of Johnny. Now he was only a part of the past, buried and laid to rest. I prayed that very soon I could convince my heart of this.

We had been on the road now for almost two weeks, moving slowly with our retinue of weary livestock. I had lost count of the days—and counted only blisters and mosquito bites and cuts from the razor-sharp grass blades.

One morning Eddie woke up hot and feverish. Was it from something he had eaten at our haphazard meals? As another tedious day of bouncing on the wagon seat behind the trudging horses began, he leaned against me, whimpering.

"Feeling poorly, babe?" I asked.

He nodded, big tears pooling in his eyes.

"Well, you just come here to me." I shifted him onto my lap and held the reins in one hand, cuddling him with my free arm so the incessant jolting would not jar him. The child was only three years old, after all. He had already seen too many changes in his young life.

Sarah, perched beside me on the wagon seat, pursed her lips and silently stared ahead at the endless prairie.

The footsore horses continued plodding up the long trail. And fortunately, by late afternoon Eddie's symptoms had all disappeared.

Sometimes we pulled in at one of the scattered settlers' cabins. "Would you sell us a few fresh vegetables and some dried corn for the horses and oxen?" Daniel would ask.

These isolated people were always thrilled to see us. "Stay with us for supper," they would say. "Sit down and visit for a spell."

One thin, sallow young woman clung to my arm desperately. "Please stay," she said, verging on tears. "It's been two months since I've talked to anyone besides my own family."

My heart went out to her. I looked at Daniel questioningly.

"I'm really sorry, but we simply can't," he said. "We still have a long trip ahead of us."

Each night when we set up camp, Daniel and the children groaned with the accumulated aches from the long trip. I was so glad to stop and climb down off that hard wagon seat, I quickly forgot my own tired muscles.

I still slept in the wagon with the children, while my new husband slept in his small tent beside the campfire. Did he dream of his lost love, his beautiful Lenore? I did not know. But I had already grown weary of the constant reminders of that model of perfection.

Come dawn, we traveled on, mile after tiresome mile. I had never realized Illinois was such a long, long state.

When finally we reached a wide, tree-bordered river, flowing leisurely through a broad, green valley, Daniel gave a shout of joy. "That's it! The Illinois! Not much farther now."

"Yippee!" I yelled, grinning at the kids. "Hear that? We're almost there!"

Their sun-kissed cheeks flushing with excitement, they jumped down and ran over to the riverbank to view the other side.

We stopped and stretched for a few moments. While I watched the sunlight glimmer on the slowly moving waters, Daniel stood studying his map. "The river's low," he said. He glanced my way and smiled, his gray eyes shining. "Maybe we can find a place to ford it after all."

"It's good to know we've almost made it."

"That's right, Nellie. Not much longer now."

He and the two boys walked alongside his wagon, urging the oxen to pick up their pace as we continued northward, following the river's high curving bank. "Is that your land over there, Papa?" Eddie asked, looking across the river to the rolling hills and the bounteous stands of thick timber.

Daniel smiled down at him. "It's over there somewhere, son. We just have to track it down."

We pressed forward. Daniel suddenly stopped and pointed to a smaller tributary spilling into the Illinois from the other side. "That must be the mouth of Spoon River!" he shouted. "Just another ten miles or so now."

"Daniel! Look!" I called. Goose bumps rose on my skin as

I stared across the river. A dozen mat-covered Indian lodges lay nearly hidden in a grove of spreading trees. Then I noticed a patch of tall corn plants in a nearby clearing, and beyond that, a herd of horses grazing peacefully in a grassy meadow. Only the twitter of birds, the ripple of the water, broke the green-washed stillness of the scene.

One by one, a handful of tawny natives, dressed only in breechclouts, wandered out and began to gather on the river-bank, watching us intently. Ugly short-haired dogs barked as Daniel waved and called to the Indians in a friendly voice that reverberated across the water.

"Daniel! Are you sure they're friendly? How can you tell?" I asked him, never taking my eyes off those nearly naked figures.

"It's all right. The land agent told me there was a village of Potawatomis at the mouth of the Spoon. He sold me some beads to use for trading with them. He assured me they wouldn't bother us. The Indians all understand that their chiefs signed a treaty and sold this land to the government."

I stared across the water, my hands tightly clutching the horses' reins. "They don't look real friendly to me. I sure hope that agent knew what he was talking about. You know, I grew up on tales of massacres and scalpings."

"Look how those women are dressed. They probably have plenty of contact with white people."

Following his gaze, I saw a few Indian women standing in the background; they were wearing skirts of bright-colored cloth. "Now where do you suppose they bought that calico?" I asked.

"There's a trading post up north in Peoria." Daniel waved again to the Indians, then turned to me with a grave smile. "Just trust me. I won't let anything happen to you or the children."

We drove our wagons forward. Upriver from the mouth of Spoon River, Daniel discovered a wide spot that looked shallow enough to ford. After wading out to check the water's depth, he called heartily, "It's all right! It's fine!" He returned, and we prepared to cross.

Unmoving as statues, the Indians stood beneath the gnarled branches of old cottonwoods on the other shore, watching as we drove our wagons, rattling and splashing, through the water, trailing the string of bawling cattle behind us.

When we reached the other side, a trio of Indians climbed into a dug-out canoe, and, with a few strokes, crossed Spoon

River to meet us on the shore opposite their village. Daniel stepped over and spoke to them, smiling and nodding, pointing and gesturing. As the dogs yapped at him from across the small river, he handed the stone-faced men some of the colorful strings of glass beads he had brought from St. Louis.

The Indians waved us on then, and we passed the village without incident. Still, I sensed the stares of all those impenetrable black eyes following us up the narrow pathway. Sarah sat bent forward, her hands clenched tightly, her whole body stiff with fear.

When we had rounded a wide curve of the Spoon River and were finally out of their sight, I exhaled a long-held breath. "See," I said, turning to her with an embarrassed smile. "Those Indians aren't going to scalp us. They're friendly, just like your pa said."

She stared ahead, not acknowledging my words, but her stiffened spine relaxed.

After days of riding through monotonously flat prairie land, I was pleased to see the rolling hills and knobs that lay on this side of the Illinois River. The banks of the Spoon presented an ever-changing scene of wooded hillsides, tangled ferns and wildflowers, fertile floodplains. At the river's edge, willow branches swayed like veils, and graceful arms of maples and cottonwoods dipped into the water, weighted by lush garlands of wild grapevines. Birds chirped their merry tunes. Black-and-golden butterflies fluttered from flower to flower. I drove on, entranced by the beauty all about me.

We had traveled for several miles upstream when Daniel stopped and once again consulted his maps, his compass, and survey notes. "Not much farther now," he said, excitement glowing in his eyes. He shouted to the oxen, and they started up the trail again.

My heart stepped up its tempo. I was not certain what lay ahead for us, but the natural beauty of this place was glorious. Everything appeared pristine, untouched. And finally this endless, jolting trip was almost over.

But, how many Indians lived around here? I had seen no white settlers' homes for days. Daniel had told me this whole area was bounty land, deeded in plots to the veterans of the War of 1812. Was he the only veteran who had come to settle his grant?

Sometime later, the gurgle of rushing water interrupted my

thoughts. Through a pale green curtain of willow branches, I glimpsed rapids tumbling and swirling over boulders and smooth-sided rocks in the stream. Daniel halted, studying his little sheaf of notes.

"Wait here while I look around," he said. "The surveyors supposedly left piles of rocks and cuts on the trees to mark the boundaries of these plots. I'll be right back." He quickly unhitched a horse from the wagon, mounted it bareback, and rode away.

Welcoming the chance to stretch, the children and I strolled the cool, green carpet of grass and ferns growing along the stream. Pleasant, serene sounds accompanied our walk—the twittering of birds in the trees, a gentle, fragrant breeze rustling the leaves, the busy murmur of water rippling over rocks. Sunlight filtered through the arching branches overhead, laying a golden filigree about our feet. My heart swelled with a flood of excitement and anticipation. Would this enchanting, idyllic spot really be my new home?

Soon Daniel returned and vaulted from the horse with a wide smile that brightened his whole face. "This is it! I can't believe it! If I'd come out and chosen it myself, I couldn't have found a more perfect spot."

The children clustered close around him. "This is our land, Papa? Right here?" Hugh said, his voice hushed with wonder.

Eddie clapped his hands and grinned. "Are there Indians here?" he asked eagerly.

"Indians," Sarah murmured, glancing over her shoulder. Her face went pale. I laid a calming hand on her shoulder.

"Not an Indian in sight. Just look at all this!" Daniel bounded up the wooded hillside and pointed far into the distance. He flung his arms out wide, laughing triumphantly, looking as young as a boy. "Timber! Water! Prairie! Everything we'll ever need is right here at our fingertips."

The children and I raced to his side. At the crest of the hill, a tall-grass prairie stretched before us, strewn with a rainbow of flowers and bordered by a heavy stand of timber.

"I've never seen a land so bountiful," Daniel said, his voice husky.

I nodded, trembling with some unfamiliar emotion. "It's really something, ain't it?"

Ain't. I must remember not to say that.

He knelt and wrapped his arms around the children. "I guess this is as close to paradise as we'll ever come in this world."

Standing to one side, I gazed greedily at the profusion of fruit and nut trees, wild berry bushes and grapevines covering the hillsides. Game and fish and wild fowl were all around us, free for the taking. "At least we know we won't go hungry here," I murmured.

He turned to me with a smile. "Always the practical one, aren't you?"

"Always had to be," I said, grinning back at him.

"Just look at all this timber." He flung his arms in a wide circle. "Maple, oak, walnut, all around us. We can build a house and furniture, anything we need, and still never lack fuel for heat and cooking. Just a little sweat and elbow grease, that's all it takes. Why, anybody could make a fine life here."

My eyes drank in the scene. This was all the paradise a body had a right to expect in this world. Silently I blessed Daniel for letting me escape from Uncle Amos. He had given me a whole new start at life.

Plenty of hard work lay ahead for us all. That didn't scare me one bit. What else had I ever known? But a new and exhilarating sense of freedom coursed through my veins. I was free here in this raw, untamed land—free to live, to speak my mind, to grow, to expand all my horizons.

And maybe here I could forget. Maybe someday I could sleep one whole night through without those confused, disturbing dreams of Johnny.

CHAPTER 7

Eden Valley, Daniel named his plot along the river. Truly, it was almost as lovely as paradise.

"But there's still a mountain of work ahead," Daniel said. "We'll have to hurry to get a cabin finished before cold weather strikes."

He searched the woods for tall, uniform, straight-trunked trees. The sound of his ax echoed through the valley steady as a drumbeat as the bright blade ate into the trees. Fibers split and ripped, and trees roared through the air, crashing down to make the earth tremble.

"I'll help strip off the branches," I said, grabbing a hatchet.

Daniel took my arm. "No, that's too heavy for you. Let me take care of it."

I shook him off. "I'm no weakling. I'm going to help. Here, kids. You gather up and pile all this brush for burning."

Together we rolled the trimmed logs to the picturesque spot Daniel had chosen; it was near the river, but yet high enough to be safe from any danger of flooding.

We camped out in the tent and wagon for over a week while we laid the rock foundation and prepared all the logs. I helped wherever I could, ignoring Daniel's protests.

Finally he readied the forked limbs needed to lift the weighty logs into place. Raising a house was a sizeable undertaking, even a crude one-room log cabin. We were nowhere near finished.

One day as I was hacking away, helping clear brush from the yard, I heard the sound of approaching hoofs. I almost dropped my hatchet from surprise. I wheeled and saw a horse coming round the bend, ridden by a shaggy, rumpled white man dressed in homemade jeans, low boots, and a cape made from an ancient, faded mackinaw blanket.

"Hey, there!" the man called out, waving a knobby hand as he neared our camp.

My blood stirred with excitement. It seemed a month since I had seen anyone other than the family. I hurried over to hear what this fellow had to say.

Daniel stood notching the ends of logs with his hatchet so their corners would fit together snugly. He wiped his sweaty brow, returning the friendly wave. "Hello yourself! Welcome!"

The stranger sat on his weary-looking horse, surveying the five of us and our belongings, which were scattered around the shady glen. A grin appeared on his weather-beaten face. "You folks sure are a sight for sore eyes," he said. "It's been quite a spell since I've seen a white man."

"You're a welcome sight yourself." Daniel shook the man's extended hand. "I'm Daniel Cranford. This is my wife Nellie and the family. We're trying to get settled in here before it turns cold. Do you live nearby?"

"I'm clearing a farm about ten miles down thataway," the man said, pointing southward. "Some Indians were riding by and told me you folks had moved in. My name's Travis Weaver. Looks like you-all could use some help."

"That I could." Daniel laid his hand on my shoulder. "My wife's been trying to do too much of this heavy work. These young ones are willing hands, too, but they're still small."

"Yeah, no bigger than a minute. My boys was more than half-growed when we came up here a year back. Never could of made it without them, neither. Was you figuring on raising that cabin by your lonesome?"

Daniel shrugged. "Well, I'm rigging up these forked logs. Nellie said she'd help me hold them steady while I raise the logs for the walls and roof."

The man's eyes dwelled for a moment on my small frame. He slowly shook his head. "Reckon I'd better stick around. I'm afeared you might be at this half the winter with just them three cubs and a skinny woman for help. Why, she don't look much older than the kids."

An awkward silence followed. "My—my first wife died."

Good Lord. Would this go on forever?

"I'll have you know I can do 'most all this stuff," I said, glaring defiantly at the man.

But I realized I should be grateful for his offer. With his help, we could quickly finish the cabin and move into it. I grinned apologetically. "You'll stay and eat with us, won't you, Mr. Weaver?"

"Thank you, missus. I'll do that. And I'll be back tomorrow with my two big boys to help you raise this here cabin. You'll have a fair heap more to do asides that before you're settled in good for winter."

True to his word, he returned the next day with his two strapping, sandy-haired sons. In short order they helped Daniel raise and roof the cabin and cut the openings for doors and windows. While they laid the split-log floor and built the fireplace with logs and mud, the children and I filled and chinked all the cracks with sticks and moss and clay mud from along the river. Daniel covered the windows with oiled paper. Just temporarily, he said, until he could buy panes of glass.

Finally the cabin was complete. Before they left, we invited the Weavers to bring their whole family back for a housewarming. Daniel and I and the children eagerly carried in all the furniture and housewares from the wagon. Surrounded by the smell of fresh-cut wood and the drone of happy voices, we arranged the furnishings to give the rustic little cabin the feel of home.

Daniel stood in the doorway frowning, rubbing his beard as he surveyed his new realm. "This isn't much. It's awfully small. Later on I'll build us a bigger, nicer house."

"After all that time in the covered wagon, this looks like a palace to me," I said.

"A palace? No, not quite." He pulled out his pocketknife and began to carve the year, 1821, in the board above the door.

As he dug the numbers into the wood, my gaze rested on his face, his intelligent gray eyes. He truly was a fine-looking man. Even though his appearance was rougher now, his hair and beard untrimmed, his hands cut and scraped from working with the logs, to me he seemed more vigorous and alive. I found him quite handsome.

It seemed so strange, being here alone with him like this. I glanced at the bedstead and feather mattress we had placed in the corner. Those walnut bedposts had traveled all the way from

New York State. Daniel and Lenore's bed, I remembered with a twinge. And I knew I could never hope to compare with her.

We pulled out chairs and sat down to rest—and to admire our fine new home. The bird's-eye maple table, flanked by six chairs, stood against the side wall, ready to be opened out at mealtimes.

The children's beds were set up in the loft. Pans and kettles rested on the hearth; ladles and tongs and stirring spoons hung from nearby pegs. There was a food safe, a rocker, a churn and spinning wheel, all kinds of heavy winter clothes, a Bible, a home medicine book, and an almanac.

"I brought a big box of books," Daniel said. "I'll have to find a place to put a shelf for them." He raised his feet and set them on a small stool.

"What a pretty needlepoint pattern," I said, pointing to the stool.

Sarah bent and ran her finger over the nubby design. "My mother made that. She made lots and lots of beautiful things."

I glanced over at the basket filled with sewing supplies. These were all Lenore's things. She and Daniel had started out for Illinois well supplied. Would I always feel her as an unseen presence here among us?

"You-all are just loaded with nice things," I said, forcing a smile, though I suddenly felt very tired. "I only brought a few clothes, and all of them are worn and faded."

Only those and my two treasures—my mother's tortoiseshell hairbrush and the pearl brooch from Johnny. But, of course, Johnny was nothing to me now.

Dismissing these dangerous thoughts with a quick shake of my head, I again surveyed the cabin. I would be mistress of this place, the first home of my own. A heady feeling came over me, filling me with a warm glow. As soon as I could sort through those bolts of material in the loft, I would make some pretty curtains to brighten up the house. I could add lots of little touches to mark this as my own.

"By the way," Daniel said hesitantly. "There's a whole trunk of Lenore's clothes and things, if you'd like to have them. Some of them are quite nice."

I froze at the very thought of wearing her clothes. No, I'd wear rags and patches rather than give him and the children further reason for comparisons. "I don't think so, Daniel," I said, swallowing back the lump in my throat. "Maybe someday I can make them over into something for Sarah."

"That would be nice of you. Yes, she would like that, wouldn't she?"

"Time to get to work." I rose from the chair, anxious for a change of scene. "I'd better go out and throw some corn to the chickens—so they don't all run wild. Come on, kids. You can help me."

They scurried out the door.

"Nellie . . ." A brick-colored flush appeared beneath the tan on Daniel's face. "I just wanted to tell you how much I appreciate everything you've done. I know it's not been easy."

"Oh, shoot." Now I was blushing, too. I shrugged to cover my embarrassment. "It ain't— It *hasn't* been so bad. At least we're here and we got the cabin raised."

His eyes, a soft dove gray beneath his straight dark brows, studied my face intently for a moment. "I never could have made it this far without your help, Nellie. I just wanted you to know."

Could it be? Was it possible that he was beginning to like me? I knew I liked him. The trip had proved to me just how brave and strong and kind he really was.

Oh, perhaps he'd never stir me to the same exhilaration I felt when Johnny kissed me, said he loved me. He had made me feel pretty and desirable.

I could never be anything but a poor second best to Daniel. Still, I knew my fate was in good hands. I trusted him. I liked him. Yes, I liked him very much.

"You've been a godsend with the children," he said, looking deeply into my eyes. I stood taut, sensing the growing tension in the air. I felt a pull between us that was real enough to touch. Would he kiss me now? At least take my hand?

His glance dropped; he drew in a long breath. "I've never forced myself on any woman," he muttered, looking greatly embarrassed. "I'll not start with you. I understand how women find these things distasteful. You can take the big bed. I'll take the trundle and push it over by the door. I'm sorry I can't offer you more privacy."

Abruptly he turned and hurried out the door. I stared after him, my cheeks fiery hot, my hands trembling.

* * *

Fresh venison was roasting in the new fireplace a few days later when the Weavers' wagon rattled into our yard. The family of six sandy-haired children, graduated in size like stair steps, scrambled down. I rushed outside to greet the first woman I had talked to in weeks.

"Well, come right in. Just make yourself at home," I said, taking her arm and leading her toward the cabin door. "My name's Nellie."

Nellie Cranford. It was still hard to accept the fact that I was really married.

"I'm Lucy Weaver." The large-boned woman wore a faded, brown homespun dress. She regarded me with weary, kindly eyes. "Sakes alive! You're nothing but a girl. These young'uns can't be yours."

"No . . ." My glance dropped to her heavy, well-worn shoes. "My husband's first wife died."

"All alone out here, ain't you, honey?"

Ain't, again. I could sense Sarah cringe.

"Not anymore." I smiled, with a sudden burst of pleasure. "You're my neighbor."

An expression of sympathy flickered across her harried face. "Well, if you ever need me, you just let me know. Though generally I'm stuck tight to home, I'm afraid. There's just no end to all the chores, you know—and the roads ain't fitten to travel half the year."

"But come and visit me whenever you get the chance," I urged, clinging to the woman's arm. "Tell me, Lucy. What do the kids do for schooling out here?"

"Why, honey, what a question. If you want schooling for your kids, you got to learn 'em yourself."

The chatter of uninterrupted conversation spilled from our cabin until far into the night. We found spots to lay quilts for all the smaller children to sleep on up in the loft. Lucy Weaver joined me in the big bed, while the two older boys and men slept on feather mattresses scattered about the floor downstairs. Eleven people packed into one sixteen-by-twenty cabin. The sound of snores and heavy, rhythmic breathing made a soothing kind of night music throughout the long, dark hours.

After a robust breakfast of eggs and bacon and fritters, the Weavers clambored aboard their wagon and took off down the trail through the trees, waving until they disappeared around the bend.

I walked back inside and stirred the fire, struck by the sudden quiet. The smell of fresh-cut wood and breakfast bacon lingered in the little cabin, but the sound of conversation and hearty laughter had disappeared. I felt a lump tighten in my chest.

How long would it be before we had visitors again? I had lived at the inn so long, the constant sounds and movement of the guests had become a part of my life. Who would have dreamed that I would miss it so?

"Are you going to give the kids some schooling here at home?" I asked Daniel that evening. "I'd help them, but I never had the chance to get much learning myself."

"Yes, I'll work with them at night. Before long we'll have enough people around here to start a real school."

"I don't know, Daniel. From the looks of things, it may be quite a spell."

In the days that followed, household tasks occupied my time from dawn till dark. I spent free moments gathering walnuts and hazelnuts from the woods and helping lay in stacks of firewood for the coming winter. By nightfall, my body ached with fatigue. So why did sleep elude me?

The distance between Daniel and me haunted me during the long and restless night hours. We were man and wife, yet strangers still.

By day he maintained a reserved distance from me, though at times I caught his eyes, those interesting gray eyes, gazing curiously at my face. I blushed, tense with silent expectation, then turned from him and tried to concentrate on my chores.

When darkness fell, he helped Hugh and Sarah with some rudimentary school lessons, while I sewed and mended and knitted by the fire. Later, I heated water in the kettle and helped the children bathe away the day's grime in the round wooden tub. Dressed in their flannel nightclothes, their faces scrubbed and shining, they ran over to their father.

"Papa, Papa! A good-night kiss!" Sarah demanded, climbing on his lap as he sat in the rocker by the fire.

Eddie scrambled up on the other knee. "Me, too!"

Laughing, Daniel wrapped an arm around Hugh and drew him into the ring, too. "So now all my chicks are clean and sweet. All ready to head up to roost.'' He kissed each brow in turn and hugged the children to him.

As I watched from across the room, a deep envy washed over me. I had never known such warmth from my father, and now I felt omitted from this circle of affection, too. Wordlessly I hustled the children up the ladder to the loft, then climbed the rungs to tuck them into their beds.

Eddie's tousled curls were dark against his pillow. ''Nellie, will you kiss me good night, too?'' he asked, reaching up his little arms.

''Why, sweetie, sure. You just bet I will.'' I sat down beside him and held him close, kissing his soft cheek. ''And you, too, little man,'' I said, bending over to plant a kiss on Hugh. He smiled, looking pleased.

I crossed over to Sarah's single bed on the other side of the slant-ceilinged loft. She watched me coming, her face set, her eyes challenging. ''How about a good night kiss?'' I asked, chucking her chin to try to get a smile.

She squeezed her lips together and shook her head from side to side.

''Oh, just this once won't hurt you,'' I said, with a forced cheerfulness, and pressed my lips against her unyielding cheek.

Would she always be like this? I glanced over to the corner. Tucked far back under the eaves lay the trunk filled with Lenore's clothes. Her ghost was always with us.

When I came back downstairs, I found Daniel sitting in the rocker, deep in thought, staring at the fire. I pulled up another chair and picked up my knitting. The long silence that followed begged to be broken.

''Think this sock will fit Hugh?'' I asked, holding up the little tube hanging from my needles.

He glanced up, his eyes distant. ''Huh? Oh, yes. That should be fine.''

''You tired? You've been working so hard—trying to get everything done before it gets too cold.''

His gaze went back to the dancing orange flames. ''I should have started sooner. If I had moved up here in late spring, I could have had a garden and a corn crop in the first year. I don't know what I was thinking of. I'm afraid we're in for a lean winter.''

''Don't worry, Daniel. We already have this fine cabin, all

warm and cozy. There's fish and game enough out there to feed an army. We have corn for corn bread, and I've made wild plum and crab apple preserves. We'll be fine.''

His eyes rested on my face. After a moment, he chuckled softly. ''I'm not sure if you're a born optimist, Nellie, or if you just don't understand the situation.''

He rose and went outside with his leather log carrier, returning with a load of firewood. My hand covered a yawn. I poured water from the kettle into a washpan and carried it behind the sheets I had hung to curtain off a tiny corner for privacy. I slipped out of my clothes, took a quick sponge bath, then pulled my long flannel gown over my head.

Reaching behind my neck, I loosened the yarn tie holding my long hair, then bent over to brush out the tangles. Johnny said he loved my hair. He said it felt like silk. Would Daniel, some-day . . . ?

Stepping out from behind the curtain, I crossed over to the big bed in the corner. Only the flickering fire lit the room. As I pulled back the coverlet and crawled between the cold sheets, Daniel rose abruptly and went outside.

I heard Shad give a joyful bark. The next bark was closer, right outside the door. Daniel was pacing the yard again. I hated that nightly habit of his. Was he brooding over Lenore? I wanted to go out and ask him to come inside, but I lay silent instead, tears of loneliness burning in my eyes.

Later, he came inside, undressed quietly, and lay down in the trundle bed across the room. Though I pretended to be fast asleep, I was acutely conscious of his every breath. I sensed his nearness with a kind of urgency and pain. Was he wakeful, too?

Goose bumps raised on my skin. An unspoken attraction, an unnamed strain and tension, coursed between us, building in intensity with every passing day. My whole being seemed filled with waiting.

One crisp fall morning, when the woods were a riot of orange and gold, Daniel and Hugh went out to chop more firewood for winter. I sat down by the table and began churning butter, rhyth-mically pounding the wooden churn handle up and down.

A short time later, I glanced up and noticed the silhouettes of two dark forms trying to peer through the oiled-paper window.

Indians. I froze, my fingers in a death clutch on the churn

handle. Images of massacres, of kidnapping and hostages flashed like bolts of lightning through my head.

Sucking in a sharp breath, I scooted Sarah and Eddie up the ladder to the loft and tried to collect my jumbled thoughts. Daniel never seemed afraid of the Indians who lived near us. I had to overcome my fear and learn to live among them, too. And there was no time like the present.

Gathering up my entire store of courage, I grabbed four corn dodgers left from breakfast and opened the door. "Good morning," I called, my chin held high as I looked squarely into the faces of the two Indians who had come walking with noiseless steps around the corner of our cabin.

The sounds of Daniel's busy ax resounded from the hilltop. My heart beat at a much faster pace.

Two pairs of jet-black eyes stared at me curiously. I stared back, awed by their towering height, their military-straight posture. Their noses were curved and aquiline, their cheekbones high and prominent. They wore long deerskin shirts and leggings trimmed with fancy geometric designs made with beads and dyed porcupine quills. On their heads were fur turbans topped with a single eagle feather. Pierced-shell necklaces hung to their chests, and decorated wampum bags were slung over their shoulders. All in all, I found them a most impressive and intimidating pair.

The Indians muttered something to me, but I could not understand. They made a move as if to come inside the house.

"No, you can't come inside now. Did you-all want to see my husband? He's up there on the hill." I held my place, blocking the doorway. "Here, take this," I said, and handed them the dodgers with trembling hands.

Sarah's panicked whimper sounded from the loft. I pointed toward the timber in the distance and folded my arms firmly across my chest.

They glanced toward the noise of ax strokes, nodded somberly, and with the greatest dignity strolled over to their horses.

As I watched them ride away, I remained standing in the doorway, silent and imperial, hoping my strong will would compensate for my small size. After all, I had defied Uncle Amos and fought off a pack of wolves. I refused to let this pair of Indians spook me. Fine sentiments, but my heart was pounding faster than a woodpecker's beak.

Daniel returned an hour later. When I heard his wagon roll up, groaning under its load of firewood, I ran outside to meet him. "Did you see those Indians? Did they go up and talk to you?"

His brow furrowed. "Indians?" he asked, rubbing his beard. "No, I haven't seen an Indian for a week or so. Probably just a hunting party passing by. Sometimes they travel long distances."

"They tried to look in our window. They wanted to come in, but I wouldn't let them."

"How did you talk to them? What did you say?"

I shrugged. "Not much. I just stared them down."

Bursting into tears, Sarah raced out the door and seized her father's sleeve as he climbed off the wagon. "Oh, Papa! Papa! I was so afraid!"

He gathered her into his arms and patted her blond curls. "I'm sorry," he said, glancing at me, apologetic. "I'll have to stay closer, so I can keep an eye on the house. You must have all been frightened to death."

"Nellie wasn't scared at all," Eddie said, with a bright grin. "The Indians are nice. She just gave them some corn dodgers."

Daniel's brows raised quizzically.

"I don't intend to live in fear," I told him, my hands planted firmly on my hips. "The Indians are practically our only neighbors here. I guess I'd better just get used to them."

Now that I had said it, I only hoped I would be able to live up to my brave words. I hurried back into the house to finish my churning.

Daniel unhitched the horse and piled the firewood in the side yard, then came inside and sat down in the rocker beside the hearth. As I stepped over to stir the kettle of bean soup simmering over the fire, he studied me with an amused, interested look in his eyes. "You're quite a girl, Nellie," he said, smiling. "You're going to do all right here, aren't you?"

A blush heated my cheeks. I glanced his way, then hung my head to concentrate on stirring beans. "Takes more than a couple of Indians to scare me," I muttered.

He nodded. "I wasn't sure, you know. I was afraid you'd want to leave when you saw how rough life is up here. In fact, it's much worse than I anticipated, with all the Indians and so few white neighbors. But I do believe you're going to be just fine."

76

And Lenore? What kind of life would this have been for a refined lady? She would have taken one look and headed straight back to New York!

That night a storm blew down from the north, whipping the gold and russet leaves from the trees, whistling around the corners of the cabin. A cold, persistent rain sluiced down, drenching the house and all the livestock in the fields. Through it all, our sturdy roof held out the torrents of water.

The hour grew late, and the fire burned low. Up in the loft, the children were long asleep. I sat by the hearth knitting socks again, feeling snug and cozy. Daniel sat near the burning candle on the table, carving and polishing a little walnut pipe rack. Overhead, the relentless rain peppered the roof.

"Time to turn in," he said, blowing out the candle. In the soft glow of firelight, he began to pull the trundle from beneath the big bed. His eyes met mine with a questioning gaze. "Nellie?" he whispered, and reached out his hand to me.

A queer trembling came over me. I stood up, my heart pounding in my temples, and gazed at his shining eyes and dark wavy hair. The very air around us seemed charged with some great tension.

"Nellie?" he repeated softly, and suddenly it snapped. With one step, I was in his warm, caressing arms, his body pressed to mine, his hot face burrowed in my neck.

Unmindful of the fury of the wind and rain outside, he pulled back the quilt and drew me into bed. His arms encircled me and held me close. "You're very special, you know," he murmured, gently smoothing my hair back from my face. His words were soothing as warmed oil against my skin.

"I try."

Outside, a limb snapped in a gust of wind and fell with a resounding crash. My nerves were taut; all my senses were heightened.

His hand slipped down and caressed my cheek. "I never wanted to force myself on you."

The manly scent, the warmth of him so near. The feel of his breath, like a summer breeze across my face. "I like you, Daniel. Really I do."

He drew me close to him, and something rose inside me, as a flower rises to the sunlight. Excitement swept through me like a flame. He kissed me, and I felt his heart pounding against mine. All my senses were ignited by the taste, the scent, the sound of him so near to me.

And so, with passion and patience, he introduced me to the mysteries of love. I crossed over to a new frontier, and then I was at peace.

Later, we lay with arms entwined. I felt somehow forged to this man, as a blacksmith with his fire joins two pieces of iron.

"Why were you so set on coming here, Daniel?" I asked, snuggling against the warmth of him.

"My land. And the freedom and opportunity out here. A man only gets such an opportunity once in a lifetime. Back East I had a nice old family home and some land just outside town. Plenty of help with the heavy chores."

"Sounds pretty good to me."

"It might have been, except that I'd had some bad financial reverses after the war. And I knew that rocky soil was nearly played out. I've always wanted to start some kind of business of my own. Out here, there's just no limit to what a man can do."

"That's true, isn't it? You can do anything you dream."

"We're a team now, Nellie," he said, his fingers playing gently in my hair. "I'm going to share it all with you. For better or worse, just like we said."

CHAPTER 8

Soon the snows came, and ice froze hard on the river. The trees stood naked, their black arms outstretched against a low, gray sky. The air inside the cabin was so frigid, my hands felt as icy as the river.

January hit the prairie like a fist. Northern gales whipped around the little house and scurried down the open chimney.

Outside, the trees cracked with sounds like gunfire through the night. A film of ice froze over our water bucket, right inside the house. My face bones ached. The cold seeped through me like a fluid. I had never felt so cold, had never dreamed anyone could feel so cold.

Our cabin was built in a protected valley. I knew out on the flatland, the arctic winds were flailing with even crueler force. Eden Valley seemed a long way from paradise in winter.

We had covered the two small, greased-paper windows with shutters. Now the inside of the cabin was dark and dreary, with only the fireplace and a few candles for light. Sometimes it seemed as if we were living in a cave.

The cold kept the children inside and inactive too long, and they began to quarrel over trifles.

"That's mine!"

"Is not!"

"Nellie, make him leave my things alone!"

"Look, here," I'd say, reaching for their primers on the bookshelf. "Who wants to read me a story?"

In my rare spare moments, I browsed through Daniel's books, flipping pages, trying to sound out the unfamiliar big words, wishing I could understand these mysterious, enticing texts. I felt my ignorance like a scar upon my face.

Daniel went out hunting, providing a steady fare of venison, squirrel, rabbit, and wild fowl. This meat, along with beans and corn bread, served as our daily fare.

On sunny days, I dressed in my warmest clothes and went outside. Just to see the woods and fields eased my growing sense of loneliness and isolation. Squirrels barked and chattered in the trees. Whole flocks of cardinals swooped down and lit on the snow, looking like a brilliant red bouquet on some rich man's white linen tablecloth.

The children, bundled in their warmest coats and scarves and mittens, ran in the snow like puppies, playing fox and geese or sliding down the hill on greased planks.

"I'm going to build a pen of saplings," Daniel said. "Something to protect our chickens from the foxes and wolves."

"What about the other animals?" I asked. "What are we going to feed them over the winter?"

"That shouldn't be a problem. The cattle and the milk cow

79

can dig through the snow for dried prairie grass and shrubs. The pigs will just forage for acorns in the woods.''

"Looks like all of us will be living off the land.''

While a blizzard raged outside, he hung rough shelves on the cabin wall to hold all our dishes. He built a stand for the water bucket and a box for firewood.

"What shall it be for supper tonight?'' he'd ask me.

"Oh, venison might taste good for a change.''

I hovered over the fire, cooking stews and roasts and soups from all the different kinds of game Daniel shot. I washed our clothes and churned our butter and pounded grains of corn with a smooth rock to make cornmeal until my hands grew callused and my shoulders ached.

"This is the same way the Indians grind their corn,'' I told Daniel. "I sure wish we had a mill nearby.''

"It's a terrible drudgery for you, isn't it? I've been giving some serious thought to building a mill here later on.''

At night, the distant, mournful wail of wolves served as a chilling lullaby, agitating Shad to bark and growl and pace around our cabin door. I snuggled close to Daniel, grateful for his comforting warmth.

His arms opened and enclosed me, drawing me near. Every day I felt the bonds between us forging stronger. He never said he loved me, never said much at all as we lay close. But he was here, and I was here, and somehow that was enough on this bitter cold night.

"I'm going out and shoot those wolves before they kill the livestock,'' he said one frigid afternoon. The boys hovered near the fire, building toy forts with blocks of wood, while Sarah played with a pretty china-faced doll.

I looked up from darning a faded woolen sock and shook my head in protest. "Oh, Daniel, it's too cold. Just wait until it warms a mite.''

He lifted his long polished rifle and powder horn from the pegs over the door. "I've waited long enough. I'll track those devils to their den.''

As he slipped on extra layers of socks and a shirt and trousers, I thought with panic of the ice-chilled wind, the stark white world outside. "Please, Daniel. Wait.''

Wordlessly he shook his head and belted his heavy woolen

80

cape. He tucked the stock of his long rifle under his arm and paused beside the door. "It's something I have to do."

When he released the latch, a gust of frigid wind tore open the door and shot through the house, chilling me to the very marrow of my bones. Shivering, I glanced outside at the high drifts of snow; those rolling hills of whiteness made my own yard unfamiliar, a strange, exotic place.

Heart in my throat, I held the door open just a crack and watched him walk through the snow, lifting his legs high with every step. His breath billowed before him in a vaporous cloud.

"Hurry back!" I called, but the harsh wind flung the words back in my face.

An hour later, snow began to fall, the white flakes whipping sideways in the wind. My skin prickled with nervousness. I paced the floor, thinking of Daniel out in the cold and snow alone.

When late afternoon arrived and he still had not returned, frightening images began pulsing through my head like bubbles in a boiling pot. What if he had fallen? What if he was injured, frozen, torn apart by ravaging wolves?

Like little mirrors, the children reflected my anxiety. "Where's Papa? Is he lost out in the snow?" Sarah asked, her chin trembling. Tears glistening in her wide, blue eyes.

"Don't you worry. He'll be back soon," I said, putting on a brave face as I patted her shoulder. She twisted away and plunked herself down in a chair beside the fire, cradling her doll in her arms.

Eddie pulled at my skirt. "Is Papa all right?"

I swallowed back the lump that rose in my throat. "Why, sure he's all right, honey." Kneeling, I wrapped my arms around the small boy. "You know your papa was the bravest soldier in the war. Nothing can hurt him. Come on, Hugh. Find your primer and read us a story."

The heirloom clock on the mantel, the one that Daniel had brought all the way from New York State, ticked away the seconds, minutes, hours. My heart was ticking double-time. Where on earth was Daniel? It was cold—bitter, killing cold—outside. He should have been home long ago.

What would I do if something happened to him? We were just learning to know each other, to appreciate what we could build

81

up here. And what about the children? Oh, I could not even bear to think the awful thoughts that nagged at my mind.

Darkness descended. I opened the door a crack for the hundredth time. Low clouds obscured the moon, but a feeble light reflected off the waves of frozen snowdrifts.

At least it's stopped snowing, I thought, peering out into the darkness. Nothing looked familiar. If drifted snow had changed our own yard so dramatically, how could Daniel ever find his way across the vast, windswept prairie?

"You kids stay here. I'm going outside for a while," I said, grabbing my high boots from the box by the door. After slipping on extra socks and a woolen shirt of Daniel's, I bundled myself in a shawl and cloak and drew on a pair of rabbit-fur mittens.

"We'll be here all alone," Sarah said in a high-pitched whine.

I drew myself up to my tallest and gave the children a long, resolute look. "I'm going to build a fire at the top of the hill, to help your papa find his way home."

When I stepped outside, the howling wind sliced through my heavy clothes as if they were lace. Shivering, I pressed forward, struggling through the high drifts toward our woodpile in back. Spurred on by the agony of cold, I quickly piled our crude sled high with logs and kindling sticks and lumbered uphill through the snow, stumbling and sliding as I dragged the loaded sled to the hilltop.

The gale blew in a frenzy across the wide prairie. It tore at my clothes and whipped the snow from drifts up into my face. Was I insane to think that I could build a fire in this?

My heart drummed painfully, my breath came in gasping pants as I quickly tented a few logs and kindling wood. With fingers stiff as icicles, I pulled out of my apron pocket the flint and steel and a little hoard of dried sticks I had snatched from the fireside basket. Would it work? It had to work!

My lungs felt frozen, each breath like the stab of an icy dagger. I knelt with my back to the wind, said a quick prayer, and struck the flint to steel. A spark flashed, then died as a gust of wind caught it.

I struck again. This time the spark caught a tiny thumb of loosened bark on a dried stick. It flickered, flared, then caught. Fed by the wind, the sticks around the flame began to smoke, then to blaze.

I smelled the welcome scent of burning wood. The fire was

like a bright golden star there in the darkness. The ice-crusted kindling wood and logs began to sputter from the heat. I had a real fire now. A fire to guide Daniel home.

The wind howled, and the flames grew, shooting orange sparks into the night sky. I flung more logs on the fire, and more, and hurried down the hill to replenish my supply. This fire must be enormous, huge enough to light the sky for miles, so Daniel could see it no matter where he was.

Numb and stiff with cold, I again piled the sled high with logs and struggled back uphill. I panted from exertion, each frigid breath like knives piercing my lungs. My hands and feet felt like chunks of ice, rigid as the logs I threw onto the fire. I was in agony, but nothing could slow my frenzied labors. As I watched the flames leap ever higher, I smiled with the certainty that Daniel could see them.

Just as I reached the crest of the hill with my sixth sledload of logs, I glimpsed a pitiful bent form stumbling through the scalloped waves of snow across the prairie. It was Daniel!

Tears stinging my eyes, I dropped the sled rope and stood speechless, overwhelmed with relief as he slowly approached.

His face was bundled with a frozen scarf. All I could see were red-rimmed eyes and icy lashes. His sleeve was ripped, his coat and hat and gloves white with frozen sleet and snow.

"Nellie," he said, and stiffly sank down on the sled beside the fire. "Oh, Nellie, thank you."

A tear rolled down my frozen cheek. I knelt in the snow beside him and took his hand. "I was afraid . . ."

"I never could have found my way without this fire." His breath was short, his voice just a rasp. "Stupid thing to do. Going out like that."

"You're home now. That's all that matters."

He gave me a long, grateful look, the blazing fire reflected in his pain-filled eyes.

I shivered from the wind—and from the depth of emotion in his face. "Did you get the wolves?"

"I got a few," he said. "Let's go home."

My hands were numb. Clenching them, I picked up the sled rope in one and slipped the other through Daniel's arm to help him down the hill.

Again his eyes met mine. "You saved my life," he said.

* * *

In late February, Travis Weaver made a trip to Springfield and brought us back some badly needed supplies. Daniel and I tapped the maple trees growing near our cabin, inserting little tubes we made from oak twigs. After the sweet sap had dripped into wooden buckets, we poured it into a kettle over an outdoor fire and boiled it down into sugar for sweetening.

Gradually the days grew warmer as winter turned to spring. Gorged by the melting snow, the river ran high, rushing past our cabin with a roar. Returning robins greedily pecked for worms, chirping as the grasses suddenly turned vivid green. The woods and prairies blossomed with the colors of spring flowers: white Solomon's seal and twinleaf and shooting star, yellow trout lily and woods poppy, pink columbine and trillium and fire pink, blue hepatica and violet.

I felt jubilant, ecstatic with the beauty that surrounded me. The whole world seemed born anew. Now Eden Valley truly deserved its name.

"Come on, kids. Let's take a walk across the prairie," I said, taking Sarah and Eddie's small hands. We climbed the flower-strewn hillside and watched as hawks and red-winged blackbirds soared gracefully across the soft blue sky. The breeze smelled sweet and fresh, laden with the fragrance of wild plum and cherry blossoms. In the distance, our herd of cattle looked like fat brown bugs as they grazed on the new growth of prairie grass. The cow bell clanged its clear metallic song to greet us.

Uttering a loud squeal, Eddie bent down to the grass. "Arrowhead! Look what I found! It's an arrowhead!" he said, displaying his find in a chubby little hand.

A glint of sparkle caught my eye. Some Indian beads lay scattered on the ground around my feet. I picked up a dozen of the colored glass spheres. "Look here!" I said, grinning at the children. "This really must be Eden, like your papa said. The plants here even grow jewels."

A giggle issued from Sarah's lips as I dropped the beads into her hand. Maybe this spring she could finally reconcile herself to her new home, rough and crude as it was. Though only six, she was a very strong-minded young lady.

My cooking, my grammar, everything about me seemed to offend her. I could understand that she did not want to call me Mother, for she idolized her dead mother as a saint. But Sarah hardly spoke to me. She avoided me, pulled away at my slightest touch.

The two boys liked me. We were friends and workmates through our countless daily chores. They turned to me for comfort and affection. But Sarah's continued distance was discomforting, to say the least.

When we returned to the cabin, I called to Hugh. "Could you bring us a bucket of water, please?"

The boy, swinging the wooden bucket to the rhythm of his whistled tune, started toward the spring that gushed from the hillside near the house. Two minutes later, he flew in the door and dropped into a chair panting, his face as white as bleached cotton.

I ran to him, wiping my hands on my apron. "Hugh, what is it?"

"A blue snake!" he said, his voice quavering. "It turned right around and chased me."

Sarah screamed, a shudder running through her slender body.

"Blue racer. Yes, I've seen them chase after people like that." I slipped my arm around his shoulder and chucked his trembling chin. "Good thing you're such as fast runner, Hugh. At least those old blue racers aren't poisonous, like prairie rattlers."

He forced a brave grin. "Yes, but I never had a rattler chase me!" Wiping his sweaty hands against his pant legs, he stared down at the floorboards. "Do you think Papa would go with me to get the water? Just this once?" he asked softly.

I hesitated just a beat, then drew in a deep breath. "Tell you what. I'll go with you." I hated snakes as much as Hugh did, but if need be I could kill one with the hoe. And the more we killed, the less there'd be to pester us.

Eyes wide with fear, Sarah watched us from the doorway; I found a hoe and started for the nearby spring with Hugh. His abandoned bucket lay in a clump of heart-leafed violets beside the path. "All right now, where's that darned blue varmit?" I demanded, my hoe raised at the ready, though I was pretty scared myself.

Giggling, Hugh retrieved his bucket. "When he saw you coming, he got scared and took off fast."

"Well, he'd just better stay away, if he knows what's good for him." I laid the hoe across my shoulder, took the boy's hand, and we walked down the path to the spring.

When we returned, I handed him the hoe. "Next time, just take this along with you. We'll get rid of those nasty critters yet."

He nodded gratefully. If his father had been near, this eight-year-old would have tried to act as fearless as a man. With me, he could be a child a little longer. I was happy to indulge him, for I knew the frontier life forced children to grow up much too fast.

Little Eddie seemed immune to fear. He was fascinated with everything about the Indians. As Daniel plowed the rich bottom-land, Eddie searched for arrowheads and other Indian trinkets in the newly turned soil. He was on constant lookout for them as we planted corn, dropping the golden grains into hills and covering them with fertile black earth.

When we had finished the planting, Eddie scampered along the crest of the hill, where the prairie began its long sweep to the west. I followed him, fearing he might get lost.

His curly little head bobbed among the growing blades of grass and stalks of flowers as he inspected the ground for long-lost relics. That child, set against the vast expanse of flatland, seemed as tiny and insignificant as a canoe out on the ocean waves.

The early May sun smiled down on me, warm and comforting as a friend. We had weathered our first winter. Though we had arrived with just a meager stock of essential supplies to carry us through months of cold and snow, we had survived.

Soon we would see our first crop of corn, and a vegetable garden, and a new calf, and fluffy baby chicks scuttling around our yard. We had our home, snug against the wind and rain, in a setting green and lush as Eden.

And I had something more. In this season, when all the earth throbbed and surged with rich fertility, when the miracle of new life was springing up all around me, I suspected—I was almost certain—I was carrying a new life of my own.

Late one green and golden afternoon, I sauntered out by the barn where Daniel was chopping firewood. He glanced up, surprised to see me, for I seldom left my work to seek him out. "Something wrong?"

"No, not at all. Just thought you might be interested to know . . ."

He laid his ax against the log and gazed intently at my face. "What's that? You're acting awfully coy."

I grinned to cover my embarrassment. "Well, Mr. Cranford, it looks like we might have a little stranger coming to visit us."

His eyes clung to mine for a long moment as he absorbed my words. "Well! Well, that's good news," he said, with a tentative smile. "And when might that be?"

"Sometime after Christmas, I'd say."

"I'll find a doctor, or a good midwife for you. I imagine you're afraid, being here alone like this."

"Afraid? Well, maybe just a little. I guess it's all just part of nature, though."

"I want to do the best I can for you, Nellie. After all, you've done so much for me."

Pushing down the fear that rose inside me, I said, "I only hope Lucy Weaver can come and help me when my time comes. She's had six. She should know what it's all about."

"Well, I don't want you to overdo. Take it easy around here. Save the heavy work for me."

"I'll be fine, Daniel. You know how tough I am. It would be a poor time for me to start getting lazy, wouldn't it?"

"Oh, Nellie," he said, grabbing my hands. "If your sons and daughters have only half your spirit, what champions they will be!"

CHAPTER 9

Summer came, stifling hot and humid on the prairie, where painted cup and wild geranium and scarlet runner were in bloom. In the bottomlands along the river valley and in his cleared field, where the timber joined the prairie, Daniel's ranks of growing cornstalks looked like slim, green soldiers.

He shook his head in wonder at the richness of the soil. "Back East I'd have to spend the first year just clearing out the rocks," he said. "We had so many rocks, we used them to build our fences. And then I'd have to layer the fields with manure. Just look at this. We already have a good crop coming up."

We have a baby coming, too, I thought, smiling to myself. In early January, as near as I could figure it.

Daniel seemed happy with our life here. Though I knew I could never be as beautiful and refined as Lenore, I felt he was content with me.

The summer days passed swiftly, filled with countless chores. We kept so busy, we learned to overlook the bothersome swarms of flies and mosquitoes. Our whole family thrived in this season of abundance, eating heartily on our garden produce, on the fish the boys caught, and game Daniel bagged. Cheeks rosy from the sun's kiss, the children gleaned buckets of wild strawberries from the prairie and blackberries from the woods.

We saw little of the Weavers and the other widely scattered settlers who had come to claim their land grant in the Military Tract. Our only social life was an occasional housewarming at some distant cabin Daniel had helped raise. Then we women would cluster together in a corner, words flowing from our mouths like water from a spring, as in one evening we made up for weeks of loneliness and isolation.

Indians still roamed freely through the unsettled country, and Daniel treated all he met with friendly courtesy as he tried to learn their language. Small bands of passing hunters often stopped by to trade him some fresh-killed game for a twist of tobacco or a handful of bullets or beads. Though they treated me with distance and reserve, they sometimes asked Daniel for some of my corn bread, a simple treat that always delighted them.

"Where do they live?" Eddie asked one day as he watched a trio of Indians ride away, their bare copper backs glistening in the dappled sunlight.

"The Potawatomis have several villages along Spoon River," Daniel said. "Remember that big one we passed when we first came here? It's down where the Spoon joins the Illinois River." He rubbed his beard thoughtfully. "Chief Raccoon has asked me to come and visit his village. Why don't we all go down there together?''

"Papa!'' Sarah shrieked in horror, drowning out Eddie's eager assent.

"They won't hurt you, honey.'' Daniel smiled and lightly tousled her silky curls. "They're our neighbors. We have to stay friendly with them. Why, they practically keep us in meat.''

"I'd be real pleased to visit their village and see how they live,'' I said. "Do you reckon they'd mind?''

"No, I think they'd like it.'' He walked over to the doorway and stood looking up and down our valley with a thoughtful expression. "You know, I'm seriously thinking about opening a trading post here. What would you think of that?''

I chuckled. "You talked earlier about a store, but looks like the Indians would be your only customers here. A trading post sounds like a fine idea.''

A few days later, the children scrambled aboard our wagon and sat on an old quilt in the back. Buoyant with anticipation, I climbed up on the seat beside Daniel. The Indians no longer frightened me. We were all neighbors here—in this area where any neighbors were as rare and precious as jewels.

Daniel flicked the reins lightly, and we started eastward, down the narrow, winding trail. The summer day flowed as lazily as the sun-dappled river between its shaded banks. Larks, robins, and bluebirds twittered from every branch, and graceful swallows skimmed insect morsels, the water's smooth surface mirroring the whole scene.

As we rode along, Eddie bubbled with eager questions. "What do the Indians eat, Papa? Why don't they wear anything but underwear in summer? Do the kids have any toys?''

"You'll see when we get there, son. Their life is very simple.'' Daniel glanced back at the children and smiled. "Now that I think of it, it's really not much different from the way we're living now.''

Sarah sat stiff and apprehensive, like someone going to the gallows. "I won't have to eat anything there, will I?'' she asked, wrinkling her nose.

"I'm going to learn to shoot a bow and arrow,'' Eddie said.

Hugh looked down his nose at his younger brother disdainfully. "A rifle's better any day. Isn't that right, Papa?''

Daniel rubbed his chin. "A rifle's better, shot for shot, but you know how long it takes to get one loaded. By the time you shake in the gunpowder and ram the bullet into place, an Indian could shoot off half a dozen arrows.''

"See?" Eddie raised his small rounded chin in triumph.

As we approached the Indian village, I saw their herd of ponies grazing in a flower-sprinkled meadow near a broad lake that extended to the high bluffs in the distance. A large, well-tended garden of corn, squash, beans, and pumpkins grew in the fertile bottomlands near the river.

A dozen lodges made of saplings lay in a ring, shaded by a grove of stately old cottonwood and maple trees. Daniel waved to the group of tall, solemn-looking men who stepped out to meet us when our wagon halted near the crackling campfire in the center of the village. My skin prickled with the sense of eyes staring at me, many curious eyes peering from the lodges and around trees and corners. With a smile and an Indian word of greeting, Daniel climbed down and handed the men a basket filled with squares of corn bread I had baked for them.

Eddie hopped off the back and stood beside his father, gazing at the Indians with fascination. The lithe, muscular men were clad only in breechclouts, with necklaces of bear claws and pierced shells at their throats. Elaborately beaded belts encircled their waists, each belt holding a carved-horn knife. The Indians' agile bodies gleamed like polished copper in the summer's heat.

With friendly gestures and mutterings, they welcomed us to their village. A tall, dignified man, his head adorned with three eagle feathers attached to a turban, stepped forward from the group, extending his hand.

"This is Chief Raccoon," Daniel told me, and stepped forward to meet the man. I smiled, nodding to the grave Indian chief.

While Daniel helped me step down from the wagon, Hugh scrambled over the side. Sarah, her face dubious and disapproving, did not budge from the quilt in the back.

"Come on and visit," Daniel told her. "You mustn't be rude."

"No, I don't want to." Her jaw clenched with a stubborn set.

Four women approached me, smiling nervously. High cheekbones, strong noses, and intelligent dark eyes gave their faces an elemental nobility. I returned their gestured greeting, taking in their loose cotton blouses, their skirts reaching halfway up their calves. They must have bargained with some trader for that bright cotton cloth. Their greased black hair hung plaited in a single long braid down their backs.

Pointing to the corn bread, they spoke to me. Their native words sounded strange and guttural, and, of course, I did not understand.

"Corn bread," I said. "I make it with cornmeal and eggs and grease." My words met only embarrassed shrugs.

One of them ran to the fire and brought back one of their Indian corn cakes, a hard, flat biscuit six inches in diameter, to show me. She laid it in my hand, then pointed to my corn bread. I nodded. "Yes, it's pretty much the same. I suppose the only difference is the eggs."

The women led me into camp, pointing out their supplies of food: baskets of corn, dried pumpkin and squash, dried venison, fat burr oak acorns, and wild berries. Lifting a handful of corn, I tried again to explain my corn bread recipe, but they only laughed at my words, as unintelligible to them as theirs were to me.

"Sarah, come down here," I called. "Let's watch them weave." The child reluctantly climbed down from the wagon and followed me over to where a group of women sat chatting beneath a shade tree, weaving baskets from strands of rushes.

I noticed lazy spirals of smoke rising from a spot down near the river. Daniel and the boys strolled in that direction with some men—to watch an Indian burning out a log to form a canoe.

With smiles and nods and gestures, I asked the women if we could see their homes, and they led us toward one of the large huts.

A young mother sat nursing a tiny baby at the doorway of the lodge. "Darling little lamb," I murmured, stopping to pat the infant's soft black hair. Its mother nodded to me with a knowing smile. A rush of tenderness surged through me as I thought of the infant growing in my womb.

We pushed aside the blanket hanging over the doorway, stepping into a lodge about half the size of our cabin. I gazed about me in the dim light, noting that the walls were made of saplings that were anchored in the ground and bent over at the top, then lashed together with strips of deerskin. Branches were woven through the sides, and everything was covered with heavy rush mats, with a hole left in the roof for escaping smoke. The interior held only sleeping benches built along both sides, all covered with trade blankets and buffalo hides. Weapons, strings of dried food, decorated deerskins, belts, and other odd pieces of clothing hung from the ceiling poles around the edges of the lodge.

"Where's their furniture?" Sarah whispered.

"Shh . . . Nice house! Real fine," I said, spreading my hands and gesturing with a wide smile. The women nodded and glanced about their lodge with pride and satisfaction.

They crowded close around Sarah and me, chuckling softly, staring unabashedly at our fair skins. We all left the lodge and walked over to a young girl working at a small loom; she was weaving a belt in a bright red-and-yellow geometric pattern.

One grandmotherly Indian reached out and stroked Sarah's shining blond curls with a quizzical smile. The child flinched and drew her head out of the woman's reach.

I met the grandmother's eyes and patted her hand in apology. "She means no harm," I murmured to Sarah. "You should be flattered. She thinks your hair is pretty."

The women led us to the central campfire, where an old woman stood stirring a simmering kettle with a long wooden paddle. She offered us wooden bowls of thick rabbit-and-vegetable stew.

"Look how everybody works together, Sarah," I said as I smiled my thanks to the cook. "The whole village is like one big family."

Hugh and Eddie joined a band of young Indian boys down by the river, trying to spear fish with long-handled, three-pronged spears, while Sarah watched a girl her age sew beads on a buckskin dress for a doll with a corncob body and a head of carved wood. Daniel strolled about the village with the men, asking the names of everything, trying to learn more of their language.

A young mother lifted her solemn, round-cheeked baby from his cradle board and handed him to me to hold. Tickling him under his chin, I finally induced a grudging smile and gurgle, though his black eyes stared warily at my unfamiliar white face.

As his mother chuckled, I felt a sisterhood with her—and wished I was smart enough, or had more opportunity, like Daniel, to learn their language, so we could really be friends.

When we later started for home, Eddie and Hugh sported small bows and a handful of arrows the Indian boys had given them. I carried a woven basket, a gift from the women, and Sarah an Indian doll with a painted pebble for a face, calico arms and legs, and a little decorated deerskin dress.

"I was so scared when you brought us here, Papa," Sarah said, her lower lip protruding. "I was sure they would scalp us."

"You're just a silly girl. The Indians won't hurt you," Eddie piped up, clutching his new bow against his chest. "They're my very best friends."

Clusters of brilliant reddish-orange flowers covered the trumpet vines that hugged the trees and undergrowth alongside the road. Leafy branches overlapped, forming a green canopy above our heads as our wagon rattled its way home. The river valley echoed with bird song, and from the distance came the tapping of a woodpecker's urgent quest.

Oblivious to the beauty around him, Daniel was strangely silent. He held the reins loosely in his hands and stared at the trail ahead. "We'd all do well to make friends with the Indians. There are a lot more of them than us."

"But more whites are coming now, aren't they, Papa?" Hugh asked.

"Yes, more and more veterans will be claiming their plots, just like we did. This big territory will likely fill up fast now."

"Oh, good! I'd like to have some little girls to play with," Sarah said.

Daniel paused, shaking his head. "You'll have them soon, I'd wager. But I don't think the Indians really understand about the surveys and the Military Tract. Poor devils. Their days here are numbered, I'm afraid. The agreement was that they can only stay until the bounty lands are claimed and settled."

I glanced at Daniel's worried face. "I guess they'll have to move to the other side of the Mississippi, won't they?"

Sadness clouded his eyes. "We called this place paradise when we first came. It's paradise for them, too. Great hunting and fishing, great land for raising corn."

"But what can we do? They sold their land."

He leaned forward, his face drawn and morose.

I longed to lift the darkness of his mood. "Well, I suppose most of the whites will feel safer when they're gone," I said, looking back toward the Indian village. "They couldn't have been friendlier to us today, but everybody always says they're savages and heathens. I still remember hearing how the Indians burned down settlers' cabins and kidnapped women and children. Not so many years ago, either.''

His voice was deep and somber. ''They hate to lose their land as much as we would. Treaty or not.''

With a long sigh, I pondered the certainty of change. As more white settlers came, the Indians would be pushed across the Mississippi River, then farther and farther west. Twinges of pain and guilt shot through me as I contemplated the dilemma.

''I'm going to be an Indian when I grow up,'' Eddie announced with boyish enthusiasm, brandishing his bow.

His bravado made us all laugh. Spirits revived, we continued along the tree-shaded path beside the meandering river.

As summer progressed, the whole earth seemed to share my pregnancy. Beneath the brassy glare of sunlight, the cornstalks tasseled and the ears formed, hidden within their green silk husks. In our garden, the beans and cabbages and pumpkins swelled and flourished.

Daniel rigged a heavy block of wood above a hollowed stump so the children could pull the rope to drop the block, which would grind corn into meal. This was a tedious and never-ending job. I yearned for the luxury of a convenient gristmill.

''We have a spot right here that would make a fine mill site,'' Daniel told me. ''If I can find someone who knows how, I think I'll build one. A mill would be a prosperous business here. This country's bound to fill up fast—once a few of us brave the way.''

A scattering of white people had begun to pass our way, settlers seeking out their grants for military service and others who had bought a piece of land. We welcomed them with open arms. ''Stay for supper. Spend the night with us,'' we said, for we were eager for the company and conversation.

Many of the newcomers were frightened and discouraged. ''We had no idea there were so many Indians still living in this area,'' they said, frowning darkly.

Some added, ''We might just be smart to go back home and wait until this place is a little more civilized.''

''These Indians are friendly,'' Daniel told them, but his words met only blank stares. Old fears died hard.

* * *

94

One afternoon while Daniel and Hugh hoed corn and I scrubbed the family's dirty clothes with lye soap, Eddie carried his new bow and arrow up to practice on the wooded hillside by the prairie. An hour passed, and he still had not returned, so I sent Sarah up to look for him.

"Come quick!" she called, dashing back down the slope, her skirt flying in the breeze. "He's not there!"

"Not there? He has to be there!"

I flew up the hill, through the maze of trees, until I reached the prairie. Overhead, cardinals, green parakeets, and blue jays sat like blossoms on tree branches heavy with leaves. Beyond the boundary of the timber, honeybees buzzed hungrily among the tall, flowering coneflowers and goldenrod and ox eye. The vast expanse of prairie grasses stood before me, their feathered heads swaying gently with the summer breeze.

But no little boy was anywhere in sight.

The grass was high. Much higher than a four-year-old child's head. I recalled the time last spring when I had thought Eddie looked like a small canoe out on an ocean of prairie. Now it was a hundred times worse.

He could be lost out there in the tall grass, confused, not knowing which way to turn, heading farther and farther away from home. Horrifying visions danced before my eyes—little Eddie, sobbing, walking on and on toward that far horizon.

"Eddie! Eddie, can you hear me?" I called frantically. My hands trembled. Beads of sweat ran down my back.

Silence was my only answer.

I started walking through grass as tall as my head, crying out his name. The prairie seemed like an impenetrable forest. Hearing my cries, Daniel ran over from the corn plot.

Sarah rushed to him, her arms outstretched. "Papa! Eddie's lost!"

His face froze. I turned and stared into his stricken eyes. The grass surrounded me, swaying with a rhythm like the pulse beat of the earth. "Don't go out there alone!" he shouted. "Wait! I'll get the horse and hunt for him."

My chest cramped with fear. "I'm going with you."

He ran down to the pasture where the horses grazed, while I called and called for Eddie, each time with more desperation. Hugh and Sarah joined in shouting the alarm, but no small boy's voice was heard in answer.

Daniel galloped up, bareback, leading the other horse. I quickly hiked up my skirt and mounted. "Hugh and Sarah, run down to the house and find Shad. He can help," Daniel said.

We rode along the edge of the prairie grass, searching for some sign of where Eddie might have entered.

I sighted a slender trail of freshly crushed grass. "Here!" I called, my breath caught in my throat. I urged my horse forward. A thousand hideous images whirled through my head. Had the Indians kidnapped him? It had happened countless times in other places. I thought of rattlesnakes and their vile poison, of vicious wolves and panthers, even bears roaming through this untamed prairie.

A long, black snake slithered across my path. My heart pounded, almost choking me. I nudged my horse into a gallop. Daniel pulled up beside me, and we rode deeper and deeper into the dense growth of grass and wildflowers. My eyes burned from the strain of searching desperately for our little child in this boundless prairie sea. From the distance, I could hear the approach of Shad's frenzied barking.

Something moved in the tall grass ahead. Just a flash of blue and white among the towering slender stems. A small boy in a striped shirt sat up. He yawned and stretched, an Indian bow still clenched in his dirt-smudged hand.

Relief washed down on me like warm spring rain. I leapt from the horse and clutched Eddie to my breast, my heart thudding a deafening roar. "Eddie! Oh, child! What are you doing way out here?"

Daniel knelt at my side. "What happened, son?" he asked, cradling the boy's head. At that moment, Shad tore through the grass, barking joyfully. He reached Eddie and eagerly began to lick his face.

Eddie blinked his eyes and stared at us, pale and confused. Dirt stains around his eyes and cheeks traced the trails of past tears. "I got lost," he said, and sniffled back a sob. "I was going to shoot a rabbit with my bow and arrow, but I got lost."

"Didn't you hear us calling you?" I asked, smoothing back his rumpled hair.

He shook his head. "I tried to find my way out. But I got so tired, I just laid down and took a nap."

I hugged him tighter to me. "Oh, Eddie, Eddie. Don't you ever go out on the prairie alone."

"I won't. Not ever," he said, and burst into a fresh torrent of tears.

Daniel hoisted him up on the horse, climbed on behind him, and turned back toward home. "I guess that's one lesson this boy's learned the hard way."

As I rode beside them, my eyes never left Eddie's tear-stained face. My heart overflowed with affection and relief. I could not love this dear child more if he had been my own. I loved the others, too. Hugh, born a somber, old man. Sarah, poor, unhappy girl. I longed to reach her, to make her smile.

"I'm sorry," Daniel murmured, glancing my way with an embarrassed grin. "My kids sure cause you a lot of toil and trouble."

"Don't you say that!"

"What?" He looked startled by my flash of temper.

"These are my kids, too."

He hesitated for just a moment. His face softened; his voice was low. "Yes, Nellie. Yes, I guess they are."

When I finally had Eddie washed and comforted, I took him outside with me while I emptied the laundry tub. "You stay right here beside me, child," I said. "I don't want you out of my sight."

My back ached, my head throbbed, and my swelling stomach rubbed irritatingly against the fabric of my old homespun dress.

I nestled my hands against the hollow of my aching back and swept my eyes over the spreading expanse of our fertile green valley. Everything within my sight pleased me. The humble log cabin, set in a spreading grove of oak and maple trees beside the clear, rippling waters of Spoon River. The garden and the cornfields. The chickens and the cattle. The three children and the baby on the way. Daniel Cranford, that grave and remote Yankee who had given me his name.

This was my life now. This was my family. Johnny Nichols, Uncle Amos, my father, and my little sisters in Kentucky—were merely fading memories.

One windy, overcast afternoon, while Daniel was out on the prairie checking on his small herd of grazing cattle, I went out to pick beans in the garden. All the plants and tree branches stirred nervously. The air smelled of approaching rain.

From the distance, I heard the faint clip-clop of horse's hoofs coming down the trail. I glanced up from my row of beans and saw a single rider, his face shadowed by a wide-brimmed hat, heading my way on a handsome sorrel stallion.

Oh, good, I thought, excited, for we had few visitors. Maybe he'll stop and eat supper with us, join us for a long conversation afterward. He can give us fresh news from the outside.

The man raised his hand in greeting. My heart stood still. Johnny. Johnny Nichols.

My body stiffened. The world began to spin. Johnny's deep blue eyes gazed down at me expectantly as he rode closer. He looked as handsome and vital as ever. His black curls lay pressed against his forehead beneath his felt hat. A fine film of road dust covered his dark brown trousers and leather vest, his short, black boots.

I stood breathless. Though my emotions soared and my heart tripped in lightning-fast beats, I could not move or speak.

He climbed down from his horse and met my astonished stare, his face and body taut as a bowstring. The faint line of the old scar on his forehead paled against his sun-bronzed skin and flushed cheeks.

We both spoke at once:

"How did you find me?"

"Why didn't you wait for me?

"Why didn't you wait?" he repeated, with a quizzical frown. "I sent you a note that I'd be coming back for you."

"What note? I didn't see a note." Was this really happening? Was this really Johnny? My beloved Johnny—here—close enough to touch? "Oh, Johnny! Did Uncle Amos hurt you real bad?"

"Bad enough. I went away to stay with relatives until I healed."

"You went away? But I thought you were over there in your house all that time! I thought you just didn't want to see me."

"I sent a note by Blanche. She said she'd put it under our special rock, where you would find it. I wrote you I was going away to find a place where we could live together in peace." His voice quavered with emotion.

"Blanche." Dizzy now, I sank down on a nearby stump and pressed my fingers to my temples. "Blanche said you hated me. She said you never wanted to see me again."

"She said *what*?" He reached for my hand. "Oh, Nellie, you knew better than that. I said I wanted to marry you."

Sarah opened the cabin door and stepped out on the stoop, glaring at us from the distance. The wind tugged at her skirt. It gusted through the leaves with a rustling sound.

I felt ill. I pushed away his hand and hung my head. Anger flared in my heart. "If you wanted me, you should have taken me with you. You left me there with my uncle. You knew how crazy he was."

"I only left so I could carve out a new life for us," he said, his voice rich as velvet. "I have a place down near St. Louis now—with the beginnings of my own herd of prize horses. It's down there waiting for you, Nellie. I did it all for you."

His eyes bore into me, those deep sapphire eyes that had haunted my dreams for an eternity. I gazed at him greedily, drinking in his youth and masculine beauty as a thirsty man drinks water. All my old love for him came flooding back in a tremendous surge. I wanted him with a yearning that shook me to my core.

"I want you to come with me," he said.

Overhead, the flat, gray clouds were gathering. We would see rain before supper. My stomach lurched with nausea. "I'm married, Johnny. I was sure you didn't want me anymore."

"I couldn't believe my ears when I came back and heard you'd gone off with some widower to watch after his kids. It wasn't easy for me to find this place, either. But I'm sure that can't be a binding marriage, not under those circumstances."

Confused, I stared at him, chewing on my lip.

Eddie joined Sarah by the cabin door. The two children, unable to hear our intense murmurs, stood watching us with unconcealed curiosity.

The wind stirred the surface of the river. Johnny gripped my arms and held me tautly. "I left my home and family for you, Nellie. Your uncle almost killed me over you."

"I can't just leave these little kids. They need me." I gestured feebly toward the cabin.

"Somebody else's kids. Nellie, you're my girl. You'll always be my girl."

The pull between us was as forceful and undeniable as the current of the river. I loved him. And yet, in a different way, I loved Daniel, too. "But—but I'm married now," I repeated.

"You made a mistake, Nellie." His voice was deep and sensual, his words warm and soothing. "I've made a few myself. For one, I never should have trusted Blanche with that note. Just climb up here and come along with me. You don't even have to look back."

Thunder rumbled in the distance. The wind whipped my hair across my face. I pulled it back with a sharp, rueful laugh. "And not even tell my husband?"

"I'm the only husband you should have. You made a mistake, that's all. I understand. You just married him to get away from Amos Barton. I'll find a lawyer and get a legal separation for you."

Huge dark clouds piled up like wads of dirty cotton. The wind lashed at the trees and grass. Lightning flickered in the sky; the thunder grumbled. My pulse drummed in my ears, a steady, rhythmic roar. I longed to go with him—more than I had ever wanted anything in my whole life.

Sucking in a deep breath, I placed my trembling hands on my gently swelling stomach. "I can't go with you, Johnny. I'm going to have a baby."

His mouth fell open. He stared at me, bewildered, as if he did not believe this possible.

An arc of lightning rent the sky. The whole earth trembled with the responding roll of thunder.

"Then—then I'll take your child as well," he said, breathing out a long sigh. "All this is my fault, too. Just come away with me, Nellie. Now."

My body and my spirit felt as heavy as lead. My gaze clung to the wind-stirred grass in front of his boots. I wished the earth would open and devour me. "I can't go anywhere. This is my home now. I can't leave those little ones out here alone. They've already lost one mother."

"But . . ." He reached out and seized my hand.

"I can't leave, Johnny. Try to understand."

The gale whipped into a fury, tearing at our clothes. Dark clouds scuttled across the sky. He tightened his grip. "You're my girl. Mine."

Pain and torment cut through me like panther claws. I wrenched away from him. "Go, Johnny. Just go. Now." I shook my head, unable to utter another word.

His face reddened as he stared at me. I could feel the heat of his building anger, like the building storm that threatened us. "Damn you. Damn you for betraying me like this."

With a noisy, ragged inhalation, he spun and leapt upon his horse. Without a backward glance, he jerked the reins, and the horse galloped away.

Hazy and numb, I watched him disappear around the bend of the river.

Sarah stood in the doorway, her skirt flapping in the wind. Eddie ran out to me, calling, "Who was that man?"

Words stuck in the lump that clogged my throat. Finally I rasped, "An old neighbor."

The first huge drops of rain splattered in the dust and on my flushed cheeks. Leaves shuddered under their weight. I stumbled toward the cabin as if in a trance, my thoughts spinning. I could not focus on what had happened. Could it be true? I had just given up the one thing I had been dreaming of ever since that fateful day. . . .

Johnny was out there in the storm, this blinding downpour that now hammered on our roof. I felt driven to run after him, shrieking I had changed my mind. But my feet refused to budge.

Daniel dashed inside, slamming the door behind him, flicking water off his drenched shirt. Sarah ran over to him. "Some man was here and talked with *her*," she said, pointing a disdainful finger in my direction.

He looked at me, alarmed. "He left already? In this storm? My God, why didn't you ask him to stay?"

I hesitated, swallowing the painful lump in my throat. "He was just passing through."

"She must have known him pretty well," Sarah said, pursing her lips as she glanced at me from the corner of her eye. "He held her hand."

Daniel's brows raised. "Oh? A friend? Someone you knew?"

I pressed my hand against my heart, trying to contain the cauldron of agony and turmoil. "An old neighbor," I murmured in a tight voice, staring at the floorboards. "Johnny Nichols."

"Oh." His intense gaze bore into me. "I see."

I slowly raised my head—and found his eyes brimming with some peculiar expression I could not fathom. Jealousy? Gratitude? Was it possible this man had actually come to care for me?

101

We stood silent, our eyes locked in a strange suspension of time. He came to me and spoke in a low murmur. "Is there something I should know?"

"He wanted me to come with him," I said, choking on the words.

He exhaled sharply. "It was all a mistake, wasn't it? Us marrying so hasty and moving way up here. I was afraid of this."

"I told him"—I looked Daniel straight in the eye, my voice firm and steady—"I told him I wanted to stay."

Daniel took my hand and squeezed it, almost to the point of pain. The deep furrows slowly faded from his brow. He cleared his throat and asked, "What's for supper?"

The wind had dropped. The rain had diminished to a pleasant patter on the roof.

I sucked in a deep breath and tried to smile. "Hugh caught us a mess of perch. I'll fry them while you're changing those wet clothes."

This was my life. I had taken this fork in the road. It was too late now to think of turning back.

CHAPTER 10

Now I knew for certain Johnny was gone from me forever. I knew I must forget that I had ever known him. I took the brooch he had given me and buried it deep in the soft earth near the spring. That chapter of my life was closed.

Time went on, and the constant round of work left me no time for brooding. I dipped tallow candles and made soap from grease and the lye I leached from the fireplace ashes. My garden yielded in abundance, a fitting reward for months of labor. My baby chicks matured into a splendid flock. I viewed them all, and our home as well, with growing attachment and pride.

Our hogs fattened on the mast they rooted from the woods; our cattle flourished on the copious prairie grass. Daniel smoked out a bee tree, and we laid in gallons of honey. He cut the high grass with a scythe, piling it on a sled to haul back for winter hay.

While hunting in the woods, he and the boys often met small groups of Indians; they spoke with them in the few words they knew of the Indian language.

Intoxicated by the beauty and abundance of this land, I scoured the woods with the children, picking countless bucketfuls of wild plums and crab apples, grapes and persimmons. Walnuts, pecans, chestnuts, hickory and hazelnuts ripened and fell in showers from the trees. And out in the fields, the golden sunshine dried the cornstalks with their burden of plump ears as summer cooled and yellowed into fall.

Throughout the woods, touches of orange and gold and russet appeared among the wash of green. The prairie in the distance looked like a tranquil golden sea. And through it all, my pregnancy advanced.

As we sat before the fire one cool evening in mid-October, Daniel turned to me with a somber frown. "I need to take the wagon down to Springfield and lay in a load of supplies before cold weather hits," he said.

I glanced up from my knitting. "We *are* running low on coffee and sugar."

"The trip will probably take a week. Do you mind if I leave you and the kids to watch over things? I hate to leave you all here alone, but somebody has to keep an eye on the livestock. Nothing heavy, of course. I don't want you to overdo, especially not now."

Alone. I would be left alone here for a week. Chill specters of Indians and wild animals immediately rose in my mind.

"I can handle the chores all right," I said, gulping back my fears. "Just be sure to leave me the extra rifle and some powder—in case I might happen to need them."

"Oh, I'll do that. I'll leave it loaded for you. I doubt that you'll need it, but I'm sure you will feel better having it ready here."

"Could you bring back some linsey-woolsey, so I can make

103

the kids some winter clothes?" I flicked my hand to the two boys in patched trousers, playing like kittens on the floor.

He nodded. "Looks like they need it. I'll find some nice lengths of cloth for you, too. You could use some new dresses."

My glance dropped to the faded green gingham I had made into a loose skirt to cover my swollen abdomen. "Reckon so."

"We've been living off the land for a long time now. You know, we've been so busy—and had so few visitors—I'd almost overlooked how badly we all need new clothes. I'm going to buy some panes of glass for these windows, too."

"Now, wouldn't that be nice."

He smiled. "I'd say we've waited long enough. Well, all the deerskins and furs I've been saving will make valuable trading stock. I have money set back, too. There's no need for us to do without. And I want to lay in extra supplies for trading with the Indians, too."

"Sounds like a fine idea. What will you bring for them?"

"Traps and bullets, blankets and cooking pots. They'll be leaving soon for their winter hunting grounds, and the chief told me they have to go clear to Peoria to trade for supplies."

"I'll help make a list of all the things we need around the house."

"While I'm there, I'll have several bags of corn ground at the mill. At least I can save you that much work."

As I thought of being left alone here in this isolated cabin—with only the little ones for company—a shiver of apprehension snaked down my spine. But surely I could handle anything that came along. It looked like I'd have to.

"I sure will appreciate having that corn ground," I said. "It's just too bad there's not a mill somewhere around here."

Daniel gazed intently at the orange flames flickering and crackling in the black mouth of the fireplace. "I've been thinking about that ever since we've been here. We have a perfect mill site right here. I'd just need to dam the river and run the water through a sluice." He tented his fingers and studied them thoughtfully.

"That's right, Daniel." I leaned forward, smiling my encouragement. "We know more new people will be moving to this territory. A mill is something everybody needs."

"Well, I'm no miller, but if we had a mill beside the river, I could sell lots and build up a whole town right here. Lord knows I've plenty of room. And who ever saw a prettier site?''

Hugh, eyes gleaming and attentive, halted his play and looked up at his father. ''Cranford Town, Papa?''

''Eden Valley,'' Daniel replied, smiling at the boy. ''That's what I called it from the first.''

I walked over to open the door and stood silently surveying the broad sweep of river and trees, of rolling hills and fertile bottomland, all gilded now by the setting sun. The thought of houses nearby, of neighbors close enough for company, filled me with a tremulous excitement. This past year, loneliness and isolation had almost become a habit.

The Weavers were our nearest white neighbors, and they lived ten miles away. Daniel had said he would go for Mrs. Weaver when my baby came, but would there be time? She told me she'd helped with lots of birthings in the past. First babies are generally slow in coming, she said. I only hoped . . .

Pushing aside my anxiety, I turned back to Daniel. ''That's all it would take, isn't it? Just a mill, and then a whole town would grow up around it.'' My voice rang with enthusiasm. ''Well, the sooner you build that mill, the better, I'd say.''

''I always planned to go into some kind of business, sooner or later. I figure we could also open a general store as soon as more people settle around here. What do you think of that idea?''

We? Did he actually look on me as a real partner now? ''Yes. Yes, that sounds like a dandy idea.''

''A mill would be the first step. That, and an Indian trading post.'' He pondered, staring at his steepled fingers. ''A mill's an intricate thing, though. I'd have to bring in someone who knows how to build one. Maybe I could locate a millwright or a sharp miller down in Springfield. I suppose we could work out some kind of partnership.'' He nodded slowly, looking satisfied.

''Will you be leaving right away, then?'' I asked, my throat suddenly feeling tight.

''Not until I've laid in a supply of venison and made sure you know how to use that rifle.'' He paused, searching my face. ''I hate to leave you here alone. I just wish there was some other way.''

''Shoot, I'm not scared,'' I said, brushing him aside. ''I've got the dog and these two brave boys here to protect me. We'll be fine.''

Sure, we would. Of course. If I repeated it enough, I might convince myself.

A few days later, he drove away under autumn-painted trees, his big farm wagon groaning with its load of bagged corn and bundled furs and deerhides. We had lived almost entirely off our own land and labor for the past year. Still, some items had to be purchased: coffee, gunpowder and lead for bullets, patent medicines, needles and sewing thread, tow linen and jeans material, a bolt of cotton flannel for baby things and underwear, wool yarn and cloth for me to knit and sew for heavy winter clothes.

The deerhides, and the beaver, raccoon, mink, and otter furs piled in his wagon would bring a good price. He felt certain they would cover most of his expenses.

As twilight settled over the valley that evening and the little cabin darkened, my nerves grew taut. Wolves and panthers, rattlesnakes and wild boars roamed freely in the woods throughout the unsettled countryside. The night was filled with a dozen chilling threats. Whole villages of Indians lay scattered up and down the winding river valley, and daily they were forced to watch the white man claim more and more of their ancestral hunting grounds.

And now we were alone here. Utterly alone. Three small children and a woman six months pregnant.

It occurred to me that Daniel, who had seemed so staid and proper when I first met him at the inn in southern Illinois—where things were halfway civilized—was actually some kind of mad adventurer. All kinds of dreams and ambitions lay hidden behind his calm and steady gray eyes.

Of course, I harbored a few dreams of my own, modest as they were. A clean and cozy home, a thriving family. I loved this land as much as he did, its glorious beauty and fertility, its prolific bounty of food and flower. This was my home now. This was my family. All thoughts of Johnny had retreated to the farthest recesses of my mind.

I gloried in my strength. The many hardships of my life had toughened me like one of these gnarled old oak trees. I would not give way to fear. I could hold my own against any wild animal or Indian.

The only Indians who came while Daniel was gone were a trio of women, wrapped in bright green blankets against the sudden chill. The children and I were picking pumpkins in the garden when the Indian women sauntered into our yard. I was startled, for they had never visited us before. Did they mean us harm?

But they approached us with a comradely wave of hand, and my wariness dissolved. My gaze lingered on their sharp, clean-lined profiles and smooth copper skin. Their shiny black hair hung plaited in long braids, held in place with bands of woven beads. Beneath their two-piece, fringed and beaded buckskin dresses, their knee-length leggings, and blanket cloaks, their bodies moved with strong and agile motion. One, like me, was swollen with pregnancy.

An older woman with strong, handsome features showed me a broken steel needle, then spoke in a jumble of words I could not comprehend. In her other hand, she held out a pair of deer-hide moccasins sewn with a single seam down the instep and decorated in a colorful beaded pattern.

"They want to trade you for a new needle," Hugh interpreted for me, for he knew some Indian language from traveling among them with Daniel.

I smiled at the women, recalling the Indians' courtesy when I had visited one of their villages. Though these faces were not familiar to me, I nodded, pointing to the house. "Come inside. I'll get a needle for you."

As we all crossed the yard and entered the cabin, the children's eyes glimmered with excitement and curiosity.

Rifling among the jumble of thread and thimbles and patches in my sewing basket, I finally found my last package of needles. "There you are," I said, pulling out one of the remaining few. "Stay and have a cup of wild mint tea with me. I just made some crullers."

The crullers were a special treat for the children, sprinkled with the last of our white sugar until Daniel returned with a fresh supply. When I passed a plate of them to the women, they frowned and pointed to the small sugar-coated globes, speaking excitedly.

"Salt. They think it's salt. They've never seen white sugar," Hugh said.

"Oh, my." With a chuckle, I popped a cruller into my mouth and smacked my lips to demonstrate its savor.

The pregnant woman, her eyes still narrowed with suspicion, gingerly reached out and plucked a cruller from the plate. She licked a tiny sample of the sugar, and her brows raised in surprise. Another lick—and then she downed the cruller in one bite! The others looked at each other, mumbling their confusion.

Within a minute, all three were laughing and reaching for crullers; the plate was soon empty. I refilled it, and with ravenous appetites, they emptied it again.

"You kids better take some of these right now," I said, unnerved as I filled the plate a third time. "Looks like this batch won't last long."

When the last grain of sugar had been captured from the plate and licked off a wet finger, I showed the Indian women around our cabin, as they had shown me their lodges. "This mahogany mantel clock came all the way from New York State," I said, pointing to our most treasured possession.

"Um . . . Ooh . . ." The three stood watching it for several minutes, fascinated by the ticking and the swinging pendulum.

Turning back to me, they stood for a moment, staring at my face, murmuring among themselves. The older woman directed a few words to me. "They want to know if you're our mother or our sister," Hugh said, with a nervous laugh.

"Tell them I'm just the second wife." How I tired of repeating those unnerving words.

Hugh had made his explanation in their language, and the Indian women nodded, their gaze resting on me with understanding and respect.

Finally they turned to leave, gesturing their gratitude for the needle. "Come back! Come back soon!" I called after them as they strolled gracefully away on silent moccasined feet.

The nearest Indian village lay over six miles from our cabin. Though a long, tiring hike lay ahead of the women, I suspected the items of gossip they carried about the white family's curious home and furnishings and food would more than compensate for all their efforts.

I envied them their close camaraderie. Compared to theirs, my life seemed steeped in utter loneliness and isolation.

That evening, an Indian hunter stopped by our cabin and presented us with a pair of freshly shot rabbits, all cleaned and ready for the pot. Perhaps my isolation was not so complete as I had feared!

All the next day, a chill west wind gusted across the prairie, playing on my nerves until I jumped at the slightest noise. My body ached with the extra bulk and weight of pregnancy. I slept fitfully that night, stirring at every owl's hoot, at the honk of wild geese winging southward through the night. Toward dawn, I awoke to the sound of Shad's barking, an insistent, warning bark.

Through the filmy translucence of the greased-paper window, an unnatural brightness glowed on the hill to the southwest. Surely it was too early for daylight. Rubbing my tired eyes, I rose from bed and crossed the room in the semidarkness to ease open the back door.

Along the crest of the hill, the entire sky was as brilliant as midday, the trees starkly silhouetted. A low, roaring noise like thunder rumbled in the distance. I smelled smoke.

"Prairie fire! Get up! Right now!" I screamed to the children in the loft, then ran to grab the blanket off my bed. They crawled to the opening, rubbing their eyes, sleepy and confused. "Come on! There's a prairie fire! Take your blankets and run to the river. You should be safe there."

"What about the house and all our things?" Hugh asked, scrambling down the ladder.

"The only thing that matters is that you're all safe. Sarah, quick! Help Eddie find his clothes while I check the livestock."

All was pandemonium. We threw on our clothes and flew out of the house. The hogs and cattle came bolting down the slope toward the river, with Shad yipping at their tails. Chickens squawked frantically inside their pen until I loosened the gate and set them free.

The fire raged in the distance across the prairie, coming ever closer. Its blaze flickered hotly as it rose and fell and rose again. Crackling flames shot up twenty feet into the night sky. They darted up in spires and exploded into sprays. The sound, the sight, the smell was monstrous, overpowering.

What could I do? Oh, God, I had to save the house. All our things, a whole year of hard work . . .

I snatched up a bucket and handed it to Hugh. I grabbed another and dashed toward the river. "Let's throw water on the roof! We'll try to save the cabin!" I yelled over my shoulder. "Come on! I'll need your help!"

Please, God. Please, God. Oh, give me strength.

The fire was moving closer with every passing second. Dipping up a sloshing bucketful of water, I sprinted back and tossed it on the cabin wall. "Hugh, climb up the ladder and throw water on the roof!"

He rushed to the barn for the ladder. Sarah and Eddie grabbed pots and pans from the hearth and ran to scoop up water from the river. All of us were scurrying like fear-crazed ants. No time for words. No time to think. Just this intense obsession with survival. Bucket after bucketful of water slashed through the air, tossed frantically on cabin roof and walls.

My head spun from the effort, from the suffocating smell of smoke. I coughed and choked as the harsh fumes seared my lungs and sent rivers of tears running from my eyes.

The fire surged closer, an enormous body of flames, leaping and plunging like ocean waves against a rocky coast. I glanced quickly at the children, praying for their safety. Macabre orange light danced across their faces, reflecting the flicker of the blaze.

I soaked blankets and towels in the river and dragged them dripping to the house. I sloshed water all around the cabin's foundation and handed bucket after bucket up for Hugh to throw on the roof.

My breath came in sharp, gasping pants. My heart thundered like the hoofbeats of a charging army. My swollen stomach seemed a clumsy burden, always in the way as I dashed about my frenzied tasks. Oh, God. I must save the house and children. That was all that mattered now.

A haystack on the hilltop exploded into flames. The fire slowed and hesitated for a moment as it reached the plowed soil of our fields and chewed its way around the grassy borders. It approached the timber, and tall columns of flames licked at the trees, spreading quickly through the drying leaves.

Closer. Every second closer.

If only the wind would shift. These fall winds were so fickle. I prayed desperately that the wind would shift away from us.

My face felt blistered from the stifling, choking heat and smoke. My lungs gasped for air. I rushed madly back and forth from the river, pouring more and more water on the soil around our home. The blaze approached. Oh, no! The flames were sweeping through the leaves overhead. The grass alongside my garden was all ablaze.

"Run!" I shrieked to the children scurrying around me. "Run to the river! Into the water! You'll be safe there!"

Eddie and Sarah hesitated, panting and confused. I grabbed their hands and raced them down to the water's edge. Then I dashed back up, dragging wet blankets to beat out the tongues of fire that ate their way toward our cabin.

I was certain all was lost. Our cabin and barn and every bit of our belongings were doomed. But I fought on. With Hugh at my side, we beat those cursed flames. The boy worked fearlessly, his slender body exerting tremendous energy throughout this crucial battle.

Suddenly the fickle wind shifted its direction, blowing now from the northwest. Its force diminished. The flames sank to a low blaze and crept along the sloping riverbank, away from our house. Now the serpentine path of the river marked the border of its devastation.

My heart thundered wildly as I watched the fire and heat gradually fade away into the distance. Was it really gone? Could it be true?

I glanced down and noticed my old blue dress was torn. My hands and arms were black with dirt and smudge. My face felt blistered from the heat. My eyes burned, my throat felt tight. Each gasp of breath was torture. But the fire—the fire had given up the battle and retreated in defeat.

Eyes filled with horror, Sarah and Eddie staggered up from the river. Their clothes were soaked and filthy. Still we stood our vigil, beating out stray licks of flame with wet towels and blankets, stomping on smoldering sticks, throwing still more water on the burning logs.

Sunrise flooded the horizon with a brilliant orange glow by the time we finally slowed our hectic pace. All the earth was stark black as far as I could see. Here and there, white plumes of smoke curled upward in lazy spirals. Prairie and timberland lay charred and desolate. An eery silence and the pungent, acrid smell of fire hung over all the land.

Exhaustion hit me like a blow. I panted for breath and shuddered with the pain of aching back and arms and legs. My knees had turned to water. I knew I must lie down.

"Can you watch over things out here?" I asked Hugh. "Call

111

me if anything starts burning again." As I started for the house, each step seemed an unbearable exertion. The heavy smell of smoke made my stomach queasy.

"I guess it's over now," he said, his voice faint and hoarse. Eddie and Sarah stared at me with wide, fear-struck eyes.

I had to lie down. Now. I could not think beyond this urgent need.

Staggering into the house, I dropped down on the bed. A deep sigh of relief breezed softly from my lips. My stinging, leaden eyes fell shut. I was so tired. So very tired.

A sudden cramp seized my midsection. I winced, biting my lip against the stab of pain.

I did not want to think. I wanted only to relax and let this blissful tide of relief wash over me. We were saved from almost certain destruction. All of us were safe. No need to struggle anymore. Everything was fine.

Oh, God! Another cramp came, fiercer than the first. I froze with shock. This one I could not ignore.

My throat knotted as an appalling thought hammered for recognition in my brain. The baby. All that frantic work and agitation had brought on my labor. It was too soon. Three months early. Oh, God! What could I do?

I heard the door creak open. Sarah's small blond head peeked in. Dirt smudges streaked her cheeks. Her eyes looked softer and more friendly than I had ever seen them. "Are you sick?"

"I have to rest awhile," I said, trying to hide the quaver in my voice. "Please stay outside. Watch after Eddie."

Frowning, still pale with fright, she opened her mouth to protest, but no words came. She stared at me for one long moment, then softly closed the door.

My heart pounded in expectation. What was happening to me? I felt caught up in the clutches of some tremendous force of nature. I writhed with the accelerating waves of viselike cramps, biting my lips to keep from crying out. What could I do? The children needed me. I must get up and fix them breakfast. I must try to calm their spirits.

But there were more agonizing cramps, coming fast and violent. I was helpless. I could do nothing but submit to their consuming power. Rivers of sweat poured down my face and chest, despite the chill in the early morning air. I gripped the

112

bedpost and pulled with all my might, trying not to cry out so I wouldn't terrify the children.

My baby was coming with an urgent force and speed as I lay there alone in that cold cabin. I could only obey my body's ancient ritual commands, like all the animals of field and forest. I had seen dogs and cows and horses lick their newborns clean. Would my instincts be wise enough to tell me what to do?

My baby came in a flood of blood and water. A boy, as tiny as a puppy. Too tiny to survive. He squirmed weakly a few times . . . and then was still.

My head spun with shock and exhaustion. My heart lay like a boulder in my chest. With infinite tenderness, I lifted my baby boy and wrapped his tiny body in a corner of my sheet. Tears rolled down my cheeks. Until this very moment, I had not realized how much I wanted him. A little boy. My firstborn son.

I gazed down at his miniature face, his doll-like hands. So vulnerable. So precious. A crushing pain welled up inside my chest; sobs began to pour from me.

Again Sarah opened the door. A look of stark horror crossed her face. She gasped and rushed over to the bed. "What is it? A baby! Oh, Nellie! Are you going to die?"

She burst into tears and threw her head upon my shoulder. Sniffing, I wiped my eyes and patted her slender, heaving back. "No, no, honey. I'm not going to die. The baby came too soon, but I'll be all right after a while." I lifted her chin and looked into her reddened eyes. "I need your help, Sarah. Can you get me a towel and basin of water, and a clean sheet? After that, we'll need to find the boys something for breakfast."

"I'll try," she said, her lips quivering. She glanced down at the baby's tiny, motionless form and burst into fresh tears. Wrapping her arms around my neck, she sobbed, "Oh, Mother, I'm so sorry."

I held her close and stroked her hair, trying to hide my own hurt. "Now, now. Don't cry. Maybe it was meant to be."

The depth of my pain was staggering. My baby, my firstborn was already come and gone. And all before Daniel could even see him. Yet as I felt the brush of Sarah's childish kiss against my cheek, a vague comfort washed over me. Sarah had called me Mother.

The fire, and the birth and loss of the baby, had left us all in a state of shock. Numbly we struggled through the rest of the

113

day. I was too weak to rise from bed, but somehow the boys and Sarah found food enough to eat.

Our Indian hunter friend returned that afternoon. After assuring himself that the fire had not harmed us, he presented us with a cut of fresh venison, nodded solemnly to our thanks, and silently strode away.

That evening I arose and slowly, painfully, tried to put some order back into our lives.

We cleared a spot in the black, charred earth, beneath a giant spreading oak, and Hugh dug a hole to hold the baby's tiny swaddled body. The boys dragged a granite boulder up from the river on a sled and grimly laid it to mark the grave.

Death was no stranger to any of us, not even the children. With disease and accident looming as constant threats, we all lived with its specter every day. Now, somehow, we must help one another find the strength to carry on.

My grief lay like a heavy stone in my chest on the gray, overcast afternoon two days later, when I heard the thud of horses' hoofs and creaking wagon wheels speeding toward the cabin. I wrapped a shawl about my shoulders and walked over to the door, watching as Daniel drove his team of exhausted horses through the blackened grass along the river road. He jerked the galloping beasts to a halt beside the door, leapt down, and rushed over to me.

"Nellie! Nellie, are you all right?" He grabbed my hands and stared into my eyes, his face working with emotion. "My God, I couldn't believe my eyes! I thought you were all goners! Everything is black clear to the river!"

The children crowded around him, pulling on his jacket sleeves. He knelt down and drew them all into his arms. "Oh, my poor little ones," he crooned.

"We threw water on the house," Hugh said in a hushed, distant voice.

Eddie nodded somberly. "Yeah. We saved it, too."

With a look of pain, Daniel shook his head and stood to wrap his arm tightly around my shoulder. "Oh, Nellie, I'm sorry. I'm so terribly sorry. I never should have left you here alone. When I saw that there had been a fire, I was afraid . . ."

I shrugged, trying to contain the turmoil in my soul. With the shawl covering me, he had not even noticed that my stomach

114

was flat. "I've lived through prairie fires before. I saw my share of them down in southern Illinois."

"Oh, God! I'm so thankful you're all right. I never should have left you here like that." He touched his children's faces gently, one by one, as if to assure himself of their survival.

"I'm just relieved we saved the house and everything. I wasn't about to let anybody get hurt. I would have dunked all the kids in the river, if the fire got too bad. Only . . ." I sank down on a nearby chair, exhausted from the effort of explaining.

Daniel came to my side and clutched my trembling hands. "You're such a brave girl, Nellie. I promise I won't leave you here alone again. I brought a fellow and his wife back with me. We're going to build a mill by the river. And that will bring lots more people here. You'll never have to be alone again."

Nodding, I hung my head.

"They'll be coming along soon. I took off at a gallop when I saw there'd been a fire." He raised my chin with a bent forefinger, gazing at me earnestly. "I promise you won't have to be here alone anymore, Nellie. And when the baby comes . . ."

Tears welled in my eyes and spilled over, cascading down my cheeks. I was not used to tenderness. Its presence weakened me. It was far better for me to be hard, for I had cruel facts to face.

"Nellie! What's wrong?"

All three children stared at me, their eyes like huge, dark caverns. Sarah began to cry.

I glanced up at Daniel, then lowered my gaze. Would his pain be as deep as mine? After all, he had three other children. But I had sacrificed Johnny for this child. It would have been my very own, my flesh and blood. I had looked forward so to holding him, to nursing him at my breast.

Drawing in a long, jagged breath, I steeled myself to go on. Still I could not bear to watch his face. I was tired. So very tired. I could not remember ever having been so tired. If only I could lie down . . .

Sarah's sobs continued, muffled as she buried her face in her hands.

"What's going on here?" Daniel demanded, his face clouded with confusion.

My heart beat in heavy, painful thuds. I forced myself to speak the bitter words. "The baby . . . He came too soon. We buried him up on the hillside."

CHAPTER 11

Daniel winced. A low groan escaped his lips. He took my hand and gripped it tightly for a long time, his face full of unspoken grief. What was there to say? Nothing could take away the loss I felt. Still, somehow I would find the strength to carry on.

Soon another wagon came rattling into the yard. I walked over to the doorway and saw a sandy-haired man of around thirty, tall and broad as a giant, crossing the charred grass toward our house. "Everything is all right here?" he asked, a German accent coloring his voice.

Daniel stood beside me, his concerned gaze lingering on my face. "Nellie's been through a terrible ordeal. She needs to go to bed and have a long rest."

"I'll be all right," I said quietly.

He hesitated for a moment. "Might as well come on in, Karl. Bring Ruth and the baby. I know Nellie will want to meet them." Turning back to me, he said, "Just lie down and take it easy. I'll see to all these other things. I'm sorry to bring all this on you just now."

"I'll rest in a little while. Right now I want to meet our company." Maybe the activity would help me to forget.

The German strode back to the wagon, lifted down a toddler in a short tow-linen dress, and held out his massive hand for support as a woman climbed down. She was plump and plain, with straight dark hair pulled back into a loose bun—and a smile that lit her hazel eyes and made her whole face radiate with friendliness. I liked her at once.

After introducing me to Karl Schulmann, his wife Ruth, and baby Cora, Daniel nodded to the man. "Karl's a miller. I asked around and found him at a mill down by Springfield."

"Ja, you came at the right time. I vas looking for a chance to move on," Karl said.

A satisfied grin crossed Daniel's face. "They packed right up and came along with me. We're going to build a combination saw- and gristmill here. Karl knows all about them."

"Ja, I should," Karl replied in his guttural-accented voice. "I've been vorking at them since I come over from Stuttgart. Ja, first I vas a bond slave for a miller back East. Seven years, just to vork off the money for my passage. That's vhere I learned the trade. Now I am happy to come build a mill in this new place."

"We're in dire need of one around here," I told him. "I've been grinding corn by hand for a year."

He planted his massive fists on his hips and gazed along the curving sweep of the river. "Looks like a first-rate spot. But before you dam the river, you must obtain permission from state authorities."

"I'll ride down to the capital and take care of that right away." Daniel hesitated, rubbing his beard. "First we'd better scout around for a good plot for your cabin. I'll give you a nice piece of land close by. After you have a place to live, we can concentrate our efforts on the dam and mill."

"Would you-all excuse me?" I asked. "I'm feeling a little weak and need to rest a minute."

"Oh, I'm sorry." Daniel took my arm. "I'm so wrapped up with all these plans, I forget myself. Here, come over to the bed."

"Let me help you, honey. I'll fix you a cup of tea," Ruth said. What a godsend it seemed to have a woman around.

I glanced down at little Cora's smiling face. The sight of her plump, pink cheeks, her small, sturdy body, opened the raw wound. I drew in a sharp breath at the stab of pain. After hesitating for a moment, I swallowed back the lump in my throat. "You—you can stay here with us until your cabin's built," I said. "It will be a treat for me to have the company."

Ruth's broad smile lit the room. She led me to the bed and

117

covered me with a quilt. "You just lay down and rest. When we get settled in, I'll help you clean up the yard and everything. Looks like that fire nearly caught you."

"The kids and I threw half the river on the house and roof." I shivered, remembering. "It was all we could do to save it."

"And you here by yourself, poor dear." Her head wagged sympathetically. "You look so pale. Have you been sick for long?"

"I lost my baby. He came too soon, after the fire." The pain of it choked me, made my head spin.

"Oh, Lordy. My, you have been through a lot, and you not much more than a girl yourself. Men just don't understand what they ask of us, do they?"

She busied herself at the hearth, then found my cannister of tea and set to brewing up a pot.

Daniel came to my side. "Just take it easy now, Nellie. I'll be with you in a minute. I only wish you could see everything I brought. All the supplies we needed, and glass panes for the windows. I brought plenty for the Indians, too—the traps and guns and bullets they'll need for their winter hunting. Iron kettles and hoes and awls. Blankets, dress goods. I even brought a present for Chief Raccoon. I'll bring it in and show you."

He went out to his overburdened wagon and returned with a long clay pipe, decorated in red, white, and blue stripes. "Think the chief will like this?" he asked.

Karl stood in the doorway, gravely studying the pipe; then he looked at the wooded landscape surrounding us. "You have many Indians here?"

"Quite a number," Daniel said. "I'm working up a regular trade with them. They asked me if I'd let them have the things they need on credit. The chief promised they'd pay me back with furs and hides come spring."

"You *did* say they're friendly . . . ?" Ruth said, with a dubious frown. She lifted cups down from my shelf as if she had lived here all her life.

"We've been here a year and have never had a bit of trouble," I assured her.

"Well, all right. I guess." Still looking dubious, she poured a cup of tea and carried it over to me.

"But there is a treaty," Karl said. "The Indians vill have to leave soon."

"Yes, there's a treaty." Fingering the dark curls of his beard, Daniel gazed off into the distance. "But that doesn't make it easy for them to leave this place."

The children hung at the door, peering at the new people with undisguised curiosity. "Papa, did you bring anything for me?" Eddie piped up in his high voice.

"You bet I did. There's something here for everybody." He glanced at me, his eyes softening. "Let me find your present first, Nellie. I've put you through so much here."

After digging through a barrel filled with assorted supplies, he drew out a small box and brought it to me with an embarrassed grin. "Here. Just for you."

My cheeks flushed as I tore open the wrapping. A necklace. A fine white cameo set in shiny black onyx hung from a slender silver chain. I gasped, lifting my gaze to Daniel's as I held the lovely piece against my heart.

Daniel gave the Schulmanns a plot of land along the river for a homesite. Karl, Ruth, and little Cora boarded with us while the men built a cabin, chopping trees across the river, where the fire had not passed. When the Schulmann's cabin was complete, we invited the Weavers over for a big house-raising celebration.

Then Daniel and Karl began to talk in earnest about constructing a mill. "Good rock foundation here," Karl said, eyeing the river bottom near the bubbling rapids. "Ve can build a tub mill vith a horizontal vheel. That's the easiest and cheapest kind. No cogs or rounds to make. There're few vearing parts, and not much friction, either."

Daniel nodded his agreement. "You're the expert. I'll leave the design up to you."

"Tub mill should do fine, as long as ve have plenty of vater. Ve must build a good high dam."

Daniel rode down to the state legislature in Vandalia and obtained permission to dam the river. Then he and Karl built a cribbing of rough-hewn logs, notched into one another on the top and bottom. When the eight-foot-high frame, slightly curving with the river current, was completed, they filled it with stones to hold the dam in place.

A band of Indians, led by Chief Raccoon, rode over one day. Frowning, they asked Daniel questions about the dam. "What did they say?" I asked him after they left.

"They weren't too happy about us damming the river," he said. "Said it was interfering with their fishing. I told them all about the mill, that they could use it to grind their corn, too. They seemed to take it pretty well in stride after that."

Throughout the winter, they painstakingly selected and cut the proper kinds of wood for building all the different parts for the combination saw- and gristmill.

While the men worked on the mill, Ruth and I exchanged daily visits. "You just don't know how glad I am to finally have a neighbor," I told her. "In fact, I already think of you more like a sister."

"Good thing we get along, isn't it?" she said, with a laugh. "We'd be in a sorry fix if we ruffled each other's feathers."

With the coming of spring, the men began the task of assembling the intricate works of the mill. They built a strong frame of heavy timber that reached out into the river stream, then laid a stout plank floor at bank level, leaving all below it open in case of high water. Next they channeled the river over to one side and constructed a large, watertight enclosure, the reservoir designed to hold the water that turned the mill wheels.

Close by, they made a planked-in enclosure three feet square for the horizontal waterwheel, with a shaft that led to the main floor, propelling the up-and-down saw. With the raising of a water gate, a forceful rush of water would strike the blades of the wheel and set it in motion, powering the saw upstairs.

Beside this wheel was a round enclosure, also adjacent to the reservoir, containing a turbine wheel. When a second water gate was lifted, the force of the falling water would turn the turbine wheel and its attached tall, upright spindle, thereby turning the slowly grinding millstone.

"Now comes the hard part," Karl said, his broad brow furrowing. "Ve have to find just the right stone to cut into mill-stones."

"We'll find it," Daniel told him. "Granite, you say?"

Karl nodded. "Ja, granite. A big boulder, it vill take."

They searched for days, traveling miles along the riverbanks until they located the perfect rock, a massive granite boulder. As they hauled it back to the mill site, the loud squealing and groaning of the wagon under the stone's weight signaled their approach from afar.

"Isn't it lucky our men get along so well, too?" Ruth said,

beaming her bright smile. "They've been working together every day for months."

"You don't know what a difference it's made to us, having you all here," I told her. "Everything seems easier now."

From his well-worn wooden toolbox, Karl carefully selected an array of hammers and chisels to form the boulder into two circular millstones. He patiently and meticulously chipped and cut until the surfaces of the top and bottom stones were each flat and perfectly smooth. Then he cut a pattern of identical curved lines on each stone, a sickle dress, so when they were finally fitted into place, the stones would act like scissors cutting on the grains of corn and wheat.

Day by day, with eager fascination, the children and I watched each step of the long and involved process. The mill beside the river, with its tall, impressive building and its intricate machinery, took shape before our eyes.

"The Indians are back," Daniel told me one clear, sunny day in early spring. "The chief said they're going to bring me furs and hides to settle up their bills from last fall."

"Wherever will we put bundles of furs?" I asked, glancing around our crowded cabin. "We don't have an extra inch here."

"Don't worry about that. I'll drive a wagonload of furs down to Springfield to sell. Later I'll put up a shed out back for all my trading stock."

And so, after his return from the week-long trip to Springfield, along with plowing and planting his fields and helping Karl build the mill, Daniel chopped logs and built a storage shed.

"These summer months are flying by," I told Ruth one steamy day in early July. "It's so good to have you living nearby. But the kids and the house chores and the garden and the baby chicks just eat up all my days. We'll never get a chance to sit down and talk."

"Honey, you just come along with me," she said. "You and me and all these little ones are going to have ourselves a picnic."

Feeling giddy as two girls let out of school, we stole an hour for a pleasant chat in the cool, dense shade along the river's edge.

That summer, some new settlers moved into the Military Tract. We thought of the families settling within twenty or thirty

121

miles of us as our neighbors, even though we rarely saw them, except when they came to use the mill.

Some travelers stopped by our house on their way past to ask directions and advice. Several families stayed over for a day or two. Most were war veterans, come to claim their plots of bounty land like Daniel, though a few had bought their tracts from veterans or land speculators. I looked forward to these visits, for the people came from every state. One man had traveled all the way from Scotland.

"I rode this here horse clear up from Kentucky, carrying this baby in my arms," one woman said. "Led this other horse, too, all loaded down with our household goods and farm tools."

Her husband smiled wanly, pointing to his young son. "That's nothing, Ma. I walked. And carried this young'un on my shoulders, too. Every step of the way."

The Indians returned frequently to check on the progress of the dam. "The river will soon be backed up enough to spill over its edges," Daniel told them one day. "We'll be grinding corn and sawing boards before you know it. And the fishing will be back as it was before."

They went away dubious, pondering the import of this strange modern gadget.

"When the mill's in operation, we'll have more people than ever moving in here, won't we?" I asked Daniel.

His eyes gleamed with anticipation. "Yes, this is a perfect spot for a town."

"We need a school." I glanced at the children's bright, alert faces. "My greatest dream is for all the kids to have a good education. If more people move in, we can hire a teacher for the children."

"Yes, we have to. I'm just too busy these days to help them with their lessons, and it looks like I'm going to be busier."

I swallowed hard and felt my cheeks grow warm. "I worked with them every afternoon all winter. You know I try to help them the best I can, but I never had the chance for much schooling. I can read and write, and that's about all."

"I agree. They must have a good education," he said, his brow furrowed. "It was all so easy back East. Out here on the frontier, it seems almost impossible."

"We'll find a way." I tried to feel optimistic, but then I spied Eddie slipping from tree to tree along the riverbank, stalking

122

some imaginary deer with his bow and arrow. These days that boy seemed more like an Indian than a white child. He caught fish in a trap, as the Indians had taught him. He played for hours with the little Indian children when their parents came to trade with Daniel. As the young ones romped together, trading their little treasures, too, Eddie quickly learned the Indian language, even though I still relied mostly on gestures.

One day Eddie came tearing into the kitchen; he was holding out a thin leather thong from which dangled three long, curved claws. "Look! Chief Raccoon gave me a bear-claw necklace," he said, his voice shrill with excitement. "He likes me, Ma. He says I'm just like a son to him."

As I studied the boy's treasure, my gaze lingered on his sun-bronzed face, his eager eyes, his strong, lean little body. With a smile, I recalled his words of another day. "I know you told us you wanted to be an Indian when you grow up," I said, bending to wrap my arms around him. "But we want to keep you here with us awhile longer. Does that sound all right with you?"

His hazel eyes grew wide. "Sure, Ma. Sure, I'm your boy. I just—I just want to wear my Indian necklace."

I slipped the thong over his neck and stood back to view the effect. "You look dandy, Eddie. Just like a real brave."

By mid-July, the mill was complete and the water spilling over the dam. We began its operation with great ceremony. All the children and Ruth and me stood in rapt attention while Karl tossed the first bag of corn into the hopper on the upper floor. Daniel, down below, threw open the water gate and a mighty thrust of water forced the horizontal waterwheel to turn, causing the attached spindle to turn the millstone above the stationery bed stone. The grains of corn, fed from the hopper to the narrow space between the stones, were crushed and spilled outward, escaping down a chute into a wooden bin. The children ran downstairs to watch as Daniel sifted the first golden grains of cornmeal and dipped them into a bag.

"That's all there is to it," he said, with a proud grin. "It took a long time for us to get to this point, but there it is."

"Show them how the sawmill works, Papa," Hugh said, as if in his nine-year-old wisdom he understood it all himself.

123

"It's too noisy in here," Sarah said, wrinkling her nose. "This whole building shakes. I want to go outside."

But I stayed, captivated by the intricacy of the mill works. I watched Karl and Daniel saw a huge log into planks, the up-and-down blade moving slowly, inch by inch, down the log securely fastened to a movable carriage. I knew this sawmill would be a marvelous timesaver for all the pioneers.

Soon settlers would be riding in from miles around to our mill, to have their corn or wheat ground. With ox and chain, they would drag entire trees to the sawmill—and leave with an aromatic supply of rough boards.

This land would build up like wildfire. Why, before long a whole new city would be sitting here beside Spoon River. I could visualize it now—store and blacksmith shop, an inn to house the travelers stopping by, a church and school, all the things that make a real community. My pulse quickened in anticipation.

Whites and Indians. Would there be room for us both in this beautiful valley? The Indians depended on hunting for food and trapping furs to trade for supplies. As more and more white settlers arrived with their axes and plows and hogs and cattle, they would transform these good hunting grounds into farmland.

The Indians would soon be moving on further west. They had signed treaties, and the government had paid them for their land rights. Still, I knew they would not leave their homes without a deep sense of loss. Would there not be resentment and hostility as well?

Was it right for us to make them leave their homeland? Though I was powerless in the face of such monumental questions, they left me with a nagging sense of guilt.

For now we could all celebrate the inauguration of our mill. I had something else to celebrate, too. I was pregnant again. Before winter came, I would be holding a new baby in my arms.

Daniel was as pleased as I. "Nellie, you really have to take things easier. Save the heavy work for me. You mustn't overdo," he said.

I nodded, grateful for his concern. This time, I promised myself, everything would go right.

The mill quickly generated a thriving business. Settlers drove in from miles around, hauling bags of corn slung over their horses' backs, driving wagons loaded with the weight of huge logs. The Indians came, too, marveling at the mill's efficiency.

"Time for me to set to work again," Daniel told me. "Now I'm going to chop more logs and build us a good-sized general store."

"I can help you in the store, Daniel. You know I like to get out and meet people."

"I only wish I could assure you I can handle everything myself," he said. "Somehow I have the feeling you'll have your chance to help before we're through."

The following week, Daniel woke one morning at dawn, shaken by chills. "Why has it turned so cold all of a sudden?" he asked, his teeth chattering as he felt around for a quilt.

A slick film of perspiration covered me that sultry August morning. Tense with apprehension, I studied his face in the dim morning light. "Daniel, you're not getting the Illinois shakes, are you?"

He threw his arm across his eyes. "Ague? Good Lord, I hope not. Not with everything I have to do around here." Another violent chill coursed through his body. "Would you bring me a blanket?"

A blanket in all this heat? Now I knew that he was coming down with ague, that scourge of the prairie. I had seen it time and time again down in southern Illinois—the chills intense enough to rattle the teeth, the raging fever that followed, the racking body pain and headache. An attack of ague could hang on for weeks, leaving the victim listless, fertile soil for other illnesses. And once you had the disease, you could expect nasty recurrences from time to time.

"Just rest," I told him, trying to mask my concern. "I'll make you some boneset tea as soon as it gets light."

So much to do, I thought as the giant brassy sun crept over the eastern horizon. So much to do, and now Daniel's sick.

At the insistent call of the rooster's crow, the children woke and climbed down the ladder from the loft, rubbing sleep from their eyes. "Hugh, bring in some firewood while I go out and milk the cow," I said. With Daniel sick, all of us would have to do double duty.

As I went about the morning chores, my thoughts dwelt on the coming baby. I had lost my first child at this point, and could not bear to think of a repeat of that horrible experience. Yet the

125

concerns of day-to-day survival pressed upon me like a crushing weight. We must see Daniel through his illness.

"I'll help you," Eddie said, his eyes sad as he finished a last bite of eggs at breakfast.

"Sure you will. We'll all pitch in." I turned to Sarah. "If you'll wash these dishes, dear, the boys and I will go out and hoe the garden before the sun gets too hot."

The thumping of the mill, the cheerful murmur of water spilling over the dam, accompanied our tasks. Karl would have to mill grain and saw boards for his customers without any help for a while. I knew Daniel was in for a siege.

A lone Indian stopped by the cabin that afternoon. "Trade Cranford," he muttered in a deep voice, his way of asking for Daniel. I pointed to the high-postered bed in the corner, where Daniel lay moaning in pain. Frowning with concern, the Indian left, returning a short time later carrying two freshly shot squirrels. He handed them to me with a grunt.

"For us? Did you want to trade them for something?" I asked.

Eddie ran to my side and spoke with the tall brave in Indian language. "It's a gift for our supper," Eddie said after a brief exchange. "Because Papa is sick."

"Oh, thank you. Thank you so much," I said, touched by his kindness. Our Indian friends had always been good neighbors, despite their different and sometimes puzzling ways.

Daniel's face was flushed now with raging fever. The Indian glanced inside the door at the man tossing and groaning on the bed, then muttered a few words.

"He says bad medicine," Eddie told me. "He says their medicine man should come over here and drive away the evil spirits."

"Evil spirits!" My hands flew to my chest as I stared at the Indian in horror. "No, no! It's just the fever. He'll soon be fine again."

A few days later, Chief Raccoon rode his fine black horse into our yard and walked up to our door with all the dignity befitting his rank. "Cranford?" he asked when I greeted him.

"Mr. Cranford is still sick," I said, glancing inside to where Daniel lay prostrate on the bed.

The Indian's solemn face drew inward in a frown.

"Come in, Chief," Daniel said, his voice barely audible from across the room. "It's always good to see you."

126

I led the Indian over to the bed and brought him a chair. He gazed at Daniel with a furrowed brow. "You want medicine man come?"

"No, thanks. I'm getting better now. But sit and talk awhile. That's the best medicine."

Chief Raccoon sat down stiffly, unaccustomed to the hardwood chair. "You ride to my village. Sweat oven help you."

"Maybe I'll try that one day. I've heard those sweat ovens are good for almost every kind of ill. But tell me, Chief. How did you learn to speak English so well?"

"In white man's war. Redcoats give Indian sharp knives. Set them like hunting dogs on white brothers."

"Yes. I fought in the war, too."

"No good for Indian. Take pay to fight in white man's war. Then Redcoat and white brother shake hands. Be friends again. Indian feel like fool."

Daniel studied the chief's dark and somber face. "The white men are coming out here in full force now, Chief," he said. "You'll be learning a lot about our ways."

"I know ways of white man." The chief nodded, his eyes sad. "White man want fences. Indian say Great Spirit made the world and its riches for all men. Sky and land and river, tree and grass and fruit, animal and fish and bird—Great Spirit gives this for all men to share."

My skin pricked with goose bumps. Daniel nodded wordlessly.

After Chief Raccoon left, I turned to Daniel anxiously. "What's going to happen around here? The government gave the war veterans these plots. You know they're going to fence the land and plow the ground."

"And that's the crux of the problem, isn't it? The Indians don't believe anybody can own land, no more than they can own the rivers or the air we breathe. And land ownership is the very basic tenent of our white society."

"Yes, and it's caused a fuss wherever whites and Indians try to live together. Oh, I just wish I knew some way to work out all these differences."

"So do I, Nellie. So do I."

Daniel's illness lingered for over two weeks. When he finally regained enough strength to step outdoors, Hugh proudly showed him how the fields had flourished under our care. Long rows of corn grew tall and green, with fat ears ripening inside each golden husk. The garden burgeoned with lush vegetables, and the chickens and cattle fattened by the day.

Daniel looked about him, slowly observing all the signs of a coming glorious harvest. "You've all been working so hard, while I've just been lounging around the house," he said, his voice tight with repressed emotion.

"You were sick, Daniel," I murmured, my hand on his arm.

"Well, now I'm going back to work. I have to finish the store."

"Oh, good! I'd like to help you. I'm really looking forward to that store."

More people were coming to the mill every day now, riding many miles to save themselves the grueling work of pounding corn or sawing boards by hand. The thump and shudder of the mill was like music accompanying my daily chores.

In late September, Daniel made a trip to Springfield to purchase stock for our new general store. He began stocking only a few basics: gunpowder and lead bullets, iron tools and utensils, some bolts of cloth and sewing notions, coffee and tea, sugar and tobacco. But we knew that as the store grew, it would attract even more business and activities and settlers to Eden Valley.

My days of loneliness and isolation were all behind me now.

By the last days of October, the air was growing chill. Corn shocks stood like golden teepees in the field, and all the potatoes, beans, cabbage, turnips, and pumpkins from our garden were stored in the root cellar behind our cabin, ready for the long, cold winter. Just as soon as freezing weather set in, the men would butcher some hogs. They cut gigantic stacks of logs for winter fuel and piled them in our backyard. The whole world seemed tense, waiting for the first snow.

And, growing bigger and more uncomfortable by the day, I was tensely awaiting my baby's arrival.

Early one crisp day in mid-November, my pains began. Daniel ran down the road for Ruth, then drove the children over to a nearby settler's house.

Ruth held tightly to my hand when the pains came. "Just

relax, honey," she said in a warm, soothing voice. "Before you know it, you'll be holding a fine new baby in your arms."

Perspiration coated my face despite the chill. "I'm so scared, Ruth. After last time . . ."

"Hush now, dear. You're going to be fine."

She found Daniel's whiskey jug on the top shelf and tilted it to pour a slug into a cup. "Here, take a sip of this when the pains come strong," she said. Sitting in a chair pulled close to my bed, she knitted on a woolen shawl, talking to me as my hours of labor passed.

The pains grew fierce and close together, and I knew my time had come. I gave birth to a baby girl, a perfectly formed child with reddish fuzz crowning her tiny head.

Her angry squawls filled the chill air and echoed back off the cabin walls. Oh, she was bound to let the whole world hear of her insult and outrage. Though I was weak and tired, I laughed at this little girl's feisty spirit. She was tough, like me. Already she was proclaiming herself a bonafide frontier girl.

"She's a beauty! A real doll baby," Ruth said, a smile irradiating her plain features. "I'll run out to the barn and tell Daniel she's here."

Joy coursed through me like a flood tide as I gazed down at my baby's tiny red face. How precious, how miraculous, she seemed. My very own flesh and blood.

When Daniel stepped inside and saw the little bundle in my arms, his eyes filled with tenderness. "Oh, Nellie, look at that. A redhead."

"I guess you could hear her yelling way out back. She wants to make sure the whole county hears her complaints." I smiled up at him, met his gaze of wonder and pride.

He was a gentle, caring father to his other children. I knew he would be good to this child, too.

My gaze lingered on his face, his high forehead and thin nose and neatly trimmed beard. I couldn't help but wish he'd say he loved me. Just this once. I was young, and still clung to my dreams of romance. I needed to feel loved, too. I longed to hear that I had come to equal Lenore's place in his heart. Yet Daniel never talked of such things. Perhaps he never would.

Emotions were a luxury here in the wilderness, as the Indians had always known. Survival depended on strength.

This strong, silent man was brave and honest and hardworking. He was good to me and the children. We lived in peace together. We worked as partners, caring for the family, and for a growing business and a farm. And now I had a darling baby of my own. What more could I ask?

Still . . . A lump tightened in my throat, swelled to fill my chest.

Still, it would be nice to know.

CHAPTER 12

We named the baby Lucinda. Everybody, Karl and Ruth and all the Weavers, agreed with us that she was nothing less than a perfect jewel. All through the bitter winter months, she was our family's special ray of sunshine, brightening the cold, dark days.

The older children delighted in her smiles. "Look here, little Cinda," Eddie called as he and Hugh made silly faces and engaged in outlandish antics to coax the baby's gurgling giggle.

"Now don't you noisy boys bother her," Sarah scolded, tucking the blanket close around the baby. "You might make her cry."

But our Cinda seldom shed tears. In the evenings, while I sewed or knitted woolen socks and sweaters, I rocked her cherrywood cradle with my foot, listening with contentment to her pleasant coo.

Winter blizzards, hurled upon us by the north gales, altered the landscape with high, wind-tossed drifts of snow. Cloaked in white, tree branches shimmered like crystal in the sunlight.

Our cattle and horses huddled in the barn, munching icy bites of the prairie hay Daniel had cut and dried for them last summer.

At night, the anguished howling of wolves out on the prairie made the long hours hideous. This frigid white world had left them desperate for food. One settler out traveling after dark was chased by a hungry wolf pack and barely escaped their snapping fangs by scurrying up a tree. He spent the whole night there, shivering and quaking, while the beasts barked and growled and lunged for him. Dawn was breaking before they finally wearied of their quest.

Deer roamed restlessly about the land, searching for tender twigs to sustain them until spring. In early morning, droves of ten or twelve passed from the prairie to the timbers, where they quickly stripped all the low-growing branches from the young trees.

Daniel, his rifle tucked under his arm, sometimes walked to the deer lick downriver and climbed a tree to wait. Within an hour or two he returned, pulling a buck home on the sled. We ate venison for supper every night for a week, drying part of the meat for keeping, Indian-style.

In the spring, the Indians returned from their winter hunting grounds. Their ponies burdened under great bundles of furs and hides, they came to trade with Daniel.

"Glory be!" I said, staring at the stacks of deerskins, and beaver, otter, raccoon, mink, and muskrat furs out in the storage shed. "Whatever are you going to do with all these?"

"There's one big buffalo hide here. I'd like to keep that and make a carriage robe. The rest I should take down and sell in St. Louis. There's a big market there. I need to buy more trade goods, too. This is going to be a big business for us, Nellie. I never realized just how much there is to it."

"I heard something that might be of help," I said. "Just yesterday Ruth told me about a man who brought a keelboat up the Spoon. Now that he's here, he just might sell that boat to you."

Daniel's face lit with interest. "Yes, a keelboat would be just the thing to haul these furs and hides downriver to St. Louis. The big markets there pay a great deal more than I can get in Springfield. I do believe I'll go down and talk to that fellow about the boat right now."

"St. Louis is a long way to travel, Daniel."

"Going down is nothing. The hard part will be coming back upriver with the load of supplies. But I'm running short of lots of things, for the whites and Indians both."

"Guess I'd better start making a list of everything we need

131

for the house. I have a few ideas of some different things you could carry in the store, too.''

He left immediately, riding down the river road to find the man with the keelboat. A short time later, Eddie came running in, his tanned cheeks flushed pink. ''The post rider's coming! Maybe he's going to stop here!''

Since the post rider only came our way twice a month, his visits always caused a stir. I stepped out on the stoop and watched the dusty horse and trail-hardened rider approach at a fast pace. He jerked his steed to a halt near our front door. ''Letter for you, ma'am,'' he said, handing me a sheet of folded and sealed paper.

My pulse raced with excitement and apprehension as I examined the missive. The mangled letter, from New York State, was addressed to Daniel. I only hoped it didn't bring him any bad news.

When Daniel returned, I rushed out to give him the letter. He ripped open the seal and quickly scanned the neatly written message. ''Listen to this! My youngest brother, Noah, is going to move out West, too, with his wife and baby boy. He's thinking of settling here.''

''Oh, wouldn't it be nice to have some kin nearby?'' My thoughts drifted to my little sisters. So many years had passed since I last saw them. I wasn't even sure where they were now. Most likely our paths would never cross again.

Daniel's face creased with a smile. ''Noah should be in St. Louis by the time I get there. I'll try to get word to him to wait for me there. They can come back with me. Oh, by the way—I bought that keelboat.''

''Well, good for you. And your brother can help pole it back upriver. That's too much work for one man alone.''

''Noah's coming. I just can't believe it,'' Daniel said. ''He's always been the flighty one in the family. It will do him good to settle down somewhere. I'll give him a piece of land, and maybe he can help me out a little. These days I'm hard put to find time for all the farming chores, what with the Indian trade and the store and trying to help Karl at the mill.''

''I'm afraid Karl's going to have to hire somebody else.''

''We've talked about that. He's thinking about taking on the oldest Weaver boy as an apprentice.''

''Good idea. Say, Daniel . . . Did I hear you say your brother

132

is flighty?" I could not imagine such a trait in anyone related to him.

"Yes. Noah's never been content to stay anywhere very long. But there's no place with more opportunity than here. He should recognize that soon enough."

Daniel poled his long, newly purchased, canoe-shaped keelboat upriver to our place and stacked its broad deck with the bulky and valuable bundles of furs. The day he pushed off with the long pole and floated away from us, Spoon River was running high, almost out of its banks with spring thaws.

The keelboat would float effortlessly downstream to the Illinois, then ride that river's current until its waters joined the Mississippi. Continuing on, it would reach St. Louis. The trip would be completed in only four or five days.

The return trip, in stark contrast, would be like a grueling uphill climb. Daniel said it would take three weeks or more, poling the keelboat slowly upstream or tying ropes to trees along the shore and pulling the boat forward by brute strength. Only when the wind was fair could he hoist the broad white sail and sit back for a welcome rest.

I stood on the bank with the baby in my arms, holding up her tiny hand to help her wave. "Good-bye! Be careful!" I called, my voice wavering as Daniel floated out of sight.

My childhood had been colored by vivid tales of river bandits, and I felt anxious for Daniel's safety on the river—especially with his rich load of furs. Though he showed no trace of fear, I knew there would be few other boats in sight during his long trip down the Illinois—or when he was continuing on down the Mississippi to St. Louis.

Daniel's courage never failed to inspire and excite me. With his long rifle, his strong arms, and iron-willed determination, he thought himself invincible. While others had quaked and turned back at the sight of all the Indians in the Military Tract, he had made friends with them, learned their language, and was now engaged in a flourishing fur trade.

Close beside me on the riverbank, Hugh, Sarah, and Eddie waved and called until their father's boat disappeared around the bend. Ruth and Karl stood nearby, watching and waving, too. How comforting to have close neighbors while Daniel was gone this time.

A fragrant spring breeze touched my cheeks and tousled my

hair. I smiled at its promise of a season filled with wildflowers and growing things. "I vill plow your fields and garden," Karl said, with a reassuring grin. "Do not give that another thought."

"Thanks, Karl. Then the kids and I can plant the corn. Spring is such a busy time. We'll have plenty to occupy us while Daniel is gone."

"That is too much vork for a voman. You got the store to tend, too. I vill do the planting for you."

The load of work lying before me seemed like a mountain to be climbed. But I was determined to show that I could manage things myself—*and* to prove my worth to Daniel.

"No, Karl. You're busy enough with the mill. I like to be outside in spring. Don't you worry about me."

Ruth squeezed my arm. "At least let me watch the baby for you."

So while Ruth cared for baby Cinda, the older children and I worked in the field in the afternoons, dropping kernels of corn into the plowed ground, hoeing bits of black soil over them. A warm spring sun smiled down on us; a south breeze wafted scents of the newly awakened land.

Long afternoon shadows lay before us when we finally returned to the cabin, passing through woods sprinkled with a rainbow-colored array of wildflowers. Bluebells and trillium, bloodroot and Dutchman's breeches all nodded dainty little heads, greeting us and brightening our way. I stopped to pick a bouquet for the table.

Our moment of respite ended as soon as we reached the cabin. "Hugh, you'd better milk the cow and chop some wood. Eddie, feed the chickens and hunt eggs. Sarah, go get the baby from Ruth's and then come help me with the kitchen chores," I said, feeling like a drill sargeant.

The kids quickly did my bidding, for they knew we all relied on each person doing his share of the chores.

The steady rumbling from the mill gave proof of its regular use. Men and boys rode in from over thirty miles around with wagonloads of logs or sacks of grain thrown across their horses' backs. While waiting for Karl to mill their corn and saw their logs into uniform planks, the farmers gossiped or fished in the water below the dam. Those traveling long distances camped overnight in tents or wagon beds in the parklike grass along the river near the mill. All stopped by our store before they headed home.

The customers kept us informed of all the latest news. "I heard there were nine thousand quarter-sections of this land advertised for sale last year," Ruth told me one day when I stopped by her house.

"That many? Lordy! Why?"

"Because the absentee owners didn't pay their taxes. When all those plots are sold, we'll see plenty of new people moving in."

"Seems like this spring has already brought a good crop of them."

"Lots of these men are just passing through, heading up to work at the lead mines in Galena."

"I've heard so much about Galena lately. Just where is that town, anyway?"

"It's way up in the northwest corner of the state. That's a long trip, and the land between here and there is plumb full of Indians, too. But from what I hear, there's a regular land rush around that town."

"So they say."

"Yes, already nearly two thousand people living around there, I've heard. All the lead mines are going great guns."

Karl, covered with fine white dust from the mill, stood in the doorway, listening to our conversation. "You think ve got Indians around here? Ja, boy! Vait till they see how many they got up north."

Ruth scooped little Cora up into her arms. "What's going to happen up there?"

"If the Indians are in the vay, the settlers vill chase them out, like alvays," Karl said. "Just like they do the rattlesnakes and panthers."

"Karl, please. That's an ugly thing to say. They're people, too." I thought of the Indian village I had visited, of the young mother nursing her bright-eyed baby. A heavy weight gathered in my heart.

"I did not say it is a good thing." Karl shrugged his massive shoulders. "I only tell you that's the vay it is."

Customers, stopping by for supplies, often had to call me in from the garden to open the store. We sold salt and sugar, tea and coffee, spices, gunpowder, and a few tools and tinwares. I

135

enjoyed meeting and visiting with the variety of people, but I always asked for silver money, produce, or hides in trade. Daniel and I didn't trust all the different kinds of paper money floating around the country.

The work surrounding me from dawn till dark weighed down on me like a heavy cloak. I had little time for thought beyond the next pressing chore.

Still, at stolen moments, I prayed for Daniel's safety. I missed his strong and quiet presence in the house. I missed the sound of his deep voice calmly relating the events of his day. I missed the comforting warmth of him beside me in the bed at night.

He had come to mean so very much to me. After he returned, I would just come out with it and tell him. Maybe then he would say he cared for me, too. How sweet those words would be to my ears. How joyful to my heart.

By the time Daniel's keelboat came back upriver, the corn had sprouted into rows of crisp, green pips, and all the garden plants were leafing out. Eddie, playing near the river, saw the boat first. He dashed into the house, flinging both arms wildly with excitement. "Come out! Come out! Papa's home!"

We all raced down to the riverbank and called and waved to Daniel. Beneath lacy overhanging willow branches, his keelboat, piled high with goods from St. Louis, hugged the shoreline. He and another man set long poles into the muddy river bottom time after time, pulling the boat forward foot by tedious foot. How could they possibly have traveled like this all the way from St. Louis? Had the winds been fair so they could use the sail at least part of the way?

A slender young woman in pink muslin stood on the deck. In one arm she held a baby, with the other she returned our welcoming waves. Shaded by a wide straw bonnet, her cheeks were pale. She looked as delicate as fine English china.

Daniel pulled the boat in to shore and tied it to an ancient sycamore along the bank. His eyes shone as his glance met mine above the eager children pressing around him. "Everything all right here while I was gone?" he asked me.

I flushed with delight at seeing him. "Everything's fine. The corn's already up." I had come to really love this stiff-backed Yankee—and longed to throw my arms around him as the children were doing now!

Our gaze held for a lingering moment. Then he nodded to the newcomers at his side. "This is my brother Noah and his wife Emily."

"Welcome! We're so glad to have family here with us," I said, clasping their hands.

The lanky young man's mouth curved in a wide infectious grin. His dark hair and gray eyes were like Daniel's, but his good-humored smile revealed a soul less grave and serious.

A faint peach colored his wife's pale cheeks as she smiled down at the baby in her arms. "And this little fellow is Benjie."

At the sound of her soft, refined voice, Sarah ran up and seized the woman's hand. "You come from New York, don't you? I can tell. You sound just like my mother."

A flicker of sympathy crossed Emily's face. She shifted her baby and slipped an arm around Sarah's slender shoulders. "I'm your Aunt Emily, dear. I knew your mother's family back East. I'm sure we're going to be great friends."

Sarah laid her head against Emily's arm, a gesture that took me completely by surprise. I had never known the child to be so demonstrative and affectionate. Was this woman really so much like Lenore? Her pretty face and graceful movements, her honey-colored hair, shining even after that grueling trip . . . Suddenly I felt homely and inadequate.

But I had no time for such foolishness. I hustled everyone into the cabin for a good hot meal and then helped the men unload the keelboat. My excitement bubbled like a boiling cauldron when I saw the wide array of goods Daniel had purchased for our store with the proceeds from the furs and hides.

"Did you bring the gingham and calico and broadcloth?" I asked, fingering eagerly through the barrels and packages.

"Yes, I brought everything on your list," he answered, with a smile. "And a little something extra, too." He reached into his pocket and handed me a dainty gold watch hanging from a slender chain.

My face flushed as I stared openmouthed at the intricate flowers carved into its oval cover. "Oh, Daniel . . ." I looked up at him, unable to go on.

Embarrassed by my show of emotion, he turned back to the barrels and searched for the gifts he had brought for the children.

We all began to unpack. Within a short time, we had stocked the store shelves with caps, boots, bolts of cloth, sewing notions, tools, and tinware. The men rolled in barrels of salt and molasses, kegs of coffee and tea. I knew that soon the settlers would be bringing in their eggs, butter, lard, bacon, homespun cloth, and hides to trade for these store goods.

"I sure hope you're figuring on making a good profit on these things," I said. "After all, you went to a bunch of trouble and danger bringing them up here."

Daniel threw me a quizzical glance. "Back where I come from, the women let their men worry about such things."

I hesitated just a moment, then grinned, taunting him. "I reckon by now you've noticed women in these parts tend to look at things a mite different."

He smiled wryly, wagging his head.

"The way I figure it, the more I know about these things, the better I'll be able to help you," I said, and turned back to the work at hand.

For the Indians, he had brought traps and guns, bullets and blankets, brass kettles and steel needles, beads and paints and silver jewelry. Unpacking and opening those dozens of barrels, marveling at all the extravagant riches, thrilled me like a hundred Christmases and birthdays rolled into one.

Noah looked over the countryside and quickly decided to set down roots. He agreed to work for Daniel, to pay off the cost of purchasing a plot of land. While the men cut logs and built a cabin a few hundred yards down the way, Emily and Noah and little Benjie stayed with us.

"When your cabin's done, we'll invite all the neighbors in and have you one grand housewarming party," I told Emily.

As we shared the house and garden work and compared notes on our babies, she and I quickly became friends. I soon discovered she was not afraid of work, despite her ladylike appearance. She helped me cook the venison and prairie chicken and wild turkey Daniel bagged. Since Benjie and Cinda were nearly the same age, we watched avidly for the cutting of their tiny, jagged baby teeth and laughed at their delightful antics. Our little ones crawled around our feet on the rough puncheon floors, while Emily and I chatted and sewed.

"I can't believe how hard you work, Nellie," Emily said, taking dainty stitches in the hem of Sarah's new dress. "Would you be upset if I told you that back East they warned me the frontier settlers were a lazy and dirty lot? They said all the men do is hunt and drink whiskey. I just wish they could see how you really live out here."

I chuckled. "Oh, I've heard my share of slander against Yankees, too. Down South they call them inhospitable and miserly and selfish. Some folks even question their honesty. 'Course, I know better, being married to one."

"No one could ever call you inhospitable." Emily paused, a fond smile lighting her face. "You've been like a real sister to me. I don't know how to thank you."

"Oh, pshaw," I said, with a wave of my hand. "Don't you know I'm just thankful for the company?"

Sarah barraged Emily with questions. "Tell me about New York. Tell me about the towns and schools and clothes the ladies wear back East."

I listened with interest and envy, for I knew these were things I would never see and could hardly imagine. "Sarah is still a New Englander," I said, forcing a smile. "Just look at the difference in Eddie."

The boy, his bear-claw necklace hung around his neck, grinned at us across the room. He had just come in from netting quails—as expertly as any native.

Emily regarded him with a smile. "Eddie is a true son of the wilds, isn't he?"

"That's our Eddie boy."

I glanced at her pale, delicate face and slender form. Was Emily strong enough for the frontier? Life was hard enough in the cities, where the air was filled with miasmas of consumption, diphtheria, pneumonia, and a hundred other diseases. But out here, even the heartiest of us faced a constant challenge.

Sure enough, soon after they moved into their new cabin— which was just down the valley near the river—Emily fell sick with a bad case of ague. For weeks I nursed her through bouts of chills and fever and watched over little Benjie at our house.

All the while, new settlers kept trickling into the territory. The rich farmland attracted them like bees to clover. "Where are you-all from?" I always asked them when the covered wagons, rolling in from the South and the East, stopped by our store for food and other supplies.

"Virginia." "New Jersey." "South Carolina," the people would reply. I had only heard about these places in travelers' tales.

"Tell me all the news from outside. Tell me all about your trip," I begged, ever delighted with the sight of new faces after the long spells of solitude I had known in Eden Valley.

Every family had a different fascinating tale of the adventures of their trip. Some I suspected of embroidering the truth a bit. But I could not doubt one tough, weather-beaten Hoosier dressed in a red flannel shirt and fur-trimmed cap.

Tears glistened in his eyes when he told of their hard journey. "Our baby girl got sick and died while we was crossing the prairie. We had to bury her in a grove of maples along the way."

"I'm so sorry," I said, knowing it was inadequate.

"All we could do was carve her name on a tree, as a marker. Hard. It's mighty hard to leave a child along the way like that." Struggling with his emotions, the man turned and left the store.

Daniel used his keelboat to ferry families and their belongings across the river, collecting a small fee for each trip. There must have been over two hundred families settled around the Military Tract now, though some prospective settlers still turned for home when they saw the Indian villages situated here and there along the waterways.

But the day was coming soon, I knew, when the white man and his plow would force the Indians to leave.

"There is a treaty," Daniel reminded me. "The Indians sold the land. They agreed to move out when the settlers come."

"Do you really think they knew what they were signing? How many can read English?" I could sense the tension gradually mounting between the settlers and the Indians and prayed it could all be handled peaceably.

Our village was growing, too, serving the needs of the outlying farm community.

A burly blacksmith bought a lot near the mill and built a house and shop. Soon the bang and clang of hammer against iron accompanied the steady song of water spilling over the dam. The blacksmith's wife was a healer, a most welcome addition to the valley, versed in all the lore of herbs and roots used to prevent and cure sickness.

The next addition was a tanner. Judson Lowder drove into town one summer day with his wife Becky and a wagon full of towheaded children. When he stopped by our place, Daniel was out working in the fields with Noah, so I left the baby with Sarah and opened the store.

"Are you from back East, too?" I asked the earnest, quiet man, glancing at his sallow skin and pale eyes.

"Me? No, I'm from down by Carlyle," he said, scratching his chin. "Right now, the good land that's opening up around here is all the talk down there. Thought I'd come up and have a look-see myself."

"Carlyle! Why, I lived not far from there. Down by Mount Vernon."

The man's thick, wiry brows raised with interest. "That so? My sister married a fellow from down that way."

"Small world, isn't it?"

He wiped a thick, square hand across his mouth. "Yep. Maybe you'd know this guy. Johnny Nichols?"

My heart lurched. I opened my mouth, but no words came.

"He's from a big family over that way. You must know them," the man insisted. "He lives down by St. Louis now."

I nodded tautly. "Yes, I know the family," I said in a faint voice.

"Johnny's doing all right for himself these days." Smiling with pride, Judson Lowder folded his arms across his chest. "He's started up a dandy horse farm. Racing stock. He and my sister got married a year or so ago. In fact, they just had a baby boy a few weeks back. Say, slice me off a pound of bacon, will you?"

My hands began to tremble. Clenching my jaw, I laid a slab of bacon on the counter and cut off some thin slices. "Anything else now?"

"Your husband owns a lot of land in these parts, I hear tell."

"Yes." I gulped and stared down at the slab of bacon. "Yes, he does."

"Looks like an up-and-coming settlement here. Pretty spot, too. I might just settle down near here and raise some cattle. I plan to start me up a tanning operation. Need to be by water for that."

"You'll have to talk to Daniel. He'll be in for dinner soon."

The man paid me and started for the door. "I think I'll ride around and look this territory over a bit. I'll be back later."

Johnny. Married. With a baby. Just the same as me.

Visions of him crowded in before me. His eyes, his smile, his deep and tender voice. He had told me he loved me. The one time in my life I had heard those precious words.

But his last words to me had been a curse.

Well, with all the work and concerns in my life, I couldn't let a thing like that upset me. I had come a long way in the last three years. I was a respectable wife and mother now. And Daniel was a good man. A fine man. I thanked my lucky stars that I had met him. What could Johnny possibly offer that I did not already have?

And the answer came as quickly as the question. Johnny had made me feel pretty and desirable. One moonlit evening, long ago and far away, Johnny said he loved me.

How I longed for Daniel, just once, to say those magic words to me. I yearned to tell him how much I loved him, but something held me back.

No, he would have to take the first step. Until then, I would feel in my heart he still preferred Lenore.

CHAPTER 13

Fall came and the woods blazed with crimson, gold, and maroon.

"Some of these Indians are riding all the way from up around Peoria to trade here with me," Daniel told me.

"I sure hope they won't forget to pay you back for the things you're selling them on credit," I said. "You've got a big investment in all those guns and traps and powder."

He frowned at me, shaking his head. "Why do you worry about such things? It's my place to take care of the money affairs. Just leave all that to me."

"You can't blame me for being interested, can you? We've both worked so hard to build the business here."

"Chief Raccoon guaranteed me they would all pay. He's a friend. I trust his word."

"Yes, I expect his word is good enough for anyone." I bit my tongue, wanting to say more. Even though I had but little education, I could understand money matters perfectly well. Was that not feminine enough for him? Had Lenore never questioned anything?

Before the days turned chill, Daniel again took his keelboat down to St. Louis to lay in supplies for the coming winter. During the weeks he was away, the house seemed empty.

It was then I approached Emily about teaching our children, all the children in Eden Valley. Her response was exactly what I'd hoped it would be.

"I could do that, couldn't I?" Her eyes gleamed as she drew in a long breath. "Yes. Teach the children. And not just yours, either. There're those Lowder children, and the other families out on farms. But what about Benjie? He's into everything these days."

I swooped down and caught the little toddler as he passed. "Tell you what. If you'll teach the kids their reading, writing, and arithmetic, I'll look after Benjie. He'll be good company for Cinda. And I'll cook supper for you and Noah while you're teaching, too."

"Oh, Nellie," she protested. "You're so busy now."

"Shoot, a couple more won't make a bit of difference."

A dandy solution, I thought as I walked back to my house with a lighter step. Emily would make a first-rate teacher, and it would be good for her, too. Homesickness was gnawing at that poor girl like a tapeworm. And yet I wished . . . Well, I just wished I weren't too ignorant to teach those kids myself.

The other families in the area were thrilled when I approached them with our plans for the school. Before long we had lined up a dozen prospective students. After Daniel returned from St. Louis, he made another trip down to Springfield to buy primers, spellers, copybooks, and slates for the makeshift school in Emily's cabin.

Every morning Noah brought Benjie to play with Cinda, while the older children walked to Emily's. Even Eddie put aside his bow and arrow and his Indian games to concentrate on reading tales from his primer. Hugh quickly became expert at ciphering, and Sarah took first prize at every spelling bee.

As winter set in, the children from outlying farms waded through deep snow to come and take their places on the rough-cut benches in Emily's cabin. She quickly won their affection with her patient, soft-voiced instruction. Though her school was nothing fancy, no teacher ever had more willing pupils.

"Come on, now. Settle down and do your lessons," I told the children in the evenings by the fireside. "Show me what you've learned today."

Secretly I hoped to learn a few new things myself.

"Don't you envy anyone with learning?" I asked Ruth one day.

She gave a nonchalant shrug. "Oh, I don't guess a fancy education means all that much for pioneer women like you and me. After all, the men handle all the business matters."

"I know," I said, frowning. "They handle all the politics and finances and everything. Why, we can't even vote!"

"By law, a married woman couldn't own a thing in her own name, you know. Not even something she inherited."

I chewed my lip to hold back my anger at the injustice of it all. "I can't see how it's true, what so many people say—that schooling is a waste of time for girls. Of course, right now I don't have time to read for pleasure, anyway. Maybe someday, when I'm an idle, rich lady, with hired girls to do all my household chores."

We laughed at the absurd picture. Still and all, my ignorance made me feel crippled and inadequate.

Soon maple sugar time rolled around again, and then spring, with its magical rebirth of the land. The Indians—the neighboring Potawatomis and the Sauk and Fox from up north—returned from winter hunting with their fat bundles of furs.

"Looks like you were right again about them paying you back for all the things you sold them on credit," I said as Daniel once more loaded his keelboat for the long trip to St. Louis.

"I told you they would pay," he replied. "The chiefs like me because I give them an honest trade. Some traders give the Indians liquor—and then cheat them out of all their furs while they're drunk."

"What low-down snakes. The Indians know you'd never stoop to anything like that."

The oldest Weaver boy was serving an apprenticeship with

Karl now, learning the miller's trade. A cooper, an Irishman named Norman Hart, moved in and built a shop. Our little settlement was gradually becoming a real town, with cabins and craftmen's shops sprinkled along the green and fertile valley of the winding Spoon River. The white curls of smoke rising from all the chimneys gave a sense of coziness to the scene.

On this trip, Daniel was able to include barrels from the cooper's shop, filled with salted pork from the outlying farms and flour from our mill.

Hugh, a very grown-up twelve now, considered himself a partner in all of Daniel's ventures. He begged until his father consented to take him along to St. Louis. As the two of them shoved off the loaded keelboat from the riverbank and began their long journey southward, Sarah and Eddie watched, looking forlorn.

"I'm sure lucky to have you two here to help me with the chores," I said, drawing them into a hug. "Things will be so much easier this year. Uncle Noah will do all the plowing and planting and watch over the cattle and sheep. All we have to worry about are the house and garden and chickens and the milk cow. Nothing to it! Of course, I'll have to tend the store, too."

The store was occupying more and more of our time, and Daniel had involved himself in so many other projects, too—the farm, the mill, the Indian trade, and selling lots to the newcomers in our fledgling town.

"I'll milk the cow," Eddie said as we sauntered back to our cabin.

Sarah grimaced. "Not me! But I can feed the chickens, and I'll help watch Cinda."

"Thanks, honey. That's a big job in itself."

I smiled, thankful that her early hostility to me had disappeared. Though she was still strong-willed and independent, we two had finally learned to be friends.

Our bright and happy little Cinda was everywhere these days, running with her clumsy toddler's gait, speaking in a never-ending stream of baby chatter. With her perky red curls and freckled nose, her effervescent personality, she was everybody's darling. But we had to watch her every minute, for I never knew just where her curiosity might lead her next.

Each time I glanced her way, a lump rose in my throat. Just the sight of her brought back long-buried memories of my care-

145

free childhood days back in Kentucky. I prayed that Cinda would always be as happy as she was now, that she would never know the hard times I had known.

With Daniel away, all the extra work made my life completely hectic. I kept store hours in the afternoons, sometimes having to wait on Judson Lowder, Johnny's brother-in-law. By this time I had practically forgotten Johnny. When I thought of him at all, it was only to wish he had found happiness with his new family, as I had found with mine.

One day, three Indian women came walking into town, their heads held high, their step light and agile. "Hello. Come in," I said when they stepped into the store. I only wished we understood each other's language better, so we could really talk.

As soon as he spied them, Eddie dropped his chores to run and play with the Indian children who had tagged along.

The three spread their woven baskets and beaded moccasins and pretty feathers out on the store counter, their black eyes shining with pride. "Trade," the eldest woman said. "See? Good. Much good here."

"Nice. Very nice things. I gestured to the filled shelves behind me. "What do you want in trade?"

They fingered lengths of calico and broadcloth rolled into colorful bolts, then pointed to a slab of bacon and some iron cooking pots.

After they chose the items they wanted—and struggled over our negotiations—I pressed a little bag of hard candy in the oldest woman's hands. "For the kids," I said, pointing toward the river where Eddie was showing the Indian boys his new fish trap.

"Good," the woman muttered. "Friend."

Our eyes met, and I felt a sudden closeness to this dignified, copper-skinned woman. "Thank you. Thank you so much. I hope you will always call me friend."

The thump and growl of the mill beside the river, the clang of the blacksmith's hammer, the thud of horse hoofs, the creak of wagon wheels traveling to and from our little village, the children's voices laughing as they searched for eggs the chickens hid under bushes near the house—these sounds gave constant reminders of the realities of my life.

As the weeks passed, I faced another reality. I was pregnant again. Another child. Another branch of my life intertwined,

146

inextricably, with Daniel. Though the prospect of a third pregnancy so soon seemed overwhelming, the wonder of new life again filled me with awe.

This spring I felt much more secure while Daniel went to St. Louis. I shrugged off fear of wolves and prairie fires, for I had neighbors nearby—Karl and Ruth, Noah and Emily, the Lowders, and others I could call. Nothing could happen to me now.

One evening just at dusk, four Indians came to my door, their faces hard and set. They were unfamiliar, not the Potawatomi Indians from our area, but from the Sauk and Fox tribes farther north. I recognized them from their shaved heads and the startling headdress attached to the remaining scalp lock. A narrow strip of red-dyed horsehair, standing straight up and several inches high, adorned with a feather, ran down their heads from front to back. Lines of white and black paint across their brows, noses, and cheeks gave them further decoration. They wore bear-claw necklaces and buckskin shirts and leggings, trimmed with beaded designs. Silver earrings dangled from their ears in a cluster from top clear down to lobe.

I soon understood they wanted me to open the store. "I'll be right over," I told them, holding Cinda in my arms. She stared at them with huge, puzzled eyes. "What do you need?"

"Whiskey," muttered a tall, surly brave with a long scar down his weathered cheek.

My body tensed. "You know the law says we can't sell you whiskey," I said, and felt four pairs of eyes like shining black stones riveted on me.

"Whiskey," the Indian repeated, his voice rough and insistent. The others nodded, murmuring among themselves.

My voice was strong and steady. "No whiskey." I closed the door, quickly slid the new iron bolt, and leaned back against the door as if to emphasize my point.

Standing by the table, Sarah stared at me, looking terrified. Cinda ran across the room to her, giggling.

Eddie frowned. "You should have let me talk to them, Ma. I know their words."

I glanced at the intrepid eight-year-old and firmly shook my head. "The Indians around here are our friends, but these are strangers to me. They might be dangerous. Especially if I cross them."

The door rattled. Grunting noisily, the Indians shook the latch

147

handle with annoying persistence. What would I do if they broke in? My mouth went dry.

"Get up in the loft!" I told the children in a harsh whisper. "Help Cinda up the ladder."

A dark shadow appeared at the window. I glimpsed an Indian's dark eyes peering in at the crack where the curtains met. My own breathing loud in my head, I pinched out the candle, grabbed the water bucket from its stand, and tossed its contents on the fire. After a momentary sputter, the only light left in the room flickered out.

The Indians kicked against the door forcefully, muttering among themselves. Then with heavy, angry footsteps, they stomped off the front porch, and all was still.

I sat in the darkened house, straining to listen, frantic to know what they would try next. All I could hear was the frenzied pounding of my heart.

The hard knot of fear kinked up inside me ever tighter. Edging my way to the side window, I cautiously peered between the curtains. Now the Indians were over at the store, kicking and beating at the plank door. Didn't anybody else in town hear them? Surely the blacksmith or the cooper or Karl or Ruth down by the mill would notice that dreadful racket. Or did the constant drone of water falling over the mill dam cover this new sound?

My fear quickly turned to anger. If those men kept on, they would kick their way right through that door. They might steal or destroy all the merchandise Daniel had brought all the way from St. Louis with so much effort. If they broke open the whiskey barrel and went on a drunken rampage, who knows what damage they might do?

No! Daniel and I had worked too hard for such a long time to establish this store. I refused to stand there like a dumb ox and see it all destroyed.

I sucked my lungs full of air. My mouth drawn tight, my fingers tensed like claws, I seized the rifle and powder horn from the antler hooks on the wall. With a burst of energy fueled with rage, I sprinkled powder into the muzzle and rammed a bullet down with the long rod. Tear down our store, would they? Well, I'd show them a thing or two!

"Sarah! Come down here and lock the door after me," I said. "Don't open it again unless you're sure it's me." My body felt rigid with fury and determination.

"Please! Don't go out there!" she cried, climbing down from the loft.

I clenched my jaw. "Lock this." Flinging open the door, I stepped outside.

Frozen openmouthed, too startled to move, the four Indians in front of the store stared at me as I strode across the yard through the dim evening mist.

"Get out of here," I ordered. My hands steady, I pointed the rifle at the stocky, older Indian who seemed to be the leader.

He laughed, a guttural sound. "Brave squaw."

My body stiffened. My pulse drummed frantically inside my head.

Another stepped toward me. Grinning smugly, he raised his hand to reach for my gun. I cocked it and glared at him, fury blazing from my eyes. He hesitated, watchful.

"This is my house. This is my store," I said. Good Lord! Would I really have to shoot them? Did I have the nerve?

"Go," I said. My glare inched from face to face. Heat burned in my cheeks, but I forced my eyes not to waver. I was certain I could stare them down. I had had plenty of practice on Uncle Amos.

The men eyed one another, scowling quizzically. "Brave squaw," the older one repeated.

A long moment of tense silence.

The Indians broke out in sudden laughter and shrugged as if embarrassed. "Brave squaw! Brave squaw!"

Then, as if they had planned it all along, the quartet turned with dignity and strode away from the store. With my rifle still trained on them, they nonchalantly mounted their ponies and rode away, laughing at their fine sport.

My heart was lodged in my throat. I stood frozen, immobile, staring at the spot where they had disappeared into the darkness. That rifle must have weighed a ton. I peered down its long barrel, as long as I was tall, and felt the muscles in my arms draw and quiver.

Finally I lowered the gun. Would they return? I had no way of knowing. But whatever happened, I would be prepared. Fear had no hold over me when I was called to protect my home and children.

I dashed over to Karl's house and told them of the episode.

He quickly rounded up a band of men to stand guard over the store through the night, lest the Indians come back.

But I never saw those four shaven-headed Sauk and Fox again.

A few days later, Daniel returned. He conferred with Chief Raccoon about the incident, and learned that the hostile quartet were from a village way up north.

"Looks like the Indians like to gossip as much as the whites," Daniel told me, with a trace of a wry smile. "Word about you and your rifle seems to have traveled like wildfire through all the Indian villages. They even have a new name for you."

"New name? What's that?" I blushed with pride, recalling my fierceness.

Daniel chuckled, an amused gleam lighting his eyes.

"Is it Brave Squaw?" I asked. "That's what those Indians who came here called me."

"No, it's *Wawasmo-queh*." His gaze played over my face, a grin teasing at the corner of his mouth. "Lightning Woman. They call you Lightning Woman."

I let the words flow over me like water. Lightning Woman. Yes. Fire and power. Something to be reckoned with. I guess it suited me.

The next time Chief Raccoon and his men stopped by the store to trade, I could see them eyeing me with new respect.

CHAPTER 14

Glowing descriptions of the fertile paradise out here in the Military Tract had circulated throughout the southern and eastern states. That summer, still more settlers arrived. One trail-worn man told us he had walked every step of the way from Ohio, while his wife and three small children rode in the wagon.

150

"Best farmland in the world," the newcomers proclaimed. "Just look at it! Black as pitch. No trees to cut, no stones to clear."

Breaking the prairie could prove to be a monumental task, though, for in some areas the tangled mass of roots extended downward many feet. We were lucky our fields were located along the river, where the soil was looser. The settlers out on the open prairie had to hire a driver with six yoke of oxen and a long, six-wheeled plow. "Gee, Bright! Haw, Brick! Git going, Spot!" the driver shouted, cracking his heavy rawhide whip as he called each ox by name.

The fresh, rich odor of the fertile soil wafted on the spring breeze. Insects, snakes, and field mice scurried from the cutting blade, which sometimes turned up arrowheads and exotic stones. When the plow had passed, flocks of red-winged blackbirds settled down to feast on worms and insects in the dark and wavy sod.

The farmers cut a small tree and dragged it to harrow the soil, then dropped golden grains of corn into the soft, dark loam. "I can raise ten bushels of corn here in Illinois with less work than raising one bushel back in Maine," one man told us.

"This corn is the best crop in the world," another said. "It's food for man and beast. You can weave the shucks into hats and scrub brushes and mats. The cobs make dandy fuel."

Indians continued to roam freely through the unclaimed land. Many of the white newcomers were nervous and suspicious, for they had brought their deep-seated fears and prejudices along with all their household goods.

"The Indians have their own growing list of complaints," Daniel told me. "They say all these plowed fields, and all these hogs scrambling through the woods for mast, are ruining the hunting. And they don't like the farmers digging up the prairie to plant apple, peach, and cherry orchards."

"I know. Things sure have changed since we came here."

"The worst part is that some of the settlers are hostile and abusive to the Indians."

I propped my hands on my hips. "Now there's no call for that. The Indians have already lost so much."

"Yes, some small bands have already abandoned their villages along the river," Daniel said. "They've moved west, over by the Mississippi."

151

If only I were wise enough to solve these weighty problems. The Indians believed the treaty they had signed gave them the right to hunt these lands. What did the treaty really say? The white man's written words remained a mystery to them. Someone had told them they could stay as long as the land belonged to the government. They thought that meant forever. Now they were learning it meant only until white settlers had come to claim the land.

"It's so unfair to take advantage of them that way. Where will it all end?" I asked.

"It boils down to the same problem everywhere," Daniel said, shaking his head. "The whites want land to own and fence and farm. The Indians want the land left open, so they can hunt where they please."

My heart clutched with regret. "Oh, Daniel . . . They'll have to leave, won't they?"

"That's what it's going to come to, I'm afraid. Fortunately there's still lots of hunting ground for them up in Wisconsin and Minnesota—and all kinds of open space across the Mississippi."

"I'll miss them. And think of poor Eddie. Think how sad he'll be."

His face clouded. "Yes, the Indians have always been our friends here. I respect them and their ways, and I'm sorry to see them leave. But remember, Nellie. Our coming has played a role in their departure, too."

I hung my head, feeling powerless, caught up in the vast tide that was sweeping across this land.

Winter set in early that year. November brought chill rains, then gales sweeping harshly from the north across the prairie, freezing the ground to stone.

But the first heavy snowfall in mid-December of 1825 crowned a momentous occasion at our house. My baby boy was born.

Tiny Joel was a handsome child, alert and inquisitive from his first cry. Beneath his cap of thick, dark hair, his face was red, for he was enraged at all this birthing business, just as his sister had been.

Ruth again served as midwife, and the other neighbor women came in to lend their support. "Well, bless my soul!" Ruth said, holding up the squalling newborn for everyone's inspection. "If he's not the spitting image of Daniel Cranford."

He was that. Despite my exhaustion, I had to laugh at the likeness this tiny fellow bore to Daniel. Our two lives were meshed completely now, wound together like the strands of a hemp rope.

The noises, the commotion of five active children, filled our little cabin throughout the frigid winter months. Every day before they all walked down to Emily's house for classes, Hugh and Eddie helped milk the cows and feed the livestock, and Sarah tossed cracked corn to the chickens and geese.

While the other children were at school, Benjie came to play with Cinda. My tireless little redhead was now at the stage where she explored everything, even digging into Sarah's box of cherished treasures in their shared loft room. Hard-pressed to keep her and Benjie out of trouble, I enlisted their help in churning butter and folding diapers, which I dried before the fire.

I sang "Barbara Allen" for them, tears misting my eyes as I recalled my mother's sweet voice.

Emily's cabin overflowed with nearly twenty students now, as more families sent their children in from the farms in the surrounding countryside. One day as spring approached, she met me at the door with a weary sigh. "This town is going to have to build a school and hire a regular teacher next year," she said. "I just can't handle all these students in this little house." Dark circles of fatigue underscored her eyes. Her body looked frail beneath her faded green linen dress.

"You've worked miracles here, Emily, but I know it's been hard. You're right. It's time we built a real schoolhouse." I pondered for a moment. "Maybe Daniel can put the word out."

That evening I mentioned the problem to Daniel. "Yes, we should bring in a teacher," he said, his eyes distant, brooding. "Emily's not strong. I'd hate to see her come down sick."

He was thinking of Lenore. From the start, Emily had reminded Sarah of her mother. Now the child clung to her aunt, imitating her genteel mannerisms and her serene tone of voice. But I refused to give in to jealousy. Emily was a friend. Certainly I did not envy her delicate health. I needed every ounce of my strength just to get through my busy days.

* * *

Summer came. Out on the small farms in the area, the new settlers were building homes, clearing land, and planting crops. The sounds of ax and log chain echoed all across the fertile prairies and down through our green river valley.

Daniel and I strolled through our village, marveling at how it had grown. Our house and store stood in the center of the town, fronted by the expansive riverside park. The large two-story mill dominated the scene, and near the mill and mill dam was Karl and Ruth's house. Beside them, a-ways down the one main street, stood the new blacksmith shop, with the owner's cabin just behind it.

Norman Hart had built his cooper shop to the east of us, and Judson Lowder his tannery farther down the road at the edge of town. Just a few craftsmen now, but we knew it was only the beginning.

I gazed over Eden Valley contentedly. "I can't believe all this has happened in only five years."

"Five years," he repeated, his eyes filled with pride. "Not long to transform a piece of wilderness into a thriving frontier village, is it? We have people traveling to our mill from farms miles out in the country. While they're waiting for their grain to be ground or their timber to be sawed, they all stock up on supplies at our store."

"And it's not just us that's prospering." I flicked my hand toward the cooper shop. "They're buying pails and churns and barrels from Norman. The blacksmith never stops, and the tannery's almost that busy, too."

The brawny, square-built blacksmith shoed the farmers' horses and oxen and repaired their broken tools. Wearing a leather apron, black smudges on his face and hands, he pumped the bellows until his forge was cherry red, turning molten metal into hinges, latches, andirons, dippers, pot hooks, and a hundred other useful tools and utensils.

Judson Lowder worked their cowhides at his tannery near the river, just outside town. He made their shoes and boots and other goods from their own leather. After soaking the hides for months in vats of a tanning solution made from oak bark, he rinsed them in the river, then dried them on racks covered by an open shed. He then thumped on the dried leather with a heavy club—to toughen and compact it.

"Before long, other people will be coming to serve this community, too," Daniel said.

154

I nodded, counting off the possibilities. "Let's see. There'll be doctors and teachers and preachers."

"Don't forget the lawyers, gunsmiths, tavernkeepers, wagonmakers. Who knows what all? Eden Valley is sure to make a name for itself in this blossoming state."

Sarah, eavesdropping on our conversation, glared down the road at the tannery. "I hate those nasty tanning vats and drying racks. Some days those bad smells carry all the way to our house." She held her nose, her little finger crooked up daintily.

"Maybe so, but you know we need that leather," Daniel replied. "People have to have shoes and boots and saddles. Belts, harnesses, straps. All those things."

I shrugged off Sarah's delicate sensibilities. "I don't reckon a little stink ever killed anybody."

Through the store and mill customers, we passed the word out into the community that the time had come to build a school.

Daniel had sold a dozen of his town lots. Now he donated one for a school. In early summer, a crew of men, both townspeople and area farmers, chopped down timber and built a one-room log schoolhouse near the cooper's shop.

When the noisy, rousting volunteers had finished their task, our whole community gathered for a celebration picnic by the river. I bustled around all morning, preparing food for this great and memorable day. My excitement and pride knew no bounds, for this was a dream come true. Eden Valley now possessed its own genuine schoolhouse. And we could use the new school building for church services on Sundays, too.

On the shady, parklike expanse of grass beside the river, the men set up long plank tables and the women loaded them with platters of ham and fried chicken, corn bread and biscuits, and bowls of garden vegetables. Lucy Weaver brought half a dozen kinds of fruit preserves.

While we were getting things set up, the little girls jumped rope and played tag in the park, their gingham and calico dresses bright streaks of color among the trees. All the boys went fishing below the dam, grateful for an hour of rest from their endless round of chores.

After dinner, Norman Hart stepped over to his rooms behind his cooper's shop and brought out his fiddle. Soon, two dozen

155

laughing, lighthearted couples were beating down the grass, dancing to his infectious melodies.

Daniel, chewing on a blade of grass, leaned back against a tree trunk and watched the dancers winding out a reel. He turned to me, pride lighting his face. "Yes, before long Eden Valley's going to be a booming town. Take my word for it."

Sharing his elation, I smiled as I laid the baby on a quilt and sat down beside him in the cool, inviting shade. "All this in only five years. Whoever would have believed it?"

I closed my eyes, basking in the fragrant breeze. The steady, pleasant hum of water falling over the dam lulled me to drowsiness. To rest . . . To drift away on some soft, cushiony cloud . . .

Daniel's voice cut through my reverie. "Next thing should be an inn. What would you think of that?" He glanced at me, his brows raised in query. "So many people pass through here, and now they have to stay wherever they can find room. We always have some farmers camping out in the park while they wait for Karl to do their milling. This is a natural place for an inn."

Another business project? My ambitious Yankee husband never lacked ideas. I suddenly recalled Uncle Amos and his inn and a chill shudder ran down my spine. But an inn here, in Eden Valley, was an entirely different matter. This one would belong to us, to our growing family. An inn of our very own might not be so bad, after all.

"I know a lot about inns. I worked at my uncle's for six years," I said, without a trace of hesitation. "But do you really think we have the time to run it? It's a lot of work, you know. Seven days a week. We still have the farm and store and Indian trade and your share of the mill."

His intense gaze softened. "You work too hard now, Nellie. I didn't marry you to make you a slave. I'll hire some help for all the extra chores. But we could build living quarters onto the inn, and have it right next to the store. That would make everything a lot handier for us."

"And use our cabin for storage?"

"Sure. That would work out fine. And later on, down the road a few years, I'll build us a fine brick house up on the hill, overlooking the whole valley." He turned to me with a confident smile. "You can live like a fine lady then. How does that sound?"

156

"Oh, Daniel, I never dreamed . . ."

"Don't you know this is the place where dreams come true? A man would be a fool to turn aside when this kind of opportunity comes knocking at his door. Now wouldn't he?"

I laughed contentedly. "Nobody ever called you a fool, Daniel Cranford."

A hint of a smile teased at the baby's lips as he gazed up from the quilt with drowsy eyes. I swept him up in my arms and hugged him to my breast. Cinda dashed across the grass toward me, her long green muslin dress and copper curls flying out behind her. "Look, Mama, look! I found some pretty flowers for you!"

Flinging herself down on the quilt, she handed me a bouquet of wildflowers, then began tickling the baby's wiggly toes. Daniel pulled her to his lap and stroked her silky hair, his face thoughtful. "I'm building all this up for the children, you know. This town is going to be the family's legacy. Just you wait and see."

"I believe you, Daniel. I've always believed in you."

"Yes. You always did."

I followed his gaze to Hugh, fishing beside the dam, an earnest, intelligent boy at twelve. Sarah, that terribly proper young lady, came walking toward us with a smile, daintily bearing a plate of ginger cakes. Eddie, still sporting his bear-claw necklace, romped with a group of young boys, laughing uproariously as he played bull pen.

All five children would someday inherit this rich legacy. I could see it now. Future generations of Cranfords—prosperous and respected far and wide. They would never have to suffer want or hardship. Somehow, that made the back-breaking labors, the pain of isolation we had known as trailblazers, all worthwhile.

Though Daniel and I were different in so many ways, we shared completely these dreams and ambitions for the family.

We spent hours discussing the plans for the inn, and Daniel drew them up with painstaking care. With help from Noah and the Weaver boys, he soon began cutting logs to construct the large new building.

A week later, he lay in bed, pale and listless, stricken again with chills and fever. "The Illinois shakes," someone had named it. I called Hannah, the blacksmith's wife, a sturdy

157

woman with sharp eyes and a soothing voice. She plied him with fever root and barks and slippery elm tea, but still his fever raged on and he moaned with agonizing headaches.

His illness robbed me of sleep. Far into the night, I lay on the trundle bed across the room from him, restless and worrying. Though people seldom died from the fever, I feared these recurrences would weaken him and leave him fair game for any other diseases that happened along.

One day Chief Raccoon and two of his men stopped by the house to trade deer hides for some tools and hunting knives. The chief looked in on Daniel and frowned deeply. "Bad medicine," he muttered, shaking his head.

The next morning, an elderly-looking Indian rode up on a black pony; he was carrying a fur-trimmed leather pouch at his side. When I answered his urgent knock at the door, he glanced over my shoulder and nodded to Daniel.

"It's the medicine man," Daniel said, stirring painfully on the bed. "Let him in. He's a friend."

The Indian strode over to the four-postered bed in the corner and announced, "Help Cranford."

He quickly dug into his pouch and brought out small leather bags of herbs, barks, and oils. With an air of unquestioned authority, he took my tongs from beside the fire, dropped hot coals into my big iron kettle, and sprinkled herbs and a handful of water over the coals to produce steam. He carried the kettle over by the bed and tented a blanket over Daniel, so that he could inhale the aromatic vapors.

"This probably would work better if I went over to the sweat oven at your village," Daniel murmured.

"Next time you come. Sweat drive out evil spirits." The Indian mixed a poultice of herbs and barks and tied it to Daniel's forehead.

The medicine man spent hours brewing teas from his assorted potions and urging them on Daniel, one after another. By late afternoon, the man appeared drained and fatigued, but Daniel's eyes were alert, his fever cooled. He even sipped a bowl of chicken soup with appetite.

As the Indian carefully packed away his herbs and prepared to leave, I looked up into his wise, sympathetic eyes. "I don't know how to thank you," I said.

He acknowledged me with a solemn nod. When he mounted

his black pony in the yard, he raised his hand to me, murmuring, "Help Cranford. Cranford friend to red man."

"And the red man is a friend to all the Cranfords, too," I said as he rode away.

Though pale and weakened, Daniel soon resumed work on the new inn. Once again we reviewed our elaborately drawn plans. The spacious building rising beside the store would have a stone foundation, two stories, and a long porch. Besides the roomy combination dining hall and lounge, the downstairs had a kitchen and our family quarters: a small parlor and three bedrooms. An open stairway in the lounge led to the second floor, where the men's and women's quarters at either end were each ample size to hold several beds. Four small private rooms also opened off the central upstairs hallway. A thick coat of plaster would cover the inside of the sturdy log walls; clapboards sawed and planed at the mill would give a quality finish to the exterior.

As I watched the impressive new inn taking shape before my eyes, I felt certain the future of our family was secure.

"We should make a list of everything we'll need for furnishings," Daniel said. "I'll take the boat down to St. Louis, buy the things, and bring them all back with me."

My mouth watered at the thought of decorating this big place. "Let's sit down and start that list right now. I just wish I could go with you and pick out those things myself."

"I wish you could, too. But the trip is so long and grueling— and what would we do about the children?"

"I know, I know." But still I wanted—I yearned—to go.

When Daniel left, his keelboat was loaded with corn, pork, walnut planks, and ginseng from the woods to sell at the thriving St. Louis markets. He returned with everything I had listed. As I helped unload all the chairs, beds, and linens, the pots and dishes and flatware for the inn, I giggled with pleasure, like a young girl. I would decorate the place all bright and cheerful, put my own special mark on it.

Our excitement reached fever pitch the day we moved our walnut bedstead, our bird's-eye maple table and chairs, our mahogany mantel clock, and all the other household goods from the cabin to our new quarters.

How enormous the inn seemed. My heart raced with pride and exhilaration as I viewed it. The children ran up and down the stairs, laughing at the sound of their voices echoing through the empty rooms.

"Come see! Come see!" Cinda said, and took me upstairs by the hand to view the lovely river valley from the window up there.

Daniel hung a swinging wooden sign out front, painted proudly with the words, CRANFORD INN. "Oh, Daniel, it's beautiful." My voice had suddenly grown husky. "Just think—a new home, a new business venture. Just look how far we've come!"

He turned to me, eyes gleaming. "We're not finished yet, Nellie. There's no limit to the opportunity in this valley."

Our gaze held. Though I knew no words to express the depth of my joy and anticipation at that moment, I sensed that words were not needed.

The older children now attended classes in the new schoolhouse just down the road. The townspeople had hired a teacher, a cadaverous, sallow-skinned young man who hailed from New Hampshire. Were all the teachers in the whole world Yankees?

"He's strict. So much stricter than Aunt Emily," Sarah complained at the end of the first day, sighing pettishly as she laid her books on the parlor table. At ten she was as slender and delicate as a willow, fastidious in dress and manner. Though she had long ago accepted me as part of the family, she still viewed me with a resigned tolerance. I knew I could never meet her exalted standards of speech and conduct.

"The teacher has to control his class," Daniel said. "These young ones around here run wild almost all year. They go barefoot all summer. A teacher has his work cut out for him just getting them to settle down for a few months in the winter. Back East, the teachers always switch the students, you know. That's just customary."

I patted Sarah's slumped shoulder. "This new teacher may seem different from Aunt Emily, but he came with the best recommendations, honey. He has a fine education." How I envied him this treasure. I vowed my children would not be denied it.

Twenty-four children, from ages six to seventeen, trudged to school each day. Some walked for miles over rugged, hilly ground, wearing only deerskin moccasins. One family sent three children riding on one pony. School cost two dollars and fifty cents per pupil for the term, and some families could only pay this fee in farm produce.

I dropped by one winter afternoon to bring Eddie's forgotten mittens and smiled at the children sitting on their rough, backless benches. The little ones' feet dangled, their legs not long enough to reach the floor. The older students in the back, too big for their bench, sat bent over, their knees almost up to their chins.

"They sure do look uncomfortable," I said, glancing quizzically at the teacher.

The young man gave me a tight smile. "That keeps them from getting drowsy, doesn't it?"

I'm glad that stiff neck isn't teaching me, I thought. As my gaze circled the room, I noticed how pretty Sarah looked, sitting there beside the other girls, like a rose in a bean patch. She was a bright girl, and already quite accomplished at needlework.

Hugh and some of the older children sat at the writing desk, a long board fastened to the south wall beneath the narrow row of windowpanes. They dipped their pens into wells of ink made from walnut husks, and the quills rasped and scratched against the paper in the copybooks as they copied the lesson the teacher had written for them on the first line.

A group of small children, including Eddie, recited aloud the letters in their spelling books, while a little Weaver boy scowled at them from his dunce stool in the corner.

The Lowder girls, dressed in identical brown homespun frocks, sat there among the other children. Those three girls were easy to pick out, for all were blonde and round-faced, like their mother, Becky.

Johnny's nieces. Had they heard from him? Of course, that was of no concern to me. I rarely thought of Johnny anymore.

But still . . . I glanced at the Lowder girls, and the image of their fair, round faces faded into another. I recalled how much Johnny had meant to me when I was young and alone and he was my only friend.

The lonely girl I remembered seemed a totally different person from the busy woman, the mother, the business partner I had become. Lightning Woman, the Indians called me.

Certainly I was far from alone these days.

CHAPTER 15

Our new family parlor, located off the kitchen in the back of the inn, was a special source of pride to me. Its wine-red, flower-patterned carpet and ecru lace curtains from St. Louis made all our other furniture look almost elegant. We set the rocking chairs before the fireplace, the maple table and chairs near the door to the kitchen. Norman Hart built us a large walnut desk, which we placed against the other wall. From its seat of honor on the mantel, Daniel's heirloom clock ticked away the hours, making us feel right at home.

A bedroom for the big boys and another for the girls opened off the parlor. Baby Joel's cradle shared our bedroom on the other side of the kitchen.

The family quarters were now complete, but I still had to finish decorating the inn rooms. When Sarah offered to help hem the curtains for all the windows, I quickly set her to work. She was only eleven, but already justly proud of her sewing and embroidery skills.

"How does this look?" she asked me a short time later, glancing up from her needle, her fair brows furrowed with a frown.

I bent to examine the length of white sheeting in her hands, wrapping my arm around her slender shoulders. "I can't believe you made those tiny little stitches! You've a real gift for needle-work, Sarah. Why, before long you'll be sewing pretty dresses for yourself. You'll put all the other girls to shame."

She blushed, and a pleased smile curled her lips as she lowered her gaze to her work.

Daniel watched her from the doorway. "Your mother loved

to sew, too. She was always sitting by a sunny window, stitching for hours.''

Sarah nodded. "Yes, Papa. I remember."

I wandered out to the kitchen, fighting the green-tasting bile of jealousy. Of course they would remember Lenore. Did I want my children to forget all about me after I was gone? I knew how much he loved her when I married him. Why should it bother me now?

Numbly I walked over to the shelves and began arranging all the cups, bowls, and dishes. Little Cinda followed at my heels. "I can help, too, Mama," she said, her green eyes wide and eager.

"Yes, darlin', you're a big help. And I need all of it I can get." I bent down and hugged her, stroking her soft copper curls. At least she didn't long for another mother. Handing her a dishtowel, I asked, "How would you like to dry those spoons and forks for me?"

Cinda was my shadow, always begging to help me, to be part of everything going on in the busy world around her. Just as she put away the second spoon, Joel woke up from his nap and began to cry. "Oh, the baby!" she said. "Can I play with him? Please, Mama?"

"Sure. That's a big help, too. Let's bring him out here with us." I changed his wet diaper, brought him out from the bedroom, and laid him on a quilt in the sunlight by the kitchen door.

"Here, baby," Cinda said, running out from her room with the rag doll I had made for her last Christmas. "You and me and Dolly will have a nice tea party here."

As Joel watched, his baby face pulled into a bemused frown, she fed him and her doll imaginary bites of sweets.

I stopped to gaze at them, drawing in a long breath to still the turmoil churning in my heart. Fine home. Fine family. Fine businesses with great prospects for the future. So much more than I had expected when I took off with a stranger. What right did I have to ask for anything more?

A short time later, Eddie dashed in the back door after playing in the woods. "Hey, this sure is a big house," he observed.

"Careful! Don't step on the baby." Though this tireless nine-year-old moved like quicksilver, I caught him by the back of his shirt as he passed. "Stop right there, boy, and wash those hands and face."

"Ah, do I have to?" he asked, with a teasing grin.

"Don't even ask. And yes, our rooms are bigger here, but I don't want you kids to think of this whole inn as your private house. You know you can't be running up and down the stairs disturbing the inn guests when they come."

Hugh, standing in the doorway, laughed at his brother's dirty face. "You don't have to worry about Eddie, Mom. He's always out playing with the Indian kids."

"Only when their parents bring them to the store or mill," Eddie protested.

"Yes, and isn't that almost every day?" I tousled his curly hair. "I'm lucky if I can ever find you when I need you to bring in firewood."

"I'll get you some right now." My quicksilver boy was out the door and gone again.

When all the new curtains were hung, we threw a big house-warming party, with Noah and Emily, Karl and Ruth, and all our other neighbors from near and far. Norman fiddled out his cheery tunes for half the night to help us celebrate.

Already weary travelers had begun laying over at the inn. "We're going to have to find you a hired girl to help with all this extra cooking, cleaning, and laundry," Daniel said.

"Oh, I'm sure I can cope myself," I answered, with a teasing grin. "All I have to do is figure out how to grow three extra pairs of hands."

"Until you do, you'll need a hired girl. I'll put out the word at the store."

I blessed my lucky stars when we found Nancy. She was an energetic, big-boned farm girl of nineteen, with a long, luxuriant mass of dark hair and a wide, ready smile. Every morning she rode a horse in from four miles away and immediately set to work, continuing all day with good-natured efficiency.

When the first light flakes of snow began drifting down one cold November afternoon, I turned to her, alarmed. "Nancy, don't try to ride home in this storm. Stay here with us overnight. There's plenty of extra room upstairs."

"Heck, this is just a puny snow. I'll be fine. My ma's bound to fret if I don't get myself home." A smile lit her rosy face. "I'm pretty tough, you know."

"But I worry, too," I said. "Tell your ma I'd sleep a whole lot better if you'd stay with us when the weather turns bad. Just

164

take one of the private rooms. They won't be filled anyway. Most people are satisfied to bunk down in the common rooms.''

She nodded, and a lock of long, dark hair escaped from the piece of yarn tied in the back. "I reckon I'd have more time to get the chores here done if I stayed over on ugly days. It's too much for you, with your babies and the store and all.''

I patted her strong shoulder gratefully. "And what would I do without you?''

"Oh, heck,'' she said, with a quick toss of her hand. "I'm the eldest of eight kids. I've been helping Ma with all those young'uns since I was knee-high to a grasshopper. Work don't scare me one bit.''

Her help seemed a godsend to me. When Daniel traveled to Indian villages on trading missions or conferred with Noah on the farm and livestock business, I had to run over and tend the store. In the spring, Daniel again left for St. Louis with a boat-load of furs from the Indians' winter hunting, and I was left in total charge of both the inn and store.

The pace was hectic, but I enjoyed meeting all the interesting new people. Most of the travelers were men: land speculators, surveyors, government people, and salesmen. Families stopped by, too, on their way west to settle, or to visit relatives. We even had a writer all the way from France, taking notes for a book about the American frontier.

A traveling Yankee peddler stopped by the inn one spring day, his bright-red, four-wheeled wagon groaning and rattling under its burden of tin pots and pans, clocks, bolts of cloth, linen tablecloths, horn buttons, umbrellas, and endless other plunder.

"Real pretty place you got here, ma'am'' he said, his shrewd eyes surveying the town and river valley as he clambered down from his wagon seat. "Don't know when I've seen a place this pretty.''

I grinned warily, for peddlers had a reputation for flattering the ladies. "Go along with you.''

"No, ma'am. I'm speaking gospel. You know, with all these new towns springing up in Illinois, I might just settle out this way myself. This traveling life gets wearisome.'' He raised his felt hat and scratched his head. "Oh, by the way, you got any knives or axes that need sharpening?'' he asked, gesturing toward the grinding wheel attached to the side of his colorful wagon.

"Sure have. I expect all the folks have some of those. You could keep busy full-time just sharpening tools. But won't you come inside and have something to eat first?"

The peddler hitched his horse to the rail and followed me into the dining hall. "Yeah, I keep busy all right. Don't mean to cut into your store business here, but some folks out on the farms don't get into town too often. Those ladies are sure happy for a chance to trade some chickens or a bag of corn for a new coffeepot or bolt of gingham."

"I know just what you mean," I said. "Why, some of the farmers living way out don't get into town for months at a time. Or just the man comes in and leaves his wife at home."

Nancy stepped out from the kitchen and set a mug of coffee, a bowl of honey, and a plate of corn bread on the table.

The salesman aimed a broad, flirtatious grin her way. "Yeah, the ladies are always glad to see me. Isn't that right, sweetheart? Why, the kids run half a mile when they hear me rattling down the road. 'Course, they know I always slip them a bit of hard candy." He sat down at the table and sipped his coffee with a satisfied groan.

"Yes, you're a popular fellow out in the country," I said.

"I guess I'm kind of like the county newspaper. I pass along all the latest news about deaths and births and marriages. And the ladies always like my pictures of the latest dress styles from back East."

"Oh, can we see them?" Nancy asked eagerly.

I glanced down at my plain calico housedress. "Yes, show them to us. Please."

"Sure will. They show all the fancy new sleeves and tucks and frills. I'll fetch them soon as I finish this corn bread." He dribbled a generous portion of honey over a golden square. "Clocks are my biggest seller. Soon as a fellow gets a little money, he wants a fancy mantel clock."

"I know. I've told Daniel we should carry more of them in the store."

The salesman looked about him with a calculating glance. "Say, you folks are doing all right here, aren't you?"

I chuckled. "My husband is a Yankee, too." Enough said. Everybody knew the reputation Yankees had for being shrewd businessmen.

He nodded sagely. "Yeah, I've learned to recognize the signs

166

of prosperity. When I drive up to some new place and see that the people have glazed windows, I know they're doing all right. And if the man wears a hat instead of a cap—or boots instead of shoes.''

"You know all the signs, don't you?"

"I do indeed. Then, too, people generally fill me in on all their neighbors up the line. Most folks aren't adverse to a bit of harmless gossip, once I get them started.'' He munched on his honeyed corn bread, a look of disappointment crossing his face as Nancy disappeared into the kitchen.

"I don't know how you can travel anywhere this time of year," I said. "The roads don't have any bottom to them. Seems to me you'd get buried in the mud."

"It's a nuisance, for a fact. As I said, I'm thinking about settling down in some likely-looking spot here in western Illinois. Say, you got a bar around this place?''

"No. We sell whiskey by the quart at the store, but we don't sell it by the glass here."

"You got some kind of moral objection?''

"It's not that. My husband is away so much—trading with the Indians and going for supplies—he doesn't want me to have to be a barmaid while he's gone.''

"Well, I guess I can see his point there.''

Just then another wagon pulled up in front of the store, so I broke away from the peddler. I saw him strolling around the valley later, seeking knives and tools to sharpen on his grinding wheel.

My daily conversations with the variety of inn guests and store customers entertained and educated me.

Norman Hart, the valley cooper, dropped by the inn every day, too, brimming with all the news and gossip from the entire area. This big, garrulous Irishman snatched up bits of news like a cow does grass. In the evening, his jolly laugh rumbled from the front porch while he sat whittling on a stick and exchanging stories with our inn guests.

One evening as I helped Nancy put away the dishes after supper, his hearty voice drifted clear into the kitchen. "Never saw the roads so muddy as they are this spring," he told the small cluster of travelers.

"I'll vouch for that," a surveyor said.

Norman warmed to his task. "Why, just the other day I bent

over to pick up a hat I saw lying in the mud. A voice came booming up from down below, 'Why did you take my hat?' "

"Go on with you."

"Well, figuring some fellow was buried in that mud, I quick-like offered to pull him out. Know what he said?"

The surveyor chuckled. "No, but I expect you'll tell us."

"Why, that fellow sounded downright insulted," Norman said. " 'I'm riding a perfectly good horse!' he told me. 'He's pulled me out of far worse mud than this.' "

The sound of laughter rumbled from the porch and warmed my heart.

Captain Joe was one store customer whose visits I did not appreciate. All my white customers departed the moment he entered the store. A towering, fierce-looking old Indian, Captain Joe brought his three wives with him when he rode into town to trade. Few of the Indians in our area had more than one wife, and none we knew had three, but this was not the only scandal surrounding Captain Joe.

People said he got his name when he fought for the British in the War of 1812. They whispered that he had grown rich from selling American scalps to the British generals. And if that weren't bad enough, he mistreated his elderly wife shamefully, making her carry packages of pelts strapped across her shoulders like some dumb beast of burden. In his younger days, Captain Joe had bitten off part of her nose in a jealous rage, and now she covered the scar with an ugly buckskin patch.

His two young wives ambled into the store, glittering and jingling with silver brooches and bracelets. Strings of glass beads tinkled at their throats. Gaily colored ribbons were braided through their long hair, and their skirts of fine blue cloth swung over elaborately decorated moccasins. As the giggling pair greedily fingered through the trinkets on the counter, the shabby older wife stood outside, slumped against the building, hiding her disfigured face behind her hand.

One day Emily stepped into the store just after the strange quartet had departed. "That's disgusting," she said.

I joined her in the doorway, watching as Captain Joe and his young wives rode off down the road on fine glossy ponies—while the older wife brought up the rear on a dilapidated nag.

Her face taut with disapproval, Emily folded her slender arms. "Back East he would be whipped in the town square for such

168

goings on. Can't anybody do anything about it? What about Daniel? The Indians all seem to look up to him."

"I'll talk to him about it," I said. "He always tries to respect their customs, but that poor old woman . . ."

"It's a disgrace. An absolute scandal."

"It is. Sometimes it's hard to understand their ways."

She stood silent for a moment, lost in thought. "Sometimes I get so homesick I could just die. I miss my books, my piano, my friends. Civilization." She glanced up at me, her eyes glistening with tears. "How can you stand it, Nellie?"

I stared at her, stunned by her sudden outburst. "Why, this is my home," I said.

"But you're so young. Just a girl, really. You're miserably overworked, and Daniel's gone so much."

"I don't mind it. Really."

"Don't mind? You don't mind the swarms of flies and mosquitoes and grasshoppers? The tornadoes and lightning storms and prairie fires? The ague and typhus and dysentery? Sometimes I think I can't stand it another day." She shook her head and pressed her fingers against her temples.

I slipped my arm around her bony shoulders. "You're just tired, honey. Why don't you leave Benjie here to play with Cinda, so you can rest awhile."

Lines of sadness and distress were drawn across her classic features. "Thank you, Nellie dear. But I'm afraid rest won't help me."

As I watched her trudge back toward her cabin, her back bent and shoulders slumped, I felt a deep uneasiness. She looked unspeakably fragile. So ill-prepared for this strenuous life. I thanked my lucky stars for every hardship I had ever endured, for I knew each one had served to make me strong.

Busy as I was that spring with Daniel gone, I stole a few free moments to search the woods for wildflowers with the girls.

Cinda was now a bubbling three-year-old. While Sarah plucked a dainty bouquet for the dining table, my little redhead dashed ahead, giggling with delight each time she spied a clump of Dutchman's-breeches or mayapples with their shiny umbrella leaves or shy wild ginger, its dark bloom hiding low beneath the leaves. She snatched up handfuls of tall bluebells and bloodroot blossoms and tiny pink spring beauties and came running back to present them to me.

Kneeling, I hugged my darling to my breast. With her red hair and green eyes, she was my miniature reflection—and I knew we shared an inner fire and fierce spirit, as well.

Irrepressible, ever-curious Cinda. She asked the name of every flower, knew the call of robin, wren, and whippoorwill. Like Eddie, she was a true child of the West, running free and fearless through the woods and fields. Just to view her filled me with boundless joy.

Finally Daniel returned from St. Louis, his keelboat loaded with fresh supplies for the store and inn and gifts for the whole family.

As spring turned to summer, an increasing stream of farmers from the area drove in to trade at our store. Men heading north to work at the lead mines in Galena, as well as new settlers moving into Illinois from southern and eastern states, stopped overnight at the inn. I hung mosquito netting over all the beds for the summer and sprinkled sassafras chips on the mattresses to chase away bedbugs.

The mill rumbled and quivered, grinding corn and wheat, sawing logs for a never-ending line of customers—and all of them stopped by our flourishing store for provisions. Indians came, too, trading deerhides and woven mats and moccasins for bullets and tobacco and other store goods.

A gunsmith and a carpenter settled in Eden Valley. A few farmers from the outlying area bought lots and built cabins in our village for convenience, too, traveling out by day to tend their fields. As the town, a long, narrow band of homes and shops following the river's bend, continued to grow, we saw all kinds of changes and improvements. Daniel was appointed postmaster, and our store now also served as the community post office. The mail arrived twice a week, carried by horse.

One day in midsummer, a traveling preacher stopped by the inn. This short, stocky man, dressed all in black, cornered Daniel after supper. "Tell me, sir. Would you call yourself a believing man?" he asked in his deep, booming voice.

Daniel studied the man's earnest face. "I would indeed," he replied. "I was an active member of my church back in New York."

"I'd like to hold a three-day camp meeting here in Eden Valley. Looks like you folks in these parts haven't had much chance for spiritual nourishment."

"I do believe the people around here would appreciate that," Daniel said. He and the preacher went out and picked a site for the camp meeting in a pretty wooded spot at the edge of town.

Word of the coming event quickly spread through the town and out into the countryside. "Are you going down to the camp meeting?" Ruth asked me as the day approached. "I hear tell folks are coming in from miles around to listen to that preacher."

"I sure hope I can get away to hear it. Part of it, at least. I've never been to a camp meeting. But you know how busy we'll be at the store with all those people coming to town."

"Don't you worry, honey. You can probably hear that preacher from down here."

From the shady glen just around the river's bend, the steady clang of hammering rang through the valley as a group of men put together benches from milled planks and the blacksmith's long, iron nails. Under a spreading oak, they built a small platform and a pulpit for the preacher. The crowd began to arrive on Friday afternoon, their teams and wagons kicking up clouds of dust as they drove in from miles around.

Daniel and Hugh kept busy ferrying the families coming from the north across the river. Soon the smell of smoke from campfires began drifting from the glen as families set up camp.

After supper Daniel and I strolled down the road, drawn to the crowds in the glen. Wagons sat everywhere, covered with canvas in preparation for the night's camp. Here and there a tent had appeared, too. Voices droned as the people milled about, talking to one another. They soon began taking their places on the rows of benches set before the pulpit. We slipped into the back row.

The preacher, his black suit freshly brushed and his white shirtfront immaculate, mounted the platform and raised his hand. The voices of the crowd were quickly stilled. "Brothers. Sisters. Let us begin."

Now everyone took seats, watching with rapt attention as the preacher began to speak.

He quickly got to the meat of his message, his deep and powerful voice rising in intensity until I swear the leaves above his head quaked at the sound. Like the others, I was soon caught up by the force of his faith and personality as he exhorted us all to lead a simple, godly life.

No frivolous amusements, he said. No fancy clothes, no

171

dancing or playing cards or drinking. I squirmed, knowing that his last admonition would be hard for my pioneer neighbors to obey.

When the preacher began describing all the unbearable heat, the torment of the fires of hell awaiting those who fell by the wayside, gasps of horror rippled through the crowd. Some swayed with emotion; tears gleamed in others' eyes.

The sermon lasted over two hours. When Daniel and I finally took our leave from the hushed crowd and started for home, we walked down the road in awed silence. Behind us, dozens of families prepared their camps for the night. I glanced back at the campfires, twinkling like stars beneath the trees.

"Sakes alive," I said, my throat tight with wonder. "That fellow is sure some preacher, isn't he?"

Daniel nodded, chuckling. "You might say that. In truth, I never heard a sermon quite like it. The ministers back in New York could never work up that much steam."

"That wasn't a sermon, Daniel. That was an experience."

The preacher spoke three times the next day and the next, each sermon more impassioned. By Sunday night, his flock swayed with his words like fields of grain in the wind. He closed by baptizing scores of converts in the river.

The people still looked numbed when they packed up camp and left for home on Monday morning.

"Do you think I might have done a little good around here?" the preacher asked me as he prepared to travel on.

"If you didn't, Reverend, nobody could," I replied.

The men from the community gathered for occasional shooting matches, with coveted prizes for the best shot. They went out in groups on wolf and rattlesnake hunts, hoping to rid the prairies of these dreaded scourges. The women, too, got together for day-long quilting and sewing bees. Though I hated to miss them, my work at the inn prevented me from joining in these pleasant social outings, except for a stolen hour or two.

When a well-educated doctor, Truman Benton, moved to town, I knew Eden Valley had really come of age. This friendly, alert-looking young man with thick, dark hair and a quick grin, rented one of the private rooms at the inn. His handsome bay horse, his fine broadcloth suit and expensively crafted boots spoke of a prosperous background. He told us he had ridden his horse all the way from Maryland, driven by a burning desire to help the sick on the frontier.

His intelligent dark eyes gleamed with good humor. I liked him from the start, for his enthusiasm and vitality enlivened any group the moment he entered the room.

"You western girls are famous back East, you know that?" he asked me one summer evening as I carried a platter of fried chicken to the guests' supper table in the dining room.

The other guests guffawed, exchanging amused glances. Daniel, playing host, watched me soberly from his place at the head of the table. Though I really had no choice, he didn't like me waiting tables, so he made certain all the guests treated me with dignity and respect.

"We're famous, are we, Doc?" I asked, pausing to glance his way.

"Why, just look at you, Mistress Cranford. Taking care of this busy place, the store, a garden, I don't know what all. Watching after five youngsters, though I swear you look like their sister. And you're probably never sick a day, either."

I blushed, embarrassed by my heartiness and good health. Everybody knew a true lady was delicate. "No time for sickness out here," I muttered wryly.

"A doctor could starve to death in these parts," he said, with a mocking smile.

Daniel's face turned grave. "Not much chance of that, I'm afraid."

A momentary chill settled over the table. I shivered, recalling the vast assortment of illnesses I had seen and heard about over the years. Typhoid, diphtheria, scarlet fever. Whooping cough, dysentery, pneumonia, consumption. Blood poisoning. Why, childhood diseases and summer complaint claimed almost half the little ones before they ever reached their fourth birthday.

A doctor was certainly a welcome and valued addition to any community. Sometimes the bleedings and violent purgings they favored might seem worse than the disease, but we all knew these were the accepted, up-to-date medical treatments.

"Say, Doc. Did you hear about when Nellie chased away the Indians?" Daniel asked, glancing my way with amused pride. "They call her Lightning Woman."

Doc grinned at me. "Lightning Woman. What a perfect name."

173

Flushing hotly from the unaccustomed attention, I lifted my chin. "Oh, the Indians were easy. Stopping the prairie fire—that was the hard job."

The roar of Doc's infectious laughter followed as I hurried back to the kitchen to check on all the children.

Later that evening, Doc sat out on the inn porch, spinning tales with Daniel and Norman Hart, the cooper. Sarah was playing with the baby and Cinda in the parlor, while Nancy and I finished the kitchen work. Just as I set the last plates on the shelf, Doc called in the door to us. "Can't you ladies come outside and sit awhile? Even western girls have to rest sometime."

I started, surprised, for I knew it was not considered proper for young ladies like Nancy to sit with a group of men. But then, Doc was anything but conventional.

Nancy tittered delightedly, as if he had told a great joke. Her pleasant features glowed with heightened color.

"Not me," I said, smiling at him. "I have to gather up my five chicks and put them in to roost. But Nancy could probably use a chance to catch her breath."

He glanced at her, and she at him. I could feel sparks fly between them, like the striking of a flint. Suddenly the air seemed charged with rippling excitement.

Doc Benton was a young man, no more than twenty-five or so. If he liked strong and spunky western girls, he couldn't do better than Nancy. I hummed a merry tune as I crossed the yard to call the big boys in from play.

After I had put the little ones to bed and settled another argument between Hugh and Sarah, I wandered back out to the porch, itching with curiosity. The small group was engrossed in conversation, with Nancy chuckling softly at Doc's every comment. Under her admiring glances, he seemed to blossom. His pleasant, even-featured face looked boyish as he joked about his recent adventures traveling through dense forests and across vast prairies on his way to Eden Valley.

Nancy blossomed, too. With her blush and glow of intense interest, her large and ordinary features took on new beauty beneath their frame of thick and shining dark hair. And with each passing moment, the transformation deepened.

As twilight settled over the valley, a cool breeze wafted from the river, carrying the scent of green leaves and the sound of

174

rippling water. We were all succumbing to yawns when Noah appeared out of the darkness, his expression tense and anxious. My breath caught in my throat. Emily? Was something wrong with Emily or Benjie? I rose, clenching my hands.

Noah stood before us in silence, glancing nervously at the doctor. Evidently he wanted to talk to us in private.

Doc rose and stretched. "Guess you'd better excuse me, folks," he said. "Think I'll go on upstairs."

"I—I'll make sure everything is finished in the kitchen," Nancy said in a low voice, and walked back inside the inn.

Daniel turned to his brother. "Is something wrong, Noah?"

"Is Emily sick?" I asked warily.

Noah rubbed his hand against his arm nervously. "No, nobody's sick. Look, Daniel . . . I don't want to make you mad. I know how much you need my help, and I don't want to leave you in the lurch, but . . ." He hesitated, glancing around as if someone might come to his aid.

"Like some coffee?" I asked in the uncomfortable silence that followed.

"No, thanks." He drew in a deep breath. "Daniel, I've been thinking about this for a long time. I'll never make a farmer. I want to move up to Galena."

"Galena?" Daniel stared at him in disbelief. "You'd rather work in the lead mines than have your own land here?"

"Galena's a boomtown now. A fellow was telling me all about it just last week. Said there's five thousand people there now, and growing every day. He even gave me a piece of lead ore." Noah's young face beamed with excitement as he held out a strange, dark, shiny rock. "There're all kinds of opportunities up there. I could start a store like yours. There's just no limit to what I could do."

Daniel slowly shook his head. "Well, far be it from me to try to hold you back. But those Indians up there are not as friendly as ours. Not by a long shot. Just look at all the trouble they've had with the Winnebagos, and with Black Hawk and his tribe up on the Rock River."

"I'm not afraid of Black Hawk. I met him and some of his men when they were hunting down here."

"You know Emily's not strong . . ."

Noah tapped his fist into his opened palm. "My mind's made up. If you can find someone to help you with the farming, I'll

175

deed my land back to you and take the cash for my work instead. I'm ready to pack up and move on."

"Well, if that is your decision, I'll gladly buy back the land. And I can hire farm help." Daniel paused, a deep frown etched in his brow. "But think about it, Noah. Do you really believe this is the right thing for Emily and little Benjie? A mining town like that? It's bound to be rough."

"Emily never complains. She'll do fine."

I felt certain he had not even discussed this move with her. She would hate it in Galena. Crude mining camps, malodorous smelting furnaces, hoards of roughneck miners. Painted harlots, too, no doubt. I could not imagine Emily in such a setting.

"Oh, Noah, don't!" I cried. Daniel's frown bid me to silence, but I forged ahead. "You're making a mistake. Don't take her there."

"My mind's made up," he repeated, and turned to leave.

Within a week, Noah and Emily had packed all their belongings into a covered wagon and begun the long journey to the northwestern tip of the state. Though it would be no farther—and no harder—than our own excursion to Eden Valley, the three of them looked incredibly young and vulnerable as they set out. And I was powerless to do anything but wish them well.

CHAPTER 16

Norman Hart still joined us every evening on the front porch. "I heard a wild hog treed a man upriver last week," he told us one night, pausing to puff on his pipe. "Lucky for him his wife heard him yelling. She came running out with a rifle and shot the creature."

"Norman, don't tell us any disaster tales tonight," I said.

"Wild hogs are devilish mean, that's true." Daniel puffed on his pipe. "Those tusks can gore a man. You've got to keep your eyes peeled for them every minute when you're in the woods."

Norman wagged his head. "Wild hogs, wildcats, wolves. No end to the troubles. I heard a wildcat got into a chicken house just outside town."

"Yeah, Norm, you told us," I said, shivering at the thought.

"And snakes! My saints alive! Yellow rattlers and copperheads. One fellow killed a swamp snake over seven feet long. Woman came in yesterday and told me she found a rattlesnake curled up between the logs in the wall of their cabin. Right beside her bed, it was."

I glanced anxiously at the planked walls of the inn. "Haven't you heard any funny stories lately?"

But Norman was just warming to his task. "Worst thing was what happened over by Lewistown. Two wee girls were playing with their baby brother on a quilt underneath an oak. All of a sudden, this giant eagle swooped down out of the blue and grabbed that baby in his beak. Would have carried him off for sure, but the father just happened to be looking their way. Grabbed his loaded rifle quick, he did, and shot that bird. Blithering creature had a seven-foot wingspan."

Goose bumps raised on my flesh. "And the baby? Was the baby hurt?"

"Nary a scratch. Miracles still happen, I do believe."

I rose and planted my hands on my hips. "That's about enough cheery tales for me tonight, Norm. Think I'd better go inside."

Sometimes on Sunday afternoons, Daniel hitched up the wagon and took the family for a drive. One lush summer day, when golden sunlight dappled through the trees and the sweet scent of new-mown hay filled the air, we decided to go out for a ride with only little Joel, while the other children played at Ruth's. As we traveled through the rolling countryside, through woods and meadow and alongside fields of tall, green corn, the rhythmic plop of horses' hoofs lulled me into a blissful state of drowsiness. Joel, just a toddler, curled over to lay his head down on my lap. He soon drifted off to sleep.

We reached the crest of a steep hill and started down the other side toward the river. Suddenly a long, black snake dropped down from a tree branch right in front of us, just missing the horse.

He reared, then took off galloping as if a pack of wolves were on his tail. "Whoa! Whoa there!" Daniel shouted, clinging fiercely to the reins.

We were pulled along at high speed, totally out of control. The narrow dirt road loomed ahead of us, weaving a crooked downhill path around huge trees and stumps.

My body froze with terror. My breath caught in my throat. I clutched Joel to my breast. The trees and stumps passed in a dizzy blur. We were speeding, speeding down the hill toward the river. We would crash into a tree. We would all be dumped into the river and drown.

In a flash of impulse, I lifted Joel over the side and dropped him as gently as I could. Maybe at least his life would be saved.

The horse's hoofs thundered down the hill. I clung on desperately as the wagon shook and rattled.

Crazed by fear, the horse raced to the bottom of the hill and plunged frantically into the river. He struggled to swim. Daniel leapt into the water, battling to grab the thrashing horse's bridle. Finally he brought the beast to a panting halt.

"Hang on!" he shouted. "I'll pull you over to the shore."

Stiff as an oak plank, I exhaled the air trapped in my lungs. My whole body trembled as I sat frozen on the seat, unable to speak, while Daniel dragged the wagon from the water.

"Looks like I'd better take a minute and try to get this fellow calmed down," he said, with a forced heartiness. "You're all right, aren't you?"

"The baby!" I shrieked, bursting into tears. "I threw the baby out!"

Had I really done that in my panic? I hardly dared to turn around and look back up the hill. But when I did, I could only stare in amazement. Here came Joel, a toddler of eighteen months, strolling down the hill with his staggering baby steps, completely unperturbed, his chubby face wreathed in smiles. He looked for all the world as if he thought this exciting interlude was just a normal part of all our Sunday drives.

"Wait!" I shouted to him, smiling through my tears. "We'll come and get you."

Joel plunked his little bottom down on a grassy plot beside

the river and sucked his thumb contentedly while Daniel waded through the chest-high water to rescue him.

By the time Joel was back in my arms, I felt giddy with relief. I could hardly believe no one was hurt. But the little fellow took it all in stride. He sighed beneath my frantic kiss, then smiled and closed his eyes for a well-earned rest.

We talked about his nonchalance for weeks. "I like to see tough little ones like that," Doc Benton told me. "That boy should be hearty enough to fight off any disease."

The doctor spent his days out on the scattered farms around the countryside, presiding over birthings, setting broken legs and binding ax cuts, treating summer complaint and ague and a hundred kinds of disease. His big bay horse was a familiar sight as it trotted down the road with two bulky leather pouches hanging from the saddle, medical bags with compartments filled with powders, liquids, and hand-rolled pills. Doc carried lances, forceps, knives, ligatures, and splints, too—a whole medical office on his horse's back.

Sometimes when he returned, his face was knotted with the strain of heat, dust, and fatigue. Still he always took a moment to stop by the kitchen for a word with me and Nancy. Romance was blossoming between this sturdy country girl and the young frontier doctor.

Our other inn guests filled our lives with variety and color, as well. A backwoods preacher often stopped by on his regular circuit, a lean, lanky man with tawny skin and thick, black hair. Dressed in homespun shirt, buckskin leggings, and an old felt hat, he looked more like a hunter than a minister. Yet when he preached at the Sunday church service in our schoolhouse, his words were moving and eloquent.

A land speculator signed the register one afternoon and told me he was on an expedition through the Military Tract, searching for unsettled claims he might be able to buy. "I just rode down from Chicago," he told us that night as all the guests sat down to supper. "Didn't see a single white face from Chicago to Peoria. Had to camp out and live off game all along the way."

"Anything doing up Chicago way?" Daniel asked, passing a platter of sliced ham.

"No. There's only a dozen white families in the whole town. Maybe fifty soldiers at Fort Dearborn. Forty or fifty wigwams along the river and lakeshore. Half a dozen Indian trading posts." The man took a swig of coffee from his mug. "I tell you, this place here looks like heaven next to Chicago. That swampy land up there is better suited for muskrats than for people."

Daniel basked in his praise. "Yes, Eden Valley is all any man could ask for. We're looking for this to develop into quite a city someday."

Early August brought a lull in the farm work, so Daniel and a crew of neighbor men went out with ox teams to drag and smooth the primitive dirt roads. The store and inn, the endless household tasks, kept me on a constant run. Though Hugh and Eddie helped with outdoor chores and Sarah watched the two little ones, some days the work seemed almost overwhelming.

Doc Benton often stopped by the kitchen to visit with Nancy and me while we podded peas or snapped beans or churned butter.

Nancy soon acquired another admirer, too. Samuel Pike had moved up when his brother settled a plot of bounty land eight miles west of Eden Valley. This nervous, long-shanked young man rode into town on any pretext, always stopping by the inn to talk with Nancy.

"You're going to have to make all these beaus draw straws for your company," I told her, laughing as her full cheeks crimsoned.

In September, another bout of chills and fever struck Daniel. At least this year we had Doc close at hand to treat him.

So many people suffered from ague, this dreadful disease that crept over the land like a giant, vicious snake. Few died from it, but the relapses year after year left its victims weak, just ripe for any other disease.

The year 1827 was a bad year for all kinds of sickness. Just as the epidemics of summer complaint and croup diminished, scarlet fever reared its ugly head.

I woke one midnight to the sound of Cinda screaming with pain. Leaping from bed, I raced into the room she shared with Sarah and snatched her up in my arms. Her skin was hot as burning coals, her face flushed red as blood. She coughed hoarsely, her throat all clogged with phlegm.

"Daniel!" I called across the kitchen to our room. "Quick! Run upstairs and ask Doc to come and look at Cinda."

180

"What is it?" he asked drowsily, slipping on his trousers. His face paled as he saw the feverish, listless child in my arms.

Scarlet fever—that dreaded disease—was spreading through the countryside. My lips froze, unable to speak the vile words.

Daniel touched Cinda's searing cheek. "I'll get Doc. He'll know what to do." He squeezed my shoulder and hurried from the room.

I lay Cinda back in her bed. She tossed and struggled. Restless and glassy-eyed, she panted for her breath, choking on her own phlegm.

When Doc Benton bent over to examine her, his face grew grim. "Put the kettle on for tea," he said. He quickly poured cool water into the washbowl, dipped in a towel, and wrapped it around the child's fiery-hot body. "That should help lower her fever."

"Maybe if I rock her . . ." I carried her over to the rocker by the parlor hearth and began a nervous, rhythmic motion. I sang "Barbara Allen," always her favorite song.

"I'll give her some medicine," he said, reaching into his leather bag. "And if we can get her to sip a little slippery elm tea, that should help clear the phlegm."

I handed her to Daniel, rushed to put the kettle on, and quickly made the tea. The poor, sick child could swallow nothing.

I realized the grim truth. We were fighting for her life. The doctor tried his whole arsenal of remedies as the hours ticked by in a dizzy whirl.

By daylight, she was gasping desperately for breath. Her small body felt like hot coals. I held her in my arms and rocked, my whole being tensed from helplessly witnessing her struggle. If only I could do something. Anything at all. I'd gladly take her illness on myself, if only I could see my child lively and laughing once again.

All the doctor's remedies seemed like useless pap. This plucky little girl, free and fearless from the moment of her birth, now clawed and fought for every breath. Each tiny gasp of air was a minor victory in this fierce battle against death.

Horrible sounds filled the room. Gasping. Choking. Groaning. I clasped my hands over my ears to shut out the hellish noise.

Finally the struggle ended. The house was silent. Silent as a tomb.

She was gone. My darling little red-haired Cinda.

I sank down on the bed and stared into space, listening to the deafening roar inside my head. The void was too immense to comprehend. Never would she see her fourth birthday. That thought angered me as I stared at her pallid, lifeless face.

If only she could have made it to four, she might have been all right. Just a little longer. Just a few months till she crossed that magic threshold where she could have resisted the disease. Oh, the insane thoughts that spun around my head.

I glanced at her little hand. Her chubby fingers still showed stains from helping me pull carrots in the garden. I flinched and trembled with the fresh onslaught of agony.

I must be strong. All the other children would look to me to help them through this hard time. Daniel and I must both be strong for their sakes, guarding our grief jealously inside us. We had no choice.

This beloved child had been with us nearly four years. From this day on, we could only cling to her memory.

The pain was like a knife plunged into my heart. My eyes stung and burned with welling tears, but I would not give way to grief. I could face the bitter tragedies of life without breaking down. I must be strong for the children.

My grief and tension exhausted me. My throat felt thick and full, but I kept my resolution as they laid my little Cinda in the plain wooden casket Karl had hastily constructed.

My face worked with repressed emotion when they buried her beside my lost firstborn on the wooded hillside. I clenched my jaw and counted off the different kinds of wildflowers by her grave. How Cinda loved the wildflowers. Now they would always keep her company.

Stiff as a martinet, I walked back to the inn, now quiet as the grave itself. A leaden feeling came over me as I entered the girls' room and began to sort through the chest of Cinda's clothes. After all, we must be practical. Someone else could use this pretty green calico dress I had sewn for her last spring. Some other little girl could wear this woolen cloak when winter came.

A glimpse of yellow in the corner caught my eye. Her doll— lying on the floor. Cinda's little rag doll. I had made it for her last Christmas, embroidered it with a wide smile and huge green eyes like Cinda's.

I remembered how her face lit up like sunrise when she tore away the wrappings and first glimpsed her new doll. How she dressed it and rocked it and sang it lullabies. Sang it "Barbara Allen."

Never again.

My face twisted. Grief surged over me like waves. I crossed the room and picked up Cinda's doll and stared down at its smudged cloth face. Suddenly I heard her sweet voice, clear as life, drowsily singing to the doll before she drifted off to sleep.

The sound of her clear, sweet voice sang inside my head. My chest heaved, and a flood of tears came coursing down my cheeks.

CHAPTER 17

Ruth and Karl, Norman Hart, the Lowders, the Weavers, all the neighbors came to visit, bringing cakes and jams, pausing to give my hand a gentle squeeze. "Life goes on," they told me.

I tried to take comfort from their presence and sympathy. So many others had endured the loss of children. Yet as the months dragged by, my grief weighed on me like a stone around my neck.

My heart raced in panic when the other children showed the slightest sign of a cough or sniffles. Before Hugh, Sarah, and Eddie started down the road for school each winter day, I fastened their coats tightly and wrapped extra scarves around their throats.

In each little girl I saw my Cinda, recalling the joy that darling child had brought to me. I hovered like a hawk over Joel, fearful that some disease would snatch him from me, too. But this sturdy, spunky boy passed his second birthday in radiant health, his gray eyes bright and curious as a chipmunk's.

During the frigid winter nights, when icy gales rattled at the windows, a hundred different worries gnawed at me, robbing me of sleep. The children's health. Daniel's continuing attacks of ague. The Indians and their problems. And how were Noah and Emily faring? Was her health holding up in that rowdy mining town? Had Benjie found new friends?

Hoards of people had poured into Galena, crazed by the news of all the riches generated from the lead mines there. Already the area's population had swollen to ten thousand, though Indian problems still plagued that whole part of the state.

Indians stirred no fear in our boys. Eddie had made friends with dozens of the Indian children who came in with their parents to the store.

Hugh, now fourteen and taller than me, even went out hunting a few times with Chief Raccoon and his men. They gave him a strong bow and a quiver full of steel-tipped arrows, which he slung over his back by a leather strap decorated with colorful designs.

One winter day when the air was chill and diamond sharp, he returned from a solitary hunting foray, dragging his first deer behind his pony through the thick, powdery snow.

I caught sight of him through the kitchen window and ran to open the door. "Looks like it's venison for supper," I shouted.

His smooth face fairly shone with pride. "I can't wait to tell Chief Raccoon about this one."

After Daniel had helped him clean the deer, they came inside and sat down near the parlor fire. Hugh fingered the lapel of his hunting shirt.

I noticed a little leather bow tied in his buttonhole. "What's that?" I asked.

"It's just a piece of deer sinew, but the chief said it's a hunting charm. He tied it on me." Hugh grinned. "Looks like it worked, too."

Daniel shrugged. "Who's to say? Where did you run across that buck, son?"

"I was out all afternoon and never saw a thing," Hugh said, warming to his story. "Just as I was heading for home, I heard something rustling in the brush ahead of me. I looked up and saw that rack of antlers. Well, I tied my pony to a tree and crept up on the buck, quiet as an Indian. I fired, but only wounded him. I ran up and cut his hamstrings, so he couldn't get away, and then I cut his throat." The boy panted, out of breath.

"You what?" Outrage flared in Daniel's eyes. "Haven't I told you how dangerous a wounded deer can be? Good Lord! He could have killed you."

The boy hung his head. "I guess my luck was really with me this time. Maybe the chief's charm took care of that, too. Anyway, I bled him out and tied him to my stirrups to bring him home."

Eddie leaned against the doorframe, listening awestruck to his older brother. "Can I go hunting with you sometime?" he asked wistfully.

"Maybe someday, kid." Hugh raised his chin and shrugged loftily. "Of course, you'll have to wait until you're older."

"I know Chief Raccoon will give me one of those charms, too," Eddie said, glancing at the little leather bow in Hugh's lapel. "He told me I'm like a son to him."

Our family looked on the Indians as friends, but many of the other white settlers resented having copper-skinned neighbors living so near. When the Indians came into our store to trade for needed supplies, the white women often turned pale and drew their children close to their side. White men grew tense and watchful, muttering among themselves.

It was foolish, of course. Daniel and I assured them that our Indian neighbors meant us no harm. I tried to be especially kind to the Indians, to make up for the others' slights.

But around countless cabin firesides throughout the Military Tract, settlers repeated tales of raids and massacres that happened years before. If anything was missing, people immediately assumed the Indians had robbed them. Farmers complained that Indian dogs chased their hogs in the woods. One man even shot some Indian dogs, then was outraged a few days later when he discovered one of his own dogs missing. And with each field the white man plowed, another parcel of the Indian's way of life disappeared.

Travelers stopping by the inn told of troubles stirring with Black Hawk and the Sauk and Fox up by their large village on the Rock River, a hundred miles to the north of us.

The same tales circulated daily at the store, and Daniel was concerned, for he had many Indian friends. He had met and talked with Black Hawk, too, when that old warrior and his band had passed through our area on a hunting foray.

Daniel always brought special gifts for the Indians when he returned from his keelboat trips to St. Louis. In turn, some of them rode great distances to trade with him, bypassing trading posts much closer to their homes because they trusted him implicitly. Before they left for their winter hunting grounds, he gave them all the supplies they needed on credit. They were scrupulous in bringing him their furs in early spring to pay him.

The Indians' mounting troubles nagged at Daniel unmercifully. "Sometimes I feel like I'm walking on a knife blade here," he told me one spring morning, drinking a quick mug of coffee in the kitchen while I cooked breakfast for our family and the inn guests.

"I know how you feel," I said. Yet in truth, since Cinda died, I could feel little emotion of any kind. What mattered now, except the family's health and survival?

He pressed his fingers to his temples. "Here I am, selling lots in town as fast as I can. My farm tenant's out there plowing up more land all the time. I even bought another farm with the profits from my fur trade." He paused, frowning. "I call myself the Indian's friend, and yet I'm helping move things along so they will have to leave."

"It's hard to figure what a person should do." I bent over the fire and turned the sizzling bacon strips with a long-handled fork.

Daniel bent his head, staring into his coffee mug. "Civilization just keeps moving westward across the country. There's really not a thing any of us can do to hold it back."

"Well, I know people say the Indians are heathens and savages," I said, reaching to the shelf for a platter. "But the more I see of things, the more I admire some of their ways."

"Yes, I just wish some of my old schoolmasters back East could see how well they raise their children. There's never a harsh word or a switch. And look how they share all their food and goods with the widows and orphans and old folks."

I grinned. "I'd hate to have Doc Benton hear me say it, but that medicine man sure did a world of good for you during your ague attack."

"Their religion is quite beautiful, too. It's different from ours,

186

of course, but it means a lot to them. They're not all bad by any means."

"Well, no use fretting, Daniel. You know as well as I do the government's going to move them across the Mississippi. I only hope they'll be happy there, where the land's not plowed and the woods are full of game."

"The whites will be settling over there, too. Mark my words. It will only be a matter of a few years."

"I suppose that's true."

"And the Indians don't want to leave their burial grounds. Those places are sacred to them. But try to explain any of that to these hothead settlers moving in now. Some fellows are just itching for a fight." Still shaking his head, he walked out to the backyard.

I sank down on a chair, aching with regret, for I remembered how much it hurt to be uprooted from your home.

When summer came, I saw the little girls from town picking wildflowers and chasing butterflies on the wooded hillside. My grief returned, sharp as a stab wound. Cinda should be there among them, skipping, laughing, her red hair inflamed by the bright shards of sunlight glancing through the leaves. Busy as I was, much as I loved the other children, nothing could fill the void of darling Cinda. All the color, all the joy had drained from my life.

Hugh was growing to look and act more like his father every day. He willingly pitched in with all the chores around the store and garden and the stable behind the inn. Though we had tenants farming our cropland now, there was still work aplenty for us all.

I ran the inn almost single-handed, for the store and Indian trade and herds of livestock demanded Daniel's attention all day. While Nancy cleaned the rooms and scrubbed the dirty clothes and linens in the washhouse out back, Sarah helped me in the kitchen and minded little Joel.

Eddie served as errand boy, running to the woodpile for firewood and to the cellar for food supplies. But as soon as chores were finished, he wandered off into the woods, tracking possums or raccoons, trying to call birds down from the highest branches as his Indian friends had taught him. Though Sarah

187

still seemed too refined for the frontier, I knew the cloak of civilization lay loosely over Eddie.

The inn meant constant work for me, but our guests amused and educated me. And they took my mind off grief and worry.

We all looked forward to Norman's front-porch tales. "Yes, I just wrote a letter to my family back in Ireland," he told the group one evening as he chewed on a strand of golden straw. "Told them out here in Illinois we have meat for supper every day."

"Why didn't you tell them the truth?" the circuit preacher asked. "Tell them you have it three times a day."

"They'd never believe such a thing," the cooper said, shifting his straw to the other side of his mouth. "If I tell them we have meat once a day, there might just be a wee chance they'd take my word for it."

Guffaws and titters filled the evening air.

"I see you have new farms springing up throughout this territory," an English traveler observed. "It amazes me that so many of you Americans can afford to own land."

"It's not so amazing," Daniel said. "Many of these settlers had a veteran's grant. For the others, the soil here is so rich and fertile, the first year's crop will almost pay for the land."

"The whole family pitches in to help," I added.

"Yes, they all work together to make the operation self-sufficient," Daniel continued. "They raise fields of corn, sometimes a bit of wheat and oats on the side. Their gardens and chickens and hogs and milk cows keep the family in food, and they grow flax to spin and weave into linen."

"And livestock," Norman said. "We *do* eat meat here three times a day, you know."

Daniel nodded. "Horses and cattle and hogs can run free here, foraging for food. The herds just naturally increase year after year. When the farmers drive them down to Springfield or to other cities to sell at market, they figure the livestock is nearly all profit. Most keep a large flock of sheep, too. They can always sell the wool they don't spin and use themselves."

"You Americans," the Englishman said, shaking his head. "You truly are an enterprising lot."

Doc Benton still roomed at the inn, though he was out on calls all hours of the day and night. During the winter he traveled cross-country on snowshoes to reach the sick who needed him.

In spring he forded flooded creeks and rivers. He delivered babies by the dozens. At times he even pulled teeth. The mail brought him the medicines he ordered from back East, and he rolled them into pills or packaged them in little squares of paper. And all was done with the same good-humored patience.

His romance with Nancy slowly ripened. One day while she was hanging towels to dry in the backyard, he sought me out in the kitchen, his head hung boyishly. "Don't you think Nancy would make me a good wife?" he asked, his cheeks flushing.

"You couldn't find a better one," I replied with a grin.

He glanced out the back door to where Nancy stood, tall and regal-looking, her dark hair gleaming in the sunlight as she draped wet towels along the split-rail fence. "She's a dear girl, isn't she? Always smiling. Blooming with health. Such a hard worker, too. A real western girl."

"She's been a great help to me."

"Probably give me a fine family of children," he mused, slowly nodding his head.

"I wouldn't be a bit surprised."

He turned back to me with a teasing grin. "Well, since you're already spoken for, Mrs. Cranford, I do believe I might just marry Miss Nancy."

A searing blush crept up my cheeks. "Go along with you, Doc." I shoved him toward the door, trying to mask my pleasure at his compliment. "If you don't hurry, Samuel Pike may beat your time."

A short time later, Nancy rushed into the kitchen, her face aglow. "Doc asked me for my hand! I'm so thrilled I could just take off and fly. You don't care, do you, if I marry him and leave?"

I clasped her strong, rough hands in mine. "Oh, honey, I'm just happy for you. Have you set the date?"

"In a month or so, I guess. First he's going to build us a house here in town." She twisted her hands together nervously. "I don't want to leave you up a creek without a paddle. Can you find somebody else to help you here?"

"I'm sure I can. But now, let's talk about your wedding."

Before the month was out, Doc's grateful patients had helped him build a three-room cabin down at the end of the town's one long, curving road. Nancy's mother and sisters sewed her a fancy wedding dress of ivory linen, all trimmed with ruffles and yards of crocheted lace.

On the morning of the big day, I decked the inn's large dining room with bouquets of wildflowers and drapes of colored ribbon. People from far and near would join us for the joyous festivities after the wedding—ham, baked beans, and frosted cake, dancing to Norman Hart's fiddle and, finally, a lively Virginia reel.

At last the grand moment arrived. I dressed the children in their best togs and donned my new frock of yellow silk. We gathered with the family and friends and neighbors, all packed into the little schoolhouse that doubled as a church on Sundays. Many of these rough, work-hardened people, their skins bronzed and creased from working in the sun, wore clothes of homespun, home-dyed cloth, sewn by some wife's busy hands.

A hush came over the murmuring crowd as Nancy, resplendent in her lace-trimmed gown, marched in the door, ready to speak her vows with all the serenity and confidence of her stalwart nature. Doc, all combed and spiffed and dressed up in his best black frock suit, took his place beside her, his face glowing with contentment.

The itinerant preacher we had garnered for the occasion looked appropriately solemn in his long frock coat, boiled shirt, and black silk tie. Bowing to the assembled congregation seated on low, backless school benches or standing at the rear, he intoned the wedding ceremony in his deep, resonant voice. At one point, he paused and asked, "Does anyone know of any reason why this marriage should not take place?"

From the jumbled mass of people packed into the small schoolhouse, young Samuel Pike's strident voice rang out, "I do!"

Everybody's eyebrows shot upward. All those widened eyes turned on him sharply—and a drone like a swarm of honeybees hummed throughout the room.

The astonished preacher stared at Samuel. "And what is that, young man?"

"Well . . ." Samuel's face flushed beet red. He shot a glance at Nancy, ran his finger under his tight collar.

"Yes. Speak up," the preacher said.

Samuel was in agony. He swallowed hard, then croaked, "I want to marry her myself."

The stunned murmurs of the guests quickly turned to ripples of laughter. I joined them, giggling with delight as the joy of the occasion washed over me like warm spring rain. Doc and Nancy. What a splendid frontier couple they would make.

I glanced at Daniel. He smiled and gave my hand a squeeze as our ringing laughter blended with the rest.

And then I realized. It was the first time I had laughed since Cinda died.

So it was true, what people said. Life really does go on.

CHAPTER 18

Several other new villages now lay scattered about our section of the Military Tract. Lewistown. Canton. Farmington. Bernadotte. The man who founded Lewistown, Ossian Ross, had been operating a ferry across the Illinois River near the mouth of the Spoon. And day by day the tension between the Indians and the settlers pulled ever tighter.

Problems with the Indians' dogs intensified. One ill-tempered farmer hated Indians—and bragged in town of how he killed their dogs at every opportunity.

When one of his hogs was mysteriously shot in the woods, the farmer's rage reached fever pitch. Two days later, a hunter discovered that an Indian had been shot, his body propped against that dead hog. The other Indians solemnly carried the body back to their village and buried it.

Smoldering with outrage, Chief Raccoon came to Daniel. "The sky is overcast with storm clouds," the chief said, standing ramrod stiff, his black eyes ablaze.

"I apologize for my neighbor. That man is a fool," Daniel replied.

"Times are bad. Dead Indian was no enemy to white man. Now I see two black clouds drawing to each other."

"I will ride down and get the marshall to put that man in jail. Will that keep the peace?"

The chief shook his head once, sharply. "Jail no help for us. Now squaw and little ones of dead Indian have no man to hunt for them. White must pay gold to squaw . . . or the rivers will run with blood."

"I will ride out right away and tell the man he must pay reparations. You have my promise."

The Indian stood silent for a moment, studying Daniel's face. "Cranford brother to red man. Your words enter my heart. You bring gold for squaw, we bury hatchet. Now I go."

Daniel quickly rounded up a committee of citizens, and they paid a call to the guilty settler, forcefully convincing him to pay stiff reparations for his crime.

Thank heavens, they averted further violence, but only by a hair. And, I feared, only for a while.

That fall, our inn served as polling place for the elections, and we soon learned that Andrew Jackson had been chosen as our new president.

"Old Hickory our president," Daniel mused when the news arrived by messenger from Springfield. "Some of these fellows around here served with him at the Battle of New Orleans. You should hear the tales they tell."

Families from outlying farms, their many children dressed in walnut-dyed homespun, thronged into town to celebrate. As Daniel ferried them across the river, someone suggested he build a bridge. The idea grew and spread until finally Daniel called a meeting at the inn to discuss the project, while Karl painstakingly drew plans and diagrams for a covered wooden bridge.

"This bridge will be a boon for the whole community," Daniel said, standing before the fireplace as he spoke to the crowd of farmers and craftsmen, still dressed in their rough work clothes. "Lots of you folks coming to the mill or store have to wait quite a while for me to ferry you across the river. With a bridge, we can eliminate that nuisance."

Karl spread his diagrams out on the table, and the men passed by to view them. Though the river itself was only thirty yards wide, the bridge—from bank to bank—would measure almost one hundred yards.

The discussion was brief. "Let's start right now, while the farm work is slack," one deep voice called from the rear. Others shouted their agreement.

Work began immediately. While the ground was frozen, oxen dragged wagonloads of rock to the bridge site. A neighborhood work crew, bundled in their heaviest woolen and buckskin clothes, assembled on sunny winter days to build the thick stone pilings, lay the long timbers across them, and construct a cover to protect the bridge from the ravages of weather.

Many of their wives came along and spent the day sewing and quilting in the dining room of the inn. The air resounded with the drone of pent-up gossip about births and weddings and the new families moving in. At noon the women set out their bounteous potluck dinner of ham, wild turkey, and fried chicken, with beans and squash and cooked cabbage, topped off with apple and pumpkin pies.

The project had the air of an extended community party. Ruth bubbled with excitement as she came into my kitchen for another pot of coffee. "Isn't this fun? And it will be real handy to have the bridge, too."

I smiled in agreement. "These fellows don't dawdle one bit, do they? They all act like they've got wasps in their britches. It's sure a welcome change from the usual gloom around here in the winter."

In spring, we had another occasion to celebrate—when Andrew Jackson was inaugurated. "You old soldiers should have a parade to celebrate Old Hickory's inauguration," I told Daniel as the big day approached.

The children voiced their loud approval. "Do it, Pa!" Hugh said. "You still have your old uniform, don't you?"

"Can I march, too?" Joel piped up in his childish soprano.

Daniel stroked his beard. "Why not a parade? I'll spread the word. And why not let all you young ones march, too? This great country belongs to you as much as anybody."

He dug through his old chest in the attic and found the uniform he had worn over fifteen years earlier. Though the jacket was wrinkled and smelled of camphor, he looked handsome and commanding when he slipped his arms into the sleeves. All the children stared at him in wonder as he strapped on his long sword and put on his hat with its big cockade at one side and two feather plumes extending high above the crown, all decked

193

out in red, white, and blue. He grinned sheepishly, a bit embarrassed by all the attention, but his eyes looked faraway, lost in memories the rest of us could never share.

"Better let me hang that jacket from the rafters, so the wrinkles will smooth out before your big parade," I told him.

"Hmm? Oh, yes. Wrinkles would never do, would they?"

On Inauguration Day, people drove in from farms miles away and lined the road in front of the inn. Talk rippled through the crowd like the drone of water over the dam. As wide-eyed little children watched, the fife and drum struck up. The war veterans, dressed in old uniforms of varying degrees of fit and preservation, commenced marching to the beat.

Women and children fell in proudly behind them, carried along by the swell of patriotism that swept through us all. Just a little over fifty years before, our grandfathers had fought the Revolution for our independence. Now this great country was settled clear up to the Mississippi River. New towns like ours were rising up everywhere; new fields were plowed to raise food for the ever-growing population.

Land of the free. Home of the brave. How we frontier people valued that precious independence. We never questioned our years spent in backbreaking labor, for we knew we were always working on our own land, for our own family.

Outsiders did not understand. Foreigners, out traveling around the frontiers of America, sometimes stopped overnight at our inn. I heard them ridicule our people, calling us coarse, uneducated, loud. They said we had to work much harder than the peasants in Europe, yet lived in worse conditions. They simply did not understand. We were free and independent. We worked only for ourselves, not for some grand lord sitting idle in his manor.

The people here were so independent, it was sometimes hard for Daniel to hire farm help. As soon as tenant farmers had accumulated the cash from a year or two's crops, they hurried out and bought their own plot of land.

After the big parade, I called to the crowd of proud and excited citizens, "Everybody come inside! We're going to have a party!"

Sarah and Ruth, and her little daughter Cora, helped me lay out cakes and cider on the tables we had pushed back to the wall. Norman Hart rosined up his fiddle bow and found a spot in a corner, where he bowed out "Miss McCall's Reel," "Weavily Wheat," and "Paw Paw Patch." Unable to resist the merry tunes, we all joined in the dance, forgetting the preacher's strict prohibitions for a while.

I talked with all my old friends—and made a few new ones. Half an hour passed before Doc and Nancy arrived, but both looked radiantly happy. Her full face glowed pink with the excitement of the celebration.

"Glad you made it, Doc," I called, hurrying to them. "I was afraid some untimely sickness would come along and make you miss the big party."

"As a matter of fact, I just got back from a birthing." His eyes twinkled as he glanced at Nancy. "This gal here would have shot me if I hadn't made it to the dance."

"I wouldn't miss this party for anything," she said, shoving his arm playfully. "I'd have just come without you. So there."

He laughed. "Sure, and danced all night with Samuel Pike."

Nancy's face blushed pinker, though we all knew he was only teasing. Such a dandy pair, I thought, glancing down at the swell of her full red calico skirt. Was she expecting yet?

"Great party! Great occasion," Doc said, his eyes skimming the throng of boisterous revelers.

"Eden Valley's a great town." Nancy took his hand. "Now, you come on and dance with me."

Yes, this was a fine town, I had to agree. And things just seemed to get better and better. I shared Daniel's pride as the originator of this bit of earthly paradise.

And today was a time for celebration. I left the dancing and walked outside to check on the children. Joel was playing tag with his little friends. Sarah and Hugh talked with schoolmates, while Eddie and other young boys played bull pen in the side yard.

All is well, I told myself, with a contented sigh.

But then, a chilling thought ran through my mind. What about the Indians? Are they saying all is well today?

CHAPTER 19

By 1830, our inn had become a popular stopping place for the hordes of new folks traveling through the territory. Land speculators came, too, out looking over the unclaimed bounty plots. Our fireside and front porch buzzed with news of Illinois' amazing progress.

"Looks like civilization's really catching up with us now," one visitor pronounced. "Some fellows from Yale University are opening a college down in Jacksonville. Who knows what's coming next?"

A stout, ruddy peddler scratched his head. "Yep, and now there're steamboats running up the Illinois River all the way to Peoria."

"I don't regret selling my keelboat," Daniel told him. "Those steamboats sure beat poling it upriver."

A dubious frown crossed the land speculator's sharp, goateed face. "Funny how things go. For years we've been trying to run off all the squatters around here. Now the government tells them they can preempt any land they've cultivated. Sure makes it hard to figure out just who owns these claims here in the Military Tract."

"Folks are swarming in like honeybees to settle here," the preacher observed. "And that's the gospel."

The peddler shook his head, wobbling his jowls. "Swarming makes it sound too durned easy. I came out that new National Corduroy Road through Indiana. Like to shook my guts loose."

Daniel's lip curled in a wry grin. "Yes, I've heard that's what they call it. Shake Gut Road."

"We're getting settlers from all over now," the lawyer said, pulling a deep draw on his pipe. "The first one's were mostly Scotch-Irish stock, you know."

The peddler chuckled. "Yep, I know them well. Irish enough to know a joke, and Scotch enough to keep it to themselves."

After the laughter dimmed, the lawyer rubbed his chin. "Well, the Indians here are going to have to give way to these settlers. Remember how President Monroe put it? 'The hunter state requires a greater extent of territory to sustain it than is compatible with progress, and the just claims of civilized life must yield to it.' "

Daniel's gaze played over the group. He slowly shook his head. "Sure makes it sound simple, doesn't he? If he lived out here awhile, he might learn it's not quite so easy."

As more settlers moved in, the stirrings of protest against the Indians increased. Some small skirmishes even flashed further up the Spoon River, when white settlers used guns to chase away Indians hunting near their farms.

Traveling on their swift ponies, the Indians could cover great distances quickly, and the settlers worried about the warlike Sauk and Fox and the Winnebagos from farther north of us. Many of the new villages had built blockhouses for protection in case of attack.

The government was deeply concerned about the Indian problems, not only for the settlers, but also for the thousands of prospectors and laborers who had poured in to the lead mining area around Galena.

We heard that a man up in that crazy boomtown, equipped with just a pickax, could earn fifteen dollars a day. Up to a few years earlier, all lead had to be imported at great cost. Now it was mined and smelted in this little corner of Illinois and shipped down the Mississippi by steamboat.

No, the government would not allow a few stubborn Indians to block the way of progress.

For some time now, all the men throughout the state had been required to join the militia and muster out each month for drill practice. At first, our local militia made a comical sight—a rabble of ill-clothed farm boys lugging their hunting rifles, laughing and joking as they awkwardly attempted to march in military formation. But with practice and dedicated effort, Daniel and the other veterans finally brought some order to the group.

The government was now pressuring all the Indians to move west of the Mississippi River.

Chief Raccoon rode up alone one morning to tell us he and his village were packing up and moving on. "Oh, Chief, we'll all miss you," I said, pain rising in my chest.

He glanced at me, then lowered his sad eyes. "Cranford and Lightning Woman red man's friends. Your sons like sons to me." He laid his gnarled copper hand on Eddie's shoulder.

"Don't leave," Eddie said, his chin quivering. "Why do you have to go?"

"No more place here to spread our blankets. We go now toward the setting sun. There woods and fields are still as the Great Spirit made them. Here white man cut trees, plow lands, drive game away."

Daniel stood stiffly, regret burning in his eyes.

"How can red man live?" the chief continued. "The bones of our ancestors lay buried here. Make our heart heavy to leave. But we must go to land where we can live as our fathers lived before."

"You have taught us many things," Daniel said. "We thank you for all of them. We admire and respect our red brothers."

The chief nodded. "Cranford our brother. But white man not good neighbor. White man think only of money. Want always more money, more land. Think only of property, to prove one man better than another."

Daniel lowered his head, chagrined.

"White man talk all the time, like woman. All talk same time. One red man talk, others listen. Then next man talk."

"I suppose we do talk a lot," I murmured.

"Whites use strong locks on all doors. I think whites must have many thieves. Red man only set corn pounder against door, so visitor will know he is away."

A lump rose in my throat. "So many things are different."

"For red man, life is meant for living. For white man, life is for getting. Better for us to live as our fathers lived before us. We go now."

I blinked to hold back the tears as Eddie turned and buried his face in his hands.

His jaw clenched, Daniel extended his hand to the chief. "Our prayers go with you. I will never forget you, my friend. But first,

I want to give you some supplies for your trip. Come inside the store with me.''

A week later, another scraggly group of Indian families traveling westward stopped by the store. The men were walking, the women, carrying small children and dragging all their belongings behind them on packs attached by long poles, rode horses.

Daniel brought them over to the inn, his face dark with anger and frustration. "These people haven't eaten all day," he told me. "Their corn has given out, and when the men tried to hunt for meat, the settlers ran them off with guns. Can you find them some food?"

"Sure I can. You just leave that to me," I replied.

A bitter hurt and sympathy rose up inside me as I added water to the stew pot bubbling over my fire, to extend it to feed all the Indians. The thin, haggard band gobbled down the soupy stew and bread and ham I gave them as if they were starving.

Before they left, I gave them a large ham from the smokehouse. I watched them fading down the road heading west, toward the Mississippi River, then rushed over to the store, bursting in on Daniel. "What's to become of them?" I asked.

"I don't know. The government has given them their last payment for their land here. That's going to be the end of them around these parts," he said, his eyes downcast.

We were painfully torn between two loyalties. "And now they're used to trading for so many things they need, instead of making everything for themselves, like they did before the whites came," I said. "I'm afraid they're worse off than ever."

Daniel wagged his head. "The Sioux tribe thinks that land in Iowa belongs to them. There'll be fighting. I would bet on it. And how long before they all have to move again? White settlers are already moving across the Mississippi, Indian country or not." He clenched his jaw and stared into the fire. "I only wish there was something we could do to help."

The hurt weighed heavy in my chest. "Oh, you know what people say. The Indians are only nomads." My voice took on a bitter edge. "They never really settle down in one spot, like we do. They're savages and heathens—and clearly God meant this beautiful land for civilized Christians. How many times have we heard that?"

His gaze was fastened on the fire, distant and unmoving. He cleared his throat and murmured, "It's not that simple, is it, Nellie?"

"No." I swallowed hard as his sad eyes lifted and met mine. "It's anything but simple."

Each one of us will remember the winter of 1830 until the day we die. Fat flakes of snow began to fall in late December, continuing on and off for more than a month. Finally the snow lay nearly four feet deep in the timber, while in some places on the windswept prairie, the drifts had piled up to over twelve feet.

The temperature huddled below zero for weeks, often plunging to twenty below. Accustomed to milder winters, the farmers had left their corn standing in shocks in the fields. Now they were buried in snow, their livestock dying from lack of food. Starvation had claimed countless deer and other wild game.

The fireplaces at the inn burned logs like eating popcorn, while travelers, trapped by the wretched weather, huddled in shawls by the hearth, playing checkers and grumbling to pass the time. The children were peevish at being penned up. My own nerves, too, were frayed almost to breaking.

One afternoon as Daniel carried in still another armload of firewood, I met him at the back door. "Some more stranded travelers found their way here. All the beds are taken. They're going to have to sleep on the floor. And how in the world am I going to feed them all? I guess bean soup will have to do until it's fit for you to go hunting for fresh meat."

His lips were blue, his cheeks crimson from his brief foray to the woodpile. "I don't think anyone will complain. At least they're all inside out of that wind." He shivered as the gale rattled the cabin door. "Poor Doc Benton. He's out answering sick calls in all of this."

I shook my head, stricken by the thought of the doctor braving the deepest snows and worst storms to tend the sick and injured in the scattered, isolated farmhouses far out on the prairie. So many people had taken sick with assorted ills, even the deadly galloping pneumonia, during this long spell of arctic weather. Jenny, my new lean and lanky hired girl, had been down sick with grippe for three days, too.

"I just don't know how Doc does it," I said, drawing my knitted shawl closer around my shoulders. "I can hardly stand

200

the cold, even here inside. My whole body is stiff and aching from it. You can sit right in front of the blazing fire in the dining room and your back will still feel freezing cold! Why, the water freezes in the washbowls upstairs.''

"Maybe I should hang blankets over the walls up there.''

"We're using all our blankets. Every bed is piled high. Now I'm going to have to make pallets on the floor for these new people, too. I've had to put the two women in Sarah's room. Everybody has been going to bed fully dressed in all their winter clothes and still they complain they can't sleep for the cold.''

The muscles in Daniel's jaw tightened as he glanced into the dining room at the large cluster of travelers huddled around the roaring fire. "All these extra people here, held just like prisoners by this wretched weather.''

"I feel like a prisoner myself, having to wait on them all. And with Jenny sick, I'm having to do everything. Just heating bricks to warm the sheets before all these people go to bed is quite a chore. They're getting snappy and irritable, too. Oh, Daniel, will it ever end?''

"Soon, I hope. The kids should be helping you more. As soon as they come home from school, I'll put them to work. But I'm afraid we're going to run short of food if this doesn't ease up pretty soon.''

"What are you saying? We have all these extra people to feed.''

"Oh, I can still bag a few prairie chickens and quail for meat. They get trapped in the snow crust when they light, and all I have to do is pick them up and bring them home. The trouble is, they're so thin now they don't amount to much for food.''

Not enough meat for the family and all the extra inn guests? What would I feed them? Even my supply of dried beans was getting low. "But there're still deer,'' I protested.

"I don't know for how long,'' he said grimly. "The deer step through the ice crust and get caught in the snow, too. Then the wolves close in and have a feast.''

I shuddered at the image. The long, mournful wail of wolves carried for miles across the prairie, haunting our nights. They ran in scavenging packs across the fields, sometimes darting into farmyards to carry off a lamb or pig. They were so starved for food they would chase a man on horseback. I worried about

Doc, out alone so often, driving his sleigh through the trackless snowdrifts of the hills and woods and prairie.

When the children came in from school that afternoon, their faces were flushed from cold. They huddled close around the kitchen fire, crying out from the sting of warmth on their chilled flesh.

An eery premonition fretted me as I stirred the pot of simmering ham and beans. "Hugh, after you get warmed, would you run down and see how Nancy is doing?" I asked. "Sometimes Doc is gone for days at a time. Maybe you could help her chop some firewood."

The long-limbed adolescent held his hands out to the crackling fire. "Sure, I'll go. Just as soon as I get thawed out here."

A short time later, he again donned his heavy woolen coat and coonskin cap and fur gloves. I looped a knitted scarf around his neck. Though Doc's house was just a-ways down the road, I knew the cold would make it seem like miles. Gusts of frigid air blasted through the kitchen when he opened the door. As he started across the yard, white frosty plumes issued from his mouth.

I stirred the beans, then stepped over to the shelves to count out icy plates. "Sarah, you'll have to help me set the table. All these extra people. So much work to do. Oh, I wish Jenny would hurry and get well."

Sarah's pale brow furrowed with concern. "Poor Jenny. It seems like everyone is sick with something these days."

My skin prickled up in goose bumps, though I wore two dresses and heavy underwear and a woolen shawl wrapped close about my shoulders and torso. "It's just too cold. I don't know how any of us can survive if this weather doesn't break soon."

The stranded travelers, all wearing winter coats and jackets and wrapped in blankets like Indians, grumbled as they clustered close around the blazing fireplace at the side of the big dining hall. Under their blanket cloaks, the two middle-aged matrons were almost impossible to distinguish from the men. Daniel served each of the men a drink of whiskey, trying to add a bit of warmth and cheer.

"If it would just warm up a little, I'd take off for Springfield tomorrow, snow or no snow," one man muttered, holding his hands out to the fire.

Another shook his head dubiously. "I don't know about that.

If you try it, you'd better ride together, two or three of you. You have to trade off taking the lead, you know. Walking through deep snow like this wears the horses out. If it's too deep, you'd have to get off and walk a-ways, to open the trail for them.''

"Yeah, and those wolves out there are starving," another said in a grim tone. "You might just make them a nice tasty supper."

I hurried back to the kitchen. All conversations these days were depressing.

As I tossed another armful of logs on my fire, Hugh burst in the back door, bringing with him fresh blasts of icy air. "Nancy's sick. She's awful sick," he said, his eyes wide with fear. "You better go down and look after her."

I sucked in a quick breath. "Oh, Lordy! I'm so shorthanded here. Sarah, you serve these beans and corn bread while I run down and see to Nancy. Hugh and Eddie, you help, too. You'll all have to do the dishes if I don't get back by then. Tell your pa not to worry. I'll be home when I can."

Ignoring their complaints, I rushed to my room and grabbed my heavy winter outer clothes. When I stepped outside the front door, my long woolen cloak and extra shawls and boots and mittens seemed poor protection from the bitter, brittle cold awaiting me.

A frenzied gale hurled itself down the snow-packed road. The river had disappeared completely, lost beneath the ice and deep drifts of snow. The trees stood stark and bare, their skeletal branches forming a pattern of black lace against the faded sky. The mill and blacksmith shop lay silent now, the only sign of life in town the fat smoke plumes feathering from all the cabin chimneys.

The short walk to Doc and Nancy's house had never seemed so grueling and forbidding. I struggled along, my feet buried in ice-crusted snow with every step. Each gasp of frigid arctic air was torture to my lungs.

Finally I reached their cabin at the end of the road. I lumbered up to their front porch and opened the door latch with my stiffened fingers. "Nancy?" I called, glancing around the neatly appointed room that served as Doc's office.

The sound of deep, hoarse coughing rattled from the bedroom at the side.

"Nancy! Are you all right?" I hurried to the bedroom—and froze in the doorway at the sight that met my eyes. My friend lay on the rumpled sheets, pale and wasted, her hair matted, her gown soiled and disheveled.

As I approached, I could feel a raging heat issuing from her, like from a fireplace. "Oh, my dear girl. How long have you been so sick like this?"

She looked up at me with sad, glazed eyes and opened her mouth to speak. Only a rumbling, choking cough burst forth.

"Well, I'm here now," I said, squeezing her trembling hand. "I'll just stay right here and take good care of you until Doc gets home."

I stirred the kitchen fire and put on a kettle for tea. Though she was too sick to speak, her anguished eyes followed me. With forced cheerfulness and brisk efficiency, I busied myself straightening her bed, changing her gown, bathing her fevered brow.

There was so little I could do. She choked with every sip of tea I urged on her. She could not eat. Spells of racking coughs awoke her when she drifted into a restless sleep.

She lay in some remote borderland between sleeping and waking. Still I stayed at her side, holding her hand, repeating tales I'd heard at the inn, making a pretense at conversation.

I knew that she was desperately ill. She needed Doc. She needed some magic potion from his medicine bag. She needed something. Now.

Her fever raged through the long night. She tossed and twisted in her bed, grasping at her throat. Her cough was now a struggle for breath. I bathed her searing face and brushed her long, dark hair. I prayed, I paced the floor, I cried out in frustration at my helplessness.

Toward dawn she gasped in one horrendous bout of choking. I rushed to raise her shoulders, tried to ease her struggle. Suddenly she was limp and still.

I stared down at her pallid, wasted face. Her large efficent hands. Only seconds before, her strongly built body had writhed in battle with the suffocating phlegm. Now all was still.

A white world loomed outside the door, but to me the whole universe seemed black. If the spark of life could abandon this hearty young woman so easily, I knew none of us was safe.

I sat there in the cold silence beside Nancy, feeling lost and empty. Grief for this dear friend weighed down on me like a blanket of lead. My family and the hordes of travelers at the inn seemed oceans removed from me as the hours slowly inched toward dawn.

A pale, hazy sun was rising over the horizon when I heard the soft thud of hoofbeats on the snow-packed road outside, then circling around back to the barn. Muffled footsteps plodded wearily across the back porch. Recalling how I felt when I lost Cinda, I steeled myself for Doc's onslaught of pain.

The door eased open. "Nancy?" Doc called in a thin, exhausted voice. "I'm finally home."

Wordlessly my lips pinched tight with tension; I blocked the bedroom doorway with my body, longing to shield him from the unhappy scene.

He stared at me, incredulous, his eyes deep hollows of fatigue. His clothes were soiled and wrinkled from days of wear. "Nellie? What on earth are you doing here at this hour? Did Nancy's cough get worse?"

A weight as heavy as a millstone filled my heart. Swallowing back the agony that welled inside me, I murmured, "She's been real sick, Doc."

"Oh, no! I've been out for days in this storm, tending to everybody else's sicknesses, and my own poor wife has to depend on the neighbors."

"She—"

Pushing beside me, he stepped into the bedroom. He gasped. "Nancy! Oh, my God!"

My chin quivered. Scalding tears coursed down my cheeks. "I tried to help her . . ."

He seized her wrist and felt frantically for a pulse. He pressed his ear against her chest, listening. He dropped to his knees beside the bed and stared at her still form. A tormented moan tore from his throat. "Oh, no! Dear God, no! How could I leave her here alone and sick?"

"You—you had no way to know . . ."

He raised his stricken eyes to me, numbly shaking his head. "She only had a little cough when I left. Nothing serious. She always seemed so strong."

I stood rigid in the doorway, unable to speak.

He eased himself onto the side of the bed and stared at Nancy's still, pale form. Tears gathered and glittered in his eyes.

"Please leave me alone awhile," he murmured, his voice

choking as he bent low and buried his face in his hands. "I don't know if I can handle this."

Doc wandered numbly through the next day, silent and pale, as the townsmen built a casket for dear Nancy. They piled brush and logs high and lit a big fire in the new cemetery atop the hill—to thaw the soil enough to dig the grave. We held a funeral service in Doc's house, singing all the favorite old hymns before we laid Nancy to her rest.

I tried to hide my own grief and give comfort to Doc, as he had comforted me not long ago. "You come down and eat your meals with us," I said after the funeral, taking his quavering arm. "No use letting yourself get run down. We all depend on you so much."

"The house. All Nancy's things. Whatever will I do now?"

"Don't worry about that now. Just come and have some coffee with us. All the rest can wait."

The weather cleared a bit, and all our stranded travelers moved on, but Doc was still floundering. For weeks he went about looking like a lost soul, hardly answering when spoken to. The sicknesses raged on throughout the area, but Doc could only give them a small part of his attention, for he was drowning in his own guilt and sorrow.

One afternoon he walked up to my back door, stomping the snow off his boots before he entered. I glanced up from my worktable to meet his sad, dark eyes. "Sit down, Doc. Have a cup of tea with me," I said.

He slowly shook his head. "I came to tell you I've decided to go back East. It's just too much for me to handle out here."

My hands flew to my heart. "Doc! Oh, Doc, sit down. Let's talk about it first."

He sank down in a chair and numbly accepted the cup of tea I poured for him. "I thought I could make it here, but I'm just not cut out of the same cloth as you, Nellie."

I sat down beside him and laid my hand on his arm. "You blame yourself. I know. I felt the same way after I lost Cinda. I was just sure there was something I could have done to save her."

"But I'm a doctor. To let my own wife die that way, alone for so long, without any care . . ."

"You were out in the storm, trying to save all those sick

206

people by yourself. Oh, Doc . . . I've heard you say yourself how fast galloping pneumonia can take a person—and how there's no medicine or treatment to fight it.''

He only shook his head.

"Please don't blame yourself. Don't you think Nancy knew why you were gone? She was so proud of you. She told me a hundred times how you had saved this one or that, when everyone had given them up for goners. She knew how much we all depend on you. What will we do if you leave?''

"I just can't bear living in that empty house. All those reminders . . . We had so many dreams. Children, a bigger house, a trip back East to see my family . . . How can I go on all alone?''

"No need to face that empty house just now. You can take one of the private rooms upstairs here, for as long as you like. Take your meals with us. You've helped us, and the whole community. Now it's time for some turnabout.''

His eyes were moist as he turned them to me. "Maybe— maybe I could try it for a while. I couldn't leave till spring, anyway.''

My eyes misted, too. I wrapped an arm about his shoulders. "Don't you dare to leave us, Doc. We need you here too bad.''

CHAPTER 20

The ghastly winter left its mark on every one of us. By the time the long-awaited spring arrived, all the settlers looked gaunt and haggard, saddened by the new graves dotting their family cemeteries. Out on the prairie, livestock by the dozens had frozen; others had been devoured by packs of ravenous wolves. Every kind of game and fish was scarce.

With Nancy gone, Doc Benton's dreams of a large and hearty

frontier family seemed to die, too. Silent and forlorn, he moved into a private room at the inn, bringing just his clothes and a few personal belongings. He used his house only for his medical office.

And now, the growing problem with Black Hawk's band threatened the whole northern part of the state. Conflict had been churning in that region for the past three years. Many villages of the Sauk and Fox tribes had moved west of the Mississippi, as designated by the treaty. Black Hawk and his band stubbornly remained, planting corn and living life as usual at their large village on the Rock River.

They left on their winter hunting foray, but returned to their village in the spring. White settlers had moved onto their land. The angry Indians raised havoc, pulling up all the fences the whites had erected and turning their horses out to graze in the settlers' wheat fields.

The outraged government sent troops who took possession of the Indian villages and set fire to their lodges. Black Hawk, an old but fiery warrior, surrendered. He sullenly agreed to move his people across the Mississippi, to land that had been given to their tribe.

Still, the settlers lived in constant fear of an attack, even down in our area, for the Indians could easily come back across the Mississippi—and their warriors could ride fast and far. Everyone talked of how Black Hawk's band and the Winnebagos up near the Wisconsin border had violently and persistently resisted the advance of the whites' frontier. Some people spoke of moving to Springfield or other points south until the Indian troubles were finally resolved. When the militia drilled that next summer, the men's faces bore a new, grim sense of purpose.

"What's going to happen with the Indians now, Pa?" Hugh asked in his newly deepened voice. At seventeen, he stood as tall as Daniel—and borrowed his father's razor to shave the crisp stubble from his upper lip and chin.

Daniel sat at the parlor table, thoughtfully fingering his beard. "I don't know, son. Everybody is so worried about Black Hawk and his band coming back and attacking us. And there's still the Winnebagos just a couple of days' ride away. Maybe if we built a blockhouse here, it would put some of their fears to rest."

"Blockhouse! You mean, like a fort?" Sarah, a pretty but headstrong young lady of fifteen, dropped the stylish blue skirt she was hemming and frowned at him. "Papa! That makes it sound more frightening than ever."

Eddie wrinkled up his face in disgust. "It's all so stupid. These Indians around here wouldn't hurt anybody. There's only a few stragglers left, anyway—and they've been friends with us for years."

"It's Black Hawk and his people that have them concerned," Daniel said. "He's very upset about having to give up his land. And I can't say I blame him. I hear his village up on Rock River is one of the most beautiful spots in the state. But the government has forced him to leave. Someone in his tribe did sign a treaty. White settlers are moving up throughout that whole area now."

"A blockhouse might be the best solution, at that," I said. "Folks around here might settle down a bit if they knew they had a place where they could go and be safe. But where would you build it?"

Daniel shrugged. "On the bluff above the town, I suppose. We could build a tower with a wide view, in case anything ever happened."

"Papa!" Sarah protested, pressing her hands to her ears. "You know I hate all this talk about Indian wars."

He stared out the window, looking sad and weary. "We might as well face facts. The people are getting tense. Things are bound to change."

"They're changing so fast now it makes my head swim," I said. "Just look around. Every day there's more and more steamboats on the Illinois. A stagecoach route now from Springfield to Peoria. Before you know it, we'll have stagecoaches coming through Eden Valley, too. Why, this place is getting downright civilized."

"Yeah. Too civilized," Eddie said morosely, fingering his Indian necklace.

Our youngest, six-year-old Joel, stood beside his father's chair, looking from face to face, a puzzled expression clouding his eyes.

But we had little time to waste in conversation. Soon Daniel and Hugh left again for St. Louis to sell the produce and furs Daniel had taken in on trade at the store. These days they traveled by steamboat, a much quicker, easier, and more comfortable mode than the old keelboat.

209

They returned with barrels and boxes of supplies and merchandise for the store, including fancy clocks, English china, and a wide array of fine cloth, ladies' bonnets, and quality wearing apparel. Sarah squealed with joy when she saw the book of illustrations of the latest ladies' styles from the big cities in the East.

"Oh, Papa, thank you!" she said, quickly fingering through the pages. "Look, Nellie! See this one with the puffy sleeves and embroidered collar and the tucks down the skirt front? I'll bet I could make myself one just like that."

"You could. I'm sure you could," I said.

Daniel brought me some special gifts, too—a length of beautiful green linen for a new Sunday dress and a stylish bonnet trimmed with bright silk flowers. I turned to Sarah with a grin. "How about if we make a deal? If you'll sew me a new dress, I'll excuse you from kitchen chores for a while."

"You know I'd never turn that offer down," she replied.

After Daniel's return, he helped the other men from the area down massive trees and build an impenetrable log blockhouse at the top of the hill behind our house.

Cold chills skittered down my spine every time I glanced out the back door and saw that square, two-story, windowless building, with its openings for rifles and its tall lookout tower. Its presence spoke to me of fear, violence, and death, in a spot where I was used to seeing only the beauty and wonders of nature. But the other settlers seemed to take great comfort in the blockhouse, knowing that in case of an Indian uprising, they could safely hide behind its solid log walls.

I thought of Doc, riding through the countryside to tend the sick, mindless of any threat or danger. He clung to his noble work as a lifeline, for it alone helped him to forget his pain and loss.

Outwardly our lives went on exactly as before. Birds wakened and sang in the woods; insects began their busy hum. The rooster crowed out in the henhouse, and the prairie chicken answered from the grasslands with his strange, hoarse whistle. The morning glories opened their pretty white and lavender faces to the sun.

Our lives went on as before, but now a nagging tension permeated every moment of the day.

* * *

Fall arrived, and with it a new schoolmaster, Forrest Henley. Although this tall, lean young man was only in his early twenties, his dignity and reserve made him appear older. He had an air of good breeding, with a long, patrician nose and eyes as sharp as flint. I welcomed this well-educated teacher with special enthusiasm, for he had arrived from Massachusetts with a whole trunkload of books.

After eyeing him in quick appraisal, I propped my hands on my hips. "How would you like to make a deal, Master Henley?" I asked.

His lips tightened, his brows raised in surprise. "A deal? I— I don't understand."

"Boarding around from family to family can't be much fun for you, I'm sure. How would you like to have permanent room and board right here at the inn?"

"Well, yes. That's very generous." He studied my face intently.

"There's just one hitch to this little proposition. Hugh here is aiming to go to Illinois College in Jacksonville next year."

"I'm getting too old for this little school here," Hugh said. "I didn't go this last year, but helped Pa at the store and with the livestock. Sometimes I lend a hand at the mill, too."

I wagged my head. "I'm sorry to admit it, but his education has been a mite sketchy up to this point. I was thinking— Well, maybe with all those books you brought, you might just tutor him a bit and bring him up to snuff before he goes."

A smile spread across Forrest Henley's long face. "I would say you have yourself a deal, Mrs. Cranford. I shall be pleased to tutor Hugh. I must admit I was not looking forward to moving to a different home every fortnight."

The following evening, Hugh joined Forrest at the table in our family parlor off the kitchen and listened to his introductory lectures on history, geography, philosophy, and literature. Their session continued far into the night.

By the end of the first week of the tutoring sessions, Sarah was visibly upset. "Why can't I listen to the teacher, too?" she asked, her jaw set and her lower lip protruding. "Just because I've spent nearly my whole life out here in the wilderness, deprived of all the benefits of civilization, doesn't mean I'm not interested in learning new things."

I studied the intense expression clouding her delicate features.

211

"Of course you're interested. You're just about the sharpest girl I've ever known. Let me talk to Master Henley about it." The dignified sound of his title brought a smile to my lips, for he really was a young man.

"Why would you want to spend your nights at classes?" Eddie asked, wrinkling his nose. "You sit in school all day. Whew! That's plenty long enough for me."

Chuckling, I ruffled his dark hair. "You'd never make a schoolmaster, would you, Eddie boy? I 'spect you'd rather be out galloping your pony across the prairie."

"Any day," he said, and took a giant swig from his mug of milk.

Daniel frowned at the boy. "Well, you need your education," he said sternly. "You'd better pay attention in school, instead of always daydreaming about hunting and fishing."

Joel, now beginning his first year at school, piped up in his high voice. "Eddie behaves in school, Papa. I turned around and watched him."

"Child! Don't you know you'll get switched if you do that?" Daniel shook his finger at Joel. "Just do your own work, son. Eddie knows enough to sit still in school. When evening comes, he can have all the exercise he wants—out chopping firewood and pitching hay!"

Eddie grimaced in disgust. I winked at him on the sly, for I understood his burning need for freedom and adventure.

That evening, when Forrest Henley came into our parlor to tutor Hugh, he had two extra pupils. I myself only came to listen, of course. Well, to tell the truth, I secretly hoped that I might learn a thing or two—*and* overcome some of my humiliating ignorance.

But Sarah. Now, there was a girl with a quick, intelligent mind. If Daniel had stayed back East, she surely would have gone on for advanced education. Her dignity and poise and sense of style made her stand out from other girls like a ruby on a plate of beans. But what kind of future would she ever find here on the frontier?

As the evening wore on, the young master's teachings totally engrossed me. I was amazed to learn how many different subjects I was ignorant about. As I listened, I could feel my mind unfolding like a blossom in the sunlight. I glanced at Sarah. Her rapt expression told me she shared my feelings of wonder.

Daniel joined us later, pulling up a chair to join our avid little group.

The hour grew late. Forrest Henley finally closed his literature book and placed it with the others on the tall stack at the center of the table. He smiled at the ring of our enthralled faces. "I must say this group is more attentive than the one I face all day in school."

The fire in the hearth crackled cozily. "Young man, you certainly are a fine addition to our little settlement here," Daniel said.

"Stay awhile," I added. "You'll have a cup of tea with us, won't you?"

"Yes. I should like that."

As we all sat sipping from my best Blue Willow cups, the young man told us of his home near the Massachusetts seacoast, of his schooling there, and of his lengthy trip out to Illinois by steamboat and stagecoach.

Sarah grew tense with excitement. "Someday I plan to go back East. I still remember the pretty towns . . . with brick houses and steepled churches."

Forrest pulled a wooden flute from his deep coat pocket. "Do you mind if I play a tune or two?" he asked.

"Please do," Sarah said, clasping her hands together. Her eyes glowed, filled with admiration for this talented young man. Without her customary disapproving frown, the girl looked almost beautiful.

A smile quivered on my lips as I poured us all another cup of tea.

Later that night, I stood in my dressing gown before our bedroom mirror and brushed out my long hair. Daniel stepped up behind me and wrapped his arms around my waist. "Things are opening up here, aren't they? One day this place won't be much different from the East."

I leaned my head back against the warmth of his strong chest, smiling at his reflection in the mirror. "Maybe this civilization business isn't so bad, after all," I murmured, and turned into his embrace.

CHAPTER 21

By the spring of 1832, most of our Potawatomi Indian neighbors had moved across the Mississippi River or to the northern part of the state. More and more white settlers were also moving into northern Illinois, and they demanded protection from the government. Fort Armstrong on Rock Island in the Mississippi River, close to Black Hawk's old village, was manned with soldiers to keep the peace.

But now rumors were rampant that Black Hawk and his band of Sauk and Fox were once again returning to their village, this time bringing six hundred warriors.

"If Black Hawk comes back across the river, it will mean war," Daniel told me. "I hate to even think about it."

One morning in late March, I was hanging laundry outside, glorying in the fragrant southern breeze that stirred the air with promise of the balmy days ahead. Suddenly the sound of galloping hoofbeats echoed through the valley. I ran out front and saw a lone rider, sweaty and disheveled, tear into town and leap off his horse. "Indians!" he shouted. "Run for your lives!"

My heart lurched painfully. "Where? Where?" I asked—in unison with the startled townspeople swarming around the stranger.

"Canton! I heard them shooting over near there! And the grass was all mashed down! Must have been a whole tribe riding through the prairie!" The man raced up the street, spreading the alarm at the inn, the mill, the cooper's, and the blacksmith shop.

My pulse raced with panic. I ran into the kitchen, yelling to

Jenny and our inn guests, then took off for the school to get the kids.

Within seconds, the whole village was in pandemonium. Students, white-faced with terror, poured out of the schoolhouse door and scrambled for home. Men and women grabbed up food and supplies and scurried up the hill to the blockhouse, hugging babies to their bosoms, dragging frightened toddlers by the hand.

All our inn guests quickly buckled saddles on their horses and fled southward, away from any threat of hostile Indians. Some families from area farms, too, threw a few possessions into wagons, hitched up, and galloped toward Havana, where the ferry crossed the Illinois River on the road to Springfield.

Sarah, Eddie, and Joel flew in from school and hovered around me, panting, their faces pallid. "How close are the Indians? What can we do?" Sarah asked, her voice quavering.

I steeled myself and tried to remain calm in the midst of all the chaos. "Don't you kids worry your heads about this. We've lived among these Indians for over ten years. You know they'd never harm us." I only wished I felt as assured as I sounded.

Daniel hurried over from the store with Hugh. "Take the kids up to the blockhouse," he said, clenching his jaw grimly. "I'll stay out here and see what happens. I know all these Indians. I can talk to them."

"I'll stay, too. They're my friends," Eddie said. This tall fourteen-year-old looked fearless as he fingered the old bear-claw necklace he still wore every day.

Hugh drew himself up soldier straight. "Count me in."

"All right, boys. We're in this together," Daniel said, gazing proudly at his sons. "Nellie, you'd better take Sarah and Joel on up to the blockhouse now."

My heart clutched with fear for them, but I knew argument was useless. I dared not think about what lay ahead. "For heaven's sake, be careful." I quickly wrapped some cold corn bread and cheese in a dishtowel, took Joel's hand, and started out the door. Sarah followed, fretting, carrying the pail of drinking water.

We slipped on the damp, muddy hillside as we ran up to the blockhouse. Inside, over a dozen families clustered in tight, milling groups, whispering as if hostile Indians were already gathering outside the thick log walls.

At intervals, the Weavers and scores of other terrified settlers poured in from outlying farms. All the men, loaded rifles in hand, took up posts at the loopholes around the log walls of the blockhouse.

Babies sensed the overriding fear and tension and squalled in shrill protest. Eyes round with panic, people massed together, speaking in strained whispers.

"You know, the Indians killed fifteen hundred whites down in southern Illinois back in the early days," Mrs. Lowder rasped, clutching her towheaded children close to her sides.

Ruth nodded shakily, her hand holding Cora's in a death grip. "Yeah, and there was all kinds of Indian troubles around here in the War of 1812. Why, the soldiers had to burn down Peoria to keep those French people there from selling arms to the Indians."

Tears welled in the stricken eyes of a young farm wife. "They take hostages! They always kidnap the women and children!" She buried her face in her hands, sobbing hysterically.

"Now, now. A hundred grizzly bears couldn't break into this blockhouse," I murmured, wrapping my arm around her quaking shoulders.

I glanced around the thick log walls surrounding us. Yes, surely we were safe here, I told myself, trying to dismiss the thought of fires set by Indians shooting burning arrows.

Karl Schulmann, still covered with mill dust, manned the lookout tower, squinting to peer into the distance. "Damned redskins," he muttered. "Ve gave them all that land across the Mississippi. Vhy can't they just stay over there vhere they belong?"

"Can't never trust them," Judson Fowler said, his fingers wrapped tight around the barrel of his gun. "They sign a treaty, take the money for this land, and still they want to claim it for their own."

Karl bobbed his head. "I told Daniel that a hundred times. But no. He thinks they're fine people. Huh! Maybe this time he'll see things different."

The level of fear and anger rose by the moment. Some settlers paced the rough floorboards, muttering to themselves. A few young girls wept and trembled. I tried to comfort them, but many others stood immobile, frozen with anxiety. I felt fear, too, but mainly confusion. And sadness that the conflicts between our two peoples had finally come to this.

216

Darkness fell. Where were Daniel and the boys? Someday his stubborn courage would be the death of him. And yet in my heart I knew I wouldn't change him for the world.

Outside the blockhouse, only the gentle night sounds of owls and ducks and frogs down by the river broke the silence. The women argued over spots where they might spread their quilts and blankets on the crowded floor and lay their overwrought children down to rest. Sarah and Joel stuck close to my side as we finally lay down, fully dressed, and tried to close our eyes and shut out all our fears.

Men massed near the loopholes, their rifles loaded and at the ready for the anticipated attack. All night the restless vigilantes tensely smoked their pipes, murmuring and growling among themselves.

Babies bawled; older children whimpered at the slightest noise. I heard Doc's soothing voice, comforting them in the dark. My thoughts and prayers were all with Daniel and the boys.

Dawn broke, pale rose and gold-streaked across the eastern sky. Outside the blockhouse, the cool, dewy air hummed with silence.

At early morn, Daniel climbed the hill to the blockhouse and tapped on the tiny wooden peep door in the gate. Karl unlocked the opening from inside. "I haven't seen or heard a thing out here," Daniel told him. "I'm going to ride over to Canton and see what happened there."

I rushed out to Daniel. "No! You mustn't go," I said. "It's too dangerous."

He took me by the shoulders and looked into my eyes. "Where's my brave Lightning Woman? You know somebody has to go. You can't all stay locked up here forever."

Lowering my eyes, I nodded reluctantly.

Karl pushed open the blockhouse gate. "Bring your boys up here to help protect these settlers. I'll ride along vith you, old friend," he said, his jaw set, his face pale as a man going to the gallows. "But I varn you, if I see any Indians, I'm not going to look on them as my friends."

After the two men rode off toward Canton, the deadly anxiety again enshrouded the milling refugees inside the walls of the blockhouse. Hours dragged by with painful slowness. Men, women, children, babies—all crowded together in that small space, their nerves like coiled springs, everyone exhausted, dirty, hungry, thirsty.

Where was Daniel? Were the Indians lying in hiding somewhere, just waiting to ambush the first whites who came by?

Hugh and Eddie scurried down to the inn and garnered baskets of food supplies for the settlers. Some men emptied the smelly slop jars, others ran to fill the water pails at the spring.

No one dared to venture a guess at how many hours—or days—we would have to spend in these impossibly cramped quarters.

By late afternoon, I felt certain my nerves could not take this suspense another second. Suddenly Norman Hart, in the lookout tower, gave a yell. "There's Daniel and Karl! They're coming! Now we'll hear what's going on!"

Someone sprang open the gate, and I dashed out, the first of our beleaguered group to meet the men as they galloped up to the blockhouse.

"Are you all right?" I asked frantically.

But everybody was shouting at the same time. "What happened?" "Is Canton still standing?" "Were many killed?"

Rubbing his beard, Daniel smiled wearily at me. He scanned the upturned, taut faces of the crowd. "Everybody's fine. The folks over there took to their blockhouse, just like we did when that fellow spread the alarm."

A voice shouted from the rear. "You mean there wasn't any massacre?"

Daniel climbed down from his horse and looked from face to face, shaking his head. "You folks won't believe me when I tell you what happened."

"Well, come on and tell us!" somebody yelled.

He blew out a long exhalation. "I asked all around. Nobody seemed to know anything about any Indian attack. Finally I discovered that those shots the fellow heard yesterday were just some hunters shooting squirrels in the timber near Canton."

My chin dropped. A murmur of disbelief swept through the crowd.

"But he saw marks in the prairie grass!" Mrs. Lowder shouted.

"Yeah! Those Indians are probably out spying right now," the blacksmith said. "Probably planning their raid for tonight."

Daniel chuckled wryly. "It didn't take me long to learn how the prairie grass got tromped down. A troop of militia from

218

Beardstown rode through there just the day before. They were on their way up to Rock Island—to fight against Black Hawk if he comes back.''

I felt relief pour over me like rain after a drought.

"You mean there're no Indians around here?" Ruth asked dubiously.

"No. That fellow just let his imagination get away from him," Daniel replied.

"Well! Of all things! We might all have died of fright," I said, my cheeks burning with rage.

Angry mutterings hummed throughout the throng of settlers. "A blasted mistake by some sniveling coward! That's all it was!"

"I'd like to get my hands on that guy."

"If he comes this way again, I'll show him an Indian raid!''

Some people laughed. Others, like me, wanted to strike out and find the villain who had spread the false alarm. Gradually the weary refugees began to gather up their blankets and the meager store of food and other belongings they had brought with them.

"I've never seen so durn much fright and turmoil over anything," I muttered to Ruth as we headed down the hill.

Clinging to little Cora's hand, she glanced back over her shoulder warily. "Next time we might not be so lucky," she replied.

I prayed fervently there would be no next time.

The children and I were giddy with relief as we settled back in our quarters at the inn. But that evening, Daniel stared morosely into the fire. "This whole top half of the state is nothing but a powder keg," he muttered.

I glanced at him, sharing his gloomy mood. "That silly episode just shows how touchy the situation really is around here.''

"All the Indians are going to have to leave for good, aren't they, Pa?" Eddie asked, his eyes sad and distant-looking. He already missed his Indian friends.

Still concentrating on the orange flames, Daniel nodded slowly. "That's the way it's going to be, son.''

"Maybe they'll be happy across the Mississippi," Sarah said. "After all, they can still hunt and fish and raise corn over there.''

"That land is not so bad, is it, Pa?" Hugh asked.

His father shrugged. "I guess that depends on which side of the fence you're standing on. The Indians resent being pushed farther and farther west. Black Hawk's tribe has had a village by the Rock River for years. They had hundreds of lodges there. Their dead are buried there, too, and you know how much that means to them."

"In their religion, burial grounds are sacred places," Eddie said softly.

Daniel nodded. "Yes, they go there and commune with the spirits of their ancestors before all the important events in their lives."

I silently chewed my lower lip, knowing nothing I could say would dilute the graveness of this matter. I felt confused, torn in two like a sheet of foolscap paper.

"I can't say I blame Black Hawk for wanting to keep his place up by Rock River," Daniel continued. "From what I've heard, they have acres of fine cornfields there, and a big bluegrass meadow for their horses. That river is just teeming with fish."

"And it's their home," I murmured.

Musing, Daniel lit his pipe and puffed. "I only wish there was something I could do to help before this turns into a real shooting war."

"Oh, Daniel . . ." The knot in my throat choked off my voice. My heart ached for him, for I shared his deep affection for the Indians. Yet those tribes had signed treaties and sold away their rights to the land. Now hoards of white settlers were pouring in to file claims, build cabins, and plow the rich Illinois soil. I knew with chill certainty this unrelenting white tide would never be stemmed.

By April, we heard scattered reports of alarming news. Black Hawk had crossed the Mississippi at Yellow Banks, into Illinois. He was heading toward his old village with over a thousand followers, many of them women and children. The men did not wear war paint and ignored any whites they saw along the way.

Still, the settlers were convinced that war and massacre were imminent. They sent down an urgent alarm to the governor, pleading for armed protection. Throughout the whole territory, the whites chopped down trees and hastily built new forts, blockhouses, and stockades.

The governor, outraged by the old warrior's defiance, immediately called out the militia. The U.S. Army, equally determined to confront and forcefully remove Black Hawk and his

people, sent heavily armed troops by steamboat up the Mississippi from St. Louis.

Hugh, just turned eighteen, was called out with his regiment
of local militia. Much as he objected to the whole idea of this
war, he had no choice but to ride off with his friends. The other
boys were jocular, looking on the expedition as a lark, an extended picnic away from spring planting chores. But Hugh's face
was pale, his lips pinched into a tight line as he packed a few
clothes and personal belongings into his saddlebags and rode
away to join the troops.

I ached with sympathy when I watched him leave, for I knew
how torn he was by this deadly conflict.

After Hugh left, Daniel stood on the front porch, staring morosely down the empty road after him. "Come inside," I said
gently, taking his arm. "I've just made a fresh pot of coffee."

His head was bowed, his back bent. His face was sallow and
gaunt from his repeated bouts of ague. Grimacing as if in pain,
he grabbed the porch rail and clung to it tightly. "It's so hard for
the boy. We've been friends with the Indians for so long."

"I know. It's tearing him apart. I only hope the thing will be
over soon. Maybe they can get Black Hawk to turn around before it's too late."

Daniel's gaze rested on my face. "I have to go up north, too,"
he said softly.

His words struck me like an ax cut. Fighting my shock, I
glared at him with all the force and anger I could muster. "Daniel Cranford! You're forty-five years old. You have three other
kids here, and a store and inn and farm to run. You've just said
how long we've been friends with the Indians. You've got no
business running off to that darned war. It's bad enough that
Hugh has to go."

"I need to go up to the fort at Rock Island. Not to fight, but
to try to help negotiate."

"What possible good can you do?" I demanded. "They've
got themselves a war going on up there now."

"If they'll just let me through, maybe I can locate Black
Hawk." He spoke rapidly, his voice urgent and determined. "I
know those Indians. I can speak their language. I can try to talk
him and his people into some kind of compromise."

"Oh, Daniel, don't go. It's terribly dangerous."

"If somebody doesn't do something quick, the soldiers and

Indians will start shooting at one another, hundreds will be killed. Men, women, children. Who knows how many will die before it's through? I have to go—to see if there is anything I can do to help prevent the death and destruction.''

When I heard the firm conviction in his voice, I knew that nothing would hold him back. This conflict of divided loyalties had been eating at him as cruelly as his yearly seige of chills and fever. He could think of nothing else until this turmoil was resolved.

"Then go," I said softly, and slipped my hand into his. "I can handle things here."

His callused fingers squeezed mine. "I depend on you so much, don't I? At least I can find you someone to help with all the heavy work while I'm gone."

Pain-narrowed eyes rested on my face, softened with gratitude for my understanding. I felt closer to him at that moment than I ever had in all our eleven years together.

Daniel and I were a team, despite our many differences, despite the fact that he was sixteen years older than me. We had shared our bed and board, had lost two little ones, had watched four other children grow and thrive under our care. The strange events that had brought us together were long forgotten in the press of daily burdens. Lenore lay buried in some secret room of his heart, just as Johnny was in mine.

Silently I filled his saddlebags with food and extra clothes for the long ride up to Rock Island. As I watched him mount his horse, my heart ached to call out to him. Daniel was a good man, through and through. How I longed to tell him of the depth of my affection, longed to hear him speak to me some tender words of love. But that was never our way.

He gazed at me with a slight smile, his gray eyes dimmed with sadness. I promised to watch over the family and the businesses. He promised he would hurry home. "Be careful," I said, choking with emotion.

"I will." His gaze held mine for a long moment. "I owe you so much, Nellie. When this mess is over, we'll take a little trip, do something special."

I nodded, blinking back tears. "Yes. Yes, we'll do that."

Tightening his lips, he waved and rode away.

* * *

Three months passed. Karl and the other townspeople avoided mention of Daniel around me, but I felt disapproval in their strained silence and taut faces. They thought he was a fool for pleading for the Indians' sake. They would all be glad to have the Indians finally gone from Illinois for good.

"The people around here think Papa is slightly mad on the subject of the Indians," Sarah told me.

Eddie's eyes blazed fire. "He is not! He's the only one with any sense!"

"We can all hold our heads real high," I said. "We're proud of your pa. Nobody else has his sense of justice, that's all. Nobody else is half as brave."

Sarah and Eddie pitched in to help me run the store and inn. My hired girl came every day, and even the schoolmaster, Forrest Henley, took over some heavy chores, rumpling his fancy broadcloth suit in the process. Still, the constant press of work occupied me sixteen hours a day. I became snappy with the kids, barely able to get through my chores for the weight of worry.

During the dark, lonely nighttime hours, I lay awake, tossing on sweat-dampened sheets. Images of young Hugh, of all the horrors of war, flashed through my head. Daniel, up there at Fort Armstrong. Or worse yet, riding across the embattled countryside, searching for Black Hawk and his desperate band.

"You're getting awfully thin, Nellie," Doc observed one day.

"I can't sleep. All this worry is eating holes in my stomach."

"Just slow down a little. Let me give you something to soothe your nerves."

But not even Doc's friendly counsel and his potions could comfort me.

The mail was unreliable, and news from the war up north was hard to come by. I heard only fragments from travelers passing through. The heavy spring rains had turned the roads into a sea of mud, slowing travel and adding to the difficulties.

In May, I heard conflicting reports about the Battle of Stillman's Run, a confused, mishmash affair. "It was a massacre!" a man passing through told me. "Over a thousand Indians attacked the troops."

"It wasn't Hugh's division, was it?" Thankfully they had not been involved in the battle.

Later I learned the truth about Stillman's Run. Only forty Indians, bellowing fearful war whoops, had chased off over three

223

hundred white troops. The inexperienced militia soldiers fled in terror, galloping full speed to Dixon's Ferry. Black Hawk, old and tired, then disappeared, and four thousand soldiers and militia rode out in all directions, searching for the aged warrior.

A short time later, the post rider brought us further news. "Indians raided a settler's place near Dixon's Ferry. Killed fifteen whites, they did. Took two young girls hostage, too."

"Have—have you heard anything about Daniel? Or Hugh?"

"No, not a word. Just try to keep your spirits up, Miz Cranford. This war will all be over soon."

But my spirits were not helped by the news he brought me on a later trip. "The Indians attacked the Apple River Fort near Galena. The place was under siege for twelve hours. Two whites were killed. We got four Indians, though."

Waves of terror and concern swept over me. Poor, delicate Emily and little Benjie—living with all that warfare going on so near Galena. How could they ever cope?

"There've been scattered attacks by small groups of Indians all over northern Illinois," the post rider said. "Clear from the Mississippi River to that little white settlement there at Chicago."

"Where is Daniel?" I was so nervous and frantic, I thought my skin would burst. "Couldn't he at least get a letter through to me? I haven't heard from him for weeks."

"Now, don't you fret, Miz Cranford. The government is sending more troops out from the East. They're not about to let that old Indian get the upper hand."

Black Hawk still evaded his pursuers. The army now thought he was hiding up in the Wisconsin territory, and the troops were searching for him there.

In early July, General Scott and his soldiers arrived by steamship in Chicago. We heard they carried the deadly Asiatic cholera aboard ship with them. Sixteen of the men had died on the way.

The general turned Fort Dearborn into a temporary hospital, but by the middle of the month fifty more men had died; another one hundred twenty were ill.

People's eyes widened with horror when they spoke of this deadly disease. A militia man, returning after his term of enlistment had expired, gave me the latest news. "General Scott won't move his soldiers out of Chicago yet," he said. "He knows the whole militia would desert—rather than mix with those men and run the risk of getting cholera."

I heard the general and his troops finally left Chicago in late July, traveling toward Galena and Rock Island. The other generals were now chasing after Black Hawk near the Wisconsin River.

One afternoon I heard shouts from the road out in front of the inn. Norman Hart stuck his head in my kitchen door. "The war's over!" he called.

"Oh, thank God!" I dashed out to join the crowd standing around a haggard-looking man on horseback. "Did Black Hawk surrender?"

"No, that old fox is still on the run," the man said. "But they got all his people, up by Bad Axe Creek. Trying to get away, they were. Sneaking back across the Mississippi, after all the damage they done up north."

I pressed nearer. "Please. Have you heard anything about my husband? Daniel Cranford?"

"Soldier, is he?" the man asked. "They'll all be coming home soon."

"No, not a soldier. He was looking for Black Hawk."

"Yeah, him and everybody else." With a gruff laugh, the man spurred his horse and headed down the road.

Karl and Ruth came over to me. She slipped her arm around my shoulder. "Daniel and Hugh will be back now," she said, leading me into the inn. "Looks like all this foolishness is finally settled."

I shuddered with a strange chill. "Did you hear what that man said? All Black Hawk's people were killed. He had women and children with him, too."

"The government promised to put an end to all of Black Hawk's threats and defiance," Karl said grimly. "Ja, I guess they had to do it any vay they could."

Ruth tweaked my chin. "The important thing is, now Hugh and Daniel will be coming home. All the boys will be coming home now."

One muggy evening a week later, when the air lay thick with the scent of summer growth, I heard the hoofbeats of a lone horse thudding up to our stable. I ran to the back door and watched as Hugh, stiff and bent as an old man, climbed off his horse and stood motionless, looking toward the inn.

Sweat slicked my palms and trickled down my spine. "Hugh!" I cried out in a strangled voice.

He stared at me, a tortured look twisting his ruddied face.

I rushed out to meet him. "Hugh! Are you all right? Is your pa on his way home, too?" I asked, grabbing his arm. "Come on inside and rest. I'll call the other kids and tell them you're home."

His glance met mine. He grimaced, then stared down at the tangle of grass around his feet. My heart lurched in apprehension. Only the steady gurgling of the mill dam broke the silence as I studied his drawn, forlorn face.

A painful lump tightened in my throat. My runaway pulse thundered in my ears. I felt frozen, unable to speak.

Silence hung like an impenetrable curtain between us. Finally he raised his eyes. He swallowed hard and met my frozen stare.

His voice quavered. "Pa died."

CHAPTER 22

"No!" Pain slashed at me like a dagger. My jaw fell open. I stared at Hugh, unable—unwilling—to absorb his words.

Driven by an urgent need for motion, I paced back and forth, shaking my head, choking back sobs, pressing my hands against my temples. I crossed the yard and blindly sank down on the back stoop, burying my face in my hands.

No. No. It could not be true. Not Daniel.

Hugh stumbled over and sat down at my side. "It was cholera," he mumbled. Reluctantly, as if each word brought agony. "Some soldiers at the fort had it. He caught it there."

Cholera. No! This was just a nightmare. I shook my head, still burrowed in my hands. "Cholera," I repeated hazily.

"I was still out in the field with the troops. By the time I got back, he was gone."

"But—but how could he get cholera?"

"Some of General Scott's troops brought it with them when they came to Rock Island. Pa went down there to protest, after the soldiers killed women and children at Bad Axe. He knew General Scott. He fought with him in the War of 1812."

"He caught the disease from the soldiers there?"

"Yeah, several men had died of it before I left. I'm lucky I got home without it. It's a horrible disease." Hugh shuddered. "It took Pa in less than twelve hours."

Daniel. Gone. It could not be true. An image of him flashed through my mind—shoulders squared, chin high, dedicated to his noble mission, riding off with just a wave. And me, standing silently, watching him leave without a word.

A sob wrenched from my throat. Hot tears coursed down my face, burning like acid. "I—I never told him that I loved him," I stuttered, heaving with sobs.

Hugh laid his trembling hand on my shoulder. "He knew."

"No! No! I should have told him." I thought of our early years together, wondered when I first began to love him. A fresh torrent of tears flooded my cheeks. My arms closed about my ribs, and I rocked back and forth. How could I endure this agony?

Immersed in his own grief, Hugh sat quietly until my racking sobs subsided. "We have to tell the others," he said hoarsely.

I drew in a quavering gasp. How could I? Where would I find the strength? Sarah, Eddie, Joel. Their father. Dead. "Give me another minute," I murmured, pulling myself upright and sucking in a painfully deep breath. Somehow I must steel myself, lay aside my own hurt long enough to comfort those poor children.

I called them all together in the parlor and I told them. I do not know how I lived through the ordeal.

Afterward, we all clung numbly to one another, unable to comprehend the enormity of this loss. No one asked about the future. We all understood that we would carry on the family businesses. With his unlimited courage and optimism, Daniel had shown us the way.

227

The shocking news quickly spread through the town. As soon as he heard, Doc Benton hurried out to the kitchen, where the children and I stood staring with empty eyes. He took my hand, his sympathetic gaze resting on my face. "It's hard, Nellie. Oh, Lord, don't I know how hard it is."

My eyes veiled with tears, I nodded my gratitude for his kindness. Nancy was gone. And now Daniel. I bit my lip, trying to dam the rush of emotion. Oh, it wasn't fair! It just wasn't fair that death should have the power to sneak in at any moment and rob us of our loved ones. I clenched my fists until my nails cut into my palms.

"If you need anything, I'll be right here," Doc said, his hand firm on my shoulder.

The muscles in my jaw tensed as I struggled to hold back another flood of tears.

That night I lay taut and restless, fighting recurring nightmares. Daniel, deathly sick and alone. Far from home. Tended only by uncaring strangers, while some hellish disease wrenched his life from him.

I recalled all the chances we had missed, moments of tenderness and intimacy when we could have spoken words of love. A weighty cloud of shyness and reserve always hung between us. I should have led the way. Surely he deserved to know how very much he meant to me. It was the finest gift I could have given him. And yet I had held back.

The next morning, as Hugh sat at the table after breakfast, still staring into his mug of coffee, I asked the question that had nagged me for weeks. "Did Daniel ever get to talk to Black Hawk?"

Hugh, pale and tense, shook his head. "No white man talked to Black Hawk. He hid out the whole time. I guess he moved up into Wisconsin while his men were riding out in small parties for flash attacks here and there."

"Oh, Lordy, what a mess that was."

"Pa pleaded with the generals to give Black Hawk and his people one more chance to cross the Mississippi peacefully. It was clear from the start he only had a few men with him. They were no match for all the thousands of militia and regular army troops we had up there."

"No one would listen to Daniel?"

"No. It was a lost cause from the first day. Black Hawk's people were trying to surrender when they all got slaughtered at Bad Axe."

"Bad Axe. Yes, we heard about a battle there."

"Ask me about it. I was there."

"Oh, Hugh. No."

His voice grew agitated. "Yes, I was a part of that grand army, shooting at a bunch of starving Indians. We didn't spare a one. Cannons blasting from a steamboat, too. Peppering the water while the Indians were trying to swim across the Mississippi to safety."

"You wouldn't."

"No. I couldn't. I shot into the air, over their heads, until the sights and sounds of all that killing made me sick. I finally had to turn away and vomit."

"My God."

"Three hundred fifty bodies strewn about the land and in the water. Men, women, children—it didn't seem to matter. The troops had been hunting those Indians for three months, had been thwarted by them at every turn. Now when they finally had them in their rifle sights, it was just like a Fourth of July shooting match."

"Our boys? Our boys did that?"

He drew in a long, shaky breath. "I saw one woman with a baby in her arms. She was cut down and fell over on top of the little one. Later, I moved her body and found the baby still alive. Took him to the Indian agent by the fort. I guess he'll know how to get the poor kid back to his own people."

I stared at him, speechless.

"Old Black Hawk is still on the run," Hugh continued numbly. "And the army won't rest a minute until they've captured him. I'm just thankful my enlistment ran out when it did."

"You've seen enough of war to last a lifetime."

"And Pa. Poor Pa. All his efforts just a waste of time."

Tears streamed down my cheeks. "You know how strong he felt about it. He just had to try."

After a few days' rest, Hugh took over the running of the store, but he was a different person now—grim, sad-eyed, and silent.

Though I tried to pick up the pieces of my life, Daniel's absence left an enormous and frightening abyss. For years I had depended on him for so many things. Now I was left to carry on alone.

At night I dreamed of Daniel. I woke up covered with sweat, haunted by the knowledge that I had never told him how I loved him.

Three weeks passed, and every day the pain grew worse. One night I saw him in my dream, so real, so close I could almost touch him. He was reaching out to me, struggling, trying to extend his hand to me, just far enough away that our fingers could not meet.

At the first pale light of dawn, I awoke trembling, frantic with grief and guilt. I must go to him. At the very least I must see that this brave man's grave was dignified and properly marked. I would cover it with flowers, plant a tree there to honor and remember him.

When Hugh came out to breakfast, his eyes hollowed with sorrow and fatigue, I glanced up from my untouched mug of coffee. "I'm going to Rock Island," I said. "I have to see Daniel's grave. Can you show me the way?"

"Ma . . ." He sighed and shook his head. "That's no place for you. All the aftermath of war. Sickness . . . God, it's horrible."

"I have to go. With you or without. In fact, it's better if you stay here and help take care of things."

Sarah, pale and wide-eyed, stood listening at the doorway. "What about us? What if something happens to you, too?"

"I'll be fine. And Jenny comes in every day. She can watch over things around here. Forrest can help check in the inn guests, and I'll ask Ruth and the other neighbors to lend a hand."

Eddie, forlorn and distant-looking, watched me from across the breakfast table. Joel ran to me and clung to my skirt, gazing up with dark-circled eyes.

My chest tightened in an iron vise of conflict. Smoothing back the small boy's rumpled hair, I glanced around the circle of intent, confused faces. "Please try to understand. I have to go."

"It's a crazy idea," Hugh muttered. "I just got home. I don't want to ride back all that way again. It's over a hundred miles of hard traveling."

"No, you stay here. I'll take Eddie with me. Just tell us how to get there."

230

My mind a swirling whirlwind, I scurried around all morning, making arrangements with the neighbors, packing a saddlebag. As Eddie and I strapped saddles on our horses, preparing to leave, Doc hurried out to the stable. "What's this I hear, Nellie?" he asked, his eyes narrowed with concern. "Do you know what you're doing? What good will it do?"

"Don't try to stop me, Doc. I have to go."

He didn't understand. Nobody understood. I had lived with Daniel for eleven years—and had never once told him that I loved him. I remembered full well how much those precious words meant to me when I heard them all those years ago from Johnny Nichols, yet I denied them to this man who had given me his name and three children and had stood beside me through years of trials and hardships.

It wasn't too late. I could tell him now. I was certain he would hear me, if I could only get there fast enough.

With Eddie riding close beside me in somber silence, I started down the dusty road. I could not have found a better traveling guide, for this stalwart fourteen-year-old knew the woods and trails better than most men.

But all my thoughts focused on remembered images of Daniel. Did he go to his grave believing I was still in love with another man? Oh, I needed so desperately for Daniel to know.

The miles sped by as we trotted our horses up the narrow trail, all rutted where wagon wheels had mired in spring muds. The sun poured down on us like melted honey. Through tranquil forest and sun-blazoned prairie, fording streams that mirrored trees and sky, we pressed onward, oblivious to the sweet fragrance of summer, to the beauty of brilliant flowers and merry bird song.

As the sunset flared orange and crimson, we reined in our horses at a lonely cabin on the edge of a maple grove. The settlers there welcomed us to share their supper and offered us a spot to spread our blankets on their rough puncheon floors. In the morning, we were on our way again, heading toward the Mississippi River.

Toward noon the second day, we rode into a sleepy village perched along the riverbank. An ominous silence hung over the jumbled collection of weathered log cabins. The air reeked with a sweet-sour smell. No sound, no sight of human inhabitants appeared. The crisp *clip-clop* of our horses' hoofs echoed down the sunbaked streets.

I turned to Eddie with an eery foreboding. "There's a general store. Let's stop and ask how far we are from Rock Island."

"Do you really think there's anybody here?" the boy asked, shifting his eyes from house to house.

A wizened old man stood behind the counter when we entered the store. "Where is everybody?" I asked him, glancing out the door at the deserted street.

He stared at me with dark, sad eyes. "Cholera. Some boy brought it back from the war with him. You better get out while you can. Whole families are being wiped out overnight."

Cholera! I gasped. My breath seemed caught in my throat.

"Look over there," he muttered, pointing a gnarled finger at the row of wooden boxes across the street in the town square.

Suddenly I recognized them as a long, staggered row of caskets.

"People are dying so fast we can't get graves dug for all of them," the man said. "Some get thrown in three or four to a grave."

Eddie's face blanched as white as swans' down. Speechless, he stared outside at the caskets.

The storekeeper wagged his head morosely. "Funny how some gets it and some don't. Nobody wants to take care of the sick ones anymore, now that they've seen how bad this cholera is. See that house next door?"

Stiff as a cornered deer, I scanned the neat little cabin adorned with wild rosebushes along its front. Waves of nausea swept over me.

The old man scratched his arm nervously. "Some people carried that woman's brother over there when he got sick. He didn't have nobody else to look out after him. She was so scared of cholera, she didn't dare to touch him. Wouldn't even let him inside the door. Just left him laying out there under that tree until he died."

I stared at the man, horrified. My sight began to blur, the room to spin.

" 'Course, he didn't last more than a few hours. Living skeleton, he was. But the stinking flux . . . Why, the bugs was just swarming around him. Even had a vulture circling over and setting on the tree branch."

"My Lord!"

"Well, you know, you can't really blame the woman," he said, with a quick shrug. "After all, she might have caught it and died herself. Yep, just from giving him a couple hours of comfort."

My nausea was now acute. Retching, I rushed outside and over to the side yard. Eddie followed wordlessly.

My heart pounded like the hoofbeats of a racehorse. The world spun in circles before my eyes. I sank down on a stump and stared dizzily across the street at the long row of caskets. Cholera. An enemy, swift and powerful and evil.

My heartsick gaze rested on Eddie, hearty and intrepid at fourteen. Surely a bright future lay ahead for him. I had no right to endanger his life like this.

Nor my own. The family depended on me now. What would they do if I got cholera and died, too?

Reality struck me like a chunk of lead ore. I flinched and gritted my teeth against the onslaught of painful truth. Daniel was gone. It was too late to tell him anything. From now on, I must think first and only of the family. The children would have to serve as Daniel's monument. They and Eden Valley.

Garnering every ounce of my strength, I stood and turned to Eddie. My throat choked on the words. "Let's go home."

CHAPTER 23

Doc Benton met us as we rode into our yard toward dusk the next day, our horses sluggish from exhaustion. Calm and deliberate, he lifted me down from the saddle. For a moment I rested my head against his shoulder, longing to give way to the agonizing pain that churned inside me.

He asked no questions, and I gave no explanation for our quick return. He was an old friend. He needed none.

Bracing myself, I turned from him and trudged across the yard toward the inn. I had children who needed me. I had work that must be done. All the responsibilities of home and inn and store and farm had suddenly been dropped into my lap. And I was only twenty-nine, more like a sister than a mother to the older children. Emotional outbursts were a luxury I could not afford.

A new and burning goal now spurred me. This family, this town, would be a living monument to the memory of Daniel Cranford.

A few days later, Hugh came to me, a frown clouding his smooth, young face. "I won't be going down to college at Jacksonville this fall," he said. "You need my help here."

I looked into his somber gray eyes with alarm. "Oh, no, Hugh. We'll make out fine. Your pa always planned for you to go to college."

He shook his head firmly. "Maybe later. You were very good to us after our mother died. Now it's my turn to pay a little back."

His words brought the sting of tears to my eyes. "You know I never looked at it that way. I was proud to be part of your family." I hesitated, blinking back the haze. "It was an adventure, wasn't it? Remember how this valley looked when we first came?"

I gazed out the front door at our shady glen. The roomy mill stood solid as a rock beside the murmuring dam. All the craftmen's shops, the school, the tannery, the row of neat homes curving below the slope of wooded hill. The covered bridge opening onto fertile green fields and tiers of rolling hills. The lush, grass-covered park beside the river, where families came from miles around to picnic on Sundays.

How beautiful it was, spreading out before my eyes. Eden Valley. So long ago, Daniel had named it Eden Valley.

"Your pa left this town as a legacy for you kids," I said, turning back to Hugh. "Now it's up to us to help it grow, just like he would have done."

A cloud of gloom had settled over Hugh. He became silent and morose, absentminded. Though he had just turned nine-

234

teen, he trudged around the store bent over like an old man. His young face was etched in a constant frown as he glumly sorted incoming stacks of letters and newspapers and stuffed them into the little wooden cubbyholes built along the back wall.

Karl Schulmann bought out Daniel's share of the mill. I managed the busy inn with the help of Jenny and a washwoman, while Sarah did our bookkeeping and Eddie took care of the stable out back. In spare moments, I rode out to confer with the tenants on our farm.

Many of my neighbors in the village and outlying community seemed shocked at the idea of a woman running a business on her own. They filled my ears with dire warnings and predictions.

"Don't you worry. I can handle things just fine," I told them, more determined than ever to succeed.

Doc Benton stayed on at the inn. One evening after supper, he came out from his sparsely furnished room and joined me in the kitchen as I dried and hung up the last pot by the hearth. "Mind if I join you for a bit?" he asked.

I hung the dishtowel on its peg, smiling at his question. "You know I'm always glad to see you, Doc. But wouldn't you rather sit with the guests on the front porch? Norman's out there. Just listen to them laugh! Sounds like they've got a regular party going on."

Doc chuckled. "I've heard old Norman's stories so many times, I could tell them all myself. I'd rather have a cup of tea with you, if you have time."

"When don't I have time to talk to an old friend? Sit down. I'll put the kettle on."

He sank down on the chair and watched as I dipped water from the pail into my smallest copper kettle and set it over the fire. "Are you feeling all right, Nellie? This has all been such a strain."

"I'm holding up, thanks." I glanced out the back door, where Hugh had gone for a solitary walk in the deepening twilight. "I worry about Hugh, though."

Doc nodded in understanding. "He's taken all this hard. He saw some awful things in the war, you know."

"If only there was something I could do to help."

"Just give him time, Nellie. You and I both know there're some things only time can heal."

I raised my head and met his kindly dark eyes.

After that, Doc spent many evenings sitting with me and the children in the parlor. We all welcomed his comradely visits, for they made the lonely evening hours more bearable. I hoped no one would gossip about us. As a businesswoman, I could ill afford any cloud on my good name. But after all, Doc was an old friend, and the children served as ever-present chaperones. Sometimes Forrest Henley joined us, too, always welcomed by Sarah's blushing smile.

But still, Daniel's absence left an aching void in my life. I missed him desperately. The dull hollowness inside me was a wound that would not heal. Often I read and studied by candlelight far into the night, trying to forget my loneliness and pain.

The war had formally ended late in August when Black Hawk was captured. He was imprisoned for a while, then sent out to Washington, at the request of President Jackson. Before returning to his tribe, now living in Iowa, he was taken on a tour of the large eastern cities, so he could see with his own eyes the vast power and resources of white America.

Of the thousand Indians who had followed Black Hawk back to Illinois last April, six hundred—men, women, and children—had been killed. Seventy-two white settlers and soldiers had also lost their lives in the conflict.

The final departure of the Indians from the state heralded a flood of settlers flowing through our area, heading north. By the next spring, the narrow, muddy roads in northern Illinois gleamed white with covered wagons. New towns sprang up overnight, new steamers plied the Illinois River, and new stagecoach lines extended to the farthest reaches of our burgeoning state.

But the constant threat of cholera still plagued us. The following summer, we received a letter from Daniel's brother Noah. I felt weak after reading it and had to sit down.

"Nellie! What is it?" Sarah asked, stunned by my sudden faintness.

"Emily. The cholera's taken her, too. And the little girl she had after they moved north."

"Do you think Uncle Noah will stay in Galena now?"

"I suppose so. He's opened a dry-goods store there. Says he's doing real well. Some neighbors are helping him look after Benjie."

Emily gone. Her sweet, refined voice forever stilled. My pulse hammering, I wadded the letter tightly in my fist and beat my hands on the table in frustration. I only wished I could beat on death with that same fury.

The toll from cholera was staggering. Down in Quincy, over thirty people died in only five days.

"This hideous disease is a curse from God," some people said.

"In some towns, folks are spraying lime on the streets to ward off the cholera," Ruth told me.

"Yes, and I've heard some keep big bonfires of tar and sulphur burning," I said. "Anything they can think of to drive the sickness away."

"You should hear people talking in the store," Hugh added. "They're using chloride of lime, and vinegar, and even coffee as preventatives. They chew garlic. They wear bags of camphor around their necks."

It seemed to me these preventatives were mostly useless, for the epidemic raged across the state, striking first one town and then another. Eden Valley, thankfully, was spared, but we lived on the edge of constant fear.

Still, life went on. Out on the prairie, bobolink and quail and whippoorwill sang their age-old songs. Black crow and hawk wheeled through the sky, and, in the woods, the illusive wild turkey marched in stately splendor, all unmindful of disease and death.

Two years passed like the blinking of an eye. The growing prosperity of our businesses filled me with a deep pride. These days, the stagecoach stopped overnight twice a week, bringing our inn a steady flow of visitors, some more welcome than others.

One afternoon a well-dressed man with sand-colored hair and beard and small dark eyes, climbed off the stage and walked up to the inn door with a clumsy, staggering gait. A strong scent of whiskey clung to him.

"Where's the proprietor of this place?" he asked me in a slurred voice.

"I'm the owner. Would you like a room?" I said.

His narrow, slitted eyes widened above his flushed cheeks. "You, honey? Well, now . . . Isn't this a nice surprise!"

237

"If you want a room, just sign this book," I said, pushing the opened register toward him. "Otherwise I have other things to do."

"Tell me, honey—just how did a pretty little thing like you get to be the proprietor of a big inn like this? You must have a man around here someplace."

"I'm a widow," I said shortly. "Sign the register, please."

He leaned closer. I drew back from him, repulsed by the reek of liquor encircling him like a cloud.

"A widow. Oh, you poor, sweet thing. Bet you get pretty lonely, don't you? Nights all alone. Bet you'd like a little company. How about tonight?" He slipped an arm around my waist.

I jerked away, glaring fire at him, and slammed the register book shut. "I'm sorry. We're full. You can't stay here."

His cheeks flushed even redder. "Now, just a minute, lady."

"Good day, sir." I walked over to the door and stood beside it, still glaring as I waited for him to leave, my arms folded tightly across my chest.

He stared at me for a moment, then smiled a silly grin. "I was just teasing you, sweetheart. You wouldn't put me out, would you? Where am I supposed to stay?"

"That's your problem, mister. I suppose you could sleep out in the barn. Maybe you can sober up before the morning stage comes by."

Gripping his hat in his hand, he turned dejectedly to leave. "You're a hard one, lady."

"I know. I've had to be."

Later, a new business opened in town. A man called Lyman Weldon bought a lot and built a small saloon. He and his wife Tillie moved into an empty cabin at the edge of town.

At first no one objected to the saloon. We had never kept a bar at the inn, but the store sold whiskey by the jug, and nearly all the men drank some now and then. In contrast to my unwelcome guest, most men controlled their drinking and it never caused a problem. In fact, many people swore it helped prevent and cure disease. A saloon might provide a friendly place for folks to get together and talk over the war or the state's growth or the old days.

One afternoon when Ruth dropped by my kitchen for tea, she wore an anxious frown. "What do you think of that Lyman

238

Weldon?'' she asked me, stirring spirals in the cup of steaming liquid with her spoon.

I hesitated for a moment. "I don't know what to make of him, to tell the truth. That fellow sure has an air of mystery about him."

His well-tailored, burgundy velvet coat and brocade vest, his shiny white hair and carefully groomed goatee, were in themselves enough to set him apart from all the other men in our village. He always wore a large pearl tiepin in his satin cravat. But every time I glimpsed his wary yellow eyes, cunning as a cat's, an uneasy sensation prickled my skin.

Ruth made a little clucking sound. "If you ask me, his wife's the biggest mystery. She must be thirty years younger than him. And where in the world does she get those fancy frilly dresses? I've never seen the likes of such."

"Tillie Weldon would be pretty, if she was just a mite less flashy."

"Have you noticed her cheeks and lips?" Ruth asked, sniffing. "I'm sure that woman uses paint."

"Well, maybe she'll add a little color to the town," I said, grinning.

I frequently noticed Tillie Weldon tripping down the street to our store, tossing her head so that her pale, frizzy curls bounced as she swung her dainty wicker basket. Within a short time, her visits to the store became an extended daily ritual.

One day at dinner, Sarah scowled angrily at Hugh. This lovely, proud young lady of eighteen looked down her patrician nose at all the local boys. Though her sharp remarks could cut like a butcher knife, she had been very patient with Hugh since he returned from the war. But now her voice took on a mocking, disapproving tone. "I see your friend Mrs. Weldon came to visit you again," she said.

My ears perked up, for I had been too busy to notice anything unusual.

Hugh's face blazed brick red. "Why are you talking?" he muttered. "You spend all your time hanging around the school-teacher, marveling at every word he utters."

Raising her brows, Sarah glared at him with all the hauteur she could muster. "For your information, sir, Mr. Henley is extremely intelligent and well-educated. It just so happens that

239

I value education very highly. I doubt if you can learn much from that awful Mrs. Weldon creature.''

"Oh, I don't know about that." He scowled at her, his eyes enraged above his crimson cheeks. "She's lived in New Orleans, and St. Louis, too. I guess she's seen a lot more of the world than you have."

Eddie surpressed a giggle. "She sure wears fancy clothes," he said. And that from a boy who never noticed anybody's clothes.

Sarah harrumphed. "Fancy is certainly the correct word." She stomped out of the kitchen.

Concerned, I studied Hugh's red face. This confused, injured young man didn't need any further emotional tangles in his life. But just as I opened my mouth to speak, the sudden ring of the inn's front bell called me to other pressing duties.

The next afternoon, when I stepped into the store to get some tea and salt for the kitchen, I saw Tillie Weldon leaning over the counter toward Hugh, her low-cut, garnet silk dress revealing a shocking expanse of soft, milk-white skin. She smiled teasingly and lay her small hand on his arm. "I wouldn't know about that, honey," she murmured, her voice low and seductive.

My step sounded smartly on the floorboards, and she turned my way, startled.

Hugh's handsome young face flushed again. He shot a quick glance at the woman, who gazed at me with a challenging half smile.

"Afternoon, Mrs. Weldon," I said, meeting her eyes squarely. She tilted her head to one side. "Ah, the Widow Cranford."

"I do hope you're finding our little town to your liking."

A light laugh gurgled in her throat. "I must admit this is a bit of a change for me. I've always lived in big cities."

"So Hugh tells me. New Orleans. St. Louis, he said."

Her smile faded. "And what else have you heard?" she demanded, frowning at Hugh.

"Why, nothing. Not a thing," I said. "We'd all like to get to know you better."

Hugh's gaze dwelled on her heart-shaped face, her porcelain skin, and reddened lips. "She really likes Eden Valley. Don't you, Mrs. Weldon?"

"Now, honey, I told you to call me Tillie," she said, patting his hand.

His blush deepened.

One glance informed me Hugh was in the throes of his first love, and that this woman was enjoying it to the hilt. An icy chill of fear snaked down my spine. I felt certain her husband, that cunning, cat-eyed man, would not take the matter quite so lightly.

Daniel, I miss you so, I thought as I stood there. Where are you now that I really need you?

"I just wanted a few things for the kitchen," I said, folding my arms and planting my feet firmly on the floor beside the counter. The pungent odors of the store enveloped me: coffee beans, mingled spices, bacon, leather, linseed oil. "Go ahead, Mrs. Weldon. I'll just wait until you're finished."

Pursing her lips, she squirmed impatiently and flipped a frizzy curl. "Oh, I guess this is all I need today. Let me pay you now, Hugh, dear, and I'll be on my way."

After she left, he avoided my eyes and busied himself straightening the shelves, but raw emotion still colored his face. I didn't know what to say to him. Although he was my stepson, I was only eleven years his senior. I remembered well the all-consuming power of first love, the compelling urge toward action, even foolish action. Hugh always appeared unruffled, but I knew his emotions ran deep and strong. He would not take love lightly.

Fear and concern for him nagged at me all through the day. He had already suffered so much from the war, and from his father's horrid death. What could I do? What could I say to him? I longed for some of Daniel's sage wisdom.

A few days later, a guest at the inn visited the saloon, then returned to join Doc and a group of other men out on our porch. Though I was talking with some women friends at the other end, I could not help but overhear the men's conversation.

"Do you folks around here know about that fellow running the saloon?" the inn guest asked. "Why, he's an old riverboat gambler. I'd know him anywhere. I watched him take a man for five hundred dollars on a trip down to New Orleans a few years back."

Doc stiffened with surprise. "You're talking about Weldon? What's a fellow like that doing way out here?"

"That's what I'm asking you. But I can tell you they didn't call him Weldon then. His name was Gates. They called him

Pearly Gates, 'cause of that pearl tiepin he always wears." The man spat tobacco into the dust of the road. "Yes, sir, I'd sure like to know what's he's doing in this little burg. He used to be real highfalutin."

A traveling millwright lowered his voice and glanced down the street toward the saloon. "Hiding out, maybe? Think things got a little too hot for him over on the Mississippi?"

The other fellow sniggered nervously. "Maybe he just wanted to settle down with that young wife of his. Did you get a peek at her? Where do you suppose he found her?"

"Plenty of fancy gals like that along the waterfront in St. Louis. They usually ain't married, though."

I glanced around to see if Hugh was within earshot, but he stood down by the river, leaning against the gnarled trunk of a cottonwood, watching the water plunge over the dam.

No one could stop the river's urgent quest. It traveled with a will and purpose of its own. And I knew Hugh must travel his own road, as well.

But still I fretted. Busy as I was with all the work around the inn, I couldn't overlook the daily spectacle of Tillie Weldon in her fancy low-cut dresses and matching parasols, tripping down to the store. I noticed, too, that she always lingered for a long while, and strolled home with the smug, satisfied smile of a woman who craved attention from men and never failed to garner it.

My first look at this woman had warned me she might spell trouble for our quiet, conservative town. Much as I had hoped the cloak of gloom left by the war would lift from Hugh's young shoulders, I had never imagined it would happen this way.

One night later that month, just after drifting off into a fitful, dream-filled sleep, I awoke to the ruckus of loud shouts from the road out front. I hurriedly slipped into a dress and rushed out to investigate.

The night was black, lit by a spattering of stars and a pale crescent moon. Shining squares of lantern light bobbed and swung back and forth as men ran along the riverbank, yelling. "See anything?" one deep voice called out.

"Not a thing! Run down this way!"

Other hastily dressed townspeople hurried out from their houses and down to the river. Doc Benton pushed his way through the milling crowd along the shore. "What's wrong here?" he asked.

"Jake Kelly got drunk and fell in the river!" The blacksmith held out his lantern, and the murky water reflected back its golden flame.

People rushed home for more lanterns, then joined in scouring the swirling water in the dim and flickering light.

"Never knew Jake to drink much," one fellow muttered, staring helplessly into the dark stream.

"He was playing cards with Weldon earlier. Guess he lost a bundle, then tried to drown his pain."

"Looks like he drowned, all right."

"Seems like he would have figured out by now nobody ever wins a game against Weldon."

When dawn finally broke, the grim, exhausted crew searched all along the winding river for any sign of Jake. They found his bloated body washed up in a snarl of driftwood two miles downstream.

A chill of shock enveloped the whole community. Accidental deaths were almost commonplace, but this one seemed very different. Ominous.

Who was this Lyman Weldon? Who was his bold, flamboyant wife? What new elements had they introduced to our quiet little village?

They wrapped Jake's body in an old quilt and carried it home in a wagon bed. As his family prepared for the funeral, I thought of Hugh—and shuddered with the sense of impotence and foreboding that surged over me.

I had saved Daniel's children from prairie fires and Indian riots. I could not save them from themselves.

ister, and deep frustration in my soul growing worse as time passes. After a while, or then, I would return to the dark, the very thought of him ...

While trying to tend to spiritual care, that Eden Valley was a vast unexplored ...

CHAPTER 24

The next summer, Johnny Nichols and his wife and children came to Eden Valley to visit her brother. I could have sworn I had forgotten all about him. When Judson Lowder told me they were coming, my acute discomfort filled me with surprise.

Johnny's horse and buggy swept past the inn one bright June afternoon, just as I was sweeping off the front porch. Glancing up at the sound of approaching hoofbeats, I noticed first the splendid pair of matched grays pulling his rig. Then I met his eyes—those mesmerizing, deep blue eyes.

I would know Johnny anywhere. Over the last thirteen years he had changed little, still as handsome as ever, in his craggy, virile-looking way.

He dropped his glance and tucked in his chin, his back held ramrod straight. Perhaps he did not recognize me, for he did not speak, wave, or even slow his horses as they trotted past the inn and on toward Lowder's place.

He could at least speak, I thought, my mind spinning with confusion. Would it hurt him to stop and introduce me to his wife and children? After all, we were old neighbors.

Then I recalled the circumstances of our last meeting—his anger, his bitter curse. Surely that anger would have faded by now. Perhaps he was so embarrassed by the whole situation, he found it easier just to ignore me.

The swishing of my broom took on new vigor, hurling clouds of road dust off the wide porch boards. Johnny Nichols. Huh! I certainly didn't need him, I assured myself, and swept all the harder. I had buried Johnny in the past years ago. He was married now, and had a family. I had a busy, fruitful life of my own here, and deep satisfaction in my ever-growing sense of independence. What was he to me? I would avoid the sight, the very thought of him.

And I really tried to keep that vow. But Eden Valley was a very small town.

On the Fourth of July, the townspeople held a lavish celebration. The militia and war veterans, wearing ill-fitting uniforms and self-conscious dignity, formed ranks behind an improvised band of two fiddlers, a drummer, and a flutist. The band could have used more practice, some spectators murmured behind their hands. Still, they all watched with avid attention while the old soldiers marched smartly down the curve of our main street, following the natural bend of Spoon River.

Solemn-faced women, each dressed in her finest, came next, marching with firm step to the drummed-out beat of "Hail Columbia." The older children followed.

The cloudless sky was ablaze with brilliant sunshine, the air heavy with humidity as the parade proceeded in all its grandeur to a clearing in the woods. There, a stout, black-suited congressman from Springfield mounted a wagon bed and gave a lengthy patriotic oration to the audience that lounged on the grass before him.

When the congressman had finally exhausted his subject, the children tore back to the village park for races, marbles, and other games. Men set up long plank tables in the shade, and we women spread out an array of food. After dinner, the men held a horse race and a shooting match across the river.

The presence of Johnny through all this holiday celebration was as hard to ignore as a blister on my toe. For days I had battled the old images that kept rushing back to me. Johnny had avoided me completely. Today I could not avoid seeing them standing by the roadside, viewing the parade. His wife had wavy brown hair and pale, round eyes, an empty, childlike expression on her face. Two children stood beside them. The boy, around ten, resembled his mother. The younger girl, a lovely child with dark gypsy curls, had skin like pale pink rose petals and Johnny's beautiful blue eyes.

I glanced again at Johnny and my pulse began to race. Stepping back into the inn's deserted dining room, I wandered over to a cane-bottomed armchair before the empty fireplace, fighting the flood of confusing memories and emotions.

This was worse than foolish. Here I was, thirty-one years old, the widow of a man I had loved and held in high esteem. I was a mother, responsible for a large family, a farm, and two businesses. Flourishing and prosperous businesses, I reminded myself with pride. The sight of some old beau should not throw me into such a dither. Whatever was wrong with me?

Footsteps on the porch. My cheeks burned; I knew my face was flushed. I gulped in a deep breath, trying to collect myself before I turned to face some inn guest returning from the celebration. Maybe that nice old lady from Philadelphia had stood too long in the hot sun.

The footsteps were now inside. A man's footsteps, hesitating near the door. A voice, deep and questioning. "Nellie?"

I turned, and looked into Johnny's eyes. My mouth went dry. I rose from the chair and clasped my hands to still their trembling as I stared at Johnny.

With a faint, quizzical smile, he crossed the room toward me. "Nellie, it's so good to see you again. I wanted a chance to talk with you before we have to leave."

Never taking my eyes from his face, I nodded stiffly. "Nice to see you, Johnny."

The jagged scar was still there on his forehead. Against the chiseled, bony structure of his tanned cheeks and jawline, his lips looked strangely soft. I suddenly recalled the touch of those lips upon mine, long, long ago.

"You look lovely, Nellie. You never change."

His voice, his nearness flustered me. Did my hair need to be brushed? Oh, I wished I'd worn a newer, nicer dress.

"I've changed a lot," I said, laughing nervously. "More than you know. The Indians called me Lightning Woman."

"Because of your red hair?"

Smiling, I shook my head. "Because I once chased them off with a rifle."

"A real frontier woman now." He tilted his head and grinned at me. "I like that."

"Life changes us all, I guess. It's been a long time."

Thirteen years. Both our lives had been completely transformed since then. But the old attraction was still there, smoldering in embers I had long believed were dead.

Our eyes fed greedily on each other, but our words came hard, stilted with embarrassment. He glanced down and studied his highly polished boots. "I wanted to apologize for what I said the last time I saw you. I was out of my head. I had no right to talk to you that way."

I nodded wordlessly. He had asked me to leave with him. What would my life have been if I had gone? Daniel, the children—all forgotten. Joel and Cinda never would have been born. Cinda. My darling little lost Cinda.

I did not regret a moment I had spent with Daniel. Our time together was a precious memory. But Daniel was dead now. And I was very much alive.

My heart pounded in my head in rapid drumbeats. How did I look in Johnny's eyes? I feared I must look a little haggard now, after all these years of hard work and responsibility.

Once you said you loved me, Johnny. Could you love me still?

He nervously fingered the brim of his straw hat. "So. You're working at an inn again, after all these years."

"This time it's different. This inn belongs to me."

"Yes. That does make a difference, doesn't it?" He paused, gazing intently into my eyes. "I've thought of you so often, Nellie. I know it was all my fault. I never should have trusted Blanche to get a message to you."

"I—I guess that's all water under the bridge now."

"I've never forgiven her. And when I've thought of you up here in the wilderness, working so hard . . ."

"It wasn't so bad. Sure, I worked hard, but never without reaping the rewards. My husband was a good man."

"And now he's gone, and you're left to take care of everything yourself."

"And doing a pretty good job of it, if I do say so myself."

A sudden grin lit his face. "Yes, I'd say you are, at that."

An old, familiar thrill coursed through me as I returned his infectious smile. "And you, Johnny?"

"I'm doing well enough. I have a big spread down by St. Louis, a nice house, a fine stable of thoroughbreds."

"Good. I'm happy for you."

"Yes." His voice sounded like a stranger's, choked and raspy. His eyes bore into mine for a moment, then he glanced down at the floor, fingering the watch chain draped across the front of his vest. "Well, we have to be heading back tomorrow."

"So soon?" My chest was tight with the tension generated by his nearness, by the burning intensity of his gaze.

247

Such foolish thoughts. I knew this long-forgotten, romantic dream of mine was never meant to be.

He turned from me, at a loss for words. Clearing his throat, he glanced at me again. "Take care of yourself, Nellie," he murmured hoarsely. "Don't work too hard."

"And you, Johnny. You take care of yourself, too." The pain of speaking those inane words. The agony of parting once again, perhaps forever.

Frowning, he studied my face intently. He reached out, as if to touch me, then abruptly dropped his hand. "Yes. Yes, I will." He wheeled and strode out the door.

Long after he had disappeared, the image of his face, of his broad shoulders pressed against that linen jacket, his slender hips and long legs encased in fawn-colored trousers, lingered in my mind.

I wanted him. In an instant, all my desire had rekindled into a blazing flame, after two years of living a solitary, virginal life.

The shamefulness of my desires brought a blush to my cheeks. Why, at heart I was no better than Tillie Weldon!

Though I tried to put aside those thoughts and bury myself in work at the inn, I knew from town gossip the exact moment he left. Now I would forget him, put aside this silly infatuation. Oh, why was it so difficult to control the wanton meanderings of my heart?

Honestly and humbly, I must remind myself of this when I broached Hugh about his dangerous and growing attachment to a married woman.

In August, as a searing sun burned down and the corn plants grew as tall as small trees, I once again urged Hugh to register at Illinois College in Jacksonville for the coming winter. We could afford to hire a clerk for the store, I told him, and Sarah could help. After all, she was a capable, intelligent girl. And she, too, hoped to rescue Hugh from Tillie Weldon's spell.

By this time, many townspeople were complaining bitterly about the nightly ruckus at the saloon. "They're at it till all hours," they said.

"How's a body to sleep?"

"That Weldon pulls some pretty shady tricks at poker. And what about them shell games he's got going at his place?"

"How about the bets he lays on horse races and cockfights?"

The men who gambled with Weldon often lost precious cash money needed to pay taxes on their farms. Some drank themselves senseless at the saloon, while others provoked fights over imagined slights, often ending in raucous brawls. People complained—asked Weldon to tighten the reins on his place—but nothing ever changed.

Weldon, or Pearly Gates, or whoever that man really was, angered the people of Eden Valley by running a rowdy saloon and shady games. His wife upset them for a different reason. Hugh was not the only object of her bold flirtations. She swung her voluptuous hips and blinked her darkened lashes at any man, young or old, who happened to cross her path.

Since modesty and decorum were customary and expected in pioneer women, Tillie's wanton behavior shocked the townspeople. And her husband was known to be jealous and possessive. The situation worried us all.

Hugh began to disappear for long periods of time in the afternoons. "Can Sarah look after the store? I'm going hunting for a while," he would tell us, and head off down the road, his rifle tucked under his arm. But he always returned home empty-handed.

Much as I had hoped he could escape the clutches of his deep depression, I dreaded seeing him further complicate his life.

One evening in early fall, after scarcely touching his supper, he quietly rose from the dining table and strode to the back door. "I'm going out," he mumbled, averting his eyes.

"Oh? Going to visit one of your friends?" I asked, trying to mask my concern.

He glared at me, annoyed. "Don't worry about me. I'm not exactly Joel's age, you know."

It was true. He was no longer a child. I could only sit silently and watch him walk away.

As I stacked the dirty dishes and carried them to Jenny in the kitchen, worry nagged at me until I felt I simply must do something or burst. I wandered out the front door and over to the dam, where the insistent gurgling water mirrored my anxiety and concern.

Doc Benton, seated on the porch bench, rose and strolled over to join me. "Pretty evening," he said casually, gazing at the last glow of sunset quivering on the river's surface. The air was crisp and cool. Soft twitterings of bird song sounded from the trees. "I never tire of this scene."

His friendly presence always comforted me—like a cup of warmed milk. I raised my eyes to his . . . and words began to pour, unbidden, from my lips. "Oh, Doc, I don't know what to do. I'm so afraid for Hugh."

A deep line appeared between his brows. "Why, Nellie. What is it?"

"That woman. Tillie Weldon. She's always chasing after him, and he's so young . . ."

"He's almost twenty-one now, isn't he? That's not so young, you know. Lots of fellows are married by that age here on the frontier." Frowning, he pondered for a moment. "Would you like for me to talk to him? I could just casually bring up the subject."

"Oh, would you? Please?"

"Sure. Those Weldons are a pair, aren't they?" He looked out over the cascading waters, glistening faintly in the dimming light. The soothing melody lulled even my tormented soul. After a long pause, he murmured, in a tone so soft and gentle I could hardly hear him, "Nellie?"

"Yes?"

"Nellie, I've been looking for the right time to say this. It just doesn't seem to come along."

I hesitated, studying his kind eyes and pleasant features for some clue to his thoughts. He had sobered, too, from the light-hearted, idealistic young fellow he had been when he came out here to the frontier.

"Daniel's been gone two years now." At my nod, he continued. "You and I have been friends for a long time."

"A long time." I smiled, secure in the contentment of his friendship. "I don't know what I would have done without you after Daniel died."

He glanced down and kicked at a tuft of coarse grass growing near his toe. Stepping over to the river's edge, he picked up a flat stone and skipped it across the water. With an embarrassed, boyish grin, he strode back to me and took my hand. "Nellie, why don't you and I get married? We'd make a good team."

After a stunned moment, joy and pride welled up inside me. How sweet, how dear he was to ask me at this time in my life.

250

Maybe if he had asked me sooner, before I saw Johnny again and started feeling so tangled and confused . . .

Tenderly I patted his strong, long-fingered hand. "I can't tell you how truly honored I am, Doc. The problem is, right now I feel like I need a good friend more than a husband. And you're probably the best friend I've ever had."

Flinching at my words, he clung to my hand. "Can't I be both? I want you for my wife, Nellie."

My cheeks blazed crimson. I lowered my eyes and stared at the bone buttons on his shirtfront. I had been such close friends with Nancy. Could I bear to be a second wife again? After all those years of living with the ghost of beautiful Lenore? And could I really give up my independence?

Or was my real concern some foolish, futile dream of Johnny Nichols? That someday, somehow, fate would finally bring us together.

Shaking my head, I gently squeezed his hand. "No, you deserve one of these pretty young girls around here, Doc. You should have a family of your own, not take over some widow's burdens."

"I want you, Nellie."

"Oh, Doc, you mean so much to me. But, really—I just can't even think of marrying again. Not now."

He gazed down at me, his face set, his eyes sad. "Well, my offer stands, if you should change your mind." His shoulders slumped as he walked back to the inn.

I could not move. Thoughts roiled and twisted in my head. So many people touched my life. They weighed on me as if all their hurts and troubles were my own. I longed to go away, to rest and sort out all these tangled problems.

That night Hugh did not return until very late. I lay awake far into the dark hours, listening to the sounds of raucous laughter drifting down the road from the saloon. Just how busy was Lyman Weldon at that place? Did he keep tabs on his flashy young wife? Was he not jealous of her brazen flirtations? Where would it all end?

A few days later, Ruth dropped in to see me as I was going over our account books at the parlor table. We sat and chatted over a cup of tea.

"What's wrong with Doc Benton these days?" she asked suddenly, peering at me over the rim of her cup.

I shrugged uncomfortably. "Doc? Who knows? Maybe he's had a problem with some patient. You know how he worries over people."

"Are you sure it doesn't have something to do with you? I've thought for a good while he was fixing to ask you to marry him."

"You sure don't let anything slip past you," I said, with a wry laugh. "As a matter of fact, he did ask me. I turned him down."

"Nellie! Now why in the world would you do a thing like that? He's such a dear, and you're all alone now."

I gazed into the tawny depths of my tea, caught in the tangled web of my thoughts. If only I could talk to someone about Johnny, it might help me to find my way through this confusion. But how could I admit I wanted some other woman's husband?

"What's wrong, honey? I know you like him," Ruth said.

"Sure. Who doesn't? I guess he's about the nicest man I've ever known. But there are so many complications."

"You're alone and he's alone. What's complicated about that?"

"There's so much to consider," I said, squirming in my chair. "He'd want his own home. I can't give up the inn here, not after we've worked so long to get it running right. And he'd want children of his own. I'm not sure I want to go through all that again."

"But anything beats being alone."

"Oh, I don't know." I faced her squarely now. "I've come to like the idea of making my own decisions. It's kind of nice to be able to go ahead without having to stop and ask permission for every little thing."

"Doc is hardly the bossy sort."

"No, but you know how the laws are. Once a woman marries, everything she owns is put into her husband's name. Legally he can do anything he wants with it. A widow has lots more rights than a married woman."

"I know, I know," Ruth said. "But you're still young. Most anything is better than being alone the rest of your life."

My memories of Johnny nagged me like a toothache. A vision

of his crooked smile flashed through my mind, crowding out all thoughts of Doc and his proposal.

In early September, Eddie hitched up the wagon and drove Hugh to Havana to catch a steamboat for another trip to St. Louis, to purchase new merchandise for the store. I rode along to see him off.

The steamer was a huge, three-tiered vessel, all gleaming white paint and filigreed gingerbread trimmings, with bright flags flapping in the breeze. I went aboard with Hugh to see the gorgeous gilt and velvet salon, filling now with smartly dressed travelers, hard-eyed gamblers, and black-coated politicians. The country people, carrying battered carpetbags, stayed on the lower deck. A gang of sweating black men scurried back and forth like ants, unloading barrels of sugar, molasses, rum, and tobacco.

Then a long, low musical whistle sounded from the tall, black stacks, and I hurried back ashore, watching as the gangplank was raised. The boat was underway, its wide paddles gulping in great mouthfuls of river water, then spitting them out again.

Hugh had been gone less than a week when I was wakened one night by the distant crack of two gunshots. I sat upright in bed, every muscle tensed, my heart hammering.

A moment later, shouts sounded from the street. I sprang from bed, slipped on a robe, and rushed out of my room just as several inn guests came scurrying down the stairs. "What happened?" someone shouted.

I shrugged and hurried out to join the puzzled crowd gathering in the road. Sleepy townsfolk looked at one another, their eyes filled with unanswered questions. The flickering lanterns in their hands cast an eery light over the shuffling, ill-clad assemblage.

Norman Hart came running from the edge of town, shouting in shocked tones, "They're dead! My God! Both of 'em dead!"

"What?" "Who?" stunned voices questioned.

"Tillie Weldon and Bill Woodward! Weldon shot them both right through the heart. Oh, saints above!" Norman leaned against a porch post and gasped for breath. "I heard some shots and ran outside—just in time to see him jump on his horse and take off."

"My God! Bill who? Vhat happened?" Karl asked in his gutteral voice.

"Bill Woodward. That farmer from over toward Lewistown. Weldon must have caught him with his wife."

A swell of murmurs traveled through the shifting crowd.

"Bound to happen."

"What did he expect?"

"Knew she was a fancy woman first time I laid eyes on her."

"It's still murder!" Judson Lowder yelled. "We'd better round up a posse and go after him!"

"No use trying that till morning."

By morning, Lyman Weldon's trail was cold. He had jammed some valuables and cash into his saddlebags and had completely disappeared. The county marshall and a posse of farmers and tradesmen combed the trails for signs of him, but by supper all had returned to their homes. Somebody walked down to the saloon and boarded the door shut; other townspeople prepared to bury Tillie.

For days a hush of shock lay over the town. People hung their heads and spoke in whispers, as if hoping to keep this scandal a secret from outsiders. After all, this was hardly St. Louis or New Orleans. Such things just didn't happen in a quiet, upright village like Eden Valley.

And then, Hugh returned.

Eddie drove our largest wagon over to Havana to meet Hugh's steamboat. I waited, nervous as a wren, watching for them. Hugh was a deep and sensitive young man. How would he take this tragic news? Shuddering, I faced the ugly fact that he himself could very well have been the dead man.

When I heard the noisy rumble of the wagon down the road, I ran outside to meet them, my stomach cramped with anxiety. Clouds of dust swirled around the wheels as the overburdened wagon pulled up in front of the store. Hugh's broad smile and wave of greeting told me Eddie had not mentioned the shooting.

Vaulting down from the wagon, Hugh handed me a deep, round box. "Look here, Ma," he said, grinning. "I brought you back a fancy bonnet from St. Louis. Latest style, too."

I swallowed back the dread that rose in my throat. "Come inside, Hugh," I murmured, avoiding his eyes.

"I can't just yet. We have to get all this merchandise unloaded. Just look at all I bought. Sarah will have a fit over these bolts of silk and velvet—and this book of dress styles, too. Well, I figure the way this town is growing, there'll soon be no need for anybody to have to wear homespun.''

"Come in. I have to tell you something.''

He recognized the ominous tone in my voice and turned to me, his eyes filled with sudden alarm. At the sight of my taut face, he dropped a box back in the wagon bed and wordlessly followed me inside the inn.

I led him into our quiet family parlor at the back, darkened by drawn damask curtains. "Sit down. I'll get you some coffee.''

His lips tightened into a thin line. "What's going on around here?'' he asked tersely.

Breathing out a deep sigh, I sank down in a chair across the table from him. No use delaying the inevitable. "Tillie Weldon's dead.''

He flinched as if I had struck him. A sharp gasp of air. His clear gray eyes grew large and round, staring but not seeing. A long, terrible silence. "How?''

The sight of his raw pain hurt me. I had to force the words from my lips. "Her husband shot her.''

His face blanched white. His hands clenched the edge of the table. Another quick breath rustled through his nostrils; the muscles around his mouth worked, but no sound emerged.

"He's gone,'' I said, as if continued conversation would somehow cushion the shock. "He found her with Bill Woodward. He shot them both and then took off. I guess he's gone for good.''

Hugh's face was frozen, a mask of disbelief and horror. A hint of moisture glistened in his eyes. "Bill Woodward? She was with Bill Woodward?''

Slowly he rose. I grasped his arm, longing to comfort him, but he shook me off. His mouth twisted as he struggled to speak. "He didn't need to shoot her.''

"No.''

"That ugly old man. She was young. So pretty. Why did she marry him?''

"I don't know, Hugh.''

"He didn't need to shoot her.''

I only shook my head. Nothing I could say would ease his

255

torment. He had truly cared for this woman, was blind to all her faults.

Stunned, his face pale and drawn, he walked into his room and closed the door. Like a wounded animal, he sought only solitude and quiet.

I stared at the whitewashed planks of his closed door, recalling the somber, intense child he had been. His pain, I feared, would linger on for years.

CHAPTER 25

All winter Hugh brooded, desolate and morose, looking like a man lost in the desert. As he waited on customers in the store, or sorted the mail into the honeycomb of little boxes on the wall behind the counter, his face was set in grim lines. He still played host at the inn guests' supper table, but spent his evenings by the fireside in the family parlor, staring silently into the flames.

Eden Valley continued to grow, a center for the settlers filing claims, building homes, and breaking the fertile soil in the surrounding prairies for cropland. Nature, though, sometimes played tricks on us all. That spring Spoon River flooded and came roaring through our valley, tossing uprooted trees about like straws. We could only watch, aghast, as the rushing waters spilled over the banks, flooding the park and reaching up to Ruth and Karl's doorstep, threatening to carry off the mill before it finally subsided.

Come storm or sunshine, our store prospered with the influx of new settlers, even though the cost of coffee and sugar had risen to a shocking twenty cents a pound. At Sarah's insistence, Hugh brought back many bolts of pretty silks, linens, and muslins from St. Louis, along with fashion plates illustrating the latest styles.

Sarah, at nineteen, was a slender, graceful girl with silky hair and skin like porcelain. She kept our account books for the store and inn with meticulous accuracy. The elegant and stylish frocks she stitched herself attracted all the local young swains, although they shied away from her sharp wit, viewing her with more than a little awe. She made no effort to conceal her disdain for their crude western manners.

"You're an artist with that needle," I told her when she modeled her newest creation, a pale blue muslin with deep blue ribbon trim around the sleeves and hem. "You're sure going to turn a lot of fellows' heads when you wear that to the church meeting next Sunday."

She shrugged, unconcerned, and flicked a stray loose thread from the skirt front.

"It's bad enough now," I said, with a teasing smile. "All those young fellows pushing and shoving, just for the chance to say hello to you."

"Clods." She flipped her shining curls. "Not one of them can even say good morning like a proper gentleman."

Eddie guffawed, his eyes bright with a sly grin. "Yeah, funny how nobody says hello quite as proper as the schoolmaster. Guess they teach that in a college course back East."

Sarah glared at him, red circles burning in her cheeks. "I'm sure you haven't noticed, but you're quite uncouth yourself, Eddie Cranford."

With an uproarious laugh, he bowed stiffly from the waist. "Oh, do forgive me. I humbly beg your pardon, ma'am."

When Forrest Henley returned after spending the summer with his family in the East, I once more offered him room and board at the inn. Needless to say, Sarah was delighted. Once again she could converse with someone other than the frontier boys she disliked so.

In truth, his lengthy conversations with us in the evenings benefited our whole family, for he opened our minds to the intriguing world of literature and learning. During the hours spent listening to Forrest, I could almost feel my mind expanding. It was a strange sensation, for the more I learned, the more I wanted to know.

Eddie was often absent, for he preferred to hunt or fish with

257

his young friends or simply walk in the woods. Sitting still had always been a torture for him. But Joel, bright for his age at ten, curious and interested in everything, loved to listen to the articulate young teacher from Massachusetts.

The spirited discussions engrossed Sarah. Her patrician face and reserved personality fairly blossomed. "Why is that true? Tell us more about it," she would say, challenging the schoolmaster with her quick perception.

Forrest Henley's brows shot up, for he was not accustomed to being questioned by his students, and especially not by a girl. He covered his consternation with a tentative smile. "To really understand this matter, you need a fuller background in the field."

"But you're a teacher. Teach us," she said, her eyes sparkling with interest.

He appeared taken aback by her persistent questioning. "Let me see now. Where should I begin?" he murmured, as if talking to himself.

"Why, at the very beginning, of course," she replied.

The give and take of their intense debate made the evening pass like the flash of lightning bugs out in the yard. And the next night, they were at it again. A flush of pink crept into Sarah's cheeks as she challenged Forrest and sent him digging through his books for a reply. This contrary girl relished a good argument as another girl might love hearing sweet talk from some admiring beau.

I smiled contentedly as I watched them, for I suspected our Sarah had finally met her match.

Doc Benton was always there in the background, a true and steadfast friend. One day that fall, after he returned from a sick call in the country, he approached me when I came down the stairs. "Welcome back, Doc," I said. "Seems like you've been gone a week."

"It has been four days, for a fact. Old Colonel Ford down the way was in real bad shape. Poor fellow, he died shortly after I got there." He paused, then his expression lightened. "Come outside, Nellie. I've got a little surprise for you."

The strange smile on his face intrigued me. Burning with curiosity, I followed him as he led me out the front door. I started, for there on a farm wagon sat a whole family of black

258

people; they were surrounded by trunks and barrels and household furnishings. Black faces were so rare in our territory, customers at the store and mill and blacksmith shop stepped outside to stare at them.

"Why, Doc, who are your friends here?" I asked.

The tall, angular black woman, her strongly built husband, and the three young boys all stared at me with frightened eyes. "Why don't you all come inside and rest awhile?" I said, hoping my pleasant tone would allay their anxieties.

Doc motioned to the family, and they wordlessly followed us into my kitchen, studying their surroundings with curious, wary eyes. "This is Tyrus and Pearl. The boys are George, Thomas, and Patrick—named after some of our country's finest patriots," Doc said.

I nodded to them, smiling. "Well, sit down, everybody. Make yourselves at home."

"I'm hoping you can help me figure something out," Doc said, dropping wearily onto a chair. "Old Colonel Ford held these good folks as slaves down South. Since Illinois is a free state, he got legal papers changing them to bond servants when he moved here. At the same time, he had papers drawn so that when he died, they would be freed."

"That sounds like a fine idea." I glanced at the ring of faces, black as coffee beans, staring at me with unabashed curiosity. I thought of Uncle Amos and a surge of sympathy coursed through me. Yes, I knew exactly how it felt to be a slave.

"The colonel's son from Vandalia was there with him when he died. I stayed over to help the son settle all the legal matters, and then I brought these people up our way. I'm hoping you can help me get them settled somewhere."

"You'll be looking for work, won't you? And a place to live?" I asked the couple. They nodded their reply.

"I was sort of counting on you, Nellie. I know you're always needing help. Thought you might have a job for Tyrus and Pearl around here." He glanced at me with a hesitant frown.

"Well, Doc, your timing couldn't be better," I replied, grinning. "Jenny's getting married next month and moving over by Lewistown. I've hired a new girl to clean the rooms, but I need someone for the kitchen work. I could use somebody to take charge of the stable, too. Do you know anything about horses, Tyrus?"

"Yes, ma'am." The man beamed an enthusiastic smile. "I allow I know 'most everything about horses."

"Well, I could sure use a good man out there. We're getting more guests all the time, and have to board their horses. We have to keep a change of horses ready for the stagecoach line, too. Pearl, you can help with the cooking and cleaning, if that's agreeable with you. There's plenty of work for us all."

Doc burst out laughing. "Here I thought I was going to have to talk you into it. Had my arguments all planned. You made it too easy, Nellie. Thanks."

"Thought you were putting something over on me, did you? Well, the thanks belong to you. It's awful hard to find help around here, you know. Most of these settlers have all they can do to keep up their own work." I glanced at the round, dark eyes of the children and smiled. "Now, the next thing we have to do is find you-all a place to live."

"There're extra rooms at my old cabin," Doc said, turning to Tyrus and Pearl. "Why don't you take a look at that? I only use the parlor for my office. There're two more rooms and a loft. You could move in there—at least until you can find something better."

Without further ado, he bustled them back into the wagon and rumbled down the road to the far side of town.

Within days, Tyrus and Pearl were like part of the family. Her cooking won raves from all the inn guests, and his skill with horses and repair work relieved many of my pressing concerns. I was soon wondering how I had ever survived without them.

At first the boys seemed shy, bewildered by the rapid changes in their lives, but Joel introduced them to his favorite climbing trees and fishing spots and before long they were joining in bull pen and ball games with the other boys from town.

When the time arrived for the new school year to begin, I paid Forrest the tuition for Pearl's boys, too, and he accepted them without a flinch. But word of it got out to the other parents, and some voiced objections. They met outside the mill or on the road, heads bent together, complaining of my audacity. Sometimes their grumbles were loud enough to reach my ears.

"Never heard of such a thing!"

"Why, where I come from it's against the law to teach their kind to read."

I steeled myself against the inevitable confrontation. It wasn't long in coming.

The parents called a special meeting at the schoolhouse to air their concerns and fears about admitting three black children to the class. I attended, too, wearing my best green silk dress and a stubborn set to my jaw.

After listening quietly to all their protests, I stood, slowly surveying the sea of grim, determined faces surrounding me. I gulped down the fear that rose like bile in my throat. These were my neighbors, my friends, and now so many had turned against me.

Drawing in a deep breath to calm the crazy pounding of my heart, I said, "You all know me. You've known me for a long time."

"Yeah." "That's right." "What's got into your head, anyway?" angry voices muttered. Their eyes glimmered, boring into me.

"Look, I was born down in slave-holding country, just like some of you," I said, swallowing back my nervousness.

Some nodded. Some merely glared at me, distrust gleaming in their narrowed eyes.

"Well, we all moved up here to Illinois, didn't we? And we knew this was a free state."

In the face of mounting murmurs, I plunged ahead. "Free people have to know how to read and write, just to keep up with all that's going on in the world. Lord knows, it's hard enough for any of us to get the proper schooling for our kids. Seems like it's pretty mean-spirited to deny that to these little boys just because they were born black."

"What good will it do them?" a farmer shouted from the back, sneering.

"Same good it will do you or me or anybody else," Doc called out.

Impatience made me see red—and gave new force to my voice. "Look, I'm willing to pay their way. I'll be responsible for them. If they cause any trouble, I'll be the first to admit I was wrong. Now, how about it? What do you say? Won't you at least just give these kids a chance?"

A heavy silence hung over the crowd. Then the murmuring began anew, this time reflecting a reluctant agreement. Doc stood, his arm extended upward. "Come on. Let's have a show of hands. All of you in favor, raise your right hand."

Slowly, one by one, here and there a hand inched up. Heads turned as people scanned their neighbors, then more hands appeared. Doc took a quick count. We had won, and by a good majority. The boys could go to school.

Sarah had been seated in the back row beside Forrest. After the meeting, she met me at the door and gave me a quick hug. "You were beautiful, Ma," she whispered. "I've never been so proud of you."

I blushed, unaccustomed to attention. "Oh, these people are my neighbors. Sometimes they get riled up, but I knew they'd be fair, once the dust was settled."

With a triumphant smile, Doc took my arm and led me toward home. "Nellie, you're a whole team—and a horse to spare! If you were just a man, we'd run you for the legislature," he said, chuckling at my reddened face.

"Oh, Doc! How you do go on!"

When the boys started school on the first day, all scrubbed and shined within an inch of their lives, I went down to their cabin to see them off. Their mother gathered them around her and admonished them with such a list of dos and don'ts, I tried to call a halt. "Lordy, Pearl. These boys will shame the other kids if they're that good."

"They hear what I tell 'em. And they better mind." She shook her finger at them to emphasize her point.

George, the eldest, tall and rangy like his mother, nodded his head solemnly. "We will. We swear it," he said.

As the boys started up the road toward the schoolhouse, Pearl turned to me, tears welling in her eyes. "I don't know how to thank you. You're a mighty good woman, Miz Cranford."

"Oh, go along with you," I said, blushing. "Come on. Let's get down to the inn. There're breakfast dishes waiting. And we have to heat a big kettle of water, too, so the washwoman can do the sheets and towels. Sure hope this sun stays out until they dry."

Back at the inn, I quickly stacked the breakfast plates, which were still sitting on the long oak dining table. Doc Benton entered the front door and smiled at me across the room. "Well, they're off to school." He approached me spritely and patted my shoulder. "I still wish we could run you for the legislature."

I smiled, shrugging off his hand. "Sometimes you sound plumb addled, Doc. I'd never think of such a thing."

"Do you ever think of getting married, Nellie? My offer still stands."

"Lord's sake, I'm an old woman now," I said, with a chuckle. "Thirty-two years old. You'd better quit your dawdling and find yourself a younger gal."

He shook his head and rested his hands lightly on my shoulders. His smile was affable, his eyes sad. "No, if I can't have you, I won't take anybody. It's on your conscience if I have to live a lonely bachelor till I die."

"Go," I said, shoving him toward the door. "Go out and cure some sick people. I don't have time to listen to this soft soap."

I must confess it gave me pleasure to know that Doc still wanted me. But if Johnny were someday free, if he came back for me again . . . Oh, how I wished that foolish dream would stop gnawing at me. Funny how a person could be haunted by a pair of pretty eyes.

Winter set in, and once again the days grew dark and gloomy. Our only bright spots were the evenings Norman Hart stopped by the inn to lead us all in singing. Doc now drove his sleigh to answer sick calls in the snowdrifted country, wearing a fur cap, his lap covered with a buffalo robe, and heated bricks at his feet to keep them from freezing.

We received a letter from Noah at Christmas. "What does he say, Ma?" Eddie asked as I ripped open the seal and scanned the neatly written lines.

"He says he's married again. Well, how about that! He and his new wife and Benjie are all doing fine."

"Is that all?"

"He says Galena just keeps growing. His store business is booming."

"Maybe I'll go up there someday," Eddie said, his eyes afire with the thought of the adventure.

Hugh still brooded, growing more and more restless. Sometimes he left Sarah to run the store while he went out hunting, spending endless hours wandering in the woods alone. I became anxious for his sanity. This sensitive young man deserved a loving wife and family. A number of his friends had married. But would he ever be able to let go of the past?

The other children thrived. Sarah's nimble fingers flew, producing exquisite needlework and frocks for her and me. She did quilling and pierced- and cut-paper designs. As her spirited discussions with Forrest Henley continued, I noticed an increasing intimacy of tone. The most intense of arguments often ended with a burst of friendly laughter.

Eddie, seventeen and in his final year at the village school, still claimed the woods and fields as his first love. Sun-bronzed, glowing with health and vitality from his long hours outdoors, he provided us with an abundance of fresh game and fish to vary our meals at the inn. Joel looked up to Eddie as his greatest hero and begged to learn his brother's woodland skills.

These three children always gave me a satisfying sense of accomplishment. Daniel would be well pleased with them, I knew. But the thought of Hugh brought a stab of pain. Added to the trauma of the war, his infatuation and disillusionment with Tillie Weldon had been almost too much for him to bear. His torment hurt me every time I looked at his drawn face.

The following spring, a stagecoach traveler passed along some disturbing news from a town eighty miles south of Eden Valley. Two men there had accused a gambler of cheating them at poker. Enraged, the gambler pulled a pistol and shot them both. Although he now used a different name, the murderer was quickly unveiled as our own Lyman Weldon. He was tried without delay and sentenced to be hanged.

Hugh listened intently as the tale unfolded. "I'm going down there," he said, with a grim frown. "I'm going down and see him hanged."

"Oh, Hugh. Why?"

"I can't explain it. I have to, that's all."

My heart went out to him. I understood too well how complex and mystifying emotions can be. "Would you like me to go with you?"

"No. This is something I have to do myself."

He was gone five days. When he returned, he stabled his horse, then trudged into the parlor and dropped wearily into a fireside chair. He seemed older, his face pale and thin, still haunted by inner ghosts.

"Do you want to talk about it?" I asked cautiously.

With a shrug, he brushed back his shock of dark hair and leaned against the chair back. "Not a pretty sight."

"We heard that lots of people went there."

"Almost three thousand, they say. Some rode over a hundred miles to see it." He glanced at me, then looked away. "You ever see a hanging?"

"Never did. Never want to."

A shudder coursed through his body. "They drove a wagon with a coffin on it right up to the jail. Then they brought old Weldon out, all dressed in a white shroud and cap. They made him ride out to the hanging place sitting on that coffin."

"Good Lord. Sitting on his own coffin. Where was the hanging place?"

"A mile or so outside of town. A whole procession of people followed that wagon, riding horses or just walking. They had the gallows built in a hollow between two hills, so everybody could have a good view."

I turned away, my face twisted with distaste.

"They made him walk up to the gallows, and then a preacher came and prayed with him. After a bit, they pulled the white cap over his eyes and sprang the trap. The whole affair was over in a few minutes."

Shuddering, I breathed a jagged sigh. "Oh, Hugh. What a thing to ride eighty miles to see. It's sickening. What good did it do? It can't bring Tillie or those other fellows back."

He stared down at his dusty boots, his mouth set in a hard line, deep furrows cutting between his brows. A heavy silence settled over him.

After a long pause, he murmured, as if talking to himself, "He didn't need to shoot her."

I had nightmares of the hanging, of the hordes of people watching it with ghoulish pleasure, of Hugh's burning need to be there.

And what good, after all, did it do?

CHAPTER 26

One warm April morning the next spring, Sarah came to me after breakfast, her face lit by an inner glow. "Now that Eddie's going off to college, you're going to need more help. Why couldn't Forrest stay and work around the place?"

Hugh, still seated at the table, frowned as he studied the vapor tendrils coiling from his coffee mug. "You just don't want him to go back to Massachusetts again this summer."

"He's not going East," she said, with a triumphant tilt of her chin. "The lawyer at Lewistown has agreed to let him read law with him this summer. Forrest still has to earn his living, though, until school starts again. I just thought . . ."

"My goodness, yes! We can always use more help, between the store and inn." I glanced at her fresh, glowing face and smiled. Sarah was in love. As her earnest discussions with the young schoolmaster had awakened her bright mind, she had blossomed physically, too, as lovely as the redbud trees in spring. I recalled the cold, peevish child she had been, and I gloried more than ever at the change.

"Do you really think Eddie will stay at the college?" Hugh asked, shaking his head. "He told me he doesn't want to go away to school. He's always been more at home in the woods than in a classroom."

I scowled at him, hands on my hips. "Now, Hugh, don't talk that way. You know how much your pa wanted you all to get a good education. I'm only sorry I couldn't talk you into going to Jacksonville. At least Eddie will have his chance."

"Did I hear my name mentioned?" Eddie asked, striding in the back door, returning from an early morning ride through the woods. He had grown into a striking young man, tall, lean, and permanently tanned, his muscles hard as iron.

When he stopped to lather his hands at the washbowl by the door, his older brother good-naturedly slapped him on the shoulder. "I guess you know they won't allow you to wear this thing down at the college," Hugh said, lifting Eddie's Indian necklace by its leather thong. "They'll have you in a coat and stiff collar every day."

Joel dashed over and pulled on Eddie's sleeve. "Can I keep your bear-claw necklace for you while you're gone?" he begged in his boyish, high-pitched voice.

"Anything but that, little brother," Eddie said, affectionately ruffling Joel's dark wavy hair. "But after I eat, we'll sort through all my old arrowheads. I'll give you a couple of those, so you won't forget me."

Later, as Sarah worked on the account books at the parlor table, she glanced up at me, a smile playing around her soft, pink lips. "Thanks for promising to give Forrest a job," she said.

I set down the basket of folded clean clothes I was carrying to the boys' room. "Shoot, that's nothing to thank me for. I enjoy having him around. He's always giving me something new to think about. That's a treat, I'll tell you, for somebody like me who never had any schooling."

Her eyes shimmered. "He's always so interesting, isn't he?" She glanced toward the open door to the kitchen, then bent close to my ear and murmured, "He's an abolitionist."

"He's what?"

"An abolitionist. He works to help get rid of slavery."

A sudden chill ran through me. "Oh, Sarah! You know I don't believe in slavery, but openly declaring yourself to be an abolitionist can be dangerous. Just look what happened down at Alton. Riots. That Lovejoy fellow got shot."

"Forrest is not afraid to stand up for what he thinks is right."

"Well, fine. But feelings run awful high on that particular subject. I'm afraid he's wading in some pretty treacherous waters there."

She glared at me, still as stubborn as when she was a child. "He believes in it. And so do I."

I recalled what I had read in the Springfield paper about Elijah Lovejoy, a brave young editor who had been killed just last fall.

First he was chased out of St. Louis for printing an antislavery paper, and when he moved across the Mississippi to Alton, the people in the free state of Illinois protested just as loudly. Mobs descended on his office several times, destroying his presses. One night last November, the mob attacked his building again and, while defending his property, Lovejoy was shot and killed.

"You know I love Pearl just like a sister," I said, glancing away from Sarah's defiant eyes. "You know how hard I fought to get her kids into the school. But there's not much little people like us can do about the slavery down South."

"Forrest says it's evil. It's against the laws of God."

"I don't know. I have more than I can do just minding my own affairs." My head began to ache. I stopped to press my hands against my throbbing temples. "I've always held that a person ought to sweep his own front porch before he calls his neighbor's dirty."

I put away the stacks of clean clothes and went out to the kitchen to help Pearl get things set out for dinner. Surely I had enough worries of my own. How could I even think of reforming the whole country?

A few days later, Forrest Henley, his face red and angry-looking, burst into the kitchen; he was leading Tyrus by the arm. "Slave hunters just rode into town," he said tersely. "Where are Pearl's boys?"

Startled, I flicked my hand in the direction of the river. "They're fishing down by the mill with Joel and his friends. What in the world is wrong with you, Forrest? Tyrus and Pearl don't have to worry about any slave hunters."

"Oh, but they do. I'm going out and find those boys." Without another word, he hastened out the door.

"Pearl?" Dubiously I turned and met her widened, alert eyes. "What's going on here, anyway?"

She kneaded her hands together tightly. "Slave hunters just as soon pick up free niggers as go chasing after runaways," she muttered, with a quick glance at Tyrus.

He peered cautiously around the red gingham window curtain. "They takes 'em down South and sells 'em. I hear tell they get more than five hundred dollars for 'em."

"But you're free," I protested. "You have legal papers. They can't take you."

Pearl shrugged and shook her head. "Don't seem to make much difference."

Forrest hurried in, leading the three boys. I quickly herded their whole family into my bedroom. "You all stay right here," I said. "I'll take care of this."

When the two slave hunters reined up in front of the inn, I was waiting for them on the front porch, my arms folded across my chest. I looked them over, taking in their dirty, trail-worn clothes, the rifles resting across their saddles, the knives and pistols stuck into their wide belts. "Something wrong, gentlemen?" I asked, exaggerating my Southern accent as I met their cold, hard eyes.

The rough-looking men silently studied me. The older of the pair spat a fat wad of tobacco juice into the dusty road and wiped his mouth with the back of his hand. "We're after a runaway. Big strapping yellow boy. Scar across one cheek."

"Some guy in Quincy said he saw him heading up this way," the other said. "You seen anybody like that, lady?"

I tried to smile and look ingenuous. Could I trick them and get them out of town? "Why yes, sir. Matter of fact, I did," I said, dropping my arms to my sides. "A fellow like that passed through here two days ago. I heard he caught a ride over to Havana. They think he might have stowed away on a steamboat heading north."

My hands—my whole insides—were quivering. Was I convincing? Would they go away?

The men looked at each other, frowning. "Who told you that, lady?"

I rubbed my chin. "Now, let me think. Land sakes, we get so many travelers here . . . Oh, yes! I heard some fellow from the stagecoach talking about it just this morning."

"Well . . ." The older man took off his mottled felt hat and scratched his head. "I suppose we'd better head over to Havana. Maybe we can pick up his trail."

"Right down that way," I said, pointing to the road along the river. "If you-all hurry, you can make it before dark."

Stiff as a soldier, I watched the repulsive pair until they disappeared from sight. Then I exhaled a long-held breath and sank down on the porch bench to mop my sweaty brow. My whole body was damp with perspiration; my stomach had tightened into a hard knot.

My own words echoed through my head, mocking me. Mind my own business? Sweep my own porch? Now, all of a sudden, it seemed that slavery had become my own concern.

June arrived, a glorious, sun-kissed month, with warm, fragrant breezes from the south. A time for lovers.

Forrest and Sarah came to me one day and told me they wanted to be married. One glance at their faces, intelligent, idealistic, and radiant with love, and I knew these young people were perfect for each other. Since there was no reason for delay, they hurried down to talk to the preacher at Eden Valley's new church; they set their wedding date for three weeks later.

As soon as Doc Benton came riding in from a sick call, I ran out to the stable to tell him. "Little Sarah, all grown up and getting married," he said, shaking his head as he climbed down from his horse. "Doesn't seem possible, does it? Where has the time gone?"

"That's what I ask myself," I said.

He stood quietly, his eyes playing over my face. "I'm glad she's found somebody she can really talk to. That's important, Nellie."

I tensed, fighting back my warm response to the intimate tone of his voice. "Oh, I have so much to do before the wedding. I'd better roll up and get to work. I don't hardly know where to begin."

"I'm glad she's marrying a Yankee," he continued, stroking his horse's shiny bay flank. "Sarah's always been a Yankee at heart. Where are they going to live?"

"They'll stay here, in one of the private rooms, until he finishes his law studies and passes the bar. He'll still be teaching school next year. Nothing much will change."

"Those kids need a break from the routine here, to celebrate their wedding. Say, I'd like to give them a trip to St. Louis, if you don't mind. Steamboat ride, fine hotel and restaurants, the whole works. That will be my gift."

"Oh, Doc, how sweet! That would be perfect. Something they can always remember."

A sudden thought flashed through my mind, and I hurried inside to find Sarah. "Come with me out to the storehouse," I said briskly. "I have something I want to give you."

Brow furrowed with curiosity, she followed me across the

270

yard to the little log building behind the store, the cabin that had been our home for years. We made our way through the barrels and boxes of store goods and climbed the ladder to the loft.

Sweating in the stifling heat, I brushed aside a cobweb and reached far back into the corner to pull out a large, dark trunk. I grabbed an old tablecloth from a pile and quickly wiped the dust off the cracked leather, gazing down at Lenore's old trunk.

"These were your mother's things," I said, my voice choked with emotion. "I've saved them all for you."

"Oh! Oh, dear! Mother's things!" Tears pooling in her eyes, Sarah reverently opened the trunk and drew out a blue silk gown, stiff and faded with age. "You saved them all these years."

"I knew you'd appreciate having them after you grew up. You'll want to share some with the boys. They'd like a remembrance of her, too."

She startled me by throwing her arms around me and sobbing on my shoulder. "Oh, thank you, Nellie. Thank you so very much for being you."

Her wedding day dawned balmy, with the scent of locust blossoms floating on the air. As the hour approached, amber sunlight filtered through the leafy-green canopy of branches, creating a lacy pattern on the whitewashed plank walls of the little church. Neighbors, all dressed in their Sunday best, filed inside and took their seats on the narrow benches. Soon Sarah and Forrest, both slender, dignified, and intensely serious, stood before the preacher and repeated their vows.

I gazed at this young woman in the dainty white silk and lace dress, stitched by her own hands, and tears filled my eyes. Part daughter, part sister, she had been a replacement for the little sisters I had left behind so many years before in Kentucky. Daniel and Lenore would have been enormously proud of her this day.

Pearl and I had set out my new English china with a pink rose pattern and decorated the dining room with flowers and bright blue ribbon bows. After the wedding ceremony, all our friends and neighbors gathered there. Even the inn guests joined in the festivities, laughing, joking, clapping as the blushing couple slid a long knife into Pearl's masterpiece of a cake.

Norman Hart settled in a vacant corner and began to bow out familiar tunes on his old fiddle. While some guests lingered at the side table around the cake and lemon punch, others took up the lively rhythm, dancing reels down the center of the floor.

Soon the whole building throbbed with wild, infectious joy. Eddie pulled Sarah and Forrest into the middle of a ring and the crowd danced around them, clapping and singing merrily. Far into the evening, strains of music and laughter overflowed the room, drifting outside through the darkened streets of Eden Valley.

At last the pink-cheeked newlyweds started up the stairs. "Time to bring out the noise makers!" Ruth Schulmann shouted.

"Ja! Best part of any vedding!" Karl added.

Townspeople dashed home for pots and pans; farmers ran out to their wagons to retrieve those they had brought with them. Soon all were beating out a deafening clamor. Cowbells appeared, their clanging loud and dissonant. Whistles tooted, women shrieked, men shouted raucously.

I stepped outside, away from this boisterous merrymaking. As I sauntered toward the river, my sympathies were all with Sarah and Forrest. They were young and in love. I knew they yearned to be alone as man and wife.

A soft rustle sounded in the grass behind me. I turned and saw Doc striding toward me in the darkness, silhouetted against the golden lamplight from the inn.

When he reached me, we walked over to the dam and stood in silence, watching the falling waters dance gaily in the moonlight. Stars flickered like bright fireflies in the sky. The murmur of the dam was a gently soothing song.

Doc gazed down at me, the contours of his face illuminated by the moonglow. He smiled, took my hand. "Next time, Nellie," he murmured, his lips close to my ear. "Next time they will be dancing at our wedding."

Warm pleasure washed over me. He was a dear and valued friend, as reliable and comfortable as an old house robe. Wasn't this a kind of love? Why not marry him? Why should we both be alone when we would probably be content together?

But then I thought of Johnny. Even after all these years, his vivid image in my mind still stirred me with sensuous excitement. I recalled his entrancing smile, his dreamy eyes, his deep, rich voice. My whole body tensed and throbbed with desire.

Doc squeezed my hand. His voice was low and tremulous. "What do you say, Nellie? Isn't it about time we took the leap?"

My gaze lingered on the cascading waters, shimmering like molten silver in the moonlight. I could not answer, could not bring myself to hurt this dear old friend.

But I had married once for convenience. Yes, I had come to love Daniel deeply, but I always felt, still felt, that I was second choice. With Johnny, I had briefly known the full-blown ecstasy of first love, of feeling beautiful and special and passionately desired.

Now Johnny was far away, married to someone else. Still, crazy as it was for a harried, overworked widow in a little backwoods town, that old dream of love refused to die.

CHAPTER 27

Eddie soon grew restless with the routine of college classes down in Jacksonville. It took all my powers of persuasion to convince him to return to school after his visit home at Christmas.

His sun-bronzed skin had faded when he arrived home at the end of the school year in late spring. The moment he stepped into the parlor with his poised, swinging stride and dropped his leather valise on the floor, I could sense his year away at college had wrought other changes, too.

His easygoing cheerfulness had disappeared. Tense as a clock spring, he frowned and clenched his jaw. "It just won't work out, Ma," he said. "I've had enough of school. I'm just not cut out for sitting around with my nose in a book."

My first thought was of Daniel; I knew what he would have wanted for his son. "Sit down, Eddie. Relax. You've probably been working too hard and simply need a rest." I nudged him into a chair and sat across the table from him. "Now, think for a minute. You've earned high marks in all your classes. The whole world's open to you. You can go into any business or trade. Law, banking. Anything.'' My head spun just thinking of all the possibilities open in this developing country for this bright young man.

He shook his head. ''Can't you just see me as a big-city banker?'' he said, with a sardonic grin. ''It's all these cities springing up around here that I hate most of all.''

''You're just tired. Probably been studying too hard. Just rest a bit, and you'll be right as rain.''

''It's not that.'' Shoulders slumped, he stared out the window toward the wooded hillsides, where new leaves trimmed all the trees like fine green lace. ''I've been thinking about it for a long time. I have to go away. Someplace where the land isn't plowed yet. I have to have some freedom.''

My mouth dropped. I leaned my head against the chair back and studied his face. ''Where would you go?''

His eyes shone with excitement as they turned to me. His lean, supple body straightened to a proud stance. ''Minnesota Territory. I've dreamed of going there since I first heard of it. They say it's full of lakes, gorgeous ones, and the woods up there are thick and beautiful, chock-full of deer, every kind of game. I've been thinking I could open a trading post with the Indians up there, like Pa did when he came here.''

Rising, he crossed to the window and gazed at the flower-strewn hillside. Almost unconsciously he pulled his bear-claw necklace from his jacket pocket and slipped it over his head.

His words stunned me. I felt a flare of anger that he could so easily abandon all of us who cared so much for him. If he went away, when would we ever see him again? My heart ached as I thought of my father and little sisters, of Noah and Emily and Benjie, of all the people who had touched my life and then disappeared forever. Not Eddie. Oh, no! Not Eddie, too!

But then I recalled Hugh's continued misery. I could not bear to see Eddie unhappy. He needed the freedom of open spaces as much as others needed food and water. It would be foolish, even cruel, to try to hold him back.

''You don't really need my help around here anymore, do you?'' he asked.

I pressed my hand against my chest to still the rising pain. ''No, Eddie. We get along just fine. Tyrus and Pearl and their boys are such good help. Forrest pitches in wherever he's needed. And Joel is getting old enough to do a lot, too.''

Another dagger of pain stabbed at my heart. Eddie was Joel's idol. How he would miss his exciting woodsman brother.

"I'll be back now and then, Ma," he said, reading my anxieties. "It's just that Illinois is getting too civilized for my tastes. I guess I've always been half-Indian at heart."

I glanced at his bear-claw necklace and nodded. Though the words seared my mouth like acid, I forced a faint smile. "I won't stand in your way, Eddie. We all have to follow our hearts. I'll see that you have a nest egg to get started up there."

Two weeks later, we all stood beside the road, waving as this lionhearted young man rode off for the wilds of Minnesota with a newly built wagon carrying supplies for Indian trade. His eyes sparked with the anticipation of adventure. Though I would miss him, I admired his courage in following his dream.

A heaviness hovered over our house like dense fog for days after Eddie left. Joel still kept up with all his chores and played games with his friends, but sometimes he seemed almost as gloomy as Hugh.

And Hugh remained a nagging worry. He seemed bored with our thriving store, though several of the local girls tried their best to cheer him. They invented excuses to make frequent trips to the store, badgering him with silly questions about the merchandise. Giggling nervously, they lingered for a bit of flirtatious conversation. He ignored them all. And if I dared tease him about one, he snapped at me impatiently.

Summer came, days of thick, golden light washed over a world of green. Hugh's strained, pained attitude continued. Then one day in late August, as I was standing on the inn's front porch watching the departing stagecoach, I heard a feminine, deep-throated, infectious laugh drifting from the store.

A moment later, a vivacious girl with wavy nut-brown hair and laughing brown eyes, dressed in bright red calico, stepped out the door, followed by a young man whose good looks identified him as her brother. Hugh trailed behind them as if reluctant to let them leave. New light, new life, glistened in his eyes.

He glanced at me, then called out heartily, "Ma, look! More new neighbors! Come and meet Josh and Liza Johnson. Their family just bought a farm not far from here."

At the sight of his smile, joy rose in me like cream on milk.

"Always glad to meet new neighbors," I said, returning the girl's sunny greeting as I approached them.

Her face radiated health and a cheerful nature as her lively eyes swept across the park and mill and the river spilling over the dam. "I do believe this is the prettiest place I've ever seen. Eden Valley. Paradise. Somebody sure picked a good name for this town."

Hugh's gaze lingered on the girl's animated face. "My father named it. He was one of the first settlers in the Military Tract."

"Well, you should be proud of him," she said, lightly tapping his arm. "Eden Valley. Why, the man's a regular poet."

Her brother chuckled. "Come on, Liza. If I know you, you'll stand here and talk all day. We have to get these things back to the farm."

"Wait. Don't go," Hugh said abruptly.

Liza's smile broadened. "Yes?"

He stared at her as if bewitched. "There's going to be a circus at Lewistown next week. Biggest event of the whole summer. Why don't you two ride over there with me?"

I shook my head in disbelief. Hugh? Going to a circus? Why, it had been ages since he had shown the slightest interest in any kind of amusement. Already I liked this bright-eyed girl with the bubbly laugh and blithe smile. A tonic, that's what she was. A tonic Hugh had needed for a long, long time.

Liza Johnson rode off with her brother, and Hugh returned, whistling, to the store. As I resumed my sweeping with new vigor, the whole world seemed a brighter place.

The swish of my broom covered the sound of approaching footsteps, and I looked up, startled, when a deep voice boomed, "Morning, Miz Cranford."

Judson Lowder. Twin spots of heat flared in my cheeks. Would I never see this local tanner without remembering that his sister was Johnny's wife? "Morning, Judson," I said, trying to brush aside my fluster. "How's the family?"

He barked out a sharp laugh. "Well, the girls are all excited now, getting ready for next week. Johnny and Clarissa and the kids are coming up again to spend a few days with us."

I tensed. My heart began to race uncontrollably. "That's nice," I said. "Excuse me, will you? I have to see to something in the kitchen." I hurried inside without another word, fearful that my emotions were naked on my face, for all the world to see.

Taut as a fiddle string, I buzzed straight to the kitchen. I had to keep busy. That would help me get myself under control.

Pearl glanced up from kneading bread on the table and wiped her hands on her apron. "Why, Miz Nellie. Whatever is the matter?" she asked, a deep frown furrowing her brow. "You's white as a ghost."

I forced a weak smile. "Must be the heat, I guess."

How can I be so stupid? I chided myself. The time for childish dreams is long past. Johnny Nichols has a family of his own now. He is as dead to me as Daniel is.

"Sit down and rest awhile. Let me fix you a nice cool drink," Pearl said.

"I'm fine. Really." I walked into the parlor. Sarah glanced up from the account books she had spread out on the parlor table, where she often worked on our bookkeeping while Forrest studied his law books in their room upstairs. "Are you all right, Nellie? You're looking pale."

"You and Pearl fret over me too much." All this unwanted attention embarrassed me. I only wanted to keep busy, to put all thoughts of Johnny from my mind.

She studied me dubiously. "You work too hard. Rest for a while. Everything is pretty quiet around here right now."

Rest? No, work seemed a better answer. I strode out to check with Tyrus on the progress of the new addition to the stable.

As I started back toward the inn, Doc Benton met me in the yard. "What's this I hear?" he asked, frowning. "I ran into Sarah on the stairs; she told me you're not feeling well."

"It's nothing, Doc," I answered, flicking my hand. "I'm probably just getting old."

"It can't be that. Not you." His pleasant smile soothed me like a warm bath. "Why, Nellie Cranford, you're as slim and sprite as a young girl. And that glorious red hair. You remind me of a poppy blossom swaying in the breeze. No, you'll never grow old."

I chuckled. "Poppy blossom, is it? I'd say I'm more like a mother hen with a passel of baby chicks chasing after her."

What would I do without Doc? He was a dear, treasured friend. But memories of Johnny kept ruffling through my head like a stiff wind over water. My body throbbed with disturbing desires. I must put him out of my mind. Completely. Once and for all.

I dove into an orgy of housecleaning at the inn, hoping Johnny's visit to the Lowders' house might escape my notice. With bursts of frenzied energy, I emptied all the shelves in the kitchen, washed all the pans and bowls and flatware and stacks of dishes. I polished furniture upstairs and down and, panting from exertion, carried mattresses and pillows out to the backyard to air. I beat the carpets, washed the windows, and laundered, starched, and ironed all the curtains.

I knew from the town gossip that Johnny and his family were at the Lowders all week. Busy as I was, I successfully avoided them.

I will not think of him, I told myself, my muscles cramped and aching from strain. No, definitely not. I will not picture his face, will not remember his bewitching eyes, intense and filled with desire, his deep voice that made my body weak.

And then one day as I was filling the water pitchers upstairs and putting out fresh towels in the rooms, I heard the tinkle of the little pewter bell on the desk beside the entry door. I started down to answer the call.

Then I saw him. Standing by the desk, shifting from one foot to the other, brushing a speck of dust from the sleeve of his dark coat.

Johnny. Handsome, tender, exciting Johnny. I stopped, frozen on the stairs.

His gaze was riveted on me, his lips curved in a warm, lingering smile. "Nellie. I just had to see you again before we start back for St. Louis. My wife's next door—buying a few things for the trip."

My heart thudded in quick, dull beats. I drew in a deep breath and moved blindly down the stairs. As I approached him, I felt drawn like iron to a magnet. "Nice to see you, Johnny." I hesitated, not knowing what came next. "You're looking good."

"And you." His mesmerizing gaze bore into me. "You look so lovely, standing there with the sunlight on your hair."

His nearness sent a tremor through me. "It's been a long time," I murmured.

"Too long."

We stood there, staring at each other. I soaked in his image as drought-stricken land soaks in rain. How long had it been?

With a shock, I realized that seventeen years had passed since that fateful day behind my uncle's house. Seventeen long, eventful years. And now it seemed like only yesterday.

As if on cue, we stepped toward each other. He grasped my hands. "Nellie," he murmured, his voice choked and husky. "I had to see you again. I've never forgotten you."

My head spun with surging emotion. "Oh, Johnny, no. You mustn't say those things."

His grasp on my hands grew tighter. "If only we could have been together—"

A quick step clicked across the porch. "Johnny?" a feminine voice called impatiently.

I wheeled to meet his wife's sharp frown. Instantly I freed my hands from his, my face burning with embarrassment and guilt. My glance dropped to the wooden floorboards at my feet.

"Johnny, it's time to go." She glared at me, her pale, round eyes aflame with fury.

"Nellie, I don't believe you've met my wife. This is Clarissa. Clarissa, Nellie."

"Yes, I've heard of you," she said. "Blanche told me all about you."

Johnny's lip curled with distaste. "You would do well not to believe anything my sister says."

Hands stiffly clenched, he bent his head to me in a formal bow. "Nellie, I'm pleased to know you and your family are doing well. I'm sorry, but we have to go now."

I nodded, unable to speak, impaled by his wife's white-hot stare. Hatred radiated from her like heat waves from a blazing fireplace. My stomach squeezed into a hard knot. She knew. Perhaps she understood the situation better than we did ourselves.

With a loud sniff, she spun and stomped out to their waiting carriage.

Moments later, they pulled away. My cheeks burned as if they had been slapped.

Grudgingly I took a last glimpse at the departing carriage as Johnny's little girl turned back and waved to the small family group clustered in front of the store. And then I saw her eyes. Deep sapphire-blue eyes, rimmed with thick, black lashes.

Eyes that could haunt you for a lifetime.

CHAPTER 28

Johnny still cared for me. Now I knew it was true. The girl who was me, and the boy who was Johnny, had changed and grown over the years, but the attraction, the passion, was still there between us, real enough to touch.

Yes, I had wonderful memories of Daniel. Nothing would ever dim my love and respect for him. But the nagging thought remained: Daniel was dead, and I was very much alive.

It made a heavy burden, the guilt of knowing that a flame of love still burned and still connected me with Johnny. He was married now. I wished his wife no ill. But almost daily something happened to remind me of all the diseases and uncertainties surrounding us. None of us could ever count on life continuing unchanged. Who could tell? Perhaps someday down the road Johnny and I would finally be together.

The thought of him fretted me like a piece of food caught between my teeth.

The years were slipping by too quickly, in days consumed by the responsibilities of managing the inn, of signing scores of travelers in and out, showing them all to their rooms, conversing pleasantly with them. I oversaw the housekeeping and stable work, smoothed over problems for irate or impatient guests, planned meals, and helped serve the food. I conferred with the farm tenant on crops, livestock, and prices and watched closely over the business at the store, too. And with it all, I managed to play the role of charming hostess at the inn.

New towns sprinkled the whole Military Tract now. The opening of the prairies to farming had been spurred by John Deere's invention of a marvelous new light steel plow. Gradually, fine brick homes began replacing the rustic one-room log cabins.

As Joel, my youngest, turned fifteen, a new interest absorbed him. This thoughtful, gentle boy now spent every spare moment with Doc Benton, helping roll pills and straighten the instruments and supplies in his office while they discussed all the mysteries of medicine.

Doc still remained a border at the inn, with only a small, monklike upstairs room to call a home. "Looks like we might have a budding doctor here," he told me one evening after supper, nodding his head in Joel's direction.

I glanced across the dining room to the boy's smooth, pleasant face, his slender frame, lanky as a young colt. "He's been wrapped up in it for months. At first I thought it was just another passing fancy, but every night he's over by the lantern, reading from my home medical book."

"He's shown a real interest," Doc said, smiling fondly at the boy. "If he likes, and if you agree, I'd be glad to let him apprentice with me after he's finished with his schooling. Lord knows we could use another doctor around here."

"I know how hard it's been for you." I studied Doc's familiar face and saw the signs of passing years that had accumulated without my noticing. A few streaks of silver gleamed in his dark hair, a few lines were etched across his brow and at the sides of his kind eyes. These days his lips lay set in a sober line, less quick to smile, to crack a joke.

As the only doctor in a wide area, his life demanded almost saintly sacrifices and hardships, and the sad condition of our dirt roads added greatly to his difficulties in traveling through the countryside. Deep sucking mire in spring, choking blow dust in summer, trackless snowdrifts in winter—all these were braved without a moment's hesitation when someone needed Doc's ministrations.

His pay for services was often delayed until the crops were harvested, and then he usually received bushels of corn or slabs of bacon in lieu of cash. Throughout the years, he had settled his accounts with me that same way, paying for his room and board by adding to our food stores in the cellar or the storage shed or smokehouse.

Doc was an unofficial member of every family, presiding over birth and death, accident and disease. All the other settlers viewed him as an angel of mercy. To me, he was a very dear and valuable friend.

When the hint of winter began to chill the amber days of late fall, Joel started back to school once more, but this term a new teacher reigned over our one-room schoolhouse. Forrest had completed his law studies; he had passed the bar examination. Now he planned to open a law office in the newly founded town of Galesburg, about forty miles northwest of Eden Valley. Sarah and he drove the buggy up there one day to inspect the town and search for a house to buy with her dowry money.

"Galesburg is going to be a first-rate town," she told me after they returned. "A group of Eastern church people moved out there to build a college, and they made plans for the city at the same time. Now everything is well underway."

I smiled at the enthusiasm radiating from our usually reserved Sarah. Her flushed cheeks fairly glowed. "Well, if it's all Easterners, I reckon you and Forrest will feel right at home," I said.

She nodded brightly. "Yes, and they have an abolitionist society there, too."

"Abolitionist society? What can they do in Galesburg? There's no slavery in our state."

"The society is working for the day when slavery is outlawed everywhere. They distribute antislavery literature and circulate petitions. Hold prayer meetings and bazaars. Collect money to help the cause. All kinds of things."

I recalled the many travelers at the inn I had heard railing long and loud against the "damned abolitionists." Hostile, angry Southern voices spoke of outsiders meddling in other people's business. Others said while they personally opposed the extension of slavery, they didn't want to interfere. One thing was for certain, tempers always ran hot and high when they argued their clashing opinions.

"Just be careful," I said, clasping Sarah's arm. "That can be dangerous business, you know."

She lifted her head proudly. "Forrest and I must do what we know is right." Bending close to my ear, she whispered, "We're going to help with the Underground Railroad, too."

"The Underground Railroad?"

Her eyes lit with an inner fire. "It's a whole network of people from all over the country. They help runaway slaves escape to the North or over into Canada."

"I've heard a bit about it. The St. Louis papers were all up in arms about people in Illinois helping hide the Missouri slaves who cross the Mississippi River."

"It's becoming widespread now, especially among the church groups that moved out here from New England," she said. "There's a very active cell up in Princeton. After Elijah Lovejoy was killed down in Alton, his brother Owen moved up there."

"Galesburg. Princeton. I guess it is spreading."

She glanced around to assure herself we were alone. "You could be part of the Railroad, too, right here in Eden Valley."

Eden Valley? My mind reeled at the thought. "You mean that's going on around here? How come I've never heard of it?"

"It's all kept very secret. But it's going on all over. Wherever people believe in the cause."

"Just think of that."

"Yes, slaves cross the Ohio River from Kentucky, or the Mississippi from Missouri. Quincy is one of the main ports of entry for slaves crossing the Mississippi. Once they've hit free soil in Illinois, the Railroad people help them find their way up to Chicago or Detroit, where they can cross by boat to Canada."

"That's a fine idea, Sarah, but there's slave catchers after them all the time. I've seen them pass by here—mean-looking varmints, armed to the teeth, a hank of rope and handcuffs hooked to their belts. Those fellows mean business. I suspect they'd sell their grandma if the price was right."

She pursed her lips and folded her arms against her waist. "Forrest and I are joining the Abolitionist Society just as soon as we move to Galesburg. You could join it, too. I know you'd like to help."

"Yes, I sure would. But I can't do anything too open," I protested. "There're so many mixed feelings in these parts. We have to try to live in peace with all our neighbors."

"I can never make peace with slavery."

A brave, strong-willed girl, Sarah. Her words haunted me for days. I knew I could never own slaves, even if it had been legal here. I treated Tyrus and Pearl and their boys as if they were my own family. What more could I do? I was much too busy to get involved in any time-consuming, dangerous "movement," no matter how much I subscribed to its principles.

After Sarah and Forrest moved to Galesburg, my life became even busier. Hugh and I depended more and more on Pearl's boys to help with the myriad of chores around the store and inn, since Joel was often out on calls with Doc.

By now stagecoaches stopped every day in Eden Valley, bringing mail and newspapers and passengers. Some stages tarried for meals or overnight, while others paused only long enough to change for fresh horses. I always tried to be on hand, along with all the small boys in the town, to greet the stage when the driver jerked it to a halt.

Out along the country roads, the double team of horses might have plodded leisurely for hours, but when they approached the town the driver cracked his whip and brought them in at a full gallop. I never tired of this thrill and drama—the thunder of sixteen galloping hoofs, the sharp crack of the whip, the hoarsely shouting driver, the top-heavy coach swaying back and forth.

The coach skidded to a quivering stop, and eight or ten passengers, men, women and children, clambered down from their cramped seats and groaned with the long-anticipated relief of stretching their legs.

"I's coming right out," Tyrus called from the stable. He brought around fresh horses and unhitched the tired, sweaty teams.

"Yeah, these fellows could use a little rest," the driver said as he climbed down from his high perch. He strode into the store to drop off the leather mailbag and pick up the outgoing mail. After returning outside, he bit off a huge chew of tobacco, then unbuckled the leather curtain and lifted out the travelers' trunks from the boot at the rear of the coach.

"Howdy, kids!" The driver waved to the straggle of wide-eyed boys clustered near the stage, silently admiring him, eyeing his long whip.

Although the man swore like a sailor, the boys loved his exciting stories of robberies and runaways. Besides that, he could spit tobacco juice eight feet and hit a nail right on the head every time. In the boys' eyes, he was a real hero.

"Time to be heading on," he said finally. He climbed back up to his seat, took his four lines in one hand and his long whip in the other, and gave his team a cluck to start them down the road. Glancing back, he raised his old felt hat in an aloof wave to his admirers, proud as any king upon his throne.

284

Our inn's thriving prosperity was matched by the store, the mill, the blacksmith, the carpenter, the tanner, the gunsmith, and the cooper. New settlers had opened operations for wagon building and brickmaking. Another reopened the saloon, this time for a more decorous operation.

Sarah and Forrest quickly established themselves in Galesburg. And from time to time, Eddie sent us a short letter saying he was well and happy in his new home in the Minnesota wilderness. I could not ask for more.

As Hugh's friendship with Liza Johnson developed, his habitual frown disappeared. Once again he took part in the community's bustling social scene, joining the many house- and barn-raising parties, the wolf hunts and shooting matches. When Norman Hart bowed out his cheerful tunes on his old fiddle, Liza, eyes shimmering and laughter bubbling up from deep within her throat, clasped hands with Hugh to dive for the oyster, duck for the clam, allemande left, and promenade.

Another year passed, like the blinking of an eye. One warm, lazy evening in early September, as I was sitting on the front porch hoping to catch a stray breeze, Doc strolled out and joined me on the bench. The music of the mill dam hummed its continuous soothing tune, lulling us into a comfortable silence.

"It's so good to sit down," he said after a pause, resting his head against the plank wall behind him. "I've been on a dead run, and now I'm expecting Cora's husband to ride up any minute, telling me her time has come."

"Little Cora Schulmann, all grown up and married." I wagged my head in amazement. "And Ruth going to be a grandma already. Just doesn't seem possible, does it?"

He chuckled. "You know what they always say. Kids and corn are Illinois' best crops."

"Reckon that's the truth." I drew in a deep breath, savoring the pleasure of the moment—the company of an old friend, the soothing song of the waterfall.

The *clip-clop* of horses' hoofs sounded from the stable around back. The noise grew louder, and I waved as Hugh rode by. With each passing year, he looked more and more like Daniel, I thought with a touch of pride.

"Going courting, is he?" Doc asked softly.

"Riding out to see Liza again, I wouldn't wonder," I said,

my gaze following the trim figure on the briskly trotting horse. "That dear girl has done a world of good for him."

"He sure looks like a different person these days. Nothing like a little romance to perk a body up, I always say."

"I wouldn't know about that."

His eyes met mine in a long, quizzical gaze. "Now that's your own fault, and you know it."

Just then another horse galloped into town, with Cora's agitated young husband astride, and Doc was off to supervise another birthing.

I knew I should go inside to the kitchen and put some beans on to soak for tomorrow, but it was sweet simply to sit and drink deeply of the gathering twilight. The air smelled of late-blooming flowers and ripening fields. Frogs garrumped down by the river, and a mourning dove cooed in the woods, a soft, peaceful note.

Judson Lowder sauntered across the park from the riverbank, carrying a string of iridescent fish. "Evening, Nellie," he said, touching his battered felt hat.

"Evening."

"Sure warm for this time of year." His voice sounded friendly, eager for conversation. "Say, I just got a letter from Clarissa."

"Oh?" Johnny's wife. I didn't want to think about her.

"Yeah. She said Johnny's going out to Texas."

My chin dropped. "Texas! Whatever for?"

"That Johnny's always been ambitious, you know. Built him up a first-rate herd of racing horses. Now he's looking for a place out in Texas to raise horses and cattle. Going to move the family down there. He figures it's just a matter of time before it gets to be a state."

"Yeah," I said numbly. "Yeah, it's sure been in the news a lot lately."

"Well, I'd best get home and get these fellows cleaned." Swinging his string of fish jauntily, he touched his hat again and strolled down the road.

"Texas," I repeated to myself, staring numbly at Judson's retreating form.

Texas. So far away. The thought of that enormous distance stunned me. St. Louis was already too far. I had only seen Johnny three times in all the years since I had left my uncle's house. Now he might be gone for good.

The breeze died, and the evening's heat closed in around me. The river flowed over the dam with an incessant drone. I sat motionless, listening to it intently. If only I could concentrate on that monotonous hum, perhaps I could shut out the thoughts that tore into me, poisonous as rattlesnake fangs.

Johnny. Texas. So far. So very, very far from me.

CHAPTER 29

Johnny was off to Texas. What concern was that to me? I had a full life here, a satisfying life with my family and my work. Yet, in my bed alone at night, why did these thoughts of him keep floating through my mind? Why did that crazy dream persist, that someday, somewhere, we would be together?

No. I must face the cold facts. Johnny had moved a thousand miles away. Only through a miracle would our paths ever cross again. The years were passing quickly, and soon I would be growing old. Romantic fantasies belonged to young folks like Hugh and Liza.

All that winter the ring of Liza's infectious laugh drifted through the frosty air as she and Hugh ice-skated on the frozen river with a group of friends. When the frost hung like lace curtains on the windows, they drove off for jolly sleigh rides over the snow-blanketed fields. Hugh's bright eyes and animated smile made him seem a new and different person.

Joel was busy with schoolwork all winter, but he still spent every spare moment helping around Doc's office. When spring arrived, he came to me one evening, his face somber and intense. "I guess you know I want to be a doctor, Ma," he said. "Do you think I can?"

"You can do anything, Joel. Anything you choose."

287

He broke into a gleaming smile, like summer sunshine on the river. "It's what I've wanted for a long time. Doc says I'm a natural."

"You know it's not an easy life, son," I said, wrapping my arm around his bony shoulder. "You've seen what Doc goes through, fighting every day against disease and death. And there's a lot to learn. You'll have to study hard here, and then at the college at Jacksonville. It's going to be a long haul. And somehow I have the feeling that won't bother you a bit."

"I've already learned a lot from helping Doc. He's going to lend me his books, too, so I'll have a head start long before I go to college. After that I can apprentice with him, and pretty soon I'll have the whole business licked."

"That you will, son," I said, chuckling at his effusive confidence. "Wildcats couldn't hold you back, could they?"

As he turned to go outside, my gaze lingered on his lanky, boyish frame. My son. Child of my heart. Daniel would have been so proud of him.

With a start, I realized how big a part Daniel still played in my life, even though he had been gone for almost ten years. The ties that bound our lives were forever intertwined. Who would have thought, all those years ago when we first met down at my uncle's inn . . .

Engrossed in memories, I walked over to the fire to set the kettle on for tea. Then I noticed a faint rustling sound outside the kitchen window.

Now who in the world was that? None of the inn guests ever bothered around the kitchen. Pearl always went home right after supper dishes. Maybe she had returned for something.

I peered outside. The night had flowed in, dark and liquid over the yard and hillside. As I stepped out on the back stoop, I immediately spied the cellar door standing open. "Pearl?" I called. An unfamiliar bustle sounded from below. "Pearl? Is that you?"

"Yes, Miz Nellie," Pearl mumbled, her voice so strained and quavering I scarcely recognized it. Whatever was wrong?

I hurried back inside to light a lantern, then carried it down the steps into the crowded, cluttered cellar. "Something the matter down here, Pearl?" I asked. The blended odor of different foods assailed my nostrils as I made my way among the bulky sacks.

Pearl stepped out from among the barrels in the corner, her eyes as big as moonflowers against her stark black skin. She glanced back with a jagged intake of air. "Oh, Miz Nellie! I needs your help!" she said breathlessly, her words echoing off the stone walls. She rushed up and grabbed my hand. "I just don't know what I can do 'bout this."

"Sakes alive, Pearl. Tell me what's ailing you."

"Just lookit here." She led me around barrels and sacks and baskets, further into the dark, odorous depths of the cellar.

My flickering lantern light reached out, illuminating the corner where six eyes stared back at me, terrified as trapped animals. As I approached, I made out the forms of a thin, haggard black woman and two ill-clothed adolescent girls, huddled together, quaking with alarm.

"They found their way as far as my house," Pearl said, fixing her frightened eyes on my face. "They heard 'bout me somewheres, and came begging me for help. Say they been running for weeks. I thought it might be safer if they stayed down here in the cellar for a while. Just to rest, you know."

My stomach knotted with distress. "Oh, Pearl . . . Maybe we should find another place. I don't know if the inn should be mixed up in this."

"Slave catchers hot on their trail."

"But this place is so open. And the law . . . The law says . . ."

The woman in the corner moaned, wiping her eyes on the edge of her wrinkled, dirty skirt.

"Miz Nellie, you can't send them away." Pearl patted the woman's shoulder as she turned to me, pleading. "You know you can't. These poor souls been hiding out in woods and traveling by night. Ain't ate nothing but green corn and fruit for days."

"I'll bring them something to eat right away. And I'll find them some decent clothes. But—"

"This woman swears she won't go back," Pearl said. "Her master's going to put these young girls on the block and sell them to Lord knows who. Ain't you heard the kind of things goes on down there?"

I looked at those three frightened faces . . . and thought of my own children. My knees felt weak. These pretty young girls—sold like cattle to the highest bidder? Who had not heard tales of the slave markets, with scores of leering patrons squeezing naked calves and thighs of girls to judge their worth.

The woman spoke up in a quavering voice. "I left one baby buried in Kentucky. That grave is a comfort to my soul. But my other boy, he got sold South. Him it hurts too much to even think on."

My gaze fixed on the woman's tormented face. I nodded briskly. "Yes, I'll help you. But first, let me fix you-all something to eat."

When I walked back up the stairs, my mind flitted in a thousand directions. What was I getting myself into? The laws forbade aiding runaways. I could be jailed or fined, my good name ruined. What about our business here? We had all worked so hard, so long, to build it up. Yet, I could not refuse them.

Pearl followed me, muttering with grim determination. "They needs to get away fast. Slave catchers coming."

What to do? Plans quickly jelled inside my mind. I turned to her abruptly. "Tyrus can drive them up to Sarah's in Galesburg. She'll know what to do from there. Run and tell him to hitch up the big farm wagon and fill some bags with straw from the barn."

While the runaways ate a quick meal of ham, fried eggs, and bread, I rushed out behind the barn and helped Tyrus arrange sacks of straw and some of cornmeal in the bed of the wagon. Peering around the corner of the barn, I glanced at the inn's darkened upstairs windows to make certain we were not being observed.

"People around here know you work for me," I whispered. "If anybody stops you, just tell them you're taking some cornmeal to Galesburg for me."

With silent stealth, Pearl led the woman and her daughters up from the cellar and across the yard, clinging to the patches of shadowed darkness beneath the trees.

"Just crawl up here and lie down," I whispered, guiding them into the wagon. Tyrus and I carefully covered the runaways with sacks of straw and tucked the bags of cornmeal around the edges of the wagon.

As Tyrus climbed up on the seat, he hesitated, scowling down at me. "This just ain't going to work, Miz Nellie," he muttered, shaking his head. "If them slave catchers come riding by and see my black face, first thing they going to do is stop me and look through this here wagon."

My heart sank. "You're right. Of course. I should have thought of that."

I stood with slumped shoulders, chewing on my fingernail. "Oh, shoot! I'll go myself," I said. "Pearl, you tell Hugh what happened when he comes to breakfast. You and him will have to look after the inn while I'm gone. Joel can help. Just tell the folks I'll be back in a couple of days."

Drawing my shawl close around my shoulders, I hiked up my skirt and climbed up on the wagon seat. Well, this was it. I set my jaw and stiffened my spine, then flicked the reins across the horse's back. For better or for worse, we were on our way.

The night was crisp and clear, the sky ablaze with stars. Ahead of me, the road stretched like a silver ribbon in the moonlight. I rode on and on, so overcome by the mystic beauty of the night, my apprehensions disappeared.

I yawned. My eyelids sagged. I shook myself alert and listened to the muted murmur of night sounds. Far in the distance, a wildcat screamed. Was it headed my way? Were there wolves lurking in those dark copses of woods?

The way seemed endless. Just before dawn, I pulled off the road beside a creek and uncovered the woman and her daughters, so they could climb out briefly to stretch their legs and get a drink. We did not dare to speak beyond a few anxious whispers, and quickly pressed on to Galesburg.

Finally I caught sight of the sparkling new town, with its impressive steepled church and college building. Already industries were springing up there: a brickyard, and shops for making wagons, plows, harnesses, pumps, and shoes.

By the time we reached Sarah's neat whitewashed house, my eyes drooped with fatigue. She ran out to greet me as I reined the wagon in near her back door. "Nellie! Is that really you? Whatever are you doing here?"

"Shh! Careful," I whispered. "Now's the time I need you to tell me more about that railroad."

"Nellie! You mean . . . ?"

"Shh! Right here in the back of this wagon. Now what's the next step, I'd like to know."

She smiled, studying me with new admiration. "Don't worry, we'll take care of that. Just drive the wagon into the barn and unload your passengers. I'll run and get Forrest. He can take over for you from here."

I returned home the next day, happy to assure Pearl that the brave fugitive woman and her girls were on their way to Chicago, and then by lake steamer to Canada.

After a short rest, I cleared and scrubbed the far end of the cellar, then brought down a supply of quilts and blankets. Joel and Hugh helped me stack barrels to form a wall.

If the fugitives were silent, this hideout should be secure enough, unless someone came with a warrant to search. We must be extra cautious during the transfer to the wagon, though, for there was always the danger that one of the inn guests might happen to be looking out a window. I would have to devise some better arrangements. Next time any runaways came our way, I intended to be well prepared.

When I walked into my room to wash my face and hands at the basin, my pale reflection in the little wall mirror stared back at me. Well, Nellie Cranford, I guess you're a full-fledged abolitionist now, I told myself.

A muddle of thoughts whirred through my head. I was proud that I had helped the runaways escape to freedom. My years with Uncle Amos had taught me what it meant to be a slave, and I cringed at the injustice of the ugly system. Yet I knew these activities must always remain strictly secret.

Would they isolate me, sever the warm bonds of friendship I had formed with my Eden Valley neighbors? Would they get me fined, or even thrown in jail? It was too late now to look back.

"Where did you disappear to?" Doc asked me as I cleared off the breakfast table the next day. "Even Joel said he didn't know where you'd gone."

"Oh, I just went to visit Sarah for a couple of days," I said, avoiding his searching eyes.

He laid a gentle hand on my arm. "Is something wrong, Nellie? You look like you have a lot on your mind. Anything I can do to help?"

Could I trust him? I glanced up into his kind eyes and knew instinctively I could tell him anything. "It—it was some friends of Pearl's. I drove them up to Galesburg," I said softly.

"Runaways." It was a statement, not a question. "I know how strongly Sarah and Forrest feel about the subject."

I glanced around the empty room, fearful someone would overhear. Still anxious, I nodded wordlessly.

"I must say I agree with them in principle," he said. "Slavery is evil, and any laws designed to protect it are evil laws. But you're messing with some dangerous business, Nellie. Safer to hold a grizzly by the tail."

"Well, this thing really has my dander up." Speaking in low tones, I told him of the woman, her daughters, and their desperate plight.

When I had finished, he took my hand and squeezed it. "You're right. We have to help wherever we can. I just wish you'd called me. I could have driven them up in my buggy. Nobody would think of stopping the country doctor on his rounds."

My brows shot upward. "They wouldn't, would they?"

"Next time let me know. Even if I'm tied up with a patient and you have to wait awhile, that's still safer than taking off by yourself."

"I will. I know you're less likely to be stopped than me." I smiled up into his eyes, feeling a surge of relief in sharing this vexing burden with a friend. "Whatever would I do without you, Doc?"

He grinned. "It's nice you have some use for me," he said, pressing my hand.

"More than you know. More than I care to admit to myself."

No other runaways appeared for weeks. Perhaps I had been all upset for nothing. I settled back into my usual routine. Our businesses were prospering with the area's burgeoning development. I ordered myself a fancy bonnet, to be brought up special on the stage from Springfield, and made myself a pretty blue silk dress for church on Sundays. A new walnut desk, crystal lamp, and wool rug graced our family parlor.

All trace of worry disappeared. My senses reveled in the glorious sights and smells and sounds of spring surrounding me. Trees leafed out and the prairie greened. A riot of red and pink and purple bloomed on all the vines and bushes on the hill.

Late one morning, as I was weeding my bed of transplanted wildflowers beside the inn, I noticed Judson Lowder trudging up the road toward the store. I stood up and waved to him with a wide smile, for the day was balmy and my flowers were blossoming in a kaleidoscope of color. But Judson's slumped shoulders and downcast face were not in tune with the irrepressible joy of that gorgeous day.

"Won't be long until we'll have fresh peas from the garden," I said, brushing back a stray lock of hair from my cheek.

He shrugged glumly. "Suppose so." His face tightened, etching deep lines between his brows. "Guess poor Clarissa will be moving up here soon."

Something in his voice made my blood chill. "Clarissa?"

"Yeah." A long, whistling sigh escaped his lips. "It's sure a sorry thing. Didn't my wife tell you? Johnny was waylaid on his way out to Texas. A pack of bandits stole every bit of money he had taken to buy land. He never even made it to the border."

I felt a falling feeling inside me, as if my heart and stomach had suddenly sunk to my feet. "Was—was he hurt?" I asked in choked tones.

He bent his head and slowly wagged it back and forth. "Damned varmints killed him. Tossed his body in a canyon. He must have been dead over a week before anybody even found him."

I stared at him, frozen. My vision blurred. It could not be true. This was a hideous nightmare.

Judson stood motionless, lost in his own thoughts. "Clarissa and the kids will have to come up here and live with us, I guess," he mumbled brokenly. "She was beside herself when she wrote me. Johnny sold every bit of their livestock and property before he started out for Texas."

Why was he going on and on? I could not comprehend his words. Nothing mattered now, except that Johnny was dead.

"Yeah, the bandits took all his money," Judson said in a flat voice. "Clarissa and the kids were left with just the furniture and household goods. I guess they don't have much choice but to move up here with us."

Shaking his head, mumbling to himself, he walked across the porch and into the store.

The whole earth and sky swirled around me. A maddening, high-pitched hum droned in my ears. Johnny. My first love. He lived on in my mind, still twenty-one, strong and handsome, his vitality as radiant as sunlight on a summer's day.

First Daniel gone. Now Johnny. The droning grew louder, and burning tears welled in my eyes. I rushed inside, straight to my bedroom, seeking only solitude. I threw myself across the bed and stuffed a corner of the quilt into my mouth to smother the sobs that came pouring from me.

No one could share this sorrow. No one could ever understand. I never wished any harm to come to his wife, but just knowing how uncertain life was, I had clung to the belief that someday, somehow, fate would bring Johnny and me together.

I felt tortured, flung about like a blade of straw caught up in a tornado. Fresh tears gushed from my eyes.

For so long, this dream had sustained me in my hours of loneliness. I knew that Johnny was somewhere in this world, thinking of me. That he loved me. Had always loved me.

Was that childish? Was it wrong? I didn't care. I had clung to it like a precious treasure, for it was all that was left to me of love.

Now I must face a frigid world with no Johnny left in it. How could I bear to see his wife and children if they moved to Eden Valley? Constant, daily reminders of him.

That girl. Those blue, blue eyes.

CHAPTER 30

A short while later, Pearl peeked into my room. "You sick, Miz Nellie?" she inquired softly. "Something I can get you?"

My eyes burned from the deluge of tears. My whole chest felt hollow. I shifted my aching body on the bed, turning from the concerned look on her face. "No. I'll be all right."

"You sure don't look all right to me. I'd better track down Doc Benton and have him take a look at you."

"No, please. I'll just rest a bit." I flung my arm across my eyes. This was my private hell, and no one could rescue me.

Johnny. Daniel. I had loved two men in my life, and now both of them were gone. It seemed that all my youth, my very life-blood, had suddenly been drained from me. What was life, after all, that it could be snuffed out in just a wink?

A light tap sounded on the door, and then Doc's deep, gentle voice. "Can I come in?" At my mumbled assent, he stepped inside and glanced at my stricken face. "Nellie! What is it?" he asked, grasping my forearm. "Tell me."

"Johnny. Johnny Nichols." I choked back a sob. "A very old friend. I just heard he died on his way to Texas."

"He was someone very special to you."

"Yes. Remember when I told you how I came to marry Daniel and move up here?"

"And this Johnny . . . ?"

"Yes. He was the boy I planned to marry."

"I'm so sorry, Nellie. I suspect this has been hanging over you all these years, like some unfinished business."

"Maybe. Yes, I suppose it has."

Doc's sympathetic gaze, the pressure of his hand on my arm, just having him there with me was a blessed comfort. I stared at the ceiling, swallowing the pain that seared like acid in my throat. "Daniel. Now Johnny. It's so hard. It's like a plague of locusts."

"I know just how you feel. I'm forced to face death all the time, and I still can't get used to it." Tenderly he lifted my chin with his forefinger. "But you're strong, Nellie. You've faced scores of troubles that would have crippled a lesser woman. Your family needs you. The inn and all of Eden Valley are depending on you. And now the Railroad, too. You'll carry on, just like you always have."

His strength and confidence seeped into me like honey on a biscuit. I drew in a deep breath, thrust the hurt into the farthest reaches of my heart. "You're right. Tears never solved a thing. I learned that long ago."

But Johnny's death left a hollowness inside me. I felt older now, stripped bare of my last illusions of love. That part of my life was all behind me now. I must learn never to think of it again.

As time went on, I gradually began to take fresh interest in the changing world around me. I still had my family, my home, the name I had built for myself as an independent business-woman in a world where most women were nameless. I had my work with the Underground Railroad. Though it must remain a secret, the knowledge of the part I played filled me with deepest pride.

Joel, now grown into a towering and fine-looking young man, spent most of his summer with Doc on his rounds. Sarah and Forrest were deeply involved in all their work and activities in Galesburg. Sometimes the mailbag from the stage brought me a letter from Eddie, who was well established with his Indian trade in Minnesota. Occasionally I heard from Noah and Benjie in Galena, too.

I noticed that Hugh now whistled as he washed his face and combed his hair with painstaking care in the evenings, before he rode off for a call at Liza Johnson's house.

After a long and busy workday, I strolled outside and let the bustling noises of our town wash over me: the thud and thump of Karl's mill, the clanging of the blacksmith's hammer, the clap of hoofs and rumble of wheels as wagons crossed our covered bridge. The merry hum of water rippling over the dam served as background music for it all.

Eden Valley was our town. The proud, immortal Cranford legacy. And from the first day, I had played a vital role in its development.

Then one day a new sound mingled with the familiar. Judson Lowder and a group of men were cutting logs and fitting them to raise a little two-room cabin at the back of Judson's lot. Since his family and leather-working business filled his own house to the rafters, he was building a new place for Johnny's wife and children when they came to live in Eden Valley.

How could I face that woman? The furious expression on her face at our last meeting was burned into my memory as if by a branding iron. His children. Johnny's own children. A constant reminder that his vitality and charm were forever stilled.

I braced myself against the fresh onslaught of pain. I would be strong. I had promised Doc I would be strong. When Clarissa came, I would simply grit my teeth and welcome her to town like any other newcomer.

The day I dreaded finally arrived.

Judson Lowder drove his wagon over to Havana to meet the

steamboat bringing Johnny's wife and children. Within a short time, they had settled in their newly built cabin.

For me, the next days passed in a nervous blur. Finally, though my stomach cramped into a hard knot, I forced myself to bake a spice cake and march it down to their house. This was the only way I could ever lay Johnny's ghost to rest.

A tense, pale-eyed boy around Joel's age answered the door. I nodded to him tautly. "Hello. I'm Nellie Cranford," I said, and held out the cake pan. "I've come to welcome you to Eden Valley."

"Oh, thanks! I'm Conrad Nichols." Though he resembled his mother, a touch of Johnny lingered in his deep, resonant voice. He turned from me and called, "Mother, there's somebody here to see you."

The girl, the one with Johnny's eyes, crossed the room toward us. A lump tightened in my throat. Was it possible that she could be so grown already? She looked sixteen, at least. The years had slipped like water through my fingers.

"Look, Rachel. Mrs. Cranford's brought us a cake," the boy said.

"How kind of you. Won't you come in? Mother will be right out." The girl's smile was warm, her voice soft and melodic.

The sight of her shook me—those unrestrained, dark gypsy curls and sapphire eyes. Johnny's daughter. She might well have been mine. Glancing away, I stepped awkwardly across the threshold into the sparsely furnished cabin, where the pungent smell of new wood hovered in the air.

Clarissa appeared in the bedroom doorway, smoothing back her wavy brown hair. She glared at me, her pale eyes narrowed into slits. A flush of red crept slowly up her neck and face. "Yes?" she uttered tersely.

"I—I brought you a cake." I paused to swallow back the lump blocking my throat. "I hope you'll like living here in Eden Valley."

She scowled, as if aghast at the mere suggestion. "We had to come. The circumstances left us no choice."

"It's really a nice little town. The young people here are always cooking up some kind of doings. Your boy and girl will soon feel right at home."

Feeling inept and clumsy, I set the cake on the table and

298

glanced up at her reddened face. "I know how hard all this has been for you," I said. "I lost my husband, too."

"So I've heard." Her hard glare oozed hostility. My cheeks grew hot as I recalled her last trip to Eden Valley, when she had seen Johnny holding my hand, our strained emotions naked on our faces. Clarissa and I both knew that gesture had signified something deeper than a casual friendship. Obviously she had no desire to see me now that he was gone.

A leaden silence hung between us. "I'd best be on my way," I murmured huskily, and waited for her reply. Sit down and stay awhile. Have some tea. Why don't we cut the cake? What kind of gracious, friendly overture had I hoped she would make?

None came. I turned and left.

What did I expect? I asked myself, hurrying back down the road, my long skirt swaying, my shoes kicking up the dust with every step. What would Johnny's wife and I have to say to each other? No woman wants to share her husband's love. Yet her hostility hung over me like some deadly miasma—and just as I was struggling to conquer my own sense of loss.

The only remedy I knew lay in concentrating on the myriad duties at hand. Our store and inn and farm had prospered beyond my wildest expectations, but the keeping of accounts and management of business affairs demanded hours of my time.

I contracted a carpenter to build a ladies' parlor on the west side of the inn, with additional bedrooms above it. Now our women guests could visit unperturbed, while the men smoked and argued politics and told grizzly hunting stories in the lounge. After furnishing and decorating the addition, I ordered comfortable new upholstered chairs and heavy damask curtains for the big dining hall, which served as the men's lounge, as well.

The hammering and activities of building the ladies' parlor helped cover another construction project.

"That cellar door on the back is too open," Hugh had warned. "Sooner or later somebody is bound to see us slip some runaways down there. Wouldn't it be safer to keep them in the barn loft?"

I pondered the question. "Seems to me a barn loft would be the first place any slave hunter would look. Anyway, it's too hot up there in the summer and too cold in the winter."

"If they come searching, you can just bet they'll be looking in the cellar, too."

"You're right. We're going to have to come up with something pretty clever to fool those guys. After all, they're looking to get a big reward. That alone will make their eyes and ears mighty sharp when they're searching around."

So Tyrus secretly fixed a trapdoor in the floor of Hugh's bedroom on the far side of our living quarters and built a stairway down to the cellar. With the woven rag rug back in place and a chair set right over the trapdoor, no one would ever suspect this new and safer access to the downstairs.

Joel and Tyrus and his boys brought in stones, hidden in potato sacks and wooden boxes, and used them to build a permanent wall that closed off the far end of the cellar, turning it into a small hideaway for the escaping slaves. After the wall was complete, they painted it with muddy water so the stones would blend in with the old ones. When they had stacked old barrels and sacks of potatoes and onions haphazardly against this new wall, it looked for all the world like the original.

We felt much safer now that this new room was situated directly under our family quarters. Any unexpected sound from below was not likely to be heard by unfriendly ears.

After dark, when all was quiet and the drapes were tightly drawn, we carried cots, benches, candles, extra clothes, and other supplies downstairs to stock our little sanctuary. We padded the stair treads with carpet scraps, draped blankets around the walls and across the ceiling to muffle the slightest noise the runaways might make. I glowed with pride at our results, for this was as secure a fortress as I could possibly provide.

"All these people coming and going around the inn just multiply the danger of detection a hundredfold," Doc said.

"That's true." I gave him a sly wink. "But on the other hand, who'd ever suspect we were doing this kind of stuff right here in the middle of town? The trick is to whisk the runaways in and out without being seen."

"We'll have to do that while it's dark, and let them rest quietly down in the cellar through the day."

Tyrus built a trellis covering the walkway from the barn to the back door. When the quick-growing vines I planted twined their way over the top, I felt assured our fugitives were safe from spying eyes when they slipped over to the inn late at night.

We used the bedroom window as a doorway, closing off the space there between the inn and store with a tall fence front and back. The stack of firewood piled there near the window would serve to answer any questions about footsteps, if a shadow of suspicion ever arose.

Late one night a young runaway couple was brought to us by the Railroad conductor down the line. We quickly slipped them through the window and down the trapdoor to our hideaway.

"You're safe here," I told them, glancing at the torn and dirty rags they wore. "I'll bring you something to eat, and then I'll find you a change of clothes. We should have some shoes to fit you, too. Looks like you've worn clean through the soles of those you're wearing."

The weary man and woman sank down on a bench, nodding gratefully. "All that walkin' is mighty hard on shoes," she said. "Lordy, the mud and rain and briars we been through."

"How much farther to Canada?" he asked.

"Just a few more nights' travel is all. Will you tell me your names?"

They hesitated for a moment, glancing at each other nervously. "I'm Jack," the man said in a low voice. "My wife here's called Patsy."

"Well, Jack and Patsy, you'll soon be in Chicago. They'll put you on a boat there, and you'll be in Canada before you know it."

Smiling shyly, the woman patted her swollen belly. "This here child goin' to be born in freedom."

"That's worth the long trip, isn't it?" I said.

"Yes, ma'am, it sure do be. My master, he say he goin' to sell Jack down South. They's needin' plenty more hands to work the cotton fields. Jack go down there, we know'd he'd never see sight of me again. Never even know if this child be a boy or girl."

"That's when I told her we is goin' up North," he said grimly. "Last year a peddler man come through, talk to all the black folks on the sly. He say we can all be free, just by crossing the river."

I nodded, urging him on.

"So the two of us took off one night, walkin' through the woods, sleepin' by day. Once we got to the Mississippi, we borrowed a little boat somebody left along the bank and rowed over to the freedom side."

"We heard tell folks in Quincy would help us get away," the

301

woman added. "Sure 'nuf, they got us started up this line. Not much farther now, you say?"

"You'll be there before you know it," I told her. "Just rest a bit, while I get you something to eat."

The next night, we moved back the chair in Hugh's bedroom, folded up the corner of the rug, lifted the trapdoor, and scooted the fugitive couple up the stairs and through the window.

Meanwhile, Doc drove his horse and buggy over to the gate. Quick as a flash, he hid the man under the buggy seat and the woman under blankets at his feet and they were on their way out of town, with Doc looking like nothing more than an ordinary country doctor answering a late call.

Less than two hours later, he dropped them off at a farmhouse, the next stop along their way to Chicago, and was on his way back home for a few hours' sleep before his new workday began.

As the months passed, the trickle of runaway slaves grew into a flowing river along the network of secret routes. I came to look on each one of my hidden guests as part of the family, a huge and troubled family. The covert activity I had begun on an impulse was now a basic part of my life.

The more I became involved, the deeper my hatred of slavery grew. Sometimes I had to bite my tongue to keep from speaking out, but I knew expressing strong opinions would be a grave mistake. I could best protect my secret by emphasizing my Southern roots. Hard as it was, I had to keep my silence while discussions and arguments about the slavery problem raged all around me. Worse yet, I had to lie about my true convictions.

A Southern preacher stopping over at the inn expounded his views one evening as he sat on the front porch. "Just think of all the good we've done for those poor heathen Africans. We've made Christians of them, civilized them, given them homes and food and honest work to do."

"That's right, Reverend. They should be grateful," I said in a thick Southern accent, though the words tasted bitter on my tongue.

Norman Hart chuckled cynically. "Now, ain't that the strangest thing? The preachers up here been telling us slavery's an evil and a scourge. Funny how you men of the cloth can look at things so different."

The preacher stiffened his back and scowled at Norman.

"Slavery is sanctioned by the Bible itself," he said, his plump cheeks turning pink.

"That so?" A traveling peddler dug at his teeth with a silver pick. "How about you quote us chapter and verse, good parson."

"Why, there's several references to people holding slaves. Now don't you think if it was wrong the Bible would tell us so? No, sir. There's not a single word condemning it, no more than there is in the U.S. Constitution. Those abolitionists don't have a leg to stand on." The preacher folded his arms across his chest and clamped his mouth shut tight.

"I 'spect some of those abolitionist preachers could give you a run for your money arguing the Bible," Norman said. "For my part, common sense just tells me it ain't right for one man to own another."

Good for you, Norman, I thought, my blood racing as I listened to the talk. Oh, if only I could add my two cents' worth. I'd love to tell them of all the ugly scars I had seen left from beatings, of the hardships and dangers these people had endured just to escape from their difficult, degrading lives in slavery.

But I dared not say a word, not even among friends, for if I was ever caught aiding runaways, I knew the law would show me no mercy. I was much too busy to be spending time in jail.

My lingering Southern accent gave me a cloak of protection. "Now, Norm. You haven't lived down South, like I have," I said mildly. "You just don't understand."

The preacher nodded his approval, beaming me a smile.

"I'm not sure how long we can go on like this before we get caught," Hugh said one day, his young face grave with concern. "Eden Valley is such a busy crossroad. All kinds of people are stopping here at the inn and store. Somebody's bound to get wind of this."

"You know I'm careful. Real careful," I said.

"You'd better be. Just think how it would look, stories in the Lewistown and Peoria and Springfield papers about the Widow Cranford of Eden Valley sitting in the county jail."

"You like to scold, but you're just as involved as I am, Hugh. You know this is something we simply have to do."

The agent in the Railroad network generally brought us escaped slaves hidden under a wagonload of hay. He drove his

303

wagon into the barn out back, and Tyrus hid the runaways up in the loft until nightfall. Then, with the greatest stealth, he quickly slipped the runaways down the trellis-covered path, through our window, down the trapdoor, and into the cellar for a hearty meal, a change of clothes, and a comfortable rest through the next day. That night Doc, or sometimes Hugh or even Joel, transported them—hidden in the bottom of a carriage, or under sacks of grain and straw in a wagon—north, to the next station up the line.

"I heard another success story for the Railroad," Doc told me one day after he returned from delivering some runaways. "Two girls had been caught by a slave hunter, and a fellow up in Princeton helped them escape."

"Now tell me—just how did he do that?" I asked.

"Well, that slave hunter stopped by an inn overnight, never suspecting that the keeper was an abolitionist. When the girls went up to bed in the women's quarters, another fellow from the church brought over a ladder and helped them climb out through the window."

I clapped my hands together. "Now wasn't that clever?"

"Yep. He drove them over to the next town to hide. The next morning, when that slave hunter found out they were gone, he was fit to be tied. Drew his gun, searched the house and barn and haystack. Stayed three days searching the whole town."

"But those girls were long gone."

"Long gone," he said, with a pleased grin. "Score two for our side."

Though I stayed in touch with members of abolitionist cells from nearby towns through notes and whispered messages, I carefully guarded the secrecy of my Railroad activities. Even among our Eden Valley people, feelings on the slavery question were hopelessly divided. In their eyes, my life continued as before.

Winter came, and the traffic on the Railroad increased, for the runaways could cross the frozen rivers easily. Our cellar offered them a welcome sanctuary from the cold and snow and slave hunters. As it grew chilly down there, I gave the weary runaways bricks heated on the fire and wrapped in towels to warm their icy hands and feet.

At times, when we received word of slave hunters working in

our territory, or when blizzards blew down from the north, my secret guests would remain hidden in our cellar for several days.

The whole situation was fraught with danger. Doc put pieces of carpet over the horses' hoofs to muffle their sound. He used his sleigh to carry the runaways during times of deep snow, hiding them under the seat, which he covered with blankets.

One woman came to us carrying a baby in her arms, holding him tightly against her body to protect him from the bitter wind. "The way north sure is a hard one for little kids," she said.

I settled the two of them on a cot downstairs and covered them with extra blankets. "I know. I guess that's why we see more men than women."

She nodded, shivering. "What mama's going to leave without her babes?"

Once in the safety of our cellar, the baby grew fussy. I ran to Doc, frantic with fear that his cries might be heard.

"I'll have to give him laudanum to keep him quiet," Doc said. "The washwoman and the inn guests heading for the stable or outhouse pass within ten feet of the cellar door. A single telltale sound from below could give us all away."

One bleak winter night, when wind-driven sleet peppered the drifted snow, Tyrus tapped on my side window. I hurried over to open the window in Hugh's room, then rushed two men and a woman down through the trapdoor to the cellar. While I ran back upstairs for a basket of food, Pearl wrapped the chilled, shuddering runaways in blankets.

"Just look at this boy's hands," Pearl muttered when I returned. "Sure as I'm born he's got frostbite."

I winced at the sight of the young man's stiff fingers. "Have you come a long way?" I asked softly, raising my gaze to his fierce, determined face.

"Halfway round the world, seems like," he mumbled, shivering. He wrapped his blanket tighter. "Came up from Arkansas through Missouri. Crossed the river on the ice. Lived on what corn and apples I could scrounge. Found some milk in a springhouse one day. Man, that was sure some treat."

Pearl headed up to the kitchen to cook a hot meal for the hungry newcomers, while I passed around the dried apple slices and cold ham and pieces of leftover corn bread I had jammed into my basket. "Did your master beat you? Is that why you ran

305

away?'' I asked the young man, struck by the angry gleam in his eye.

''My first master, he was good enough. He ran short of cash, though, and sold me off to an old devil of a man. That new master, he used me so bad and beat me so hard. One day I just took off with his horse. Rode back to my old home, I did. Asked my old master to take me back.''

''And then?'' I urged.

''My old master, he say he ain't got no right to me no more. Say I better just keep right on runnin'. Showed me the North Star. Say keep goin' till I crossed the river into free land. That's what I done.''

''Your new master didn't come after you?''

''I left on a Saturday night. I knowed that way they wouldn't miss me till Monday mornin'. I allow he's after me by now.''

''But you had a horse. That probably was a big help.''

''No, ma'am. No way I could keep that. Why, anybody see me know that ain't my horse. I just went on foot by night, hid out in barns by day. Wore my shoes clean through. I tell you, on cloudy nights it's mighty hard to follow any star.''

''But look how far you've come already. I'll get Doc to come down and take care of your hands.''

''Just wait,'' the man said, reaching for more corn bread. ''I went three days without eating nothing. Felt hollow clean down to my shoes. Now seems like I can't never get enough.''

When Pearl brought down the fried eggs and ham and leftover bean soup, the fierce young man ate and ate and ate for nearly an hour, while the others, long sated, sat and watched him in amazement.

The next night, Doc spirited them out of the cellar, into his carriage, and off to the next Railroad station.

Our involvement with the Railroad carried heavy costs—in time, effort, anxiety, and money. Tyrus built hidden compartments into the bottom of a big farm wagon, to hide our secret human cargo. I bought warm woolen blankets and extra clothing in all sizes. By the evening firelight, I knitted socks and scarves and shawls to shield the fugitives from cold and snow as they traveled northward.

I kept a large supply of extra food on hand, never knowing how many would be eating or how famished they would be. During the day I complained loud and long about Joel and Hugh's ravenous appetites, just in case any inn guests wondered about the smell of cooking late at night.

One evening the next fall, as Doc and I sat in the parlor discussing the latest Railroad news in hushed whispers, Hugh and Liza came walking through the kitchen toward us. Their two young faces glowed with the unmistakable radiance of love.

Clinging to Liza's hand, Hugh paused before my chair and smiled down at me. "Ma, we want to tell you something."

"Should I leave?" Doc asked, chuckling. "I think I can guess what this is."

Liza blushed, nervously adjusting the horn comb in her long hair. She glanced up at Hugh with a deep-throated laugh. "There's no keeping a secret in this town, is there?"

"Don't say that!" I sputtered, for at that very moment we were sitting right over our secret room.

"Well, some secrets are different from others," Liza said.

Hugh smiled at her. "I've told Liza about our connection with the Railroad."

I blanched. She was a dear girl. Surely we could trust her. And yet . . .

He slipped his arm around her waist. "She needs to know, if she's going to be part of this family. I just want to make it official now. We want to get married. Soon, I hope."

"Oh, Hugh! Liza, dear!" My fear forgotten, I jumped up and clasped my arms around the pair. "I'm so happy for you both. We'll have to build you a new house. A nice big brick one. You should start looking for a spot for it."

"We're way ahead of you. We have a place all picked out," Hugh said, meeting Liza's delighted smile. "Down in that oak grove along the river bend."

"That's perfect, Hugh. Just first-rate. Your father would be so pleased. Oh, Liza . . . I'll be tickled to have a daughter around again."

"I want to be a real part of the family." She glanced down at the floor, beneath which lay our secret room. "In every way."

I could hardly contain my happiness. Was this smiling young man the same one who had spent months in silent brooding? My worries about him seemed laughable now that this captivating girl had entered his life.

When the young couple left, Doc turned, eyes shimmering,

and studied me with a sly grin. "Pitiful, isn't it? So young and vulnerable. I wouldn't want to go back for a minute."

"Come on, now. You're not so old," I said, patting his hand. This dear man. How invaluable his friendship had been to me over the years. How constant his concern and affection.

"No." He raised my hand to his lips and pressed a warm kiss on my palm. "No, my dear girl. Right this minute I don't feel one bit old. In fact, if you don't watch out—"

"Oh, Doc, you are the darndest tease!" My giggle surprised me. Why, I sounded exactly like a young girl. Me, with all my worries and responsibilities.

But strange as it might seem, right at that moment, with the warmth of his lips lingering on my skin, I suddenly felt young again, and vividly alive.

CHAPTER 31

Hugh and Liza were married in early June. After the gala wedding festivities, friends gathered for a clamorous shiveree, shouting and banging pots and pans for half the night outside the beseiged couple's new brick house in the oak grove. The next morning, the newlyweds rode the stagecoach to Havana and boarded a huge, white, gingerbread-trimmed steamboat for a honeymoon in St. Louis.

While they were gone, Joel tended the store, with help from Pearl's youngest boy. Her other sons were now working with Karl at the mill.

Joel was nineteen already, trim and muscular, with wavy dark hair and Daniel's intelligent gray eyes. Soon he would be starting college in Jacksonville, and then would apprentice medicine with Doc Benton.

In the meantime, he spent hours helping Doc at his office, sweeping, rolling pills, cleaning instruments, washing empty jars and bottles. Sometimes he accompanied Doc on sick calls and held the basin for a patient being bled. He steadied legs so Doc could set broken bones, held arms so he could stitch nasty cuts. Already Joel had seen more accidents and illnesses than most people would in a lifetime. Still, nothing could dampen his determination to learn the art of medicine.

"The boy's a natural. Got a real healer's touch," Doc told me. He had been with us so long, his eyes shone with as much pride as mine.

Over the next year, our clandestine labors for the Underground Railroad grew, bringing added risk and danger. The numbers of passing slave hunters multiplied as well. They tacked up posters on the front of our store that described the assorted runaways and promised rewards of five hundred or a thousand dollars.

Steering clear from all slave hunters, Tyrus and his sons dug a tunnel from the cellar to the barn to help conceal the nocturnal transfers of the runaways who stopped by our place.

The secret life exacted a high toll from Joel and Hugh and me. And now Liza was included, too. I became watchful and suspicious of my neighbors, never certain who I could trust. Only with Doc could I feel truly comfortable.

The Springfield paper carried the story when Owen Lovejoy was arrested for harboring two runaways up in Princeton. I must confess the news shook me. This was no child's game we were playing.

But Sarah wore a triumphant smile when she and Forrest rode down to bring me an update. "His trial ended in acquittal!" she whispered the moment we were alone in our parlor.

"An antislavery lawyer from Chicago represented him," Forrest said. "He argued that the owner brought the women into Illinois on his way from Kentucky to Missouri. Since Illinois is a free state, the slaves became free the minute they set their feet on Illinois soil."

I clapped my hands together. "And the jury let him off! A big victory for our side."

Forrest rubbed his chin thoughtfully. "We still have to be very cautious. Others have not been so fortunate as Owen, you know.

One man in Quincy was arrested and fined for hiding runaways. The same thing happened in Jacksonville, too."

"But still the Railroad runs on," I said, feeling a glow of pride at the small part I played.

"And it will continue until the scourge of slavery is abolished." Sarah's zeal burned like a flame. "Our organization may be loosely knit, but there are hundreds of us—ministers, farmers, shopkeepers, lawyers, teachers, businessmen. Every one of us stands ready to receive runaways at any time. We'll feed and hide them as long as necessary, and then help them along their way to Canada."

I felt awed that here in this small village I could play a part in such a widespread and committed movement. "Pearl asked me about the route they take," I said. "I had to admit I don't know much about the whole picture."

"The Railroad tries to keep it that way." Forrest's voice was low. "The less each person knows, the better—in case we're ever questioned. There's constant danger of detection."

I nodded tensely. "Of course. I understand that."

"At least we do have common signals, so we can communicate with the others along the network," he said. "You learned them from the start. When somebody arrives with a load of runaways, he gives the sign to ask if the place is safe, then indicates the number of people he is carrying by raising that many fingers."

"Right," I said, interrupting him. "Hello means all is well. A hand raised palm outward is a warning. And then there are all those other passwords we use."

Sarah bent in closer to me. "We have cells all over now—Chester, Alton, Vandalia, Princeton, Bloomington. Why, in Galesburg we use the pastor's house, and even the galleries and cupola of the church for hiding places."

I chuckled. "You should see Pearl and Tyrus. Sometimes they figure out disguises for the runaways. They've dressed men as women, and women as men. Once Tyrus even packed a man in a big wooden box, and we shipped him north by steamboat from Havana."

"Some single fugitives have traveled openly by carriage from Galesburg to Chicago," Forrest said. "They simply pose as a servant to one of our conductors. Once they get to Chicago, they know they will be safe. The abolitionist sentiment there is strong and powerful."

"It's harder here, 'cause Pearl and Tyrus and their boys are the only blacks around," I said. "Anybody else would be noticed right away."

My muscles tensed at the thought of the constant dangers we all faced. I spied on the slave hunters when those rough-looking men, armed to the teeth, sometimes stopped overnight at the inn. "Let me serve them supper," I would murmur to Pearl.

While I hovered over the table, serving bowls and platters of her famous cooking, I strained to listen to their conversations, hoping for clues to their activities and plans. And more than once, the runaways they were seeking were at that very moment hiding down in our cellar, practically beneath their feet.

My luck in avoiding any suspicion made me feel some special angel was watching over me.

I worried, though, when Joel and Pearl's boys helped with the runaways. Young as they were, they might sometime let an idle word slip out to one of their friends and give us all away. The political turmoil over slavery grew daily more devisive and volatile. Some people would feel positively righteous for turning in a neighbor for harboring and aiding fugitive slaves.

Clarissa Nichols, for example, hated me. Though she had lived in Eden Valley for over two years now, earning a meager living by dressmaking, she still refused to speak to me. Our paths frequently crossed at the store or funerals or community picnics, but even at church services on Sundays, she always drew aside her skirts and swept by me as if I were invisible. She strictly forbade Conrad and Rachel to associate with Joel.

If she had any clue to my Railroad connections, I was certain she would rush to the county sheriff over in Lewistown to have me arrested. At the very least, I would face a stiff fine.

And so I lived, tense as a tightrope walker, constantly in danger of detection.

At last the time arrived for Joel to register at the college in Jacksonville. As his departure day approached, I felt a twinge of guilt for the strain my Railroad activities had added to his life. This secret, noble as we felt it was, weighed as a heavy burden on us all. "I want to have a going-away party for you," I told him. "You can invite all your friends."

On the evening of the party, I hustled my inn guests from the tables after supper, then pushed all the furniture over to the sides. Pearl made a dozen trips from the kitchen, her hands laden with bowls of punch and platters of meats and breads and fancy cakes. Soon scores of young people, and many of their parents, all dressed in their finest, swarmed in from town and countryside to take part in the merriment.

Once again, Norman Hart and his magic fiddle enlivened the festive occasion. Liza's brother joined him with a banjo. As the inn guests and older folks grouped along the sides, keeping time to the music with their clapping hands, long lines of boys and girls faced one another, each couple in turn gaily dancing down the length of the room.

Colorful gingham and calico and muslin skirts billowed out, giving all the boys enticing glimpses of trim ankles. Explosions of laughter and ripples of bright conversation carried over the merry tunes.

Doc strolled over to me, his eyes sparkling as he nodded toward the dancers. "Why don't we give that a try, Nellie?"

"A little later," I replied. "It's so much fun just watching all the young folks."

Liza's deep-throated laughter rang across the room as she and Hugh danced down the row, both their faces radiant with happiness. I could hardly recall those years when Hugh had been as gloomy as a rain cloud.

Suddenly I heard Joel's voice cry out with delight, "Rachel!"

Johnny's daughter, lovely as a princess in a deep blue linen dress that matched her eyes, stood in the doorway, her brother close at her side. How had they ever managed to escape from Clarissa's watchful eye? Dark gypsy curls framed the pale oval of the girl's face. She lowered her thick fringe of lashes, then raised them to face Joel with a blushing smile.

I had never seen Joel so unnerved. He hurried over to her. "Come on in, Rachel! Let me get you some punch and cake." As an afterthought, he turned to her brother. "You, too, Conrad. Come have some sandwiches or something."

The trio ambled over to the table, laughing with lighthearted banter. I could not take my eyes from pretty Rachel, for she so resembled her father when he was young. Somehow it comforted me to know that even though Johnny was gone, his shining jewel-blue eyes still looked out on the world and smiled.

Doc bent his head and murmured in my ear, "All kinds of new romances these days."

"Don't be silly. Joel's still awfully young," I said. "Anyway, he's leaving now for school." But my gaze lingered on the handsome pair. Could it be possible?

The roisterous clamor of laughing voices and lively fiddle and banjo music filled the crowded room. Talk bubbled all around me like sweet, sparkling wine. But I was intoxicated with a new wine of my own. Joel and Rachel? Was it fate? A fitting ending to my bittersweet tale?

The tune ended just as a sharp, rapid click of footsteps sounded on the porch. All faces turned toward the door. Boisterous laughter dropped to a low, nervous murmur. Clarissa stood planted in the doorway, eyes widened, cheeks blazing, face pinched tight with rage.

Breathing in rasping pants, she stomped across the silent room and grabbed Rachel by the arm. "Sneak out on me, will you?"

"But, Mother! It's just a party," the red-faced girl protested, tears welling in her eyes.

"You're coming home. We don't associate with this kind of trash," Clarissa snarled, and led Rachel roughly toward the door. Conrad followed them, glancing back at the stunned crowd with an embarrassed shrug.

A heavy fog of silence hung over the crowd. Their faces filled with startled confusion; people stared at one another across the warm stuffy room. Clarissa had left, but her hatred lingered like a hissing coil of snakes.

My heart thundered wildly in my chest. I wanted to run away. I wished the floor would open up and swallow me. But, no. I would not give her such an easy victory.

"Well!" I said, and swallowed hard. Inhaling a deep breath, I raised my chin so high the back of my neck cramped. "Well, come on, Norman! What are you waiting for? Let's get that fiddle going. Doc said he wants to dance."

CHAPTER 32

When Joel went away to college, his cousin Ben came down from Galena to accompany him. The boys would be roommates at school in Jacksonville.

"You should see Galena now," Ben told us. I could hardly believe this bright and pleasant young man, bearing himself with that grave Cranford dignity, was our little Benjie all grown up.

"I've heard it's quite the place to be," I said.

His gray eyes gleamed with enthusiasm. "Believe everything you've heard and then some. Riding down here through those prairie flatlands makes me appreciate our high hills even more. It's got to be the prettiest spot in all of Illinois. And now there're big brick mansions on the hilltops, overlooking the whole river valley."

"I'd like to see it someday," Joel said. "Who lives in all those mansions?"

"Plenty of men have made fortunes from the lead mines up there. The smelters run full blast. They have whole crews of men loading the bricks of lead on ox carts and taking them down to the steamboats on the river. Why, we're producing almost eighty-five percent of the country's lead supply now."

"Sakes alive!" I said. "And this country sure couldn't get far without lead, now could it? Lord, just bullets alone must use up tons of it. Just think of all the men out hunting and target shooting. It fairly boggles the mind."

Ben's voice rang with pride. "Galena has more than that, too. It's the commerce center for the whole upper Mississippi now. We get merchandise from New Orleans by steamboat up the Mississippi, and from the East Coast brought through the Great

314

Lakes to Chicago and then overland by wagon. Pa's is just one of a dozen big stores. Why, we have a hotel that's five stories high."

"No! Five stories?" I shook my head in wonder. "Galena sounds almost like New York City."

"Before long, it probably will be," he replied, smiling at the thought.

Ben spent three days with us before they left, catching up on the long years of separation. Finally the time came for the two boys to board the stagecoach and head south to Illinois College at Jacksonville for the winter term.

I wondered if Rachel had seen Joel leave. She spent her days helping Clarissa sew shirts and coats and fancy Sunday frocks for paying customers. In their spare time, they also stitched supple deerhide gloves and mittens, which Judson Lowder sold in his leather shop. Conrad worked with his uncle in the many facets of the tanning operation.

Since ours was the only general store in town, Clarissa had no choice except to buy her cloth, buttons, thread, and other sewing notions from Hugh. Her grudging visits disturbed him as much as they did her.

"That Mrs. Nichols must be the worst crab in three counties. Nothing I do, nothing I have to sell ever suits her," Hugh grumbled when I stepped into the store one crisp day in late fall. "Do you think Rachel is adopted? I can't believe that hateful woman could really be her mother."

"Mrs. Nichols has had her share of problems," I said mildly. In truth, the woman's malice toward me nettled like a toothache. Even if she judged me guilty of misplaced affection, it wasn't fair that my whole family should suffer for my crime.

Hugh bridled, his jaw hardening. "I just cannot understand that woman. When Joel was home, she absolutely forbade Rachel to go to any parties or dances where he might be. She acted petrified if Joel even spoke to Rachel. What does she have against him?"

"Oh, I don't know." My heart lay heavy as a millstone. "Somehow it reminds me of my uncle's feud with his neighbor down in southern Illinois so long ago."

"She can't keep them apart forever."

But Hugh's concern was short-lived, for the hour had come when he could close the store and hurry home to his pretty Liza.

Throughout the winter months, the Underground Railroad continued running, despite the added dangers of footsteps in the snow. Queen Victoria had now declared that all slaves were free when they entered Canada, creating turmoil among the opposing political interests out in Washington.

We still had need for constant stealth and secrecy in our Railroad activities. Up in Galesburg, Sarah could openly host meetings of the Abolitionist Society in her home, but the people in Eden Valley remained bitterly divided on the question. Around the guests' supper table at the inn, conversations about slavery or harboring runaways inevitably ended in shouting matches.

"I just wish they'd free them all and get this damn thing settled," one circuit lawyer said.

His colleague shook his head. "It's not that easy, and you know it. We're talking about private property, bought by perfectly legal means. You can't just confiscate it without just compensation."

"Haven't you read the Declaration of Independence? It says there all men are created equal."

"And did you ever count how many of the men who helped write the Declaration and the Constitution were slave owners themselves?"

The townspeople were equally divided. The sound of their arguments filled the air wherever small crowds congregated. "Why are they always persecuting the Southerners?" Judson Fowler asked. "Most of those slaves are treated well. Better than the factory workers in the East."

The blacksmith nodded, sucking on his pipe. "Yeah. I'd never own a slave myself, but I say we all should mind our own business as far as other states are concerned."

A brawny farm boy grinned slyly. "If I ever get a chance to catch a runaway and collect one of those big rewards, I don't reckon I'll take much time to stop and ponder over all the pros and cons of it."

My blood ran cold, for I feared many people would agree with him.

I listened to them all, keeping my peace out of fear of arousing suspicion, though I ached to tell them exactly how I felt.

316

* * *

By spring, Sarah was awaiting the birth of her first child up in Galesburg. Joel and Ben returned from college, bursting with plans for their future.

"I'm heading right back to Galena," Ben said as he relaxed that evening on the front porch. "Things are booming up there these days."

I glanced at his fair hair and finely chiseled features and thought of his mother Emily, dead these many years. "Noah will be glad to have you back with him," I said.

He nodded, grinning with youthful eagerness. "Yes, that's the place to be. After I graduate, I'm going to start some kind of business up there. Dad has certainly done all right with his dry-goods store. Hey, Joel! You should come up to Galena with me."

Joel's brows shot up. "Galena? Me?" He shook his head and glanced down the street, past Judson Lowder's tannery—to the little house where Rachel lived. "No, I guess I'll stay right here in Eden Valley."

"Still planning to apprentice with Doc?" I asked gently.

"Yes. That." A look of intense yearning darkened his young face. His gaze—and his thoughts—remained far off down the road.

I could not bear that he should suffer futilely, as I had suffered longing for Johnny. Surely young love was not meant to be a torment. It should bring happiness and contentment, the kind Hugh had found with his merry Liza.

But Joel was almost twenty-one now. He must hack his own path through these mystifying jungles of emotion. There was little I could say or do to help.

Joel tapped his fingers rhythmically against his thigh as he stared down the curving river road. "Guess I'll take a walk," he said absently. "Seems like I've been gone for a hundred years."

While Ben and I sat on the porch bench watching, Joel sauntered through the white clover buds in the park and stopped to gaze at the water bubbling over the mill dam. A wren chirped, scolding, from a leafy branch. "He's going down to see Rachel," I murmured to the passing breeze.

"He likes her an awful lot, Aunt Nellie," Ben said softly.

317

I exhaled a sharp breath. "Trouble. Nothing but trouble there."

At that moment, Doc breezed through the door and joined us. "Ben! It's sure nice to have you boys back again. Where's Joel?"

Clenching my jaw, I pointed my thumb toward the slender figure disappearing down the road.

Ben glanced around him to assure our privacy. "Have you and Doc been busy, Aunt Nellie?" he asked in a low voice. "On that other business, I mean."

I started at his words. "Oh! Did Joel tell you? We have to be so careful, you know."

"I know all about it. My pa's been helping with it up north, too."

"We've been real busy here," Doc said, his voice grim. "I don't know where all this is going to end."

My hands clenched into fists. "It will never end until all the slaves are freed. The lines are drawn now."

Doc gazed far into the distance, frowning. "I only hope it won't take a war. I've seen what happens in a war."

"Then why don't they do something out in Washington? This country can't go on this way—half slave and half free."

"Shh!" Doc raised his hand in caution as a traveling book salesman stepped out the inn door and joined us on the porch. I glanced down the road. Joel stood talking with Conrad Nichols, heads bent together like conspirators.

What kind of mischief were they planning? I was certain Clarissa would never willingly let Joel see Rachel.

Now the Underground Railroad and the runaways were only part of my concerns. I feared another war was brewing, and this one very close to home.

That summer Joel worked and studied with Doc each morning, then helped Hugh at the store several hours in the afternoon. Rachel came to see him there, somehow escaping her mother's watchful eye. Perhaps Clarissa, tied up with her demanding sewing business, thought Joel worked with Doc the entire day. Whatever the circumstances, almost every afternoon Rachel strolled down to the store, a wicker basket over her arm, her lithe body swaying to the graceful rhythm of her stride, her

318

gypsy hair escaping from the sides of her red gingham sunbon-net.

Sometimes I glimpsed them talking softly over the store counter, when no one else was around. I saw the yearning in their eyes, heard the wistful murmur of their voices. How I wished for them the right to happiness in the fullness of their youth. There was suffering enough in this brief life, without losing this rare opportunity for joy. And yet, it was not mine to give.

Clarissa despised me. Would I never be free of Johnny Nichols? All my life he had been nothing but a cherished girlhood dream. He had married her, not me. Yet, in my heart, I knew he married her because my uncle would not let him marry me. And so I was condemned to endure this wretched woman's hatred.

One day in early August, Rachel suddenly stopped coming to the store. Overnight, Joel turned pale and wan.

"What's the matter with that boy?" Pearl asked me, perturbed, her hands planted on her ample hips. "Looks like he needs a tonic."

I glanced out to the backyard, where Joel leaned against a tree, lost in a fog of morose silence. His eyes were downcast, his face drained and pale. "I don't know, Pearl. I just don't know."

For more than a week, I fretted and fumed, not knowing what to do or where to turn. The anxiety stewing in my heart exhausted me, and yet I could not sleep. Was not the pain I suffered over Johnny enough? Must my son suffer, too?

On Sunday afternoon, I gathered all my courage and determination and started down the road under a blazing sun. Townspeople, sitting under shade trees, seeking relief from the heat, waved to me as I passed. I walked on, my teeth clenched with resolve.

When I reached Clarissa's cabin behind the tannery, I knocked sharply on the frame of the opened door. A rustle of skirts sounded; I heard a light tap of steps from inside.

Clarissa appeared, wearing her habitual frown. Her eyes narrowed—and the lines around her mouth deepened—when she saw me standing at the door. "You," she spat out, glaring furiously at me. She sucked in a deep, noisy gasp, like a steam

319

engine building a head before it burst into action. "What do you want?"

"I'd like to talk to you, Clarissa," I said mildly, hoping to break the growing tension.

"You would? Well, talk!" Her eyes were like a wildcat's, impaling me within their piercing stare.

"Could I come in for a minute?" I saw Rachel standing over by the table, looking terrified.

Clarissa snorted, her nostrils flaring. "Come in, then. But I can't spare you much time."

As I stepped through the door, Rachel's lovely eyes widened. She stood stiffly, chewing on her lower lip, her glance shifting back and forth from me to her mother. Her pale face looked as miserable as Joel's. Was Clarissa holding her a prisoner in this house, just to keep her from seeing him?

Baskets overflowing with lengths of cloths and thread and sewing notions lay scattered around the small cabin. A massive cherry-wood china cupboard and a walnut desk gave mute evidence of the family's more prosperous days. Clarissa stationed herself like a commanding general before the china cupboard, her arms held rigid at her sides.

"Rachel, go outside," she said curtly, never taking her piercing eyes from my face. "And don't you dare leave the yard."

With a rustle of long skirts, the frightened girl was gone.

"How old is Rachel now?" I asked.

"Nineteen. Acts more like twelve." Clarissa sniffed. "What do you want here?"

My mouth was dry as parchment. I swallowed hard, drew in a deep breath. This was hellishly difficult, and she refused to make it one bit easier. "Can't we sit down for a minute?"

"I'm busy. I have to earn a living, you know. If you have something to say to me, you'd better say it quick."

My stomach felt hollow. "I just wanted—" Oh, this was so hard. Where would I find the words? "Why can't we be friends, Clarissa?"

Her face reddened and contorted with rage. "Friends! I'll tell you why. Every time we came up here, you were chasing after my husband. I couldn't turn my back—"

I shook my head, fighting back the flood of memories, the pain, the shame. "We were old neighbors . . ."

"Don't give me that! I know he planned to marry you. His

320

sister told me how your uncle almost killed him. That's why he moved to St. Louis. I know all about it."

"Good Lord. How long ago was that? Twenty-five years. Twenty-five years, Clarissa."

The fury in her glare blazed on, relentless as a prairie fire. The sound of her quick breathing filled the hot, humid air.

My vision blurred with the spin of jumbled feelings. "I married Daniel and raised a family," I said. "Johnny married you. I hardly saw him after I left my uncle's place. We were all busy with our own lives."

Her face twisted with bitterness. "I saw you and him that day, whispering and holding hands. After that, he changed. He said he wanted to move away from this part of the country. He sold out everything we had and took off for Texas. And I never saw him again." Her face crumpled; tears gathered in her eyes. "It's all your fault."

"Oh, no, Clarissa, no!" I stepped over to touch her arm. "We were friends, that's all. Old neighbors. Please believe me."

She buried her face in her hands and began to sob wretchedly. "He's gone. I'm all alone."

"I'm sorry, Clarissa. I know how hard it is." I laid my hand on her shoulder.

She twisted away from me. "He never loved me. I knew that. It was always you."

"Oh, no. I don't believe that. No. You were a good wife. And you gave him such beautiful children."

She shook her head miserably. "I won't let your boy have Rachel, too. I won't! Not ever."

An icicle stabbed my heart and twisted. I suddenly felt hollow. I waited numbly for Clarissa's outburst to calm. Finally, avoiding my eyes, she wiped her red and tear-stained face on a frayed handkerchief.

I took her trembling hand and held it firmly. "You must let Rachel see Joel if she wants to. It's a cruel thing to keep young people apart because of some old family feud."

She shook her head, clenched her lips into a tight line.

"Clarissa, listen to me," I said urgently. "When my uncle wouldn't let me see Johnny, I ran away. I never went back. Never once saw him again. Not ever."

Her eyes widened. She watched my face warily.

"Think how you and I would feel if Rachel and Joel ran away

321

like that.'' My head sunk at the thought. ''Never see your child again? Never see your grandchildren? Could you stand that?''

She blanched. Her lips quivered. ''No, but—''

''You know, Doc Benton sees an awful lot of birth and death,'' I said softly. ''He keeps reminding me how pitifully short life is. Too short to bear grudges, he always says.''

As she continued to stare at me, her face gradually began to soften.

''Can't we be friends, Clarissa?'' I asked, gently squeezing her hand. ''Can't we at least let our kids be friends?''

Reluctantly, as if I had squeezed that out of her, too, her face and shoulders began to relax. Her frown melted; the corners of her lips curved with just a tiny glimmer of a smile.

She raised her round, pale eyes to mine and nodded faintly. ''I—I'll try.''

A long-held breath whistled slowly through my lips. Relief and hope flowed through me like a warm summer breeze. Now it was possible. Finally, at long last, I could let Johnny rest in peace.

CHAPTER 33

That evening, Joel took Rachel for a stroll along the river. As a setting sun gilded their young faces, glimmered on their hair, they stood and talked, oblivious to the droning dam.

I tried to quash the flood of joy that rushed through me at the sight of that handsome couple silhouetted against the glowing copper sky. After all, now that their meetings were no longer forbidden, they might well discover they didn't even like each other. And Joel still had to finish college.

But who could tell? Someday down the road, I just might

possibly be rocking grandchildren with thick, dark lashes and jewel-blue eyes.

As Joel worked with Doc, he gained valuable knowledge and experience. All the accidents and diseases so prevalent on the frontier made each day stir with some new drama, yet Joel seemed to thrive on this diet of crisis and involvement.

One afternoon, however, he returned home pale and distant-looking. "Something wrong?" I asked, glancing up from my account books spread out on the parlor table.

He stopped and leaned against the door frame. "Those new people out by Weaver's place. Their two-year-old just died of diphtheria."

"Oh, Joel. How terrible."

"Doc tried to save her. There's so little he can do."

"He's helped a lot of people in his time."

"We need more medicines. New ones. Strong ones. Why can't they hurry up and invent some more?"

"We have quinine now. Just look what that's done to get rid of the ague."

"We need more. Fast. People around here have a dozen babies—and lose half of them before they're five years old!"

A dagger of pain stabbed me as I recalled my darling Cinda. I hung my head, biting on my lip. "That's how it is, Joel. Only the strong survive."

Wordlessly he trudged into his bedroom and lay across the bed, staring at the ceiling, his eyes hollow, his face drawn. His melancholy wove itself like a spiderweb over the whole room.

I stood near the door, at a loss for words. "Are you sure you want to do this, son?" I asked him softly.

His dark brows drew together, his mouth worked as he struggled to contain his emotions. "I want to save them, Ma. I want to make a difference."

"You'll help, I'm sure." I sighed, feeling his anguish as if it were my own. "But nobody can save them all."

He clenched his jaw. "Well, I can try."

And the next day, he went out with Doc again.

That fall, after Joel returned to college, I noticed an increase in the number of runaway slaves heading northward. The abolitionist voices across the land had gained strength, and the pro-slavery forces were equally adamant. As I secretly shuttled all who came my way on to the next station, one persistent question nagged at me. How would this all end?

One night a young mulatto woman was brought to us, drooping with fatigue. Pearl and I whisked open the trapdoor and scooted her downstairs to our hideaway. "Just rest here," I said. "I'll bring you down a nice hot meal."

She lay down on the cot, her arm flung across her eyes. "I'm too sick to eat." Her voice was barely audible. "All I ask is a place to rest."

I laid my hand on her forehead, but quickly drew back from the searing heat. "You're burning up with fever. Have you been sick long?"

"More than a week. It's all down here," she said, pressing on her chest. "I been travelin' with three others. I got to draggin' so, I told them to go on without me."

"It's cold here in the cellar. I can't leave you down here when you're so sick." I hesitated for a moment. "I'm going to put you upstairs in Hugh's old room. We'll have Doc take a look and see what's wrong with you."

"That's dangerous, Miz Nellie," Pearl said. "You know that's mighty dangerous."

"Oh, shoot! Nobody suspects us. They always look for runaways out in the country someplace, not in the middle of town. Especially not in a busy inn."

We installed the woman upstairs and fixed her some broth and strong tea. "Will you tell me your name?" I asked her as she sipped the hot brew.

"It's Rea, ma'am. You-all are mighty good to help me like this."

"You've come a long way by yourself. Just think, you'll soon be free."

"Free. That's a pretty word, ain't it? Can't hardly think what it must really mean."

"Did you have a hard life where you came from?"

"Not as bad as some. All my sisters work out in the cotton fields. I was a housemaid. Polishin' silver, dustin', makin' beds. Easy stuff. But then Old Master starts to botherin' round me. I fought him off. Yes, ma'am. Kicked him hard, I did."

Pearl whistled softly through her teeth. "Lands! I reckon you got beat for that."

"Beat, and worse. He say he goin' to sell me to a house down

324

in New Orleans. You know what kind of house he mean." She trembled with intensity. "That's when I run away. Two field hands from our place was leavin', so I took off with them. The day before the slave trader was comin' for me, it was."

"Just rest now, Rea," I said, patting her arm. "I'll have Doc check you first thing in the morning. You need to get well before you go on any further."

"I don't dare to tarry, ma'am. Old Master sure to have hunters out lookin' for me. He don't fool with none that cross him."

"You're safe here. The most important thing is for you to get well."

The very next day, Eddie rode down from Minnesota for a surprise visit, the first in two years. When I heard his deep voice at the back door, all other thoughts flew from my mind. I rushed out to greet this lean, hard-muscled young man, dressed in buckskins, his hazel eyes gleaming against his sun-bronzed skin.

"Eddie! My sakes, what a sight for sore eyes!" I said, flinging my arms around him in a hug.

Pearl hurried to his side and patted his weathered cheek. "Yes, sir! We're goin' to have us a celebration, sure."

"Where's my baby brother?" Eddie asked in a hearty voice, glancing around the room and out the open door.

I smiled with pride. "Joel's back at college now, but he worked with Doc all summer long. I'd say he's well on his way to becoming a real doctor. Come on. Let's run over and see Hugh."

Grabbing his arm, I led him next door to the store. We found Hugh standing on a stool, hooking cast-iron skillets on nails protruding from the wall. At the first glimpse of his brother, he vaulted to the floor. "Eddie, you old devil! Sneaking in without a word," he said, pounding him on the shoulder. "Here, let's get a note off to Sarah on the noon stage. She and Forrest will want to come down right away to show off their new baby. They named him Daniel, you know. After Pa."

Eddie, grinning appraisingly, studied his brother's face. "How about you? Don't you and Liza have anything to show off yet?"

Hugh chuckled. "Not quite yet. You'll have to come back in January to see ours."

That evening, the runaway still lay hidden in the back bedroom, swallowing the potions Doc had given her. Nearby, our parlor bubbled with noisy, happy conversation. "How have the years been treating you?" Hugh asked his younger brother.

Eddie leaned back in his chair, smiling contentedly. "My trading post is going full steam. Those Chippewas are first-rate hunters and trappers, so they bring in all kinds of furs to trade. I'm serving a huge area of that wilderness up north."

"You like it up there?" I asked him.

"Love it. There's enough room for a fellow to spread out."

A spurt of laughter rippled from Liza, vivacious and glowing with pregnancy. "I'm doing a bit of spreading myself, with this baby coming."

"And getting prettier every day," Hugh said, winking at her.

Doc appeared in the doorway from the kitchen. "Come in and join us," I called. "After all these years, you're like one of the family."

He smiled. "I'd be happy to hear all about the wonders of Minnesota. Just as soon as I check on my patient here."

"You have a runaway downstairs?" Eddie asked in a low voice.

"In Hugh's old room," I said. "She's been real sick."

"Ma! You're going to get yourself locked up one of these days."

I brushed him off with a flick of my hand. "You know no jail could ever hold me."

The next day, Sarah and Forrest drove down from Galesburg. She stepped down from their buggy, holding her three-month-old baby as cautiously as if he were royalty. As she eased back his blanket so I could view his face, I must admit he did look as handsome as a little prince. A deep sense of satisfaction surged through me at the sight of my Daniel's namesake, for this tiny Daniel bore the same proud, courageous mien and clear gray eyes as his grandfather.

"We can only stay until tomorrow, but we just had to run down to see Eddie," Sarah said, flashing a quick smile at her younger brother. "How are things up in the wilds of Minnesota? Ready to move back to civilization?"

Chuckling, Eddie shook his head. "Not me. I know where I belong."

Their lively conversations echoed off the parlor walls until far into the night. I hoped my ill and secret guest could rest through all the noise.

In the morning after breakfast, Sarah took the baby back to their upstairs room to dress him in his traveling clothes. "Can't you stay longer?" I asked, tickling the baby's tiny toes.

She tied little Daniel's knitted booties. "No, I really must get back. Things have been so rushed up there." Glancing at me, she lowered her voice to a whisper. "The Railroad, you know. More and more all the time. Where will it end?"

"I only wish I knew." I held my finger out, and the baby gripped it tightly. "I guess those folks in Washington are trying to get things settled. In the meantime, we just keep doing what we can."

Sarah kneaded her hands. "I get so impatient with it all."

"I know what you mean." I leaned in closer to her. "I didn't want to say anything to you, with all the other excitement around here, but I've had a woman hiding in Hugh's old room for three days now."

Her eyes widened with alarm. "Hugh's room? Right there beside the parlor? Don't you realize how dangerous that is?"

"The poor soul's been sick. A terrible cold and fever. At first Doc feared it might be pneumonia. The cellar's too cold, sick as she was. His room was the only place I could think of. Doc can slip in through the kitchen and treat her there without being seen. I hope she's well enough to move soon, though. If any slave hunters are on her trail, they're bound to be getting close by now."

"You have to be extremely careful," Sarah said, her face somber. "Your help is so valuable to the movement. If you get caught—"

"I know, I know. But this woman is so light, she could pass for white. She's much lighter than Eddie, with his dark suntan. Why, I'd almost be willing to put her on the stagecoach. Come downstairs. I'll introduce you. Her name is Rea."

Sarah followed me down the stairs and through the kitchen, where Pearl glanced up from the bowl of potatoes she was peeling at the table. Our eyes met, and her brows narrowed in an anxious frown. "Here. Let me hold that pretty baby," she said, wiping her hands on her apron.

Doc met us at the bedroom door. "Rea's cold is much better today," he murmured. "If it weren't so chilly, I'd move her on to the next stop tonight. I'm just afraid she still isn't well enough to be out in the cold, damp night air."

Sarah and I stepped into the room with Doc, closing the door behind us. Hollow-cheeked and weak-looking, the woman in the bed eased herself into a sitting position. "I'm so glad you're feeling better, Rea," I said. "You've had quite a spell."

She clenched her jaw with grim determination. "No time to waste bein' sick. My master's a hard man. I know he goin' to be sendin' somebody chasin' after me. I got to be on my way."

"It's been too cold at night," Doc protested. "We'll have to wait for a warm spell."

I studied the woman's face. "She could pass for white," I said, turning to Sarah for affirmation. "I do believe you could take her out in a carriage in broad daylight and none would be the wiser."

Sarah frowned dubiously. Doc grinned as if I had told a fine joke.

"I'm serious," I said. "I'll just lend her some of my clothes and drive out with her this afternoon, after Sarah leaves."

He shook his head emphatically. "You'll do no such thing, Nellie Cranford. That's much too dangerous. If you really think she'll pass, I'll drive her myself."

Rea's thin face tightened under the focus of our stares. "Look, you-all been mighty good to me, but I got to be movin' on."

Sarah gasped a quick intake of air. "The baby! You could take the baby—and carry him on your lap while you're riding in the carriage. His skin and eyes are very light. If someone stops you, they would think he was your baby."

"Yes!" I said. "And you could wear a bonnet with a widow's veil. Then I'm sure you'll get through without a whit of trouble."

"Well, Doc," Sarah said, turning to him with a smile. "If you can drive her up to Galesburg, we'll take care of her from there on."

He nodded briskly. "I'll do it. I'll drive her up this very afternoon. I'll just leave a note on my office door saying I'm out on an emergency. We'll have that baby back at your house by the time you get there."

I rushed over to the store to get a lady's black bonnet and some heavy black lace for a veil. Within moments, we had Rea dressed as a grieving widow. When Doc had pulled his carriage around to the back door, we handed baby Daniel over to Rea's arms and slipped them both out to the waiting vehicle. Doc

328

snapped the whip, and his spirited bay horse trotted proudly down the road and across the covered bridge, on its way to Galesburg.

Sarah and I stepped into the family parlor, covering our mouths to muffle our laughter, for we were well pleased with our cleverness and ingenuity.

A short time later, as she and Forrest climbed into their buggy to leave, we exchanged the knowing wink of conspirators. Relief settled over me like the warm hand of a friend, for I knew Rea was now one step closer to Canada—and freedom.

Just a half hour later, I heard the rapid staccato of hoofs down the road. Hurrying to the front door, I saw three hard-eyed men coming at full gallop from the south. When they reached the inn, one jumped from his horse, wrapped the reins over the hitching post, and stomped onto the porch.

Slave hunter. I recognized him from the handcuffs hooked to his belt.

CHAPTER 34

I waited for the slave hunter in the doorway, my body tight with tension. "Can I help you-all?" I asked in a thick Southern accent.

The squat man with loose, bulldog features glared at me suspiciously. "Runaway. Young mulatto wench. Somebody saw her getting rowed across the Mississippi at Quincy. Thought she might be headed this way."

"Not here," I said, shaking my head. My heart was beating so hard, I was certain he could hear it. "I'd surely remember if anyone like that passed through here. Is there a reward for her?"

The man growled cynically. "You bet there's a reward. Two

thousand dollars. This is one I can guarantee you we're goin' to collect. We've made up our minds we're not goin' back without this gal.''

"Yes, I can surely understand that.''

He scowled at me with narrowed eyes. "Lady, we've heard some mighty strange tales down the line about this place. Heard you might by one of those nigger-stealing abolitionists.''

"Me?'' My hands flew to my chest. "Lordy me, I'm from the South. You surely know my sentiments.''

"You got niggers living 'round here, ain't you?''

"I have a couple working for me. You have no idea how hard it is to get help in these parts.''

He studied me for a long moment. "I don't suppose you'd mind if we took a look around your place? . . .''

I drew in a deep breath. This is what I had been dreading for so long. "Of course not. This is a public inn. But just one of you, if you don't mind. I wouldn't want to disturb my guests.''

With a sniff, he followed me into the dining hall and up the stairs. "What are in all these rooms?''

"You're welcome to look around. There're the men's quarters and the ladies' quarters and some private rooms. The local doctor lives in one.''

The door to the ladies' room cracked open. A well-dressed, middle-aged woman peeked out, looking alarmed. "Is something the matter, Mrs. Cranford?''

I smiled nervously, glad to see this traveler who was waiting for the Springfield stage. "It's nothing, Mrs. Andrews. Sorry to disturb you.''

Chagrined, the slave hunter stomped down the stairs. "Let's see about that barn and those outbuildings.''

I followed him into the kitchen. Eddie rose from a chair in the parlor. "What's going on here?'' he demanded.

"Nothing, honey,'' I said, motioning him to silence. "I'll take care of this.''

The slave hunter stormed out the back door and across the yard. Tyrus was standing stiffly by the barn door, his hands clenched into fists. I met his intense, angry glare. "This gentleman would like to have a look around,'' I said mildly. "Now, Tyrus, you just go ahead and clean that tack.''

Grabbing a pitchfork hanging from a nail, the slave hunter headed for the loft. With furious jabs, he pierced the piles of hay and straw. Frustrated at finding nothing, he stormed downstairs and searched the stalls, then paced the yard while I went back inside for the keys to the smokehouse and storage building.

Pearl stared at me, her eyes wide with anxiety. "What now, Miz Nellie?"

"Just act like it's nothing out of the ordinary. This will give Doc more time to get farther along his way."

I clasped my hands together to stop their trembling. I was walking a tightrope. If the slave hunters stayed, they might discover our hideaway. If they left, they were almost certain to catch up with Doc. It was a nightmare come true.

After stalling around looking for the keys, I went back outside, unlocked the doors, and watched the man poke and pry angrily around the smokehouse and storage building. His lack of success fed his frustration. He turned to me with a vicious snarl. "The cellar. Let me see that cellar. What you got down there?"

By now my nerves were stretched until I feared I would explode. I gritted my teeth, then smiled at the man with my most gracious Southern charm. "Why, certainly, sir. And then I do hope you will be satisfied that I have nothing to hide."

Swearing under his breath, he yanked open the outside cellar door and rushed down the steps. I lit a candle in the kitchen and followed him downstairs. The musky odor of onions and cabbages surrounded us in the dim, flickering light. "Just look around, sir. Help yourself," I said, my glance shifting nervously to the false wall at the far end of the cellar.

My breath held captive in my throat, I watched as he poked the potato sacks and peeked into the empty barrels. Finally he threw his hands up in disgust. "Nothing here. I can't figure how that rumor got started."

"I simply can't imagine." Though I felt faint with relief, my heart refused to slow its thunderous hammering. "Here, let me get you-all a cup of coffee and some bread and jam before you travel on."

"God, no! We've lost too much time here already. If we miss out on that reward . . . Say, that road out front leads to Galesburg, don't it?"

I gulped down the new fear rising in my throat. "Or Havana," I said, pointing in the other direction. Would my luck hold out? Could I really keep on fooling him? "I'd say Havana would be

331

the place to look for runaways. Yes, you-all should try there first. All those boats heading north up the river . . .''

He shook his head roughly. ''Galesburg's the best bet. Regular den of damned abolitionist fanatics, from what I hear.''

''No, really, I think Havana—''

Without another word, the slave hunter mounted his horse and motioned to his companions. They all galloped over the bridge. I stood frozen in the doorway, watching in horror as they disappeared into the green rolling hills in the direction of Galesburg.

How long had they been here? Fifteen or twenty minutes at the most. Though my hideaway room had evaded them, I knew Doc was now in grave peril. A rumble of thunder sounded in the west. Dark clouds were gathering and roiling in the western sky.

My entire world was tumbling down around me. My stomach churned with nausea. Doc. Baby Daniel. How could I have been so reckless as to send them off in broad daylight on such a dangerous mission? Those two people were unspeakably precious to me. And poor Rea. She had gambled her whole future on this one attempt to escape.

And now, all because I was so foolhardy, they would surely be caught. I couldn't bear to think of it.

I paced back and forth across the dining hall, my thoughts as scattered as a swarm of bees. No use to discuss this with Hugh or Eddie or Pearl. There was nothing anyone could do. The onerous burden was load enough on me.

That hideous slave hunter, with his menacing long rifle strapped across his saddle, with his handcuffs, his shining pistols and knife stuck in his heavy leather belt. His treacherous-looking face loomed before me, like a vision of the devil.

The cruel look in his narrow eyes convinced me that this animal would do anything to capture Rea and claim the reward. I was certain those men would even kill Doc and the baby, if they got in the way.

I had to stop them. If I started now and galloped hard, I might be able to pass them and warn Doc first.

I was already out the back door, running toward the stable, when I suddenly stopped. I was hysterical—not thinking straight. It would be so obvious—a lone woman galloping along the road. A clear admission of some pressing emergency. And those slave hunters were bound to recognize me.

Heartsick, I breathed a quavering sigh and started back toward the inn. I would force myself to stay calm. Surely Doc's wisdom and long experience in these secret transfers would carry him through.

Rea's disguise was an expert job, I had to admit. With her black dress and heavy black veil, I was certain anybody passing by would take her for a recently bereaved widow. Fair-skinned, gray-eyed little Daniel was the perfect foil to complete her disguise.

And Doc knew what he was doing. He was cool, intelligent, dependable. He was everything a man should be.

Yet I could not calm down. My fear continued to intensify. My mouth went dry, my body stiff. How could I pass the hours without knowing? How could I bear the waiting, the tension, the paralyzing fear?

Oh, God! What would I do if anything happened to Doc? He had been a part of my life for so many years. A valued—yes, an essential part. The very thought of life without him was unthinkable.

Beads of sweat broke out on my brow. A weight, a sickness lay upon my heart. I brushed my hair off my forehead. My hand came away wet with perspiration.

My stomach cramped, not from hunger, but from worry. Suppertime came and Pearl quietly served the meal. I could not even think of eating.

Doc. That dear, brave, beloved man. In all my life, I had never known such a loyal friend. He accepted me and cared for me with all my faults and shortcomings. When I was with him, I felt somehow complete.

He had to be all right. Over and over, I kept repeating it. He had to be. That slave hunter would simply pass him by—never notice the veiled woman with a baby at his side.

But still my fear would not relent. I had already lost Daniel and Johnny. To lose Doc, too, was more than I could bear to contemplate.

It was all my fault. I thought I was so clever, creating that disguise. And now . . .

Come back, Doc. Oh, God! Please come back to me. Scald-

333

ing tears rolled down my cheeks. I threw myself across the bed and cried in painful, desperate sobs.

The darkness thickened; the hours passed with maddening slowness. God! Where was he?

Restlessly I rose and wandered through the dimly lit dining room and outside to the porch. The hour was late. Eddie and the few inn guests had retired to their beds. A veil of clouds hid the moon and stars and left the world shrouded in black gauze. I was angry that I couldn't see. Maybe, even now, he was coming back. Safe. Oh, please, God. Please.

The night was still, the only sound the ripple of water cascading over the dam. A chill breeze ruffled my hair. It rustled through the inky shadows beneath the trees as I paced across the park and to the river's edge, closer to the bridge where I prayed Doc would soon be crossing.

The water glowed darkly. My throat ached; my eyes burned from dried tears. Come back, Doc. Oh, God, please come home safely. I love you so.

I stopped abruptly. My breath caught in my throat. Could it be true?

I sank down on a log and stared at the dark, rippling water. Yes. Oh, yes! Why had I never recognized it before?

All these years, I had been so stubbornly attached to my romantic dreams of Johnny, I had refused Doc's genuine affection. How could I have been so blind? I loved Doc. I needed him. I could not bear to go on living without him.

My heart thudded a rapid drumbeat in my chest. All the sorrows of my life weighed down on me like a heavy mantle. All the deaths and loss and hardships I had known. Now, at last, I finally admitted to myself how very much I loved and depended on Doc.

And now he was in the gravest danger. Had the knowledge come too late, as it had with Daniel?

I must be strong. All through the years, I had been invincible. Lightning Woman, the Indians called me. Now was no time for weakness. And yet . . . And yet . . . Oh, Doc, it's true. I love you so terribly much, I thought.

I sat there for hours, fearful, cursing my foolishness. A heavy mist rose over the river. Deep in the pitch-black woods on the other side, an owl's hoot cut through the nervous rustling of fall leaves. A horse's nicker sounded from the cooper's barn.

The citizens of Eden Valley rested. Norman Hart, our Irish cooper and illustrious fiddler. Karl and Ruth Schulmann, weary from their long labors at the mill and cabin. Judson Lowder, with his tannery and leathermaking enterprises. The blacksmith, the preacher, the gunsmith, the schoolmaster, and all the others. The farmers out in the surrounding countryside.

These people all had helped build Eden Valley. Yet now I could only rely on Doc.

Eden Valley, idyllic spot beside the serene waters of Spoon River. A noble monument to Daniel Cranford, a legacy for all his children and grandchildren, for generations far into the future.

Tonight, all that meant little to me. My one burning concern was Doc. I admired him so, for only he had shown the courage and conviction to help in this grueling battle against slavery. I needed him here, to share the rest of my life with me.

Veils of dark mist drifted from the river, enveloping the silent trees. The woods were steeped in quiet, teeming with mysterious forebodings.

Rising from the log, I stretched my aching muscles. Should I go back inside the inn? What was the use of sitting out here all night, shivering in the cold?

And then I heard a faint *clip-clop*ping. I strained to listen.

The sound grew louder, each *clip-clop* intensifying as it gradually drew nearer. My heart clutched. Doc! It had to be him!

I dashed across the covered bridge, my long skirt flying out behind me, my footsteps echoing off the planks. I raced onward, through swirls of fog hovering over the dirt road on the other side.

Now the sounds of the approaching horse and buggy drowned my panting breath as I ran forward to meet Doc. Suddenly the dark silhouette of a buggy appeared through the mist on the road ahead of me.

It must be him!

"Doc! Doc!" I shouted frantically.

The carriage pulled to a halt. "Nellie? Is that you?" Doc's familiar voice called out.

A flood of relief washed over me. I ran to him. "Are . . ." My voice cracked. "Are you all right?"

"I'm fine. Just fine. No need for you to worry so."

As he stepped down from the carriage, I flung my arms around

335

his neck. "Oh, Doc! I'm so glad you're home. So glad. So awful glad."

He held me close. His arms felt gloriously warm and comforting. "Well, if this is how you welcome me, I'll have to go running off to Galesburg more often. Whatever is the matter?"

"A slave hunter. After Rea." I sobbed, burying my face in his shoulder. "Oh, God . . . I was so afraid he'd catch you."

"Now, now. I'm just fine. There were three tough-looking guys who galloped up to us, hell-bent for leather. They stopped and gave us the once-over. Your disguise was perfect. They looked at me and Rea and the baby for a minute, then took off without a word."

"I've been worried sick. I was so afraid . . ."

He smoothed my tousled, sweaty hair back from my brow. "No problem, Nellie. I'm just fine."

"I have to tell you something, before another minute passes." Drawing in a long, quavering breath, I gazed up at his kind eyes, the familiar, comforting features of his face. "I love you, Doc. I think I've loved you for years."

A low chuckle gurgled in his throat. "Do you, now? What brought all this on?"

"If anything happened to you . . ." My stomach knotted. "Oh, Doc, if anything happened to you, I just couldn't go on."

He pressed a warm kiss on my brow, held my face tenderly between his hands. His eyes gleamed in the dim light. "And does this mean . . . Dare I hope you'll finally agree to marry me?"

"I will! Right now. Tomorrow at the latest. We've wasted too much time already." My arms entwined around his neck. I drew him closer to me, enraptured by the magic of his embrace. I felt young again. Newborn. My blood sang in my ears. All my senses throbbed and surged with yearning.

His breathing quickened. I could feel his heart pounding rapidly against mine. Our lips met in a fiery, lingering kiss. He broke away and murmured in my ear. "This time the honeymoon trip to St. Louis will be for you and me."

"Yes!" I laughed with delight. "For you and me. But how can we get away from all this work here?"

"We'll make arrangements somehow. We both deserve to get away." He tilted back his head and gazed into my eyes. Even

336

in the dim light, the silver streaks at his temples glistened. His face looked strong, dependable. His eyes, incredibly kind.

A thought struck me, and I hesitated. "Should we leave, with all this Railroad business going on? Everything is so uncertain now."

"It will be uncertain until they abolish slavery for good," he said. "But we have a right to our lives, too. We'll get married, then take the biggest, fanciest steamboat we can find. And when we get down to St. Louis, we're going to do the town up right. My dear girl, do you know how long it's been since you or I have had a day off?"

I grinned up at him. "What's a day off?"

He placed his hands at my waist and lifted me up off the ground. Bursting out with a loud laugh, he whirled us both around in a wide circle. "That's what we're going to find out, Nellie girl. There's a new day coming. You and I are going to make a better life together than either one of us has ever dared to dream before."

"A new day. Oh, yes! Yes, I can feel it in my bones."

About the Author

Susan Hatton McCoy grew up in a small town near New Salem, Illinois. She traces her roots in America back to the years before the Revolution and is a student of Lincoln, of Illinois history, and of frontier life. McCoy is a popular speaker before clubs, bookstore audiences, library and school groups, and history buffs. A former teacher, a mother and grandmother, she lives with her husband in Pekin, Illinois.

Log cabins,
Wood-burning stoves,
Hill Country

JAMES ALEXANDER THOM